BAYOU CHRISTMAS DISAPPEARANCE

DENISE N. WHEATLEY

AGENT COLTON'S TAKEDOWN

BEVERLY LONG

MILLS & BOON

First Published in Great Britain 2021
by Mills & Boon, an imprint of HarperCollins*Publishers* Ltd
1 London Bridge Street, London, SE1 9GF

www.harpercollins.co.uk

HarperCollins*Publishers*
1st Floor, Watermarque Building,
Ringsend Road, Dublin 4, Ireland

Bayou Christmas Disappearance © 2021 Denise N. Wheatley
Agent Colton's Takedown © 2021 Harlequin Books S.A.

Special thanks and acknowledgement are given to Beverly Long for her contribution to the *The Coltons of Grave Gulch* series.

ISBN: 978-0-263-28363-1

1121

MIX
Paper from
responsible sources
FSC™ C007454

This book is produced from independently certified FSC™ paper to ensure responsible forest management.

For more information visit: www.harpercollins.co.uk/green

Printed and Bound in Spain using 100% Renewable electricity at CPI Black Print, Barcelona

Denise N. Wheatley loves happy endings and the art of storytelling. Her novels run the romance gamut, and she strives to pen entertaining books that embody matters of the heart. She's an RWA member and holds a BA in English from the University of Illinois. When Denise isn't writing, she enjoys watching true crime TV and chatting with readers. Follow her on social media.

Instagram: @Denise_Wheatley_Writer
Twitter: @DeniseWheatley
BookBub: @DeniseNWheatley
Goodreads: Denise N. Wheatley

Beverly Long enjoys the opportunity to write her own stories. She has both a bachelor's and master's degree in business and more than twenty years of experience as a human resources director. She considers her books to be a great success if they compel the reader to stay up way past their bedtime. Beverly loves to hear from readers. Visit beverlylong.com, or like her author fan page at Facebook.com/beverlylong.romance

Also by Denise N. Wheatley

Cold Case True Crime

Also by Beverly Long

A Firefighter's Ultimate Duty
A Colton Target
Power Play
Bodyguard Reunion
Snowbound Security
Protecting the Boss

Discover more at millsandboon.co.uk

BAYOU CHRISTMAS DISAPPEARANCE

DENISE N. WHEATLEY

This book is dedicated to all my fellow true crime junkies, armchair detectives and faux forensic scientists.

Keep sleuthing, friends!

Chapter One

Mona Avery tightened the grip on her handbag as she hurried down the dark, hazy street.

"*Where* is that bed-and-breakfast?" she muttered into the night air.

The investigative journalist peered through the dense gray fog that had descended upon Lake Landry, Louisiana. A haunting stillness lurked along the desolate road.

She picked up speed, walking at a brisk pace. The heels on her tan suede ankle boots clicked loudly against the uneven gray pavement, reverberating through her eardrums.

A feeling of dread rumbled through her body. Mona struggled to fight it off, willing her legs to move faster as they grew heavy with angst.

She studied the shadows looming over unkempt lawns surrounding the few shuttered businesses lining the block. Not a stream of light shone from the shabby wooden structures.

Mona had arrived in Lake Landry less than a week ago to investigate the disappearance of her old college roommate, Olivia Whitman. She hadn't been back to the small, swampy town since they'd graduated.

A feeling of guilt pulled inside her chest. Mona regretted canceling their annual girls trip to Sedona, Arizona, that summer. It was a tradition they'd established years ago in an effort to stay connected.

But Mona's hectic life in Los Angeles, where she worked for the esteemed Cable News Broadcast outlet, didn't leave much time for a personal life. Keeping up with friends was a challenge. And now, it was too late. Olivia was gone.

Think positive, she told herself. *Olivia is not gone for good...*

Returning to Lake Landry should've evoked feelings of warmth and nostalgia. Mona had nothing but good memories of the town where she'd spent four years at the prestigious Emmanuel University, party hopping with Olivia while still managing to ace her courses.

But instead, she was overcome by a chilling sense of fear after her friend had disappeared.

A gust of whistling wind blew through Mona's shoulder-length curls. She brushed them away from her face, struggling to focus on the barren path ahead.

Mona had just filmed a live on-air broadcast near Olivia's last known location. When shooting wrapped, she felt anxious and hoped that the drive back to The Bayou Inn would help ease her frazzled nerves. But after the rental car ran out of gas and she decided to walk, she got turned around in the bleak, unfamiliar area.

Mona emitted a trembling groan. She loosened the belt on her chocolate brown blazer, then pressed her hand against her slender stomach, willing the nervous churn to cease.

Mona forged ahead, running the facts of Olivia's case through her mind.

Maybe that'll alleviate this eerie sense of panic...

Olivia was last seen exiting the LLL Water Quality Laboratory, where she worked as an environmental scientist. Her coworkers said she was heading to the Beechtree neighborhood to gather samples of residential water sources. When Mona asked why, she discovered that Olivia was checking for traces of lead and chromium.

Mona questioned several people who lived and worked in the dismal Beechtree area off camera. They claimed to have never seen her.

Mona decided to film her latest segment in the vicinity of the water source, hoping that the broadcast would jar someone's memory. Shortly after it ended, she received a strange text message.

Stop your investigation into Olivia Whitman's disappearance and get out of Lake Landry!

The message was disturbing to say the least. And now, as Mona hurried through the dim haze, she couldn't help but feel as though she was in danger.

Stay calm. Breathe. You're fine...

The meditative affirmations didn't help. Because Mona felt far from fine.

She curled her hands into tight fists, wondering who would have done something to Olivia. And why.

Mona as well as everyone else in town had their suspicions.

Blake Carter.

Blake was Olivia's cold, narcissistic husband. His arrogance stemmed from the wealth his family had garnered through their mega successful Transformation Cosmetics company. He and Olivia had been together since college. Even then, Mona despised his cocky demeanor.

She'd tried to convince Olivia that she deserved better. It wasn't as if her own family didn't have their fair share of wealth. The Whitmans had collected a vast fortune thanks to Elevate Realty Group, their powerful real estate development firm.

Through the years, Blake's behavior had only worsened. Once he became president of Transformation Cosmetics, his level of egotism reached an all-time high.

But Olivia believed in the relationship and thought she could change him. So she stayed in it.

That fateful decision may have cost Olivia her life.

Mona snapped out of her thoughts as she approached the end of the pitch-black road.

She stopped abruptly.

"Oh!" Mona breathed, suddenly remembering the walking directions app on her cell phone.

She snatched the phone from her pocket and pounded the home button. The screen was blank. Her cell was dead.

"Dammit!" she screeched.

Mona resisted the urge to throw the phone down onto the ground and stomp her heel through the screen.

"Come on, come on. Where is this place…?"

She spun around, her eyes darting back and forth. Despite the steamy temperature, a piercing chill shot up her spine.

She crossed her arms in front of her and glanced up, noticing that the bulb inside of a rusted green streetlamp had burned out.

Of course, she thought while struggling to peer through the darkness.

Her head swiveled right, then left.

Which way…which way…?

Mona closed her eyes. Took a deep breath.

She opened them, made a swift left turn and hoped for the best.

Just when she thought she'd caught a glimpse of The

Bayou Inn's dimly lit cedarwood sign, a pair of glaring yellow headlights sped around the corner.

A dark blue SUV careened toward her. Its lights flickered in her direction.

Mona froze.

Stinging pricks of fear shot up her calves.

The driver of the vehicle blew the shrill horn.

She recoiled and stumbled backward. Her boot's slim heel slid inside a crack in the sidewalk, causing her to fall into a lamppost.

The truck pulled toward the side of the road. Mona's eyes squinted. She struggled to see inside. But the tinted windows kept the driver's identity hidden.

When the SUV stopped right next to her, Mona reached around and gripped the lamppost.

Rusted-out edges of chipped paint scraped against her fingertips. She ignored the pain, digging deeper for fear of what was to come.

The driver slowly opened the door.

Mona held her breath, contemplating making a run for it. But her legs, leaden with fear, wouldn't allow her to budge.

She flinched at the sound of the car door slamming shut. Heavy footsteps pounded the asphalt.

"Hey, are you okay?" a deep male voice boomed.

"What do you want?" Mona screeched, cringing at the sound of alarm in her voice.

"I, uh… I noticed you out here wandering around and just wanted to make sure you're all right. Seems like you need some help."

"I—I'm fine," she stammered.

"You sure? Because you don't appear to be fine…"

The sound of footsteps drew closer. Mona backed farther into the lamppost.

"Despite what you may think," the man continued, "I'm willing to help you."

Mona held her breath. Then, she realized that the man's voice sounded familiar.

Standing in front of her was Detective Dillon Reed.

"Detective Reed!" she shrieked, pressing her hand against her forehead. "You just scared me half to death! What are you doing out here, creeping up on me like that?"

The ruggedly handsome detective's wide-set eyes lowered curiously. He chuckled, then tilted his head to the side.

"Well, first of all, my apologies," he replied smugly. "I certainly didn't mean to scare you. And I wasn't creeping up on you. Like I said, I was just checking to make sure you're okay. Now if I may ask, what are *you* doing out here? I'm surprised to see you roaming around this desolate area by yourself."

Mona dabbed the perspiration from her face and straightened her blazer. She looked directly at the detective, noticing that his full, sexy lips had curled into an amused smirk.

"You're really getting a kick out of this, aren't you?" she asked. "Are you some sort of sadist? Do you enjoy the fact that you almost gave me a heart attack just now?"

"Not at all," Dillon snorted, covering his mouth while clearly stifling a snicker.

Mona glared at him. The pair hadn't exactly hit it off since she'd arrived in Lake Landry. He was heading up Olivia's missing person investigation and feared her coverage would turn it into a media circus.

Even though he clearly didn't want her there, she couldn't seem to fight off her inherent attraction to him.

"But you still haven't answered my question," Dillon said. "What are you doing out here?"

"I just got done filming my latest news segment over by the water source where Olivia was testing for chemicals.

As you know, that area was allegedly her last known location. I'm hoping the broadcast will jar someone's memory. Then as I was heading to the inn, my car ran out of gas."

Mona paused, throwing her hand on her hip while peering at Dillon.

"Wait," she continued. "You must not have checked your texts. I sent you a message last night asking if you'd be willing to go live on air with me today to discuss the case."

Or did you just choose to ignore it? she was tempted to add.

Dillon sighed deeply, running his hand over his dark, short hair.

"Mona, you already know how I feel about blasting this investigation all over the media. I'm trying to maintain the case's integrity without tainting it with the public's opinion. It's bad enough all these salacious blogs and podcasts are putting out false information."

"But the public could very well help solve this case, Detective Reed. Someone may have seen something that the authorities missed."

"Tuh," Dillon grunted, turning away from her.

Mona watched as his scowl caused wrinkles of skepticism to invade his deep brown skin. She could sense angry waves of heat coming off his body. She knew he wanted nothing more than for her to pack up and go back to Los Angeles.

Lucky for her, Dillon's boss felt differently.

Mona had forged a close relationship with Chief Richard Boyer back when she was still in college, interning at Lake Landry's local news station. He was an eager police officer who'd oftentimes acted as the department's spokesperson. Whenever the pair worked together, the chief would commend Mona's talents and predict that she'd go far in her career.

After Mona arrived in Lake Landry to cover Olivia's case, Chief Boyer welcomed her with open arms. He'd encouraged Dillon to partner with her in his investigation since she was familiar with the town and had a friendship with Olivia.

He'd initially refused. But eventually, albeit reluctantly, he gave in to the chief's request.

But Dillon had yet to really let her in. And Mona found herself struggling to crack his hardened demeanor.

"Listen, Detective," Mona said softly. "Olivia is beautiful. Her family is well-known and wealthy. Her husband's family owns one of the most popular cosmetic companies in the country. The fact that she just up and vanished is baffling. Her case is going to attract attention. Unfortunately, there isn't much you can do about that."

"Yeah, well, I can certainly try to regulate the media that comes to town trying to get me involved in their unsolicited investigations."

Mona took a step back. She opened her mouth to speak, but no words came out. She was getting tired of trying to convince Dillon that she was there to help rather than hinder Olivia's case.

"Do you know how many anonymous tips I've gotten," he began, "accusing Olivia's husband of murdering her? None of them have held any merit. Yet thanks to all the salacious media coverage, Blake Carter's name is being dragged through every mud puddle across the country. I've even had to send a squad car out to his house just to keep an eye on things."

Mona stared at Dillon and sighed.

"Well, have you bothered to look into any of those tips?" she asked. "Maybe there's some merit to them. I've got a slew of stories I could share with you about Olivia and Blake's relationship. But that would require you to actually

sit down and talk with me about the case. Which you've refused to do. *Despite the chief's request for you to do so...*"
she added under her breath.

"I heard that. And going off of rumors and hearsay isn't
going to solve this investigation. I need solid evidence."

Mona paused, struggling to come up with a snappy
comeback. But she couldn't. Because Dillon was right.
She didn't have any solid evidence. *Yet.*

"Look," she told him, "all I'm saying is that two heads
are better than one. I know Lake Landry. I know Olivia.
And I know Blake. Let me help you with this. I know I
can—"

"May I offer you a ride somewhere, Ms. Avery?" Dillon interrupted.

Mona threw her arms out at her sides.

"So that's it? You're just gonna shut me out? Go against
Chief Boyer's request that we work together on this case to
try to figure out what happened to Olivia?"

He turned around and headed toward the curb.

"If you want that ride, I'll meet you in the truck."

"You have got to be kidding me," Mona muttered, watching as Dillon hopped inside the SUV and slammed the
door shut.

She entertained the idea of storming off and taking her
chances on getting back to the inn alone.

Don't be ridiculous, she thought. Despite being frustrated with the ornery detective, wandering around in the
dark would be worse than being in his presence.

Mona strutted over to the passenger side of the truck
and climbed in. She barely clicked her seat belt before Dillon peeled away from the curb and sped down the street.

"Whoa," Mona uttered, grabbing the door handle. She
glanced over at him and rolled her eyes. "Sorry that my
being here pisses you off so badly."

"Oh, you're far from sorry. I think you're actually happy to be here interfering in my investigation. You know, with all the cases you've covered this year, I would think you'd be eager to take a break from work and head home to Evergreen, Colorado, to spend the holidays with your family."

Mona snickered while staring straight ahead. "For you to be so irritated by my presence, you certainly know a lot about me."

When he fell silent, she knew she'd hit a nerve. Because one thing she'd learned about Dillon, he was never at a loss for words.

"You're staying at The Bayou Inn, right?" he asked.

"Right. And way to change the subject."

"What do you want me to say?" Dillon shot back. "That I looked you up when Chief Boyer told me that some famous investigative journalist was coming to town to insert herself in my investigation? Of course I did. I guess that's just the detective in me."

Mona leaned her head against the back of her seat in exasperation.

"Come on, Dillon! I'm on your side. I wanna find out what happened to Olivia just as badly as you do. As soon as I heard that she'd gone missing, I *ran* to my boss's office and insisted that I come to Lake Landry and cover this case. When he gave me the green light, I immediately nixed my holiday plans and flew straight here."

"Humph," Dillon grumbled. He pressed down on the accelerator, the engine roaring as he flew down the winding pitch-black roads. "I wish you would've consulted with me before you canceled those plans."

She reached up and gripped the grab handle, bracing herself when the SUV careened around a corner.

"Detective Reed, I'm going to do all that I can to find out what happened to my friend, with or without your blessing. Don't forget, your boss happily welcomed me into this investigation. So I have every right to be here. Now, I can either be your biggest ally or the sharpest thorn in your side. The choice is yours."

Dillon's lips twisted with irritation. He remained silent, slowing down while approaching the inn.

Mona looked out at The Bayou Inn's beautiful yellow Victorian exterior. Its festive holiday decor was a stark contrast from the gloomy mood inside the truck.

Lush evergreen wreaths adorned with bright gold bows lined the windows. Sweet-smelling garland made of fresh eucalyptus, bay leaves and red berries hung from the porch's white railings. Colorful icicle string lights flickered along the roof's shingles. The majestic Atlas cedar that stood in the middle of the yard twinkled with sparkling lights, highlighting the tree's silvery blue foliage.

For Mona, staying at the inn felt bittersweet. On one hand, it brought back fond memories of her college years. But on the other hand, it was a constant reminder that Olivia was gone.

The Whitman family owned The Bayou Inn. During their time at the university, the two friends earned extra cash by working there on weekends.

They'd help prepare the ornately decorated rooms for guests by setting up welcome gift baskets and dusting off the beautiful Parisian furnishings, contemporary artwork and low-country antiques.

Mona was jolted out of her thoughts when Dillon stopped in front of the entrance.

Just as he put the truck in Park, a streak of lightning flashed across the sky. It was followed by a roaring crackle of thunder, then a sudden downpour of rain.

"Oh *wow*," Mona gasped, staring out at the torrential shower as raindrops crashed against the windshield.

"Oh wow is right. Looks like I came to your rescue just in time. Imagine roaming around out there in the dark and then, *boom*! A monsoon hits."

Mona waved off Dillon's dramatics and grabbed her purse. "I'm sure I would've survived. But nevertheless, thanks for the ride."

Before she opened the door, Dillon put the truck in Drive and tapped the accelerator, making sure that he was parked directly underneath the inn's awning.

"So you won't get wet," he told her.

Mona paused, surprised by the considerate gesture.

"Thanks," she responded quietly. "I appreciate it."

Dillon's softened expression left her wondering whether she should invite him inside. Moments alone with him like this were rare. She wanted to take advantage of it. Maybe he'd open up to her in front of the inn's cozy fireplace over a mug of hot apple cider and a plate of Cajun ginger cookies.

What do you have to lose? she asked herself. *Just go for it...*

Mona turned to him and cleared her throat. "Hey, would you like to—"

Before she could finish, Dillon's cell phone rang.

"Excuse me," he said, reaching down into the cup holder and grabbing his cell.

Mona slumped back into her seat, instinctively knowing that the chance to invite him in had passed her by.

"Detective Reed," he said into the phone. "What's up, Officer Freeman?... Yes, Olivia's car was recovered outside of Jefferson Parish... Exactly. Nowhere near the area where she went missing... We did turn it over to Forensics. Came back clean... Oh, you got a new tip? What time did it come in?... Yeah, we should definitely look into it now. I'll swing by the station and pick you up in a few. Thanks."

Dillon disconnected the call and turned to Mona. "I need

to get going. But before I leave, a word of advice. Be sure to keep that gas tank full."

"Do you think that tip you just received will lead to some solid evidence?" Mona asked, ignoring his unsolicited suggestion. She crossed her fingers underneath her purse, hoping Dillon would give in and share the details.

"I don't know yet. We'll see."

She waited for him to elaborate. When he didn't, she parted her lips to ask another question. But before she could, Dillon threw open his door and hopped out of the truck.

He jogged over to the passenger side and opened her door. Mona just sat there staring at him, irritated that the conversation had ended so abruptly.

He extended his hand in an attempt to help her out of the truck. She ignored it, climbing out on her own and brushing past him.

"Oh, so it's like that?" he asked.

Mona spun around and faced him. "Yes. It's definitely like that. You set the tone, Detective. I'm just following your lead. But like I said, I'm going to be involved in this investigation whether you like it or not. I'll actually be down at the station tomorrow to meet with Chief Boyer."

"But...*why?*"

"Thanks again for the ride," Mona told him, ignoring his question. "Have a good night."

And with that, she swiveled on her heels and strutted toward the inn's white wooden door.

Right before going inside, Mona glanced back at Dillon. He was still standing there, a stern expression on his face as he watched her walk away.

Stay on the case, she told herself, now even more determined to find Olivia. *With or without Dillon's help...*

Chapter Two

Dillon sat down and slid his rolling mesh chair closer toward his cluttered cherrywood desk. Normally the messy files strewn about and printouts of his latest reports were neatly tucked away in a drawer. But ever since he'd begun investigating Olivia's disappearance, he couldn't seem to keep organized.

Dillon had arrived in Lake Landry a couple of months ago by way of Baton Rouge's police department. After ten years of working on its force, the city's high crime rate had finally gotten the best of him.

He'd made the move to Lake Landry in hopes of settling into a quieter, more peaceful life. The last thing he had expected was for a high-profile missing person case to land on his desk. But that's exactly what happened when Chief Boyer named him lead detective in the Olivia Whitman investigation.

"Are you sure about this?" Dillon remembered asking the chief. "You've got a couple of detectives in this department who grew up in Lake Landry and know Olivia's family very well, along with her husband's. Don't you think one of them would be better suited to take the lead on this case?"

"Those are all the reasons why they *wouldn't* be better suited to handle this case," the chief had rebutted. "These guys are too close to the Whitman and Carter families. They all have preconceived notions on Olivia's disappearance. Who did it. Why it was done. I need a fresh, unbiased mind on this."

"But, sir, I literally just arrived in Lake Landry. I don't know the town. I don't know the people. I'm not familiar with—"

"Your unfamiliarity with this town and everyone in it could very well be the key to solving the case," Chief Boyer interrupted. "Not to mention your impeccable track record in Baton Rouge. I don't have that level of experience here in this town. So congratulations, Detective Reed. You're it."

Dillon had just stood there in the chief's office, peering at the enthusiastic grin on his round, jovial face. As Chief Boyer stared back at him, silently running his chubby hand over the gray stubble on his cheeks, Dillon realized the decision was final.

The dinging of Dillon's email inbox snapped him out of his thoughts. He ignored the incoming message and grabbed the photos of the area where Olivia had allegedly gone missing, studying every angle closely.

The dark water appeared still, almost haunting. Barren branches hung from the shrubbery, skimming the lake's edge. When Olivia disappeared, the first thing Dillon had done was hire rescue divers to search the water. Thankfully, her body hadn't been recovered.

"Come on, Olivia," he muttered. "Talk to me. Where are you? What happened to you?"

He examined the pictures for several minutes, struggling to discover a new clue. When nothing jumped out at him, he turned to his laptop and pulled up the internet.

"CNBNews.com," he said aloud, typing in the web address to Mona's network.

CNB's blue-and-white pyramid logo appeared on the

screen. Dillon hovered the cursor over the menu prompt. He searched for a list of journalists, then double-clicked on Mona's name.

"Latest broadcast," he mumbled, tapping on the video she'd shot near the Beechtree residential water source the night before.

When Mona's image popped up on the screen, Dillon felt a sizzling burn ignite in the pit of his stomach.

Come on, dude, he told himself. *Chill out...*

Dillon still remembered the moment Chief Boyer walked Mona into his office to introduce the pair. He'd been given a heads-up that she would be arriving in Lake Landry to cover Olivia's case.

Dillon didn't hold back when telling the chief she was not welcome in his investigation. But Chief Boyer had a soft spot for Mona. He'd watched her go from an eager small-town network intern to a reputable, hotshot LA journalist.

In the end, Dillon had no choice but to accept his boss's wishes.

What he didn't expect was the jolt of sexual energy that shot through his body when the beautiful journalist sauntered up to his desk.

He'd looked her up online prior to her arrival and was aware of her obvious beauty. But in person, Mona's cascading jet-black curls, flawless caramel-toned skin, brown doe eyes and pouty lips took the normally cool detective's breath away.

Dillon somehow managed to hide his admiration while watching her long, lean legs, which were covered in black leather leggings that day, move with the grace of a ballerina.

When Mona spoke, her voice resembled that of a charismatic radio host while she carried the look of a runway model. Both her confidence and intelligence were apparent, as was her passion for finding Olivia.

A lesser man would've easily been intimidated. But not Dillon. In that moment, his irritation overrode his awe. Rather than thinking of ways to get to know her better, he was contemplating ways to send her packing.

The sound of Mona's broadcast boomed from Dillon's speakers, bringing him back to the present. He focused on the screen.

"Take a good look at this location where I'm standing," Mona said into the camera.

Her knuckles appeared white as she gripped the microphone. The protruding vein running down the middle of her forehead revealed her concern.

"If you remember seeing anything out of the ordinary in this area the day that Olivia Whitman went missing," Mona continued, "or have any information on her disappearance, I urge you to please call local authorities. The telephone number to the anonymous tip line is running along the bottom of the screen."

As Dillon continued watching the broadcast, he felt his mouth go dry. He grabbed his mug of black coffee and went to take a sip. When nothing but air flowed through his lips, he realized the cup was empty.

"I'm Mona Avery, signing off. Until next time, remember, if you see something, say something."

Dillon stared at the screen until the video went black. He sat there for a moment, gathering himself before heading to the break room for his third cup of coffee.

"Hey, Detective Reed!"

Dillon's shiny black oxford shoes screeched along the wooden floor when he came to an abrupt halt. He spun around and glanced inside Chief Boyer's office.

"Can I see you for a quick sec?" the chief asked.

"Of course."

Dillon strolled through the doorway, stepping carefully through the stacks of files lining the floor.

"Be careful. Don't slip on those piles. Mildred is re-organizing my cabinets. Close the door and have a seat, will you?"

Uh-oh, he thought. Whenever the chief asked him to step into his office, close the door and have a seat, he usually followed up with something Dillon didn't want to hear.

"What's going on, sir?" Dillon asked after slowly sitting down across from him.

"Well, I wanted to follow up with you on the Olivia Whitman investigation. How's it going?"

"It's going. I've been meticulously reviewing all the evidence that I've collected and pursuing new leads. Officer Freeman and I followed up on a tip we received that sounded pretty promising, too."

"Oh yeah?" Chief Boyer asked, his unruly salt-and-pepper eyebrows shooting up toward his forehead. "What did it entail?"

"There was an alleged sighting of Olivia at the King Cake Café. So Freeman and I went to the bistro, questioned some of the workers and patrons, and reviewed surveillance footage. Unfortunately, nothing came of it."

"Hmm…" Chief Boyer propped his hands underneath his chin and rested his elbows on his chair. "What about Mona? Have you two had a chance to sit down and discuss the case yet?"

Dillon's gaze diverted from the chief's probing stare and focused on his training certificates hanging along the back wall.

"I, uh—we've chatted a bit here and there, but, um…"

Dillon's voice trailed off. Silence filled the office.

Chief Boyer lowered his head and eyed Dillon over the top of his black rectangle bifocals.

"Listen, Reed. Mona is a top-notch investigative journalist. Her skills are impeccable, bar none. She's helped law enforcement agencies all over the country solve some pretty complicated cases. Now, I know you're a proud detective who's capable of handling this investigation on your own. But this is a high-profile case that just so happens to be close to my heart. We need all the help we can get to solve it as quickly as possible."

"But, sir, I don't need some—"

"With all due respect, Detective," the chief interrupted, "this isn't up for debate. This is an order."

The finality in Chief Boyer's low tone convinced Dillon that the conversation was indeed over. There was no way out of this. He was officially stuck working with Mona.

Dillon slumped down in the hard wooden chair and swiped his thumb along his perspiring brow. As he waited for his boss to dismiss him, there was a knock at the door.

Chief Boyer glanced up at the clock, then over at Dillon. When the chief tightened his lips and nodded his head, Dillon automatically knew who was on the other side.

Mona Avery.

"Come in!" Chief Boyer called out.

Dillon gripped the arms of his chair. He clenched his jaws as the creaking door slowly opened.

"Good morning, gentlemen."

The sound of Mona's silky voice flowed through his eardrums. He shifted in his seat and inhaled sharply.

"Detective Reed," she continued. "This is a surprise. I didn't expect to see you in our meeting."

"Yeah, neither did I," Dillon shot back defensively, swiveling in his chair. When he laid eyes on her, his demeanor immediately softened.

Mona looked beautiful, almost angelic, dressed in a cream suede blazer and fitted cream pants. Her hair was wrapped in a bun, with soft tendrils framing her face. Matte red lipstick highlighting her perfectly straight teeth. The subtle scent of rose perfume floated through the stuffy office.

Dillon felt himself growing mesmerized by her presence.

Stop it! he told himself, irritated by his uncontrollable reaction.

"Good morning, Mona," Chief Boyer boomed. "Please, have a seat. Can Detective Reed get you anything? Coffee? Tea? Water?"

Dillon's head jerked toward the chief. He noticed a glimmer of mischief in his boss's eyes.

"No, thank you," Mona replied. "I'm fine. I think I drank a whole pot of coffee earlier this morning back at the inn."

"Oh yeah," Chief Boyer uttered, rubbing his hands together. "Isn't The Bayou Inn's manager, Evelyn, serving up their holiday blend this time of year? Medium roast with touches of cinnamon and vanilla?"

"Yes, sir, she is," Mona responded before she and the chief chuckled in unison.

Dillon groaned underneath his breath, annoyed with their friendly banter.

"Hey," Chief Boyer continued, "I was just asking Detective Reed whether you two have had a chance to sit down and discuss Olivia's case yet. He's informed me that you in fact have not. So we're gonna work to make that happen. Isn't that right, Detective?"

Dillon turned to Mona. She stared back at him, the slight smirk on her face oozing with self-satisfaction.

"Yes, sir," he said stiffly. "That's right..."

"Good. Now, Mona, you said you've got some information on Olivia's husband, Blake, that you wanted to share with me?"

"I do."

Dillon watched as she pulled a leather binder from her tote bag and placed it on the desk.

"So as you both know," Mona began, "Blake Carter is one of the main suspects in this case."

"That has not been made official," Dillon interjected. "We have yet to name any suspects or persons of interest in this case."

"Okay," Mona replied. "Well, let me rephrase that, then. Hypothetically speaking, Blake *may* be a suspect in this case."

When Dillon opened his mouth to speak, Chief Boyer held up his hand. "Please. Let her finish."

Dillon resisted the urge to jump up and walk out of the office. Instead he sat back in his chair and tightened his lips in frustration.

"Look," Mona continued, "all I'm saying is that I think we should take a closer look at Blake. There are so many things he's done, even before Olivia disappeared, that seem suspicious."

"And I'm assuming you have a list of those things tucked away in your little binder?" Dillon asked sarcastically.

"As a matter of fact, I do. First of all, Blake—"

Mona was interrupted by a knock at the door.

"Hold that thought," Chief Boyer told her before calling out, "Yes?"

Dillon turned around and saw Officer Freeman stick his head in the doorway.

"Sorry to interrupt. Chief, the officers are in the briefing room waiting on you."

"Waiting on me for what?" he asked before turning toward his computer and clicking on the mouse. "Oh! I forgot I've got the ethics training update."

Dillon watched as the chief grabbed his notebook and jumped up from behind the desk.

Thank goodness...he thought, grateful for the interruption.

"Mona, Detective Reed, I'm so sorry. But I've gotta cut this meeting short. I'll tell you what. Why don't you two continue this conversation over an early lunch? Then I'll circle back with the both of you later."

Dillon clenched his teeth at the thought of having to sit across from Mona, one-on-one, and discuss a case he wished to keep close to the vest.

When he glanced over at her, he sensed that she felt the exact same way as she shoved her papers back inside the binder. Her movements were stiff and expression was tight.

"No worries, Chief," Mona uttered. "Hopefully you and I can reschedule our meeting. I'd still like to go over my thoughts on Olivia's disappearance with you."

Dillon almost felt guilty underneath the weight of her strained tone.

You've gotta lighten up, man, he told himself.

But when a wave of doubt overcame him, he gripped the arms of his chair and stood up.

Or at least try...

"I look forward to hearing your thoughts on the case, Mona," Chief Boyer told her. "But in the meantime, go ahead and share them with Detective Reed. I have no doubt that if the two of you put your heads together, you'll have this case solved in no time."

And with that, the chief shuffled out the door.

"So, um," Dillon began, his voice cracking awkwardly, "are you hungry?"

"I could eat." Mona shrugged. She slipped her binder inside her tote without making eye contact with him. "Do you have a taste for anything in particular?"

As Mona stood up, Dillon rushed to pull out her chair. "I was actually thinking of getting a spicy grilled shrimp salad from The Weeping Willow Bistro."

"Mmm, that sounds good. Weeping Willow's has the best hot water corn bread and mango lemonade in town."

"I have to agree with you there."

Dillon watched as Mona sauntered out of the office. The sight of her long, lithe legs caused a tingling to swirl inside his chest.

He coughed loudly and followed her toward the exit.

"After my experience last night," she said, "I made sure to fill up the gas tank on my rental. So I can just drive over to the bistro and meet you there."

"No need for that," Dillon blurted out before thinking twice. "Just leave your car here. I can drive us, then bring you back after we're done."

Mona stared at him through wide eyes. It was obvious his suggestion had come as a surprise. Hell, the idea had even shocked him.

What are you doing? he asked himself. *You're slipping, man...*

"Are you sure?" she asked, her high-pitched tone filled with uncertainty. "I don't want to inconvenience you."

"It's no inconvenience at all. Should we head out?"

"Yep. Let's go."

MONA TOOK A bite of her corn bread and closed her eyes. "Mmm, this is good. Oh, how I've missed it. By the time I get back to LA, I'll probably be a good ten pounds heavier."

"I highly doubt that," Dillon said, discreetly eyeing her slim figure. "It's obvious you take great care of yourself."

"Thank you. I try."

An awkward silence fell over the pair. Dillon curled his hands into tight fists underneath the table, hoping his comment hadn't come across flirtatiously.

He took a sip of lemonade and glanced around the lively Cajun-style restaurant. Crowds gathered around the redbrick walls, admiring glittery feathered Mardi Gras masks. Patrons were seated in pub stools, their distressed wooden high-top tables overflowing with platters of boiled crawfish and bowls of jambalaya.

"So tell me, Detective Reed," Mona asked, "what brought you to Lake Landry? From what I've heard, you were next in line to becoming chief of police back in Baton Rouge."

Dillon felt his hands slowly unravel. He was seldom rattled by the presence of others, if ever. He chalked it up to working in law enforcement for so many years.

But there was something about Mona that knocked him off his square.

"From what you've heard?" he asked. "Does that mean you've been asking about me?"

The right corner of Mona's lips curled into a slight smile. "Maybe. Well, actually…yes."

"Oh, okay. Now see, I wasn't the only one making inquiries. You were asking about me, too, huh?"

"It wasn't even like that, Detective. I had to know who I'd be partnering with after Chief Boyer sang your praises. Or who I *thought* I'd be partnering with…"

A sliver of guilt jabbed at Dillon's side. His eyes squinted thoughtfully as he watched Mona stare down at her plate, stabbing a piece of romaine lettuce with her fork.

"To answer your question," Dillon said, "the high rate of violent crimes occurring back in Baton Rouge got to be too much for me. I needed a slower pace. I thought a smaller, quieter town would help lower my anxiety level *and* blood pressure. And I'm single, so I figured the move would be easy. But then, the minute I get to town, *boom*. I'm assigned a case that's caught the attention of the entire nation."

"Lucky for you, you've got help all around you. Lake Landry's police department is extremely capable. They've always had an all-hands-on-deck type of attitude. At least they used to."

"And they still do. I'm getting plenty of input from other officers. And I'm open to it. But I'm the lead detective in Olivia's case. So at the end of the day, I'm going to investigate it my way."

"Understood. But I do have some information on Olivia's husband, Blake, that you may not know."

"And what would make you think that?"

Mona leaned into the table and tapped her index finger in front of Dillon.

"Blake Carter comes from a powerful family, Detective. People in this town are afraid of him. He's always been a cold narcissist who thinks his money can buy him out of any situation. They don't want to get involved and end up like Olivia."

"That's why we've got the anonymous tip line," Dillon told her. "If the townspeople feel uneasy speaking with law enforcement directly, they should feel comfortable utilizing it."

"It's not that simple. The townspeople believe that some members of law enforcement are on Blake's payroll."

"Oh, come on," he huffed, throwing up his hand. "Look, I may be new to Lake Landry PD, but I don't believe that for one second. This town's police department is known for having a pristine reputation throughout the state of Louisiana. Now, you claim to know things about Blake that I don't. What would those things be? Because I know plenty."

Mona crossed her arms in front of her. "Did you know that Blake wasn't seen around Transformation Cosmetics' offices the day that Olivia went missing?"

Dillon paused. He'd heard all about how Blake was an egotistical maniac who arrogantly flashed his wealth and mistreated his wife. But he didn't know the man hadn't shown up for work that day.

"Are you sure?" he asked skeptically. "Because Blake stated he was at work. And Blake's executive assistant was one of the first people I questioned after I spoke to him. She assured me he was in the office all day."

"Did she really," Mona uttered sarcastically, tilting her head to the side. "So I guess you also haven't heard that Blake and his assistant Ayana are having an affair. In addition to a couple of other women within the company."

Dillon leaned back in his chair, his eyes fixated on Mona's knowing expression. *"Wow,"* he breathed. "Are you serious?"

"Very. See why teaming up with me might not be such a bad thing? I have access to inside information swirling around town that you simply don't, Detective Reed."

He just sat there, dumbfounded. His lips parted, but nothing came out. Because he realized that Mona just might be right.

Dillon propped his elbow on top of the table and fidgeted with his perfectly trimmed goatee. He studied Mona's face, searching for any signs of salaciousness or deceit. He saw none. Her look of determination appeared pure. He could sense that she was really there to help find her friend rather than gain more popularity through sensational reporting on the case.

"You, um…you may be right, Ms. Avery. Maybe I could use your assistance with this investigation. But if I do agree to this partnership, it's gonna come with some terms and conditions."

"Such as?"

"Well, first off, you have to stop referring to me as Detective Reed and start calling me Dillon."

"Deal. So long as you call me Mona instead of Ms. Avery."

"You got it. Second, I'm going to need for you to keep in mind that this is *my* investigation. I take the lead on this case. And what I say goes. While I do respect your opinion and I'm open to hearing you out, I don't want us bumping heads and debating nonstop. We have to work together. Respectfully."

"I can do that," Mona replied, tapping her rose-colored fingernails against the glass of lemonade. "What else?"

"Third, and most important, no going behind my back and conducting your own personal investigations. You need to keep me in the loop on whatever plans you have to speak with people and search certain areas."

As soon as the words were out of Dillon's mouth, Mona threw her head back and stared up at the ceiling.

"Come on, now," she moaned. "Are you serious? I'm an investigative journalist, Dillon. This is what I do."

"Not on my watch. Once again, this is *my* investigation. So we're going to do things my way. This can get dangerous, Mona. I know that all eyes are on Blake right now, but we don't know if he's truly behind Olivia's disappearance. So, until we figure out exactly who and what we're dealing with, I'm making it my responsibility to keep you safe. Understand?"

Dillon almost laughed out loud as he watched Mona squirm in her chair. Clearly she wasn't used to being told what to do.

"Fine," she blurted out. "But do I even have any other choice?"

"Nope. You don't."

Just when Dillon took the last bite of his salad, their server approached the table.

"How's it going, you two?" she asked through a toothy grin. "Are those salads and slices of corn bread making those taste buds happy?"

"Ecstatic," Mona told her, placing her hand over her stomach. "Everything was delicious. I almost ordered another slice of corn bread. But I figured I'd better stop while I'm ahead."

"Would you two like a cup of coffee? Or how about a plate of dessert? We're serving up bananas Foster, pecan pralines, king cakes…"

"Mmm, sounds amazing," Dillon said, "but I'm going to have to pass. Mona? Would you like anything?"

"I'd better not. I'll definitely be back for a bowl of bananas Foster before I leave town, though."

"Oh, we've got a tourist!" the server chirped, her Southern drawl dripping with cheer. "What brings you to town?"

Before Mona could respond, the woman gasped and pointed at her.

"Wait a minute, I knew I recognized you from somewhere! You're Mona Avery! I always watch your broadcasts. Honey, let me tell you, I am a true-crime fanatic."

"Aww, well, thank you. I appreciate that."

The server dropped her arms down by her sides and stared directly at Dillon. "I really do hope you two nail that Blake Carter. All of Lake Landry knows he did something to that sweet wife of his."

Dillon quickly cleared his throat and held up his finger. "If you wouldn't mind bringing us the check, that would be great. Thanks."

He noticed the server's hands trembling when she reached up and tucked a strand of hair behind her ear.

"Comin' right up," she muttered, side-eyeing him before slinking off.

"Oh boy," Mona sighed. She tossed her napkin down onto the table. "We've got our hands full with this case and the townspeople. I'm telling you, the Whitman family is loved by this community. And Olivia is like a star in Lake

Landry. I was in awe of her when we first met. Funny how her twin brother Oliver is the complete opposite."

"Yeah, what's up with him? I've tried to get him to come down to the station on numerous occasions. I thought he'd be happy to share some insight into Olivia's disappearance with me. But so far he's been completely uncooperative."

Mona shook her head and stared down at the table.

"That doesn't surprise me. Oliver is the black sheep of the Whitman family. Oddly enough, he seems to relish in that. He attended college with us for one semester but dropped out after that."

"He's definitely a bit strange. What was he like back when you were living here?"

"Oliver's always been this detached loner who wasn't interested in academics. He always said he'd rather attend the school of life, as if he was too good for a traditional education. But he never had any real goals or aspirations. The only thing he was interested in was laying up in his parents' mansion and playing video games."

"Well, from what I've heard, the Whitmans are fed up with Oliver. They forced him to get a job in Transformation Cosmetics' warehouse."

Mona threw her head back and laughed profusely. "The thought of Oliver doing any sort of manual labor is hilarious. I'm actually surprised he's lasted this long at the company."

"Lucky for him, his brother-in-law runs it."

"I know, right? Without that little perk, I seriously doubt he would've even gotten the job." Mona paused, peering at Dillon from across the table. "You asked for full disclosure when it comes to Olivia's case, right?"

"I did. Why?"

"Well, *full disclosure*, Blake has agreed to meet with

me this afternoon. I told him I just want to have a casual conversation. As old friends."

"Okay. What time are we meeting with him?" Dillon asked.

Mona's eyes shifted around the restaurant. "*I'm* scheduled to meet with him at two o'clock."

"Didn't we just talk about this? I don't want you conducting these little side investigations on your own. It's not safe, Mona. Can't you understand that?"

"Of course I understand that. But Blake and I go way back. Now, is he a jerk? Absolutely. We haven't always been on the best of terms. I've checked him on numerous occasions over the way he's treated Olivia. But he would never—"

She paused when the server set the check down on the table.

"Thanks again for stopping in," she mumbled. Gone was the chipper tone in her voice. "Looking forward to that arrest being made…"

"Thank you for everything," Mona quickly interjected before Dillon could respond. "Detective, are you ready to go?"

"Definitely."

He pulled out his wallet and paid the bill, then followed Mona toward the exit.

Once the pair were outside, he inhaled the warm, humid air, squinting in the bright sunlight.

Christmastime in Lake Landry was in full swing. The sound of festive music lingered in the breeze. Local stores lining the streets were heavily decorated with colorful ornaments. Shoppers carrying bags filled with gifts packed the walkways.

But despite all the merriment, Dillon was completely unplugged from the holiday season. The only thing on his mind was finding Olivia.

"So where are you meeting Blake?" he asked Mona as they approached his car.

"At Kimmy's Coffee and Cake Shop. It's right across the street from Transformation Cosmetics."

"Yeah, I know that place."

Dillon wanted to revisit the idea of Mona not going alone. But he knew the suggestion would fall on deaf ears.

He opened the passenger door. Mona stepped forward, pausing before slipping inside. Her hand brushed against his when she gripped the doorframe. He swallowed the stream of heat that shot up his throat.

The pair locked eyes. Dillon noticed a fiery look in Mona's gaze, as if she were still waiting for him to challenge her meetup with Blake.

Just back off, he told himself. *Let the woman do her thing.*

"I—" both Dillon and Mona said simultaneously.

They paused, emitting awkward chuckles.

"Please," Dillon said, "may I speak first?"

"Of course."

"Thank you. Now, if I'm being honest, I am not comfortable with you meeting Blake alone."

"But I—"

Dillon gently placed his hand on her shoulder, quieting her.

She jumped slightly, appearing surprised.

"Sorry," he blurted out, quickly removing his grasp. He cleared his throat, then continued.

"I understand that you and Blake go way back. You two have established a rapport. Honestly, you may be able to get more out of him than I did. So, with that being said, I'll give you a pass and let you meet up with him. *This* time."

"Oh gee, thanks," Mona quipped.

She climbed inside the car and grabbed the door handle. After a silent staredown, Dillon backed away.

Just leave it alone, he told himself before getting in and pulling off.

"Look, Dillon, you seem skeptical of every move I make. Now, I may not be a law enforcement officer, but I am a very capable, experienced investigative journalist. My track record speaks for itself."

"That it does. And listen, it's not that I'm skeptical. It's just… I'm not used to partnering up with anyone outside of law enforcement. Especially someone linked to the media. I had several run-ins with Baton Rouge's news outlets during some of the most important investigations of my life. I don't wanna keep going through that. It's one of the reasons why I left the department."

"I understand that. But I work for a very reputable news outlet. And have you researched the cases I've worked on? Trust me, you're in good hands."

Dillon nodded his head while turning down Statewood Avenue. He had in fact looked into Mona's previous casework. And it was impressive to say the least.

She had assisted law enforcement agencies all over the United States in solving numerous investigations, from human trafficking rings to murder-for-hire plots. Her skillset and contributions could not be denied.

"Okay," Dillon said. "I'll fall back on this meetup with Blake. Just promise me you'll reach out as soon as it's over and let me know how it went."

"I will absolutely do that. And hopefully this is just the beginning. My main goal is to get an on-air interview with him. Maybe seeing his face on national television will encourage people who know more than what they're saying to come forward."

"If only it were that easy…"

Chapter Three

The silver bell hovering over Kimmy's Coffee and Cakes' white wood-framed door jingled loudly.

Mona glanced up at the entrance, expecting to see Blake enter the café. But instead a group of chatty mothers and their young children walked inside.

The pastel-themed sweet shop was packed. Charming curved metal tables and chairs with red bows tied across their backs were filled with Christmas shoppers. Twig wreaths intertwined with holly hung from the walls. A silver tree adorned with crystal ornaments stood in the front window. And trays of mocha lattes, hot chocolate and pastries were being served to the festive patrons.

Mona checked the time. It was almost 2:30 p.m. Blake was practically thirty minutes late. She grabbed her cell phone, opened their text message thread and began typing.

Hey, I'm at Kimmy's. Been here since 2. Are you still planning on meeting—

The bell over the door jingled again. Mona's head shot up. Blake finally came strolling through the door.

In all the years she'd known him, nothing had changed. Judging from the size of his biceps, which appeared well-defined underneath his dark gray blazer, Blake had still been hitting the gym religiously. His dark hair and perfectly trimmed mustache appeared freshly cut. She raised her hand and caught his attention. He looked over and nodded his head, then made a beeline toward her table.

All eyes were on Blake as he swaggered through the café. Mona had chosen a table in the back corner, hoping they'd have some privacy. But considering the size of the small shop, discretion was practically impossible.

He appeared oblivious to the patrons' stares and whispers, staring straight ahead while he made his way through the maze of tables. But judging from the slight smirk on his face, he was aware of the attention and seemed to enjoy it.

Typical Blake...

Mona stood up when he approached her table.

"Well, well, well," Blake said, his deep voice tinged with a touch of cynicism. "If it isn't the infamous Mona Avery. How've you been, M-Boogie?" he asked, referring to her old college moniker.

"I'm hanging in there," she replied coolly. "How are you?"

"I'm doing all right, considering the circumstances."

Mona cringed slightly when he reached out and embraced her. She barely wrapped her arms around him before patting his back, then quickly stepping away.

When Blake adjusted the gold links attached to his crisp white cuffs, Mona noticed his manicured hands and his diamond-embellished luxury watch.

Just as flashy as ever, Mona thought.

He gripped a chair and pulled it away from the table, flinching at the sound of its clawed feet screeching against the white marble floor.

It was then that Mona realized Blake wasn't as composed as he appeared.

"Are you okay?" she asked.

He slowly sat down and folded his hands on top of the table. "I'm just trying to maintain some sense of normalcy in the midst of all this madness. My wife is missing. Almost everybody in town suspects that I had something to do with it. Which of course I didn't."

Mona took a seat across from Blake. She studied his expression. Gone was the arrogant smirk. It'd been replaced by a tight frown. His face was lined with worry. She was surprised by his outward show of concern. Blake had never been the type to let people see him sweat.

But it could all just be an act, she told herself.

"Well," she sighed, "I am so sorry that this has happened. We're all hurting over Olivia's disappearance. That's why I'm here. I'm going to do all that I can to help get to the bottom of this and bring Olivia home safely."

"And I appreciate that. Hopefully you'll be adding this case to your long list of success stories."

"Let's hope so," Mona replied, side-eyeing Blake skeptically. She still couldn't get a grasp on whether or not he was being sincere. "You and I certainly have a lot to catch up on."

"That we do," Blake muttered before glancing down at his watch. "But unfortunately, we may have to save some of that catching up for another day. I've got a meeting with a new PR consultant that my director of operations set up in twenty minutes."

"*Twenty minutes?* That won't give us enough time to talk."

"Sorry," he said with a shrug, sitting back in his chair. "It'll have to do for now. We're preparing for Transformation Cosmetics' annual Christmas toy drive, and this year's event is gonna be huge. It's even being covered by the national news."

There he is, Mona thought. *Back to the Blake I know. All about the business and his image.*

"I don't know if you're familiar with the guy who runs my operations department, Leo Mendez," Blake continued. "He's like my right-hand man. Keeps the wheels spinning at the company. He is great at keeping Transformation's name in the media, and—"

"Blake," Mona interrupted. "I didn't come here to talk about Transformation Cosmetics. I'm here to discuss Olivia, and what you think may have happened to her."

He cleared his throat, staring across the table at Mona while rubbing his hands together. She could've sworn there was a glimmer of irritation in his eyes.

"My apologies," he said. "I just get carried away by the good that my company is doing. It's a nice distraction from everything else that's going on."

"You mean the fact that your wife is missing? I'd think that finding her would be your number one priority. Not indulging in things to take your mind off of it."

"You're right." Blake's face began to redden as he fiddled with his mustache. "And it is. You said you wanted to catch up. So I was just explaining what I've got going on and why I have to cut this meeting short. I hope you didn't take it as me wanting CNB News to cover the toy drive or anything."

When he raised his eyebrows expectantly, Mona realized that's exactly what he was doing.

Mona sat straight up in her chair, struggling to maintain her composure.

"Considering the fact that your wife is missing, I seriously doubt that CNB's viewers would be interested in your company's toy drive. They would, however, want to hear your take on Olivia's disappearance. Would you be willing to do an on-air interview with me to discuss that?"

Blake turned in his seat, crossing his legs and propping his folded hands over his knee.

Mona noticed that he wasn't wearing his wedding ring.

"I would give it some thought," he told her.

She'd heard that wavering tone time and time again. It reeked of insincerity.

"But," Blake continued, "I'd have to discuss the potential interview with my attorney before I agree to something like that."

"Oh? So you've hired an attorney?"

"Of course I have. I'd be a fool not to." Blake paused, running his hand down his impeccably pressed slacks. "Listen, Mona, I know you think I had something to do with Olivia's disappearance. But I can assure you that I didn't."

"Can you?"

Mona pulled a red leather-bound notebook from her purse and slid the slim silver ink pen from its holder. She flipped to a blank page, then stared up at Blake, tapping the pen against the table.

"How was Olivia's mood the day that she went missing? Was she sad? Stressed? Seemingly normal?"

He paused, his jaws clenching as he turned toward the window. "I didn't actually see Olivia the day she went missing."

"What do you mean? You didn't see her that morning before you two left for work?"

"No. I didn't."

"But how could you—"

Mona stopped abruptly. She studied the crumpled look of guilt on Blake's face.

"So I'm assuming you weren't home that morning?" she probed.

"No… I wasn't."

Mona took a deep breath. She grabbed her cup of maple hot chocolate and took a long sip.

"Did Olivia know you were having an affair?" she boldly asked.

Which would've been the perfect motive for you to harm her if you did, she was tempted to add.

"I don't believe so. If she did, she never questioned me about it."

"Of course not. Olivia's always been too sweet and passive for her own good."

Blake eyed Mona, appearing as though he wanted to refute her statement. But before he could, his cell phone rang.

"Could you please excuse me?"

He didn't wait for Mona to respond before picking up the call.

"This is Blake. Yes, I'm still over at Kimmy's. Okay, I'll be there in a few minutes."

Blake disconnected the call, then stood up.

"Sorry to cut our little chat short, but the PR consultant has arrived at my office. I need to get back for our meeting."

"There's a lot more I'd like to discuss with you, Blake. You could have information that will help us find Olivia."

"Have you talked to her brother yet?"

"No. Why would I? Olivia and Oliver aren't close. Never have been."

"Yeah, well, he may know more than you think."

Mona slowly leaned into the table. "What makes you say that? Has he been acting strange around the office?"

"I wouldn't know. I fired him two months ago."

"Really? Why?"

"Because of that hot temper of his. He throws tantrums like a two-year-old child. And I blame his parents for that. Thanks to all their coddling, Oliver is out of control."

"What exactly did he do to get fired?" Mona asked.

"He snapped on Leo, who was his boss, mind you, one too many times. During the last incident, Oliver got mad because Leo asked him to recount a shipment of boxes. The confrontation got so heated that Oliver swung a fist at Leo. That was it for me. I don't care if Oliver is my brother-in-law. He needs help. I'm talking serious anger management."

"Hmm, sounds like he's gotten worse since college."

"Oh, trust me," Blake quipped, "he has. And you know how jealous he is of Olivia. If he could get that angry over a warehouse delivery, imagine what his resentment toward her could drive him to do."

Mona studied Blake's stern expression. She wondered whether he really believed Oliver was involved in Olivia's disappearance, or if he was trying to pin it on him to take the heat off himself.

"Listen, I know you're really busy," Mona said, "especially during this time of the year. But I also know how important finding Olivia is to you."

She paused, waiting for Blake to agree with her. But he just stood there, staring back at her blankly.

Several moments passed before he finally spoke up.

"Yeah, yeah," he muttered. "Of course."

"Well, I would really like to sit down and talk with you again. And if possible, conduct that interview live on air—"

Mona was once again interrupted by the ringing of Blake's cell phone.

"That's Leo again," he told her. "I've gotta get back to the office. I'll reconnect with you soon. And don't forget," Blake reminded her as he headed toward the exit, "reach out to Oliver and see what he has to say for himself!"

Mona watched as Blake spun around and jogged out of the shop. She immediately grabbed her phone and composed a text message to Dillon.

Just wrapped up the meeting with Blake. Are you available to talk? Got a lot to catch you up on.

Dillon responded within seconds.

Can we catch up early this evening? I've got my hands full down here at the station.

Sure, Mona wrote back. Just call me whenever you're free.

She closed out the text message thread and opened her Instagram account. Mona searched for Oliver's page, which he posted to regularly with various celebrity conspiracy theories.

She found it and clicked on the most recent post.

Think your favorite celebrity is dead? Well think again! Many of our beloved entertainers INTEN-TIONALLY disappeared in order to escape the evils of HOLLYWOOD! Swipe left to check out the celebs I KNOW are still alive!

"This man is ridiculous," Mona mumbled.

She tapped the direct message link and began composing a private message to Oliver.

Hi there. Mona Avery here. It's been a while. I hope you're well. I'm in town covering Olivia's disappearance and would love to get together and talk with you. Please reach out and let me know if you're up for it, and if so, when. Hope to hear from you soon...

She sent the message, then sighed deeply, disappointed in the outcome of her meeting with Blake. It was too short and he was too vague. While she had gotten him to admit to having an affair, that wasn't much of a secret to many in Lake Landry.

She drained her cup of maple hot chocolate and checked her emails. After responding to a few, she opened Instagram again and checked her direct messages. No response from Oliver yet.

"Ugh," she sighed, worried that she wouldn't hear back from him.

Mona gathered her things and headed toward the exit. On the way out, she saw Kimmy standing behind the counter, filling a tray with wreath-shaped tea cakes.

"Great seeing you, Kimmy," she called out, smiling at the woman known as Lake Landry's surrogate grandmother. "The holiday hot chocolate special was delicious."

"You're so welcome, Mona! It was wonderful seeing you, too. And hey, *please* find out what happened to our girl."

"I will. I promise."

A few customers standing at the counter turned toward her. Before they could get started with a slew of questions, she hurried out the door.

"WHAT ARE YOU DOING?" Mona asked herself. "What exactly are you doing?"

She glanced out the window. No one was around. No cars were parked along the curbs, nor were they driving down the desolate road.

Mona had once again returned to the Beechtree neighborhood where Olivia had supposedly gone missing. The last time she'd visited the area, it was pitch-black. Now it was the middle of the day, and sunlight shone down on the bleak, deserted area. This meant she could get a better look at the alleged crime scene and hopefully find evidence that law enforcement overlooked.

Come on, Mona, she thought. *You promised Dillon you wouldn't do this...*

But Dillon was tied up at the station, and she was itching to do something that would help move the investigation forward.

Mona pulled over near the body of water. She turned off the engine and stepped out of the car.

A strong gust of wind whipped past her and slammed the door shut. She looked up at the sky. The bright sun had suddenly been concealed by looming gray clouds.

"Please don't rain," she groaned, realizing she hadn't packed an umbrella.

Mona contemplated getting back inside the car, heading to the inn and waiting for Dillon to contact her.

But that just isn't who you are, the headstrong journalist reminded herself before setting off toward the body of water.

She stared down at her cream outfit and tan suede ankle boots.

"The least you could've done is gone back and changed," she muttered to herself.

But it was too late now. Adrenaline was pumping through her veins. She was officially in investigative mode.

Mona trudged through the damp marsh. Her eyes darted around the field, focusing on every patch of grass and lump of mud around her.

She stopped abruptly when she noticed an obscure-looking pile of branches up ahead.

A pang of terror thumped in the pit of her stomach. The thought of finding Olivia's body flashed through her mind.

Stop that! she thought, raising her hands to her temples and squeezing tightly. *Stop it now!*

The words reverberated through Mona's head like a shrill scream. She couldn't believe her mind had gone there.

She was used to having more control of herself during these investigations. But this case was different. It was personal.

Nevertheless, Mona reminded herself she had to keep calm and remain in work mode.

Toughen up. Focus on the facts. Keep it business.

She took a deep breath and approached the pile of branches. She began sifting through them, bracing herself for what may come. A shoe. A lock of hair. A piece of clothing. Anything that would indicate that Olivia may have met her demise out there near the water.

But she reached the bottom of the pile without finding anything.

"Thank goodness," Mona breathed, wiping her damp forehead before forging ahead.

She continued searching for any bits of evidence or disturbed areas of land. Cleared marsh. A gathering of leaves. A pile of rocks. Nothing appeared out of place.

When she reached the edge of the water, Mona's cell phone buzzed. She pulled it out and tapped the notification. A text message appeared. It had been sent from an unknown number.

LEAVE LAKE LANDRY!

Mona's hand trembled as she quickly shoved the phone back inside her pocket.

"Ignore it," she told herself. "Don't give in to the threats. Stay focused on finding Olivia."

Mona closed her eyes and took a deep breath. She stared down at the gravel-filled soil. A surge of energy shot up her calves. She willed the land to speak to her. Show her a sign of something. *Anything.* Footprints. An earring. A glass test tube Olivia may have been using to collect water samples.

But there was nothing.

Mona continued along the water's edge. She pulled her phone back out and began filming a video of the area. If she couldn't find anything now, maybe she could zoom in on the video and something would pop out at her that she'd missed.

Just when Mona laid eyes on a silver chain twisted within the dirt, she heard tree branches rustling behind her.

She spun around. Bald cypress tree leaves swayed erratically in the wind. Mona squinted her eyes, studying the bright green foliage.

Within the brush, she could've sworn she'd seen a blur of blackness fumbling about.

"What in the…?"

She turned her phone toward the image and continued filming. A sharp tingling crept through her fingertips, making its way up her arms, then quickly washing over her entire body.

Mona knew the sensation all too well. It was a feeling of regret.

I shouldn't have come here…

"Hey!" she yelled, "who's out there?"

No one responded. But as she continued to observe the brush, Mona noticed a shadowy figure. And then, a flash of silver metal.

She gasped.

A gun?

Mona's mouth fell open. She almost let out a scream before quickly tightening her lips. Despite her hand's violent trembling, she continued filming the area.

"I can see you!" she shouted. "And I'm filming you!"

Slowly backing away from the water, she prayed that her heels wouldn't catch on the uneven earth. She waited for whomever was loitering in the brush to step forward or run away. Neither happened.

Fear sucked the breath from Mona's lungs. She tried to inhale but felt as though she were being suffocated.

She contemplated making a run for it. Then Mona remembered the chain buried in the dirt.

You've got to get that necklace!

She kept her phone's camera rolling while slowly inching her way back toward the chain. She kept her head up while glancing down at the ground.

Found it!

Just as she bent her knees and reached for it, Mona's heel sank down into a mudhole.

She fell backward, crashing onto the dank wetland.

Dammit!

As she struggled to stand up, tree limbs once again crackled in the distance.

Mona froze, expecting someone to jump out and rush her.

She watched in horror as a pair of black leather gloves pulled the branches apart.

Just when a black combat boot appeared, the shrill sound of a car horn blew in the distance.

The combat boot paused. It quickly disappeared back into the brush along with the black leather gloves.

A wave of relief ripped through Mona's chest. She dug her fingers into the dirt, pulling her heels up while scrambling to get on her feet. Her legs shook as she steadied herself.

She studied the wooded area where the lurker stood, hoping he'd fled the scene. When Mona felt safe enough to make a run for it, she darted toward her car.

Wait! The necklace!

She stopped abruptly, emitting a dread-filled whimper. She spun around, praying that the man was gone while retracing her steps.

"Where is it? Where is it?" she hissed.

Mona stared down at the ground, seeing double as her eyes filled with tears. Her head twisted frantically while searching for the silver chain amid tall blades of grass, scatters of pebbles and pockets of water.

Come on...come on...where is it?

A stifling panic filled Mona's chest at the thought of the lurker reappearing.

But despite her fear, she refused to leave until she found the chain.

She hobbled closer toward the water's edge, stumbling through the muddy gravel. Her boots were covered in dirt. She bent down and clawed at the soil, her frustration growing.

She wondered if Olivia felt the same level of fear right before she went missing. In that moment, Mona felt more connected to her friend than ever.

I am going to find you, Olivia...

A shrill car horn once again filled the air. Mona jumped at the startling sound. She contemplated leaving the necklace behind and coming back for it tomorrow with backup.

Just when she turned to rush off, a flash of metal caught her eye.

It was the necklace.

She quickly pulled a tissue from her pocket and grabbed the chain, careful not to taint it with her fingerprints.

Once she'd slipped it securely inside her pocket, Mona ran toward the street.

Boom!

She stopped in her tracks at the sound of a loud explosion.

Oh no. Oh no.

Mona looked up as flames blazed through the air. She stumbled to the curb.

Her car had been set on fire. The words *GET OUT* were spray-painted across the hood.

"What the…?" Mona uttered, shocked at the sight.

She caught a glimpse of a man dressed in all black, charging into the woods.

Mona slowly backed away from the scene, then spun around and took off running toward a nearby thrift store.

"Somebody help me!"

Chapter Four

Dillon pulled up in front of the inn and strolled inside the lobby. He glanced around the cozy French-themed room, admiring the colorful Christmas decorations while searching for Mona.

He walked past a group of chatty, overly made-up women. They squealed loudly while ranting over a new eyeshadow palette that had launched just in time for the holidays.

Dillon chuckled at their enthusiasm. Their joyful demeanor, along with the festive cream-colored berry wreaths hanging from the walls, gold garland lining the railings, and Fraser fir Christmas tree standing in the corner of the room, made for quite a merry atmosphere.

He glanced over toward the fireplace. There, sitting underneath a row of white satin stockings hanging from the mantel, was Mona.

Dillon felt an abrupt pounding inside his chest. He cleared his throat, rubbing his neck before walking toward her.

Even dressed in a white tank and navy blue leggings, Mona looked beautiful. Her head was propped against the back of an emerald green Louis XVI–style chair. She was staring up at the wood beams adorning the inn's vaulted ceiling.

As he got closer, Dillon noticed Mona's delicate face was plagued with a melancholy expression.

He was hit with a sense of alarm.

"Detective Reed!" he heard someone call out.

He turned and waved at Evelyn, The Bayou Inn's manager.

"Hey, Ev. How are you?"

"I'm great! It's so good to see you!"

The short, stout woman giggled while running her fingers through her chestnut brown pixie haircut. She pressed her thin lips together, spreading burgundy-stained gloss even farther outside of her lip line.

"Good to see you, too," he replied, smiling graciously at her blatant flirting.

Dillon turned his attention back to Mona. She was staring directly at him.

They locked eyes. For a few brief moments, it felt as though everything around them had stopped.

He inhaled, his breath catching in his throat as he sauntered toward her.

"Hello, Mona," he said, hoping the thumping in his chest didn't resonate in his voice.

Mona sat straight up and placed her cup down onto the coffee table.

"Hey, Dillon. How was your day?"

Dillon tilted his head, observing her rigid demeanor.

"My day was long. And busy. May I?" he asked, pointing over at the chair next to hers.

"Of course. Please, have a seat."

As he sat down, Dillon noticed Mona shifting awkwardly in her chair, now seemingly unable to look directly at him.

"Are you okay?" he asked her.

"I, um, not exactly," she muttered, picking up her cup and staring down at its contents.

Before Dillon could ask why, Evelyn came bouncing over.

"Detective *Reeeed*," she sang while rubbing her hands together. "I know you're always looking out for that waist-line of yours, but have you had dinner yet?"

"No, actually. I haven't. And I already know you've probably cooked up something spectacular tonight."

"I most certainly have. Would you like to hear about it?"

"I most certainly would," he said.

Dillon glanced over at Mona. He noticed she'd placed her hand over her stomach.

"Hey," he said to her, "are you all right?"

"I'm fine," she replied a bit too quickly. "I'm just feeling a bit under the weather. Evelyn was nice enough to make me a cup of ginger tea in hopes of settling my stomach."

"Oh, okay," he replied, eyeing her suspiciously. He could sense that something wasn't quite right.

"I'm so sorry you're not feeling good, dear," Evelyn chimed in. "I hate that you're gonna miss out on my spicy Cajun chili and creole corn bread. I added extra jalapeno peppers and cheddar cheese to give it that good ole Bayou Inn *oomph*."

"Ooh," Mona moaned, placing her hand over her fore-head and closing her eyes.

Dillon could see that her reaction had hurt Evelyn's feelings.

"I'll tell you what, Ev," he said. "If it's not too much trou-ble, why don't you bring me a cup of eggnog hot chocolate for now. And I'll take a bowl of chili, side of corn bread and a few peppermint beignets to go."

"That wouldn't be any trouble at all. Mona, can I get

you anything else other than the tea? A glass of ice water? A few crackers or a piece of toast?"

"Thanks, but I'm fine for now."

"Okay, hon. Just let me know if you change your mind. Detective Reed, I'll be right back with that hot chocolate and will put in the to-go order for you."

"I appreciate it."

Dillon watched as Evelyn hurried off. As soon as she was out of earshot, he turned to Mona.

"Hey, what's going on with you?"

"I just had a really rough day," she sighed.

"So I'm guessing your conversation with Blake didn't go very well?"

Mona hesitated, pulling at a piece of thread hanging from her leggings.

"I guess you could say that."

"Do you wanna talk about it? Maybe put our heads together and decipher whatever information you were able to pull out of him?"

She remained silent, still staring down at her lap. When Dillon noticed her eyes welling up with tears, he knew there was something she wasn't telling him.

He reached over and gently placed his hand over hers.

"Hey," he said, "I know this isn't easy for you. Your friend has gone missing. That's tough. And even though you and Blake don't have the best relationship, you've known him for a long time. The thought of him harming someone you care about hurts. But that's why you're here. To help find out what happened to Olivia. So hang in there. Together, you and I are going to solve this case. Okay?"

"Okay," Mona whispered.

Dillon's detective instincts kicked in. He sensed that there was something more going on than what Mona was telling him.

But his interrogative skills told him to back off. Whatever she was holding in, he knew she wasn't ready to discuss it.

"Well I've got some pretty interesting news to share with you," he told her.

She finally looked up at him. "You do?"

When her damp, doe-like eyes connected with his, Dillon felt the urge to lean over and kiss her.

Reel it in, man...

The moment was interrupted when Evelyn came over and handed him a cup of hot chocolate.

"Here you go, Detective Reed. I just whipped up a fresh batch for you."

"Thank you so much."

When Evelyn just stood there, running her hands down the front of her frilly red-and-white apron, Dillon realized she was waiting for him to take a sip. He immediately placed the mug to his lips and tasted the sweet drink.

"Mmm, this is absolutely delicious," he told her.

Evelyn leaned back and rapidly clapped her hands. "Ooh, I just love hearing that! Thank you!"

"You're welcome."

An awkward silence fell over the threesome. After a few moments, Evelyn pulled a stack of beverage napkins decorated with boughs of holly from her pocket. She placed them down onto the coffee table, then cleared her throat.

"Well, if there's anything else I can get for you two, just give me a holler. And, Detective, I'll bring out your to-go order whenever you're ready to go!"

"Thanks again, Ev," he chuckled.

Both Mona and Dillon watched as she practically skipped back to the kitchen.

"Someone's got a little crush on you," Mona teased.

"Nah, I'm just the new guy in town. When the next one moves here, Evelyn will forget all about me."

"I doubt that. You're not the forgettable type."

Dillon's head shot up so quickly that he almost spilled his hot chocolate. He eyed Mona intently, wondering whether she was flirting with him.

"So," she continued, "what is it that you were going to tell me?"

"I received a call from Olivia's mother this afternoon. She shared some pretty interesting information with me."

"Really? I've been trying to get by there to see the Whitmans. But we just can't seem to coordinate our schedules. I honestly think they're hesitant to speak with me because of my ties to the media. Like you, they're probably convinced my involvement will turn this case into a media circus."

"Correction," Dillon pointed out, "I *used* to think that. But I don't anymore. Anyway, I'll see what I can do to get you in front of them. I'm sure they trust you enough to know that you wouldn't say or do anything to jeopardize the investigation."

Mona gripped the mug and gulped her tea so quickly that she began to choke.

"Are you okay?" he asked, hopping up and patting her back.

"I—I'm fine," she insisted, waving her hand. "Go ahead. Continue with what you were saying."

Dillon slowly sat back down. He waited until her coughing fit was over before continuing.

"So in addition to speaking with Mrs. Whitman today, I also met with Chief Boyer. Between the two of them, I discovered a couple of details about this case that were missing from Olivia's file."

"Really? Such as?"

"First of all, Blake wasn't the one who reported Olivia

missing. Mrs. Whitman did. On top of that, Olivia had been gone for an entire *week* before the call came in."

Mona's eyes widened as they darted around the room.

"Are you serious? Those are two extremely important facts that could change the course of this investigation."

"They most certainly could. As you know, the first forty-eight hours into an investigation are the most critical. We lost a lot of precious time during the week Olivia went missing. Law enforcement could've been fresh on the assailant's trail, gathering clues and crucial evidence, and collecting video surveillance that's probably been taped over by now. Not to mention witnesses who may have been willing to come forward back then have since disappeared."

Mona groaned loudly, crossing her arms in front of her.

"But wait," she said. "How is it that Olivia was gone for an entire week before anyone thought to call the police?"

"Well, according to Mrs. Whitman, she and her daughter only talk about once a week. Between Olivia's demanding work hours and her parents' various business and personal endeavors, everybody's extremely busy. So her absence went unnoticed. Everybody thought everybody else was keeping up with her."

"And Blake *certainly* couldn't be counted on to keep up with his wife."

"What do you mean?"

"He was so busy running around with one of his mistresses that he didn't even see Olivia the morning she went missing."

"And I'm assuming you found that out during your meeting with him today?"

Mona paused.

Dillon noticed her eyes had glazed over, as if she were lost in thought.

"*Hello*. Mona? You still there?"

"Oh!" she uttered, grabbing the arms on her chair and sitting straight up. "Yeah, I'm here. Sorry, I just…so, anyway, what were you saying?"

Dillon observed her fidgety behavior. He ran his fingertips down his goatee, growing more concerned with her strange demeanor.

"I was asking if Blake told you he wasn't at home the morning that Olivia went missing."

"Yes. He did."

He waited for her to elaborate. When she didn't, he continued.

"When I spoke with Mrs. Whitman, she told me that she'd received a call from a friend who works for Sage Insurance. That's the company that issued Olivia's and Blake's life insurance policies. About a month before Olivia's disappearance, Blake met with their agent and upped the amount of her policy."

"Did he up the amount of his, as well?"

"No, he did not."

"Of course he didn't," Mona said, slamming her hands against her thighs. "I can't believe Blake's greedy ass. It's not like his family isn't loaded. Wait, no. Actually, I can believe him. Too much is never enough. That man has always been excessive when it comes to every aspect of his life. From his collection of sports cars to his fancy watches and ridiculously expensive vacations, he's always done the absolute most."

"Yeah, I can see that. During this investigation, I've learned that Blake is all about his powerful, lavish image."

"Period. His image is the only reason he married Olivia. Blake, along with his father and Mr. Whitman, couldn't wait to merge their two families and create this powerful empire."

Dillon sat back and took a long sip of hot chocolate. "I

think we can both agree that when it comes to this case, all roads are leading back to Blake. We're gathering a good amount of circumstantial evidence against him. But we still need more. Something solid enough to really pin this on him. I'm hoping we can—"

"Dillon," Mona interrupted, her voice strained. "There's something I need to tell you."

He slid toward the edge of his chair, giving her his undivided attention.

"I'm listening. What's going on?"

She once again diverted her gaze away from him.

"After my meeting with Blake, I went back to the Beechtree area where Olivia was collecting water samples."

Dillon froze, completely dumbfounded. He blinked rapidly, struggling to focus on Mona as if that would help him better understand what she'd just said.

"Hold on," he said. "You did *what*?"

"I went back to Beechtree this afternoon."

"But…*why?* You and I had an agreement. You promised me that you wouldn't make any more moves without my knowledge, did you not?"

"Yes," Mona croaked, her voice barely a whisper. "I did."

Dillon set his mug down, no longer in the mood for hot chocolate.

A seething anger brewed deep within him. He almost blurted out how this was the reason he didn't want to team up with her in the first place.

"So what happened while you were there? Obviously something went down. I noticed how rattled you were the minute I walked through the door."

Mona pulled a tissue out of her tote bag and placed it on the table.

"The good news is," she began, "I found a necklace

buried in the soil near the water source. It may belong to Olivia. Do you think you could take it down to the lab and have it tested for prints?"

Dillon leaned forward, watching while Mona carefully opened the tissue and revealed a silver chain.

"Of course," he replied. "*Wow*. How did you even spot that?"

"A better question is, how did you and your fellow officers miss it?"

He shot Mona a look.

"Careful. Now's not the time for you to get snarky. You're already on thin ice for returning to a possible crime scene without me. You've managed to violate the terms of our partnership before it really even got off the ground."

"You're right. I'm sorry."

Dillon got the attention of the inn's bellhop and asked for a plastic baggie, then turned back to Mona.

"Nevertheless, this was a great find. So thank you. I obviously need to have my crime scene investigators process that Beechtree area again."

"I think that would be a good idea. Hopefully the necklace will produce DNA evidence that'll give us some answers as to who's involved in this."

"That would be ideal," Dillon said. "Because so far, I've been hitting one dead end after another. The people I've questioned. The areas I've searched… It's as if Olivia just vanished into thin air. There's been no activity on her credit cards and bank accounts, no pings on her cell phone, nothing."

Mona pressed her fingertips against her temples.

"That's what is so frustrating about this case. I thought I'd come to town, reconnect with the Whitmans and other townspeople, and get some real leads on what may have happened to Olivia. But no one's talking. It's as if the entire Lake Landry community is afraid to speak on the record."

"But people seem to really trust and like you. Maybe you should start talking to possible witnesses off the record and maintain their anonymity."

"Good idea. It's just more credible when witnesses show their faces and reveal their identity." Mona sighed heavily and slid down in her chair. "Hopefully when I report on that necklace, the community will find that encouraging. It'll be a sign that the investigation's moving forward. You never know. That could lead to someone coming forward with information they may be withholding."

Dillon held up his hand.

"Hold on. You're planning on telling the public about the necklace?"

"Yes. Why?"

"I don't think that's a good idea, Mona. The public doesn't need to know those types of intricate details. It could bring about a lot of chaos. Plus we don't want the suspect to think we're closing in on him just yet. If he's been sloppy and left key evidence behind, I'd like to go in and recover it before he does."

"But *I* collected this evidence. And as a reporter, it's my job to break news and keep the public updated on the status of the investigation."

"I understand that. However, you don't want to compromise our progress, do you? Plus the integrity of this entire operation could be jeopardized as a result of oversharing. Our suspect could even flee Lake Landry before we're able to apprehend him if we reveal too much too soon."

"Fine," Mona muttered, throwing her hands out at her sides. "But you do understand that I'm known for revealing exclusive details that no other journalists have, don't you?"

"I do understand that. Nevertheless, we are not going to compromise this investigation for the sake of your reputation."

Mona opened her mouth to speak. Dillon quickly continued before she could interject.

"Why don't we change the subject? You mentioned that finding this necklace was the good news. Does that mean you also have bad news?"

He watched as Mona rocked back in her chair. She hunched her shoulders, once again staring down at her lap.

Dillon felt as though she was coming unhinged. She picked up her cup, slowly taking several sips of tea as if she were stalling.

This woman is about to drop a bomb on me...

"While I was at the water source," Mona said, her voice wavering uncontrollably, "I received a threatening text message."

"Really? Saying what?"

"To leave Lake Landry. It was actually similar to a text I received shortly after I began covering this case. But I ignored them both. I refuse to be bullied into quitting this investigation."

"Why didn't you report the initial message to law enforcement?" Dillon asked.

"Because I was afraid you'd use that as ammunition to have me removed from the case."

Before he could refute her claim, Mona continued.

"So, anyway, while I was in Beechtree this afternoon, I decided to film a video of the area while searching for evidence. Right when I saw the necklace buried in the soil, I noticed a shadowy figure lurking in the trees."

Dillon's muscles immediately constricted. His body grew hot underneath his tan leather moto jacket.

Don't say a word, he told himself. *Just hear her out.*

"So the next thing I knew," Mona continued, "a pair of hands covered in black gloves appeared from the brush, then a black combat boot. After that? I'm pretty sure I saw a gun."

He glared at Mona, unable to speak. He was overcome by a wave of nausea. The thought of her being in danger turned his stomach.

Mona paused when the bellhop approached the table and handed Dillon a small plastic bag.

"Thanks," he said, throwing her a stare as he dropped the necklace inside.

As soon as the bellhop was out of earshot, Dillon pointed at Mona.

"Please," he muttered through clenched teeth, "continue."

She drained her cup and took a deep breath, blinking rapidly as if she were fighting back more tears.

"I was torn between retrieving the necklace and getting out of there. Then I thought about Olivia, and how desperate I am to help solve her case. That's what forced me to stay and get that chain."

"So let me get this straight. You put your life on the line for something that probably would've still been there had you just gone back the next day with the safety of law enforcement by your side?"

Mona focused on her fidgeting hands rather than his furious stare. "Well, when you put it that way, I guess it doesn't sound like I made the smartest decision."

"Ya think?"

"And that's, um…that's not all that happened."

He groaned loudly. "What else, Mona?"

"When I got back to my car, I saw that it had been set on fire. And the words *GET OUT* were spray-painted across the hood."

Dillon dropped his head in his hands. "I cannot believe this. You know, at the rate you're going, you won't be alive to help solve this case." He jumped up from his chair. "I can't do this anymore. I *knew* this partnership was a bad idea. And you just confirmed that."

"Dillon, wait. Don't leave. I was just trying to—"

"You gave me your word, then completely went against it," he interrupted, unable to hold back his anger. "You're here in Lake Landry assisting in *my* investigation. Which puts you on *my* watch. Yet you decided to go against me and put yourself in an incredibly dangerous situation. I'm done."

"Dillon! Please don't…"

Mona's voice faded in the background as he stormed toward the door. On the way there, he heard Evelyn call out his name.

"Detective Reed! Don't forget your to-go order!"

She ran up behind him and handed over his dinner.

"Thanks, Ev. How much do I owe you?"

"All the great work you're doing for this town? It's on the house. Have a great night!"

"That's really nice of you. Thank you."

When Dillon reached the door, he paused, glancing over at Mona. She stared back at him. The soft, solemn expression on her face was filled with remorse. It almost turned him around and led him back inside the lobby.

Don't give in to it. You don't need these problems.

Dillon turned around, ignoring the pull in his chest while walking out the door.

Chapter Five

Hey, Oliver, Mona typed. I hope you're doing well in spite of everything that's going on. This is my third time reaching out to you. I'd really love to speak with you about Olivia's disappearance. I'm convinced your input could help solve this case. I hope you'll agree to talk with me. Hope to hear from you soon. ~Mona

She sent the message, then glanced down at the clock on her car's dashboard. It was a few minutes before noon.

Mona took a deep breath and stared out at LLL Water Quality Laboratory. No one had exited the stark, redbrick building in the past thirty minutes.

She leaned forward, struggling to see inside the tinted square windows. Not even a shadow of a figure loomed behind the smoky glass.

A haunting feeling came over her. She eyed the four-story structure, which looked more like a penitentiary than an environmental lab.

Mona tried to shake off the chill. But thoughts of Olivia leaving the building for the last time invaded her mind, worsening her fear.

Where are you, friend? What happened to you?

She glanced down at the clock once again. It was now after twelve.

Mona was hoping to run into Bonnie Young, who was one of Olivia's closest work confidants, on her way to lunch.

She was growing desperate to connect with Olivia's inner circle. Since no one was talking, she'd resorted to staking out potential witnesses.

When another chill swept over Mona, she reached down and turned off the air conditioner. Her hand brushed past her cell phone. She grabbed it, hoping that a missed call or text message from Dillon would appear on the screen.

It didn't.

Mona hadn't heard from Dillon since he'd walked out on her at the inn. She had tried reaching out to him over the past several days, to no avail.

The thought of losing Dillon's trust made Mona sick to her stomach. At this point, he had completely iced her out. She was operating on her own.

You shouldn't have told him what happened out there in Beechtree...

"No," Mona said aloud, immediately pushing the thought out of her mind.

Despite her regrets and the result of her actions, she knew she had done the right thing by reporting the attack.

Chief Boyer had reached out to her the day after the crime took place, letting her know law enforcement was doing all that they could to catch the criminal. But so far, no persons of interest had been named.

During the conversation, Mona was tempted to ask the chief why Dillon hadn't contacted her personally to share that information. But she didn't because she already knew the answer. Plus she wanted to mend the rift between her and Dillon privately, without getting Chief Boyer involved.

"Ugh," Mona groaned, slouching down in her seat.

Her frustration level was at an all-time high. She still couldn't believe that Dillon refused to speak to her. Her live broadcasts weren't generating any new leads. She was anxious to speak with Oliver, who'd so far refused to respond to her messages. The Whitmans still hadn't gotten back to her regarding an interview or even an off-camera conversation. And getting Blake to talk to her again seemed like a lost cause.

"This is not going the way I planned…" Mona groaned.

Her stomach rumbled profusely. She hadn't eaten since the afternoon before. But food was the last thing on her mind.

Mona once again glanced up at the lab's entrance. There was still no sign of Bonnie or anyone else.

"This is a waste of time. I'm outta here."

She turned on the engine, deciding that her time would be better spent back at the inn, planning her next broadcast over a glass of white wine and a bowl of crawfish étouffée.

Just when she put the car in Drive, the door to the lab swung open. A tall, slender woman dressed in baggy blue jeans and an oversize white blouse shuffled down the stairs.

Mona leaned forward, her eyes squinting as she studied the woman.

Is that Bonnie? she asked herself, mentally comparing her to the image she'd seen in Bonnie's bio on LLL's website.

Mona watched as the woman brushed her frizzy red bob away from her face, then slipped on a pair of black cat-eye sunglasses.

As she got closer, Mona realized that it was in fact Bonnie.

She quickly put the car in Park and turned off the engine. She climbed out, following Bonnie as she approached a burgundy minivan.

"Excuse me, Bonnie? Bonnie Young?"

The woman paused, dropping her head while staring at Mona over the top of her sunglasses.

"Yes? I'm Bonnie Young. I'm sorry. Do I know you?"

"My name is Mona Avery. I'm an investigative journalist for CNB News. I'm also a good friend of Olivia Whitman's."

Bonnie's eyes lowered. "Oh…yes. I recognize you now."

"I'm in town covering Olivia's case. And I've teamed up with the Lake Landry PD to assist in the investigation."

"I know. I've been keeping up with your broadcasts. You're doing a great job of bringing awareness to her disappearance."

"Thank you. I've done some pretty extensive research online and saw that you and Olivia work closely together here at the lab. I was hoping you'd be willing to sit down and talk with me. Maybe share some insight into what was going on with Olivia before she went missing."

Bonnie nodded her head, then glanced down at her watch. "I'm actually heading to a doctor's appointment."

When she hesitated, Mona held her breath, hoping she'd find the time to speak with her.

"But I guess I do have a few minutes to spare."

Yes! Mona thought triumphantly.

Bonnie's eyes darted around the parking lot.

"I don't want anyone to see me out here talking to you, though. Hop in your car and follow me a couple of blocks over. We can talk there."

Mona held her hand to her chest. "I will do that. Thanks, Bonnie."

She rushed back to her car and followed Bonnie out of the lot. They drove toward the quiet residential area located behind the lab, where rows of charming bungalow-style homes stood among lush, manicured lawns.

Bonnie pulled over in front of Rosehill Park. Mona

parked behind her, their cars discreetly hidden beneath a row of sweet olive trees.

Mona stared out at the park's lush green lawn, watching as young children chased one another around a water lily pond.

Just as Bonnie jumped out of her van, a gust of wind whipped through her wiry curls. Evergreen leaves and yellow flower petals fell from the trees and dusted the hood of the car. Bonnie looked around frantically, as if worried someone were watching.

Mona could see the fear in her eyes. She quickly unlocked the car door.

Bonnie frantically opened the passenger door before climbing inside.

"Whew," she breathed, vigorously rubbing her hands over her makeup-free face. "I can't believe I'm actually sitting here with you, discussing Olivia's disappearance."

"Well, I really appreciate you finding the courage to talk to me."

Bonnie's head swiveled from side to side.

"Just making sure no one followed us here," she said before turning to Mona. "Listen, I want to share with you what I know. Or at least what I think I know. But you have to promise me that you'll keep my identity anonymous. I do not want to get caught up with the Carter family. You know how powerful they are. And apparently, dangerous…"

Mona pulled out her phone and began recording the conversation. "You have my word. I will not, under any circumstances, reveal your identity during my reporting."

"Thank you."

Bonnie stared down at her wringing hands. She took a deep breath, then cleared her throat. "Did you know that Blake is having an affair with at least two female employees at Transformation Cosmetics?"

"I've heard that. The main one being with his executive assistant, Ayana."

"That's only half-true. He is having an affair with Ayana, but she's not his main mistress."

"Really? Then who is?"

"Cyndi Porter. His marketing manager."

"Cyndi Porter," Mona muttered.

She opened her cell phone's web browser and searched the name. A photo of a woman who resembled a young Naomi Campbell popped up on the screen.

"Oh wow," Mona said. "She's beautiful. But in all my research, I've never heard of her. Is she a new employee?"

"She is. According to Olivia, she started working at Transformation a little over two months ago."

"So Olivia knows about her?"

"Olivia knows about everything that goes on in Blake's life," Bonnie quipped. "She just plays like she doesn't. But trust me, the file she was building on that man before she went missing was pretty damning. She was days away from turning it over to a divorce attorney."

"Hmm, interesting. So back to this Cyndi Porter. Where did she come from?"

"Apparently, Blake met her at a beauty convention in Atlanta over the summer. She was there working as an independent makeup artist."

"Wait," Mona interjected, "the woman went from being a makeup artist to a marketing manager at Transformation Cosmetics? That's quite a promotion."

"Well, I guess it helps when you start off by sleeping with the president of the company the same day you meet him. The situation quickly escalated into a full-blown affair. Then things got so hot and heavy that Blake moved her to Lake Landry and handed her the coveted marketing manager position. According to Olivia, Cyndi is giving Transformation's vice president of marketing hell, too."

"Isn't the VP of marketing Lenora King?" Mona asked.

"Yes. And she and Olivia are really good friends."

"I'm guessing Lenora's the one who's been reporting all of Blake's indiscretions back to her?"

"You got it," Bonnie confirmed. "And Olivia would in turn confide in me. She and I were like work sisters, and—"

Her voice broke. She paused, almost choking when her words caught in her throat.

Mona instinctively reached over and grabbed her hand. Pangs of sympathy filled her chest as she watched Bonnie's eyes fill with tears.

"I understand," Mona whispered. "Olivia was like a sister to me, too."

Bonnie's eyelids lowered. She looked out at the children running through the playground.

"Olivia suspected that Blake was being unfaithful for years," she said quietly. "But she tolerated him. Until Cyndi came along. There was something about that woman that made him lose control. When they began their affair, Blake got sloppy. The town started talking. And Olivia was no longer able to turn a blind eye."

"I can only imagine how hurt and embarrassed she must've been."

"Oh, she was livid. And I'm not sure if she'd shared this with you, but Blake was really pressuring Olivia to have a baby. All he cared about was continuing the Carter legacy. But she refused. There was no way Olivia would've brought a child into that toxic marriage."

Mona felt herself growing hot with anger. She rolled down the window, inhaling the cool air.

"This is *so* frustrating," she spat. "I can't understand why Olivia hadn't filed for divorce and left that vile man a long time ago. She has a great job, plenty of her own money... What was it? What was keeping her in that terrible situation?"

"I think she was hoping he would change. But his affair with Cyndi was the last straw. She'd already begun contacting attorneys. And then, mysteriously, she just up and vanished without a trace."

"I knew things were bad between them," Mona said. "But I had no idea they'd gotten that extreme. I wish I would've known all this before I met with Blake."

"He actually sat down and talked to you? I'm surprised."

"Don't be. He knew what he was doing. I got nothing out of him."

Bonnie snorted sarcastically. "That man is the slickest, most narcissistic human being I have ever encountered."

"That he is. So, let me ask you this. Did you see Olivia the day that she went missing?"

"I did."

"What type of mood was she in? Did she seem worried? Or anxious? Or consumed by what was going on in her personal life?"

"Not at all," Bonnie told her. "She was in a great mood. Almost giddy. The fact that she'd finally decided to leave Blake had her feeling empowered. And I was so happy for her. I couldn't wait to see Olivia shine once she freed herself from that man. But then..."

Bonnie once again became choked up.

"I know," Mona said softly, now struggling to hold herself together. "Don't worry. We're going to get to the bottom of this. Lake Landry's police force is working hard to solve this case. And I'm right there with them."

Mona seethed as the words escaped her lips. She felt a sudden urge to pull up in front of the police station, drag Dillon out and force him to arrest Blake.

"I'm glad to hear that," Bonnie sighed. She glanced down at her watch. "I need to get going before I'm late for my doctor's appointment. Do you have a business card?"

"I do." Mona pulled a card out of her purse and handed it to Bonnie. "Please, feel free to call or text me anytime. And if you think of anything you may have forgotten to tell me, reach out. I don't care how small it may seem. We need all the help we can get."

"I will. Thank you."

"You're welcome. And thank *you*."

Bonnie grabbed the door handle. Before stepping out of the car, she looked around, making sure the coast was clear.

The road was empty. Bonnie climbed out and rushed to her van, climbing in and speeding off just as soon as she turned on the ignition.

"Poor woman..." Mona said to herself.

When she reached down to start the car, her cell phone buzzed. A notification popped up on the screen.

Please let this be Dillon...

But when she picked up the phone, Mona saw that it was a direct message on Instagram.

Oliver!

She frantically entered her password and opened the app.

Come on, Oliver, she thought, waiting for his message to load. *Don't let me down. Let's get this meeting scheduled...*

But when she scanned the message, her hopes were quickly dashed.

Dear Ms. Avery,
Rest assured I have received your messages. With that being said, please understand that I do not wish to speak with you. I've seen your boastful broadcasts on television. If you, along with the Lake Landry Police Department, are as skilled as you think you are, then you should be able to

solve my sister's disappearance without my assistance. I
want no part of your investigation. Be well.

Regards,

Oliver Bernard Whitman

Mona's mouth fell open. She reread the message two
more times before closing it out and shoving her phone
back inside her purse.

"You *jerk*," she muttered through clenched teeth.

Before pulling off, Mona felt compelled to check Oliver's Instagram page. She pulled her phone back out and
reopened the app, curious as to whether or not he'd posted
about Olivia's disappearance.

She scrolled through his feed. Interestingly enough,
there was no mention of his missing sister.

Just as stubborn as he's always been...

"All right," Mona sighed. "Time for some wine and
crawfish étouffée."

Right before she closed out the app, Mona noticed a
photo of Allgood's Bookstore posted to Oliver's page. The
caption read, *FINALLY! AN EVENT WORTH ATTENDING!*

Curious, she clicked on it.

*My prayers to the universe have been answered! Con-
spiracy theorist extraordinaire Michael Graham is
coming to Lake Landry to discuss his latest book,
THE CONSPIRACY CODES UNLOCKED! Meet me
at Allgood's this Saturday at 3:00 p.m. I'll be challenging Mr. Graham with a few theories of my own.
Trust me, it'll be interesting to say the least. See you
there!*

"Yes, you will," Mona said, smiling mischievously.
She took a screenshot of the post and saved it in her

phone's file folder. If Oliver didn't want to meet with her, then she'd just coincidentally run into him at the event.

Mona felt her shoulders relax a bit. Today was turning out to be a decent day. She'd received some good intel from Bonnie, and now had a plan to get in front of Oliver. It was progress.

There was just one thing missing. Her partner, Dillon.

Mona tightened her grip on the steering wheel, pulling away from the curb. And then, instinctively, she pressed the voice command button on her touch screen.

"Call Dillon Reed."

Her heartbeat stuttered as the call connected. After four rings, it went to voice mail.

"Dillon, hi. It's Mona. I know we haven't spoken, but, um… I have some new information about Olivia's case that I'd like to share with you. There's also an event coming up that Olivia's brother will be attending. Since he's refusing to talk with me, I figured I'd try speaking to him in person. Maybe, uh, maybe you can come with me."

She paused, swallowing hard as she pressed her fingernails into the steering wheel. She felt as though she was pleading with Dillon. She wasn't used to that, nor was she comfortable with it.

"I really want to help get to the bottom of Olivia's disappearance, Dillon," Mona continued. "And for the hundredth time, I apologize for going back to Beechtree. Please…give me a call. Thanks."

She disconnected the call and exhaled.

"Come on, Dillon. Do the right thing," she muttered while heading back to the inn.

Chapter Six

"Hey, Detective Reed," Chief Boyer said. "How're things going with the Olivia Whitman case? You and Mona got any new leads?"

Dillon paused in the chief's doorway. He was hoping to sneak out of the station before being noticed by him.

He hadn't told his boss about his falling-out with Mona. Now that she and Dillon had spoken and finally cleared the air, he had no intention of doing so.

"Things are actually going well, sir. I turned that necklace Mona found at the alleged crime scene over to the forensics lab. Since this case is our top priority, the tech is working to get the DNA results back as soon as possible. Oh, and Mona received some interesting new information from one of Olivia's coworkers that was pretty insightful."

"Did she really," the chief stated, a crooked smirk spreading across his chubby face.

Dillon chuckled. He leaned against the doorframe and crossed his arms, bracing himself for his boss's inevitable smack talk.

"Come on," Dillon said, "let's hear it. Get it all out. Go ahead and gloat over my partnership with Mona."

"*Me?* Gloat? Why would I do such a thing? All I'm gonna say is, teaming up with her hasn't been such a bad thing, now has it?"

If only you knew... Dillon thought.

But he resisted the urge to tell Chief Boyer about how his beloved Mona had gone rogue on him.

"No, sir," he said. "It hasn't been such a bad thing at all. I'm actually heading to an event with her now."

"Really? Is it related to Olivia's investigation?"

"It is. Well, sort of. As you know, Olivia's brother, Oliver, has refused to talk to law enforcement. He's also turned down Mona's numerous requests to meet with her. So we're going to *coincidentally* run into him at a book-signing event he'll be attending. Hopefully he will speak to us once we're face-to-face."

"Interesting plan," Chief Boyer replied. "I hope it works. I really want to know Oliver's thoughts on his sister's disappearance. I've known his family for many years. I still can't believe he won't talk to us."

"Yeah, I'm pretty surprised by that, too. But he does seem a bit strange."

"And reclusive. I'm actually surprised to hear he's even attending a social event." The chief paused, pointing up at Dillon. "Wait, how do you and Mona know he's going to be there?"

"She's been monitoring his Instagram account. According to his latest post, he really wants to meet some conspiracy theory author who'll be at Allgood's Bookstore this afternoon."

The chief propped his elbows up on his desk and slowly shook his head. "You know, as a competent, well-respected detective, I can understand why you were resistant when I initially brought Mona on board to help out with this investigation. But you have to admit, she's good. And resourceful. She's able to move through Lake Landry and connect with the community in ways that law enforcement can't. I really do think she's going to help us solve this case."

"I believe you may be right, Chief. And on that note, I'd better get out of here. I have to stop by The Bayou Inn to pick her up on the way to the signing."

"All right. I'm expecting a full report on that new intel Mona received from Olivia's coworker as well as a recap on this book event."

"You'll have that report on your desk first thing in the morning."

"Great. And good luck trying to get anything out of Oliver."

"Thanks," Dillon chuckled. "I have a feeling I'm gonna need it."

As he left the station and walked to his car, he felt a tingling energy creep up his legs. He tried to shake it off. But instead of dissipating, the sensation traveled up his arms and settled in his chest.

And that's when it dawned on him. Dillon was experiencing the thrill of seeing Mona.

Dillon parked in front of the inn and got out of the car. Right before he reached the door, Mona came strolling out.

He stopped in his tracks at the sight of her. She was dressed in a black denim miniskirt and fitted red turtleneck. Her black suede boots clung to her shapely calves.

As she moved in closer, the scent of rose and vanilla wafted from her neck.

Dillon was so mesmerized that he almost lost his balance. He reached behind him and leaned into the passenger door.

"Hello, Detective Reed," Mona murmured, her red-stained lips spreading into an inviting smile. "It's good to see you. Dare I say, I've actually missed you?"

He was struck by her cool, confident demeanor. It urged him to stand straight up and pull himself together.

Dillon straightened the cuffs on his pale blue button-down shirt and ran his damp palms down his dark jeans.

"It's good to see you, too," he said. "And I'm sorry, but did you just say that you've *missed* me?"

"Yes. I did."

Mona approached the car, her arm brushing against Dillon's chest as she waited for him to open the door.

Keep your composure, he told himself.

"Okay," he replied, unable to restrain his flattered grin. "I guess I can admit that I've missed you, too."

"Well, moving forward, I promise to behave myself. So hopefully you won't shut me out again."

"I would appreciate that," Dillon chuckled.

He stepped to the side and opened the passenger door. When Mona climbed inside, he diverted his eyes in an effort to avoid ogling her curvaceous backside.

This is gonna be a long afternoon, he thought before hopping in the car and pulling off.

"I know you told me I can stop apologizing," Mona began, "so I'll just say that I'm glad you finally returned my call. For a minute there, I thought you might report me to Chief Boyer and have him send me packing."

"I thought about it, especially after I saw that the only information you provided in your police report was that someone set your car on fire. I seem to remember far more happening out there in Beechtree that afternoon."

Mona reached over and playfully swiped his arm.

"Nah, I'm kidding," Dillon teased. "I didn't even tell the chief about our disagreement. I knew I'd allow you back in my good graces at some point. I just needed some time to cool off."

"Allow me back in your good graces? Gee, thanks."

"Don't mention it," he quipped as he turned down Jackson Street. "So, did you get everything settled with the rental car's insurance company?"

"I did. And I've already gotten a new rental."

"Good. By the way, we had your original rental processed down at the crime lab. Unfortunately, any DNA evidence that may have been present was destroyed in the fire."

"Ugh," Mona groaned. "Of course it was."

"Don't get discouraged. Trust me, we're going to catch the assailant. Now, let's talk about this whole 'funny running into you here' thing you're trying to pull off with Oliver today. What's your plan? What are you hoping to get out of it?"

"Well, I'm hoping that seeing me in person will pull at his heartstrings a bit. Maybe remind him of the old days, back when we were young and life wasn't so complicated. I don't know if it'll work. But nothing beats a failure but a try."

"Didn't you say you two weren't very fond of each other back in the day?"

"I did," Mona sighed. "But we're adults now. And this is a serious matter. So I'm hoping we can move past all that. I bet you Oliver heard all types of buzz about Blake around Transformation Cosmetics while he was still working there."

"And you think he'd share that with you after making it clear he doesn't wanna talk to you?"

Mona threw her hands in the air.

"Like I said, it's worth a try. At this point, what've we got to lose? I'm convinced Oliver's harboring information that could help solve this case. You know he still lives at home with his parents. Olivia and her mother are extremely close. I can assure you he's overheard plenty about the state of their marriage and problems they're having."

"You're probably right. I just hope you can get him to

talk to you. When I told Chief Boyer about the event, he got pretty excited since Oliver hasn't been willing to talk to law enforcement. I promised I'd have a report on his desk first thing in the morning recapping all this new info we're gathering. Or should I say *you're* gathering."

"No. You got it right the first time. *We're* gathering. Partner."

Dillon stopped at a red light and glanced over at Mona. She gave him a reassuring wink.

"Thanks, *partner*," he replied.

That tingling sensation came rushing back.

Keep your cool, big fella...

He made a right turn down Austin Avenue and let up on the accelerator when Allgood's Bookstore came into view.

The busy street was lined with cars. A large group of attendees were making their way inside the store.

"Wow," Dillon said. "Looks like this conspiracy theorist is pretty popular."

Mona turned and stared out the window.

"It does. I just hope Oliver shows up."

"Trust me," he chortled, eyeing the colorfully dressed patrons bouncing around frantically as they entered the store. "From the looks of this crowd, he'll be here."

Dillon pulled into a space near the end of the block. He hopped out and jogged over to the passenger side, opening Mona's door.

When she stepped out of the car, he watched her intently. His grip on the handle tightened when she ran her fingers through her curls, then straightened her skirt before heading toward the store.

"Um, are you coming?" she turned and asked him.

"Oh! Y-yes," he stammered. "Right behind you."

Dillon joined Mona on the sidewalk. As they headed

toward the bookstore, he was suddenly hit with a feeling of nostalgia.

He couldn't remember the last time he'd actually been out on a date. It had been more than three years since he'd been in a relationship. He missed that feeling of companionship.

But this isn't a date, he quickly reminded himself.

Nevertheless, their outing certainly felt reminiscent of one.

Stay focused. This woman is here to help solve a case, not fill a void in your personal life...

"Here we are," Mona said, pulling Dillon out of his thoughts as they approached the bookstore.

He stared up at the shop's faded black-and-white sign. The family-owned business had been around for years and was a popular tourist attraction. From rare books on New Orleans culture to vintage costume jewelry once worn by local entertainers, the store was known for its unique finds.

"I've been meaning to stop by this place," Dillon said, peering through the frosted windows at the books on display. "Seems pretty interesting."

"Oh, you'll be blown away by Allgood's. It's a Lake Landry staple. Glad I was able to help you knock an item off your bucket list."

"Yeah, me, too," he murmured.

He held the heavy wooden door open for Mona and followed her inside. The small, stuffy establishment was packed with an eclectic crowd. Dark wooden shelves lining the walls were filled with rows of books, antiques and odd memorabilia.

An older, balding man sat at a table in the front of the store. He was posing for selfies in between signing books for the enthusiastic fans. His wide grin revealed crooked, yellow-stained teeth. Wiry patches of gray hairs were scattered across his scalp and jawline. His tattered beige tweed blazer had seen better days.

Considering the man's prestigious best-seller status, he wasn't what Dillon had expected.

"That must be the author, Michael Graham," Mona said, pointing toward the table. "He definitely seems…different."

"I agree."

Dillon watched as the author pushed his thick black bifocal glasses up the bridge of his long nose while handing a book to a customer.

"You're wrong, young man!" Michael boomed. "Plain and simple. *Wrong.*"

"No, *you're* wrong!" someone shouted back. "I have proof that all these A-list celebrities who claim to be dead are still alive. *Government* proof!"

"Ha! Sure you do. I'd love to see it."

Dillon craned his neck, peering through the crowd, trying to catch a glimpse of whom the author was arguing with. When he saw a man step up to the table and lean in closer to the author, Mona grabbed his arm.

"Hey!" she whispered. "There he is. That's Oliver up there fussing with Michael."

"*Humph.* Figures."

Dillon eyed Oliver, whose wild, wavy hair had been pulled back into a messy ponytail. His pale complexion appeared sallow and blotchy. He was wearing a black graphic T-shirt with ripped skinny jeans and white laceless sneakers.

Mona leaned over and whispered in Dillon's ear.

"Oliver looks bad. I remember back when his hazel eyes used to sparkle. Now they just look dull and vacant. And from the looks of those bags underneath them, he hasn't slept in days."

"Yeah, he does look pretty rough," Dillon agreed, forcing himself to focus on Mona's words rather than her lips being so close to his ear. "He appears to be the complete opposite of Olivia. You would never know he comes from such a wealthy family."

A man who appeared to be a store employee approached Oliver and placed his hand on his shoulder.

"Okay, Mr. Whitman," the man told him. "There will be plenty of time for questions after Mr. Graham is done signing books. Let's be respectful and allow other customers a chance to meet the author."

Oliver jerked his arm, forcing the employee's hand off him before pointing down at Michael. "We're not done with this conversation. So don't think you're off the hook. You're gonna hear me out on this."

"Wow," Mona breathed. "He is so irrational."

"Yes, he is. Do you still think it's a good idea to approach him here?"

"Absolutely. It's now or never. Maybe seeing me will make him think I'm interested in all this madness, too. He'll let his guard down, and I can try to get some information out of him about Olivia."

"Good luck with that," Dillon said, watching as Oliver continued to make a spectacle of himself while customers looked on.

"Let's get in line and grab a book," Mona suggested. "I'll let Oliver notice me rather than approaching him first. That way our encounter will seem more natural and coincidental."

"Good idea. I'll follow your lead."

Dillon walked behind Mona as she joined the crowd. He discreetly kept an eye on Oliver, who was now holding court with a group of people over in the corner.

"No!" Oliver yelled. "He did not die in a car crash. His bandmates decided to replace him after they gained international fame. They were worried his drug habit would ruin their reputation. Trust me, that man is still alive. He lives near the Baltic Sea. And I'm here to prove that to Michael today!"

"Do you hear this man?" Mona asked. "He needs to pipe down and stop harassing these people."

"Yeah, he seems to have quite a temper. It's pretty obvious why he got fired from Transformation Cosmetics."

"Can you imagine the rants he probably went on with his coworkers? I bet he had a slew of theories about what was really going on within the company."

Dillon nodded his head. "And within his sister's marriage, too."

"Good point."

As Mona and Dillon reached the front of the line, he noticed Oliver glance over at them.

"Don't look now," he whispered to Mona, "but I think we've been spotted."

"I noticed. Just play it cool."

She and Dillon approached the table. Mona picked up a book while he pulled out his cell phone.

"Mr. Graham," she gushed, "it's such a pleasure to meet you. I am a huge fan."

The author sat back in his chair and ogled Mona from head to toe.

"Well, well, well," he began, "I can certainly say the same, Ms. Avery. I'm a regular viewer of your broadcasts. 'If you see something, say something.' Isn't that your signature sign-off?"

"It most certainly is."

Dillon looked on amusingly, almost bursting out laughing when Michael licked his thin, cracked lips.

While the author and Mona continued bantering, Dillon peeked over at the corner.

Oliver was watching Mona and Michael curiously. His feet shuffled back and forth as he tapped his fingertips against his forehead.

"Here," Michael said, reaching out and taking his book from Mona's hands. "Let me sign that for you. And I'd be happy to take a photo with you, if you'd like."

"Sure, I'd love that. Thank you."

"I can give you my cell phone number, too," Michael continued, "so you can text that picture to me after we take it. Maybe we can snap a few, then look them over while we discuss my book at dinner tonight?"

Before Mona could respond, Dillon stepped in and cleared his throat.

"Are you two ready for that photo?" he asked, throwing the author a look before holding up his cell phone.

Michael glanced at him, then over at Mona. A red veil of embarrassment covered his face.

"Oh…my, uh—my apologies," he sputtered. "I didn't realize you were here with someone."

"No worries," Mona replied cheerily. She smiled coolly for the camera as Dillon snapped their picture.

"I'll just make this out to Mona Avery," the author croaked, his head now buried in the book.

"I appreciate that, Michael. It was very nice meeting you."

"You, as well," he muttered. *"Next!"*

Dillon followed Mona as she strolled past the table.

"Should we grab a little wine and cheese?" she asked.

He realized that Oliver was standing near the hors d'oeuvres station.

"Sure, sounds good."

Mona approached the table and grabbed two plastic cups of red wine without looking in Oliver's direction. She handed one to Dillon.

Through the corner of his eye, he could see Oliver watching their every move.

"Does he see us?" Mona muttered.

"He does. And it looks like he's heading our way."

"All right," she replied, the excitement in her voice apparent. "It's showtime."

Just as Mona and Dillon turned away from the table and faced the crowd, Oliver walked up.

"Are my eyes deceiving me," he scoffed, "or is Mona Avery actually at a conspiracy theory book signing?"

"Your eyes are not deceiving you," she replied smoothly. "Hello, Oliver."

"What's up, Mona? I'm surprised to see a bougie, semifamous journalist such as yourself at an event like this. What are you doing here? Stalking me?"

"*Stalking* you?" Mona shot back. "Of course not. I didn't even know you'd be here."

"*Sure* you didn't. So you showing up has nothing to do with the post I blasted all over Instagram about the event? Because you were certainly stalking me on that app."

"Don't flatter yourself, Oliver. I just so happen to be a fan of Michael Graham and came to get a signed copy of his book."

Dillon stood there, his head swiveling back and forth between the pair. Oliver remained silent while rocking back on his heels as he glared at Mona. The intensity in his eyes was frightening.

"So," Oliver finally uttered, "you're suddenly a fan of Michael Graham?"

"Not suddenly. But yes, I am."

"Well, what did you think of his last book, *What You Don't Know Can Hurt You*? Particularly the chapter where he broke down the disappearance of—"

"Hello, Oliver," Dillon interrupted, stepping in before

Mona's cover was blown. "I'm Detective Reed. I've reached out to you on a few occasions, but we haven't actually met."

"I know who you are," Oliver shot back. He ignored Dillon's extended hand without taking his eyes off Mona.

"So how long have you been in town?" Oliver asked her.

"About two weeks. As you know, I'm here investigating Olivia's disappearance. I've teamed up with Detective Reed, and together we're working really hard to try to find her. Thus far, we've hit a lot of dead ends."

Oliver grabbed a cup of wine from the table and took a long sip.

"*Humph.* How dreadful for the two of you. Maybe Chief Boyer needs a smarter detective on the case."

Dillon took another step forward, preparing to check him. But Mona grabbed his arm before he could speak.

"Oliver," she said, "I really would like to sit down and talk with you. You're obviously a very intelligent and insightful man. I'm sure you're holding on to some invaluable information that could help solve this case."

Dillon abruptly turned toward Mona, shocked by her comments. But when he noticed the sly glimmer in her eyes, he realized she was simply stroking Oliver's ego in hopes of getting a sit-down.

"I'm listening…" Oliver told her, relaxing his shoulders while shuffling his feet.

And it's working, Dillon thought. *This woman is good.*

"You're a deep-thinking man," Mona continued. "I can only imagine the things that must've flown through your mind after hearing all the chatter among your coworkers at Transformation Cosmetics—"

"I don't work there anymore," he declared.

"I know. But when you did, I'm sure the staff was buzzing. And then there's your mom. Surely she's casually mentioned conversations between her and Olivia around the house that you can recall. Maybe about the state of her and Blake's marriage?"

"Maybe…" Oliver mumbled. He drained his cup, then set it down on the table and picked up another.

"This probably isn't the best time and place for us to talk," Mona told him. "So why don't we exchange numbers and arrange a meeting in the next couple of days? How does that sound?"

Oliver chugged the second cup of wine, then pulled out his phone. "I'll need to check my schedule. But yeah, we may be able to work something out. *Maybe.*"

"Awesome," Mona replied.

She took his phone and typed in her number, then sent herself a text message from it so she'd have his.

"Wait," Oliver said, nodding his head toward Dillon in disgust. "If I do agree to meet with you, does he have to come?"

Mona discreetly nudged Dillon's arm, as if she could sense his patience wearing thin.

"Not if you don't want him to."

"Good. Because I don't."

Dillon took a deep breath and turned away from Oliver. *Let it go*, he told himself. *Don't say a word. Do not buy a ticket to this clown's circus.*

He raised his cup of wine to his lips. But when he got a whiff of the overly sweet scent of blackberry, he discreetly tossed the cup in the trash.

"Now that we've exchanged contact information," Mona told Oliver, "I'll be in touch to set up that meeting."

He shrugged his shoulders indifferently.

"It's not like I know much," Oliver said. "After all, I am the black sheep of the Whitman family. And ever since I was *unjustly* fired from Transformation Cosmetics for refusing to bow down to that horrendous Leo Mendez, I've really been on the outs."

"I bet you know more than you think," Mona assured him. "Don't worry. I'll ask all the right questions."

"I'm honestly more interested in discussing Michael Graham's conspiracy theories with you rather than my missing sister. Speaking of which, what do you think of his idea that an extraterrestrial spacecraft really did crash in Roswell, New Mexico, back in 1947—"

"Hey," Dillon interrupted, glancing down at his watch, "we'd better get back down to the police station, Mona. Chief Boyer is expecting us to update him on that, uh…"

"On that report we were working on earlier, right?" Mona chimed in. "Yes. He sure is waiting on us." She tossed her cup of wine in the trash bin, then turned to Oliver. "I'm so glad I bumped into you. I'll be in touch soon."

He threw up a peace sign and slowly backed away from the pair. "Don't get too confident, now. I said I *might* meet with you. Nothing's definite. And hey, if I know something, *maybe* I'll say something," he smirked.

Dillon glanced at Mona. She remained stoic, seemingly unmoved by the taunting jab at her catchphrase.

Before she could respond, Oliver crossed his right foot over his left and spun around dramatically, then marched off.

"What a fool," Dillon muttered. "He doesn't even seem to care that his own sister is missing." He glanced around the room, watching as patrons waved their hands in the air while debating the obscure contents of Michael's book. "This was a complete waste of time."

"No," Mona rebutted, shaking her head emphatically. "It wasn't. Just be patient. By the time I'm done with Oliver, he'll be telling me everything I need to know, plus more. Trust me on that."

"All right, then. I'm glad you're so confident. Because I have no faith in him whatsoever."

"That confidence worked on you, didn't it?" Mona sassed back. "When I first got to town you would barely even speak to me. And look at you now. I've got you calling me your partner and everything."

Dillon leaned back, staring at Mona through the corner of his eye. "You're right," he chuckled, unable to stop gazing at her lush lips. A swirl of arousal shot through his groin as a result of her self-assured swag.

Get your mind right...

He shoved his hands in his pockets and took a deep breath. "I think our work here is done. Would you like to go over and say goodbye to your friend?" he asked, nodding in Michael's direction. "Or should we get out of here before someone questions you about the aliens that the government is housing in some undisclosed underground location?"

"Um, the latter," Mona snickered, swatting Dillon's arm before heading toward the exit.

He followed closely behind her.

Eyes up, he told himself, determined to keep his focus on the case rather than her swaying hips.

Chapter Seven

Hello, Oliver, Mona typed. Texting you once again hoping you'll respond this time. Still looking to conduct an on-air interview with you. We can start with an in-person meeting if you'd like. Looking forward to hearing back and getting on your schedule. Thanks.

She sent the message, then slid her phone across the desk.

"Ugh," Mona groaned, throwing her head back and vigorously rubbing her eyes. She knew solving Olivia's disappearance wouldn't be easy. But she had no idea it would be this frustrating.

She sat straight up and glanced around her hotel room. Clothes were strewn everywhere. She hadn't bothered to sit last night's dinner tray outside the door to be picked up. Her lack of progress in the investigation was weighing so heavily on her that Mona hadn't had the energy to pick up after herself.

But you've gotta keep going...

Mona stared down at her phone and instinctively picked it up. She scrolled through her contacts list in search of Olivia's mother's phone number.

"Being a pest is part of my job," she told herself.

Mona wasn't about to let the fact that the Whitmans had

yet to return her calls deter her from reaching out. She was determined to get them involved in her efforts.

Dillon had explained on numerous occasions that they were hesitant to speak publicly. The Whitmans were convinced that their high profile would attract unwanted attention, false leads and scammers.

Mrs. Whitman trusted that someone would eventually come forward with answers leading them to Olivia.

Mr. Whitman, however, felt differently. He feared the worst. Ever since Olivia went missing, he'd been waiting by the phone for kidnappers to call him demanding ransom money. And he constantly questioned whether or not his daughter was even still alive.

Mona tapped on the Whitmans' phone number and said a silent prayer, hoping they'd pick up this time.

After four rings, the call went to voice mail.

"Dammit," she murmured.

At the sound of a beep, she cleared her throat and put a smile on her face.

"Hello, Mr. and Mrs. Whitman," she said pleasantly. "This is Mona Avery again. I understand that you're both extremely busy and going through a lot right now. But I'm still in town, reporting on Olivia's disappearance and working alongside Detective Reed. I'm hoping to sit down and speak with you. We can do so off camera if you'd prefer. Whatever you're most comfortable with. I just want to help find your daughter."

Mona paused, debating whether or not she should mention the necklace she'd found. That bit of information could prove to the Whitmans that she was making progress in the investigation and worthy of a meeting.

But the sound of Dillon's voice quickly echoed inside her head. She remembered that he didn't want her divulging the details of the case.

Mona had already betrayed him once by going to Beech-tree without his knowledge. She didn't want to go against him again.

"So please," she continued, "I hope that you'll return my call. I look forward to hearing from you. Thank you."

Right before she hung up, Mona thought about her run-in with Oliver at the book signing. She didn't know whether mentioning it would give her some leverage. But she figured it was worth a try. The Whitmans were always pleased when their reclusive son actually interacted with other human beings.

"Oh, and by the way, I ran into Oliver at Allgood's Book-store on Saturday. It was so good seeing him. I'm hoping we can reconnect and catch up. But, anyway, sorry for the long message. Hope to talk to you soon."

Mona disconnected the call. She sighed deeply, taking the last sip of her gingerbread mocha latte. Just as she began to feel ashamed of herself for lying, setting up fake run-ins and withholding information from grieving parents, her cell phone buzzed.

"Please be Mrs. Whitman," she said aloud. "Please be Mrs. Whitman…"

When she grabbed the cell, Dillon's number was displayed on the screen.

Instead of feeling disappointed, a tingling thrill of excitement shot through the pit of her stomach.

What was that? Mona asked herself before picking up the call.

"Hey," she said, her casual tone a total contradiction of the flutters floating inside her chest. "What's up?"

"A lot." Dillon puffed.

"Are you okay? It sounds like you're completely out of breath."

"I am. I just got a call from Martha down at the forensics lab."

Mona jumped up from her chair.

"You did? What'd she say?"

"She got a hit on the necklace. She wants me to come down to the lab to discuss the results."

"Oh my goodness," Mona uttered, her heart beating so rapidly that she could barely breathe. She hurried over to the bed, slipped out of her boy shorts and threw on a pair of beige skinny jeans. "You're taking me with you, right?"

"Of course. I'm on my way to pick you up now."

Mona frantically wiggled her hips as she zipped her pants, then threw on a beige cable-knit off-the-shoulder sweater. She ran over to the mirror and fluffed out her day-old curls, wishing she had time to run her hot wand through them.

"Okay, good. When will you be here?"

"I'm actually turning down the block now. I'll be pulling up in a second."

Mona grabbed her makeup bag, quickly swiping gold gloss across her lips and peach blush over her cheeks.

"I'm on my way down."

"Great. See you in a few."

Mona hung up the phone and tossed it inside her tote bag, along with her notebook and sterling silver pen. She applied another layer of deodorant underneath her arms as she had already begun to sweat, then sprayed citrus perfume on her neck and wrists.

"Wait, what are you doing?" she asked herself. "This is not a date."

She tossed the perfume down onto the bed, rolling her eyes at her own behavior.

Get in work mode. This is business...

Mona slipped on her tan ankle boots and grabbed her

bag. She gave herself a brief once-over in the mirror, then ran down to the lobby.

"Hey, Evelyn!" she said while rushing past the front desk.

"Hey! No breakfast today?"

"No, the mocha latte was more than enough. It was delicious."

"Oh good. But you missed out on my famous strawberry-and-creole-cream-cheese crepes."

"Mmm, sounds delicious. I'll be sure to have them next time they're on the menu," Mona told her as she hurried toward the door.

"Sounds good. Well, make sure you're here for dinner tonight. I'm whipping up a batch of my Louisiana beef stew and pecan bread. Hopefully Detective Reed will be able to join you!"

"I'll be here, and I'll see if he's available," Mona chuckled, tickled by Evelyn's crush on Dillon. "See you tonight."

She hurried outside. Dillon was already standing on the passenger side of the car with the door open.

"Hey, thanks for letting me tag along with you," she told him.

"Of course. You're the one who found the necklace. There's no way I would've gone to get those results without you."

Mona paused before sliding inside the car, smiling at Dillon. While she wasn't easily moved, she'd found his statement touching.

"Thank you, Detective Reed."

The pair gazed at one another. She stood so close to him that the scent of cinnamon candy rolling along his tongue filled her nostrils.

"We'd better get going," Dillon whispered. "Martha is waiting on us."

"Y-yes, we…we'd better," she stammered, feeling as though he'd just broken a hypnotic spell.

The twosome climbed inside the car and Dillon drove off. Mona grabbed the door handle as he whipped around the corner and flew down the street.

She glanced over at him, noticing that he was vigorously running his hand down his goatee. His eyes were darting. His chest was heaving. There was an intensity in his expression that she'd never seen before.

"Are you okay?" she asked him.

"Yeah. I'm good. Just anxious to get the DNA results on that necklace."

"Me, too. Hopefully they'll give us some answers. Or at least lead us in the right direction."

Dillon remained silent as he sped through an orange light and made a sharp left turn down Armstrong Avenue.

When he hit the expressway, Mona pulled out her cell phone, hoping that someone in the Whitman family had gotten back to her.

No new notifications appeared on the screen.

"Unreal…" she moaned.

"What's unreal?"

"I texted Oliver asking if we could get together and talk. He didn't respond. Then I called the Whitmans and left a voice mail, once again asking if they'd meet with me."

"They haven't gotten back to you either?"

"Nope. And I poured it on thick in my message, too. Even mentioned seeing Oliver at the book signing. I was hoping that hearing their son had a conversation with someone outside of his video game headphones would encourage them to talk to me."

"Yeah, well, I already told you where the Whitmans stand. They're trying to keep a low profile through all of this. They don't want the public scrutiny. The family trusts that the police will find their daughter."

"I just wish they understood that I'm an integral part of this investigation, too."

Dillon tapped his turn signal and exited the expressway.

"That you are," he told her. "We wouldn't be heading to the lab right now if it weren't for you. Your contributions to this case have been invaluable. Don't worry. I'm convinced the Whitmans will eventually come around."

"Thanks. I hope so," she replied quietly before turning and staring out the window.

The forensics lab was located in Vincent Parish. It was utilized by law enforcement agencies in several surrounding towns, including Lake Landry.

Businesses and residential homes were few and far between in the rural area. Vast fields of grass lined the long stretch of road leading to the laboratory.

When Dillon stopped at a red light near a row of fast-food restaurants, Mona knew they were almost there.

Her stomach turned nervously. She contemplated the necklace's DNA results.

Please bring back something significant, she thought.

"Hey," Dillon said. "You okay over there? Keep wringing your hands like that and you're gonna rub the skin right off."

Mona stretched her fingers out and rubbed them over her thighs.

"Wow. I didn't even realize I was doing that. I'm fine. Just anxious to find out the results on the necklace."

"Yeah. Same here."

She looked up and saw Volution Technology's dull gray cement building come into view. The sterile structure took up almost half a block. Its thick, narrow windows were tinted, making it impossible to see inside. A few sparse bushes lined the front of the building. The intimidating establishment appeared far from welcoming.

When Dillon pulled into the parking lot, Mona noticed a couple of men dressed in dark suits stepping out of an unmarked car. Their foreheads wrinkled as they clutched file folders while rushing inside the building.

"This place feels more like a prison than a crime lab," Mona said.

"It does. Reminds me of the Louisiana State Penitentiary."

Dillon parked the car and hopped out, running around and throwing open Mona's door.

"You ready to do this?" he asked her.

"I'm ready," she said, taking a deep breath and following him inside.

The pair stopped at the security desk and showed the attendant their IDs.

"Detective Reed and Mona Avery," Dillon said. "We're here to see Martha Scott."

The attendant turned to her computer and entered their names into the system. "Thank you, Detective Reed and Ms. Avery. Please have a seat in the lobby. I will let Martha know that you're here."

"Thanks."

Dillon spun around and placed his hand on the small of Mona's back, leading her toward a row of black plastic chairs.

She gasped slightly, surprised by the rousing feel of his touch. When Mona glanced over at him, Dillon was staring straight ahead. He appeared oblivious to the effect his intimate gesture had on her.

Mona's gait stiffened as her boots clicked loudly along the white speckled tile. She looked around the stark lobby, feeling as though all eyes were on them. But the few people who were scattered around weren't paying any attention to the pair.

"So," Dillon said after they took a seat, "I hope you're not getting discouraged because you haven't heard back from the Whitmans. Just give them some time. They're scared, and still trying to wrap their heads around the fact that their daughter is missing."

"I know," Mona sighed. "But I'm convinced they know something that could help crack this case. I've known them for years. I can get them to open up. I just have to get in front of them."

"And you will. When you do, I have no doubt you'll pull things out of them that no one else could."

"You think so?" Mona asked, surprised that he believed the family would confide in her over him.

"Absolutely. Between your history with the Whitmans and journalistic prowess, you may solve this case all on your own."

"Oh, now you're just trying to win cool points with me," she laughed.

"And? So what if I am?" Dillon asked, glancing over at her with a sly smile.

Mona was seldom at a loss for words. But in that moment, she had no comeback.

She was distracted by the sound of approaching shoe soles squeaking against the tile.

"Detective Reed, so good to see you."

Mona looked up and saw a slender older woman walking toward them. She assumed it was Martha considering she was wearing a white lab coat and holding a file folder.

"Martha, it's good to see you, too," Dillon said, standing up and shaking her hand.

Mona stood up as well, unable to take her eyes off the forensic scientist.

Martha's style was eclectic to say the least. Her hair had been cut into a silver mohawk. Humungous red square eyeglasses covered the top half of her square-shaped face. She was wearing fuzzy purple socks, which were stuffed inside a pair of dingy brown Birkenstocks.

"Martha, I'd like for you to meet Mona Avery."

"Oh, I *know* who Miss Avery is," Martha said, grinning.

She reached out and shook Mona's hand so hard that she felt as though her bones might break.

"I'm a huge fan," Martha continued. "I never miss a broadcast. You are so good at what you do."

"Thank you very much. I appreciate that."

"You're welcome. So, I've got the results back on that necklace. Why don't we go back to my office and discuss my findings?"

"Sounds good," Dillon told her. "Lead the way."

Mona's stomach rumbled as she followed Martha and Dillon down a long white hallway. She bit her tongue, resisting the urge to ask for the results right there on the spot.

When they reached the end of the corridor, Martha led the pair inside her cluttered office.

Her expansive desk was covered with lab tubes, stacks of paper, a microscope and UV lamps.

"Sorry about the mess," Martha said. She pointed to a set of gray tweed chairs. "Please, have a seat."

Mona's thighs quivered as she gripped the chair's arms and slowly sat down. She held her breath, waiting to hear the findings.

Martha appeared to be moving in slow motion. She set the file folder down on the desk and thumbed through the pages.

"So," she finally began, "I was able to pull DNA evidence from the necklace and make a positive identification. Two, actually."

Mona slid to the edge of her seat. Her fingernails dug into the soft wood, chipping away at the chair arms.

When Dillon reached over and gently placed his hand on her arm, she relaxed a bit, appreciative of his unspoken support.

"You know," he said, "I'm surprised the evidence wasn't contaminated despite the necklace being outside in the elements for what I'm assuming may have been several days."

"Same here," Martha replied. "I chalk that up to the universe wanting these results to be found."

The pressure of anticipation pounded inside Mona's head.

"And what were those results?" she blurted out, unable to control herself.

Martha looked over at Mona with a pained expression on her face. Her hands trembled slightly when she picked up the report and slid it across the desk.

"DNA evidence shows that the necklace belongs to Olivia Whitman."

Mona swallowed hard, crossing her arms in front of her tightly. She glanced down at the report, unable to read the words on the paper.

"What exactly did you find?" she whispered.

"There was a hair caught in the necklace's clasp. The follicle that was attached proved it belonged to Olivia. There were also droplets of dried blood collected."

"Olivia's blood?" Dillon asked.

"Yes."

"Oh my God," Mona whispered.

Dillon slid his chair closer to hers and held her hand. She leaned into him. Violent thoughts of what may have happened to Olivia flew through her mind.

Stop it, she told herself. *Stay positive. Do not fall apart.*

"And that's not all," Martha continued. "There was

also evidence of fingerprints and skin cells present on the necklace."

"Did you get a hit on who they belong to?" Dillon asked.

"I did. They belong to Olivia. And Blake Carter."

Mona tried to take a deep breath but choked when the gust of air hit her lungs. She felt Dillon's hand squeeze her shoulder as he tried to make sense of the situation.

"And no one else's DNA was found besides Olivia's and Blake's?" he asked.

"No," Martha said quietly. Her somber tone was filled with remorse. "Just those two."

Mona abruptly turned to Dillon as tears streamed down her face.

"He did it," she insisted. Her voice trembled with pain. "He did it. I *knew* he did it."

"Calm down, Mona," Dillon said soothingly. "Let's not jump to conclusions. It does make sense that Blake's DNA would be on the necklace. He could have given it to her. Or put it on for her."

"But what about the blood evidence?" she pressed. "Why was Olivia's blood on the chain? What happened to my friend?"

"That's what we need to figure out. And this conclusive evidence is a good start. It confirms that Beechtree was most likely the area where Olivia encountered some sort of danger."

Mona held her hand to her forehead. She felt faint at the thought of Olivia being dead.

"Come on," he said quietly. "Don't get discouraged. I know this case is personal to you. But you've got to remain objective. Stay in investigative mode."

"Easier said than done."

"I know it is. But together we will press on and get to

the bottom of Olivia's disappearance. You never know. She could turn up safe and sound tomorrow."

Mona nodded. "You're right. I've got to stay positive."

Martha cleared her throat and closed the file folder.

"I'm so sorry to interrupt you two. But I've got a couple of detectives from Ellis Parish here to meet with me."

She handed Dillon a file and paper bag.

"Here's a copy of my findings as well as the necklace. I really am hoping for a positive outcome in all this. The entire town is. Actually, thanks to Mona's reporting, seems like the whole country is."

Mona took a deep breath and sat straight up in her chair.

"Thank you, Martha. That's the goal. Hopefully bringing awareness to Olivia's disappearance will generate more leads."

As soon as the words were out of her mouth, Mona's cell phone buzzed. She pulled it from her tote and stared down at the screen.

Her stomach dropped when a text message from Mrs. Whitman appeared.

"Thank you again for getting these results back to us so soon," Dillon told Martha before standing up. "I really appreciate it."

"Anytime, Detective Reed."

Mona jumped up from her chair and rushed toward the door.

"Yes, thank you, Martha. It was really nice meeting you."

"Same here. Looking forward to your future broadcasts. Best of luck in solving this case."

"Thanks!"

Mona practically pushed Dillon out of the office.

"I can walk you out if you'd like," Martha called out.

"We're fine," Mona told her. She could feel Dillon eyeing her curiously as she tapped her security code into her cell phone.

"What is going on?" he asked her. "Are you all right?"

"Yes. I'm more than all right. Mrs. Whitman just texted me."

"She did? What'd she say?"

"I'm about to find out."

Mona pulled Dillon to the side when they reached the lobby and opened the message.

"'Hello, Mona. Thank you for reaching out to us. We've been hesitant to speak with anyone regarding Olivia's disappearance for fear of drawing unwanted attention onto the family. But after receiving your voice mail this morning, Mr. Whitman and I have had a change of heart. We'd like to talk with you, off camera. If you are free this afternoon, you're more than welcome to come by our house. Thank you.'"

"This is good," Dillon said as they headed toward the exit. "After receiving those DNA results, I'm really interested to hear what they have to say."

"I'll confirm that I'm available to meet with them this afternoon and ask if it's okay that I bring you along. I'm sure it will be, but proper etiquette tells me I should get permission."

"I agree. I wonder if Oliver will be there."

"And if he is, I wonder if he'll be willing to talk with us."

Dillon glanced over at Mona, his eyes narrowing skeptically.

"Judging by what I've seen of him so far? I doubt it. But you never know. I guess we'll just have to wait and see. Hey, are you hungry?"

"I am, actually," Mona said. "I skipped breakfast this morning."

"Yeah, me, too. Why don't we go and grab lunch while we wait to hear back from Mrs. Whitman?"

"That sounds good."

Mona and Dillon climbed inside his car in silence. Her body buzzed with a plethora of emotions, from worrying about Olivia to eagerly anticipating her conversation with the Whitmans.

But one thing was for certain. Through it all, she was glad to have Dillon by her side.

Chapter Eight

Dillon sat on one end of the Whitmans' yellow silk couch in the middle of their elaborate great room, sipping a glass of sparkling water. Mona sat beside him, holding a delicate bone china cup filled with mint tea.

Mr. and Mrs. Whitman sat across from the pair in a set of cream silk Victorian-style chairs. She was dressed in a black long-sleeved shift dress and matching pumps. He was wearing a dark blue suit and deep red tie. They both appeared as though they were heading to a funeral.

"Again," Mrs. Whitman said, "my apologies for the delay in getting back to you, Mona. I've just been…we've been so distraught. I'm still in shock that my Olivia is missing."

"So am I, Mrs. Whitman. Trust me, Detective Reed and I are doing all that we can to find her."

Dillon felt his body tensing up. During their lunch, he'd stressed to Mona that she needed to keep the DNA findings of the necklace confidential. He knew that she was emotional and feared that in the moment, while facing Olivia's parents, she'd slip up and mention the results.

Mrs. Whitman sat straight up in her chair, her back rigid. Olivia's disappearance had clearly taken a toll on the regal, attractive older woman. Her light brown complexion appeared washed-out. Newly formed wrinkles of worry lined the corners of her eyes and thin, downturned lips. Her voluminous brunette hair, which normally hung down her back in a soft cascade of waves, had been pulled back in a severe bun.

The distinguished-looking Mr. Whitman, however, appeared cool and calm. It was obvious he was struggling to remain strong for them both. His short, silverish gray hair was neatly trimmed. His wide-set hazel eyes were clear and alert. He came across ready and willing to share whatever he could to help find his daughter.

When Mona pulled her notepad and pen out of her tote bag, Mrs. Whitman turned to her with fear in her eyes.

"You do understand that this conversation is off-the-record, don't you?" she asked. "Mr. Whitman and I *do not* want the details of our family's personal life being dragged into the public eye."

Dillon shifted in his seat at the shrill tone in her voice.

"Oh yes, of course, Mrs. Whitman," Mona replied. "I'm just taking notes for the sake of the investigation. Whatever we discuss today will absolutely remain confidential."

"Good. Thank you."

The corners of Mrs. Whitman's mouth formed a tight smile. Dillon interpreted it as a silent apology for her abrasiveness.

"The fact that our daughter has gone missing," Mr. Whitman added, "is excruciatingly painful, as I'm sure you can both imagine."

"Absolutely," Dillon told him.

"So I apologize if either Mrs. Whitman or I appear harsh. We're just hurting."

"We understand," Mona empathized. "I hope you know you've got so much support around you."

"Yes, well, not from everyone," Mrs. Whitman rebutted.

"What do you mean?" Dillon asked.

"That damn Blake Carter. The despicable way in which

he treated my daughter? I know he had something to do with her disappearance!"

Mr. Whitman reached over and clutched her hand.

"Honey, come on, now. Let's not get ahead of ourselves. We said we weren't going to do that, remember? We promised to be objective and lay out the facts rather than speculate on what we think may be going on in our daughter's marriage."

Mrs. Whitman snatched her hand from her husband's grip.

"Speculate?" she spat. "Oh, this is far from speculation. I heard from my own daughter's mouth how miserable she was in that relationship. Blake is an emotionally abusive philanderer. He's been having affairs with multiple women, shows my daughter no affection unless he wants to have sex with her—"

"Okay, dear," Mr. Whitman interrupted, holding his hand in the air in a bid to quiet her. "Let's maintain some decorum here."

"Decorum..." she sniffed before turning her nose up at her husband. "Believe me, I am working overtime trying to maintain my dignity. But that becomes difficult when discussing such a sorry excuse for a man. If having his cake and eating it, too, were a person, it'd be Blake Carter—"

"Sweetheart, *please*," Mr. Whitman interjected. "Detective Reed and Mona didn't come here for this. They want facts, not the lewd personal details of our daughter's relationship. All that's irrelevant to her disappearance."

Dillon wanted to tell Mr. Whitman that his wife's claims were far from irrelevant. He'd seen numerous cases where infidelity was the motive behind domestic violence incidents. But the pair were so fired up that he decided to keep it to himself for the time being.

Mrs. Whitman glared at her husband before turning to Dillon and Mona.

"As you can see, my husband is in denial. He's also more concerned about preserving the Carter family's upstanding reputation within the community than he is finding our daughter."

"That is *not* true—"

"Detective Reed," Mrs. Whitman continued, ignoring her husband, "I would like for Blake to be questioned as to whether or not he is involved in Olivia's disappearance. Because I for one am convinced that he is."

Dillon scooted to the edge of the couch and cleared his throat. "Well, Blake has been brought down to the station and questioned on more than one occasion. Now, I can't reveal the specifics of the interrogation. But I can tell you that he has a rock-solid alibi on the day that Olivia went missing."

"Of course," Mrs. Whitman sniffed, turning her nose up at Dillon. "That's because he probably hired someone to do his dirty work."

Mr. Whitman's eyes widened as he threw his wife a look of disdain. But this time, he kept quiet.

"Mrs. Whitman," Mona began, "I understand that you don't want to speak publicly about Olivia's disappearance. But in my experience as a journalist, a family's pleas can oftentimes encourage witnesses to come forward with information they'd otherwise keep to themselves. There's something about seeing a parent's pain that motivates people to open up."

"I can attest to that," Dillon chimed in. "Back when I was working on the Baton Rouge police force, I dealt with violent offenders, gang members…all sorts of criminals. Witnesses were afraid to come forward for fear of retaliation. But when the victims' families showed up, pleading with the public for information, tips would start pouring in."

"And when there's a reward attached to these missing person cases," Mona added, "that gives people even more incentive to provide law enforcement with information."

"So wait," Mrs. Whitman said, her sharp tone filled with panic, "has Blake been ruled out?"

"We haven't ruled anyone out," Dillon told her.

Mr. Whitman pressed his hand against his forehead and sighed deeply. "I can just see it now. This entire situation is going to turn into a dog and pony show. The offer of a reward will lead to false tips and con men providing fake information. I watch all those true-crime television shows. I've seen it happen time and time again."

Dillon was surprised when Mrs. Whitman leaned over and gently patted her husband's arm.

"My husband is convinced that whoever kidnapped Olivia is holding her hostage somewhere."

"And if we go public," Mr. Whitman said, "behaving as though we're hurt and weak, this criminal will demand ransom money. Mark my words."

Mrs. Whitman pulled her hand away from her husband. "If that's the case, and Olivia is still alive, I'd give away every dime we have to bring her home."

"As would I," Mr. Whitman shot back. "I just don't want to get scammed out of a fortune without recovering my child."

"Yeah, I don't want us to get scammed out of our fortune either!" Dillon heard someone shout.

The sound of sneaker soles screeching across the foyer's marble floor filled the air. Dillon and Mona spun around simultaneously as Oliver came traipsing into the room.

Mrs. Whitman quickly stood up and rushed over to him.

"Oliver," she hissed, "didn't your father and I tell you

to stay upstairs in your bedroom until Mona and Detective Reed left?"

"Yep, you did."

Dillon watched in awe while Oliver brushed past his mother, flopped down onto the love seat next to the couch and propped his shoes on top of the vintage crystal coffee table.

"Oliver!" Mrs. Whitman continued, "please remove your feet from my table!"

He chuckled arrogantly, nibbling at his cuticles. After a minutes-long staredown with his parents, Oliver finally plopped his feet down onto the dark hardwood floor.

Mrs. Whitman's lips tightened. She walked stiffly back to her chair and sat down. Mr. Whitman shook his head. He ignored Oliver while remaining focused on Mona and Dillon.

"As I was saying," Mr. Whitman continued, "I'm just concerned about all of the fraudulent criminals out here who'd try to take advantage of my family. I don't want to appear vulnerable. That's what going public would feel like to me."

Oliver, who was chewing a massive wad of pink bubblegum, threw his head back and blew a huge bubble into the air. All eyes turned to him right before it popped loudly and splattered all over his face.

"Oliver," Mrs. Whitman uttered, "must you? Especially in front of company?"

"Yes. I must," he insisted before turning toward Dillon and Mona. "So, I've been thinking. I may be willing to do that on-air interview."

Dillon looked over at Mr. and Mrs. Whitman. They both stared at their son warily but remained silent.

"Really?" Mona asked hesitantly, her eyes darting back and forth between his parents and him. "What brought on the change of heart?"

"Welp, obviously this investigation has stalled thanks to you and Inspector Gadget over here," he snorted, waving his hand at Dillon.

"*Excuse* me?" Dillon said. "Who do you think you're—"

He paused when he felt Mona's warm touch on his forearm. It immediately silenced him.

"Oliver," Mona continued, "Detective Reed and I are working extremely hard on this case. Keep in mind there are details surrounding the investigation that we're not at liberty to discuss at this time. But trust me when I tell you that things are moving in the right direction."

"Wait," Mrs. Whitman interjected, her eyes brightening with hope. "There are new details that we don't yet know about?"

"Yes," Mona confirmed, "there are. But not enough to make an arrest. We still need all the help we can get from the public. So please, reconsider doing an on-air interview with me."

Oliver hopped up from the love seat and began frantically pacing the floor. "I just said I'd be willing to do an interview. Why am I being ignored?"

"I'm all for you doing an interview," Mona told him. Her gaze shifted toward his parents. "We just need to make sure everyone's on the same page."

Mrs. Whitman stood up again and motioned for her husband to do the same. "Mona, Detective Reed, thank you very much for stopping by. But I think that'll be all for now."

"Oh, so you all are just gonna ice me out like you always do?" Oliver shouted. "I'm sick of being treated like an outcast! Don't forget, I worked with Blake at Transformation Cosmetics. I've seen and heard things that you two know nothing about!"

"Oliver, *please*," Mrs. Whitman begged, walking toward him with her arms outstretched. "Your father and I just want to—"

"I don't wanna hear it!" he yelled, quickly backing away from her. "Keep counting me out. But I'll tell you what. If you and Dad decide to dangle a reward over a witness's head? You may as well write the check out to me now. Because *I'm* gonna be the one who ends up solving this case."

Mrs. Whitman spun around and marched across the room.

"I'll walk you two out," she said to Mona and Dillon while ushering them toward the door.

Mr. Whitman stayed behind with their son, who continued to unravel.

"Mark my words!" Oliver hollered. "It's gonna be *me* who ends up finding out what happened to my sister. *Me!*"

"I am so sorry about all this," Mrs. Whitman breathed.

Dillon was surprised to see her practically jogging to the front door. When she opened it, he noticed tears streaming down her face. She pressed her hand against her cheeks, dabbing away the streaking black mascara.

"No worries, Mrs. Whitman," he told her. "We can only imagine the pain and stress your family is under right now. It's hard to hold it together during times like these."

"And I've known Oliver for years," Mona said, her soothing voice appearing to put Mrs. Whitman at ease. "So I understand his behavior. I know he's hurting. He just has a *strange* way of showing it."

"To put it nicely," Mrs. Whitman replied before chuckling a bit. "Ah, I guess I needed that little laugh."

"I think you did, too." Dillon smiled. "Listen, you have my contact information as well as Mona's. If you think of anything or just want to talk, please don't hesitate to reach out to either of us."

"And not to be overly persistent or anything," Mona added, "but please, just think about doing that interview. As crazy as this may sound, consider allowing Oliver to participate, as well. I know he marches to the beat of a different drummer, but you have to admit, he is engaging. Like he said, he could be integral in solving this case."

Mrs. Whitman remained silent, looking away while crossing her arms in front of her.

"We, uh, we should be leaving," Dillon said as he led Mona out onto the porch. "Thank you again for your time."

"Listen, before you go," Mrs. Whitman said before stepping outside, "can you tell me more about that new evidence you'd mentioned?"

"Unfortunately, we have to keep the details confidential," Dillon replied quietly. "At least for now. But when we're able to, we certainly will."

"I understand. Well, I'll think about what you said regarding the on-air interview. And Mr. Whitman and I will consider allowing Oliver to participate. But he may need some sort of media training in order to do so."

"And that's what I'm here for," Mona said. "I can teach him everything he needs to know before getting in front of the camera. So don't worry. By the time we go live, he'll be a pro."

"A pro?" Mrs. Whitman asked skeptically. "That impulsive son of mine? *Please.* That child will get on air and say anything." She squinted her eyes and stared out at the weeping willow tree standing in the middle of her vast front yard. "But again, I'll think about it. At this point I'm willing to do whatever I can to find my daughter."

"Good," Dillon said. "Again, call us if you need anything."

"I will. Take care."

"You, too," Dillon and Mona replied in unison.

The pair headed to the car, then left the residence in silence.

As Dillon drove back to the inn, he glanced over at

Mona. She was looking out at the bleak stretch of grassy swampland, her forehead creased with worry.

"Hey," he said, reaching over and gently nudging her thigh. "Why don't we go out tonight and have a nice dinner? I think we could both use a night off. Maybe talk about something other than this investigation."

"That actually sounds amazing. I definitely need a break from all of this. And as a matter of fact, Evelyn is serving up her Louisiana beef stew and pecan bread tonight at the inn. *And* she extended a special invite just for you."

"Did she?"

"She sure did."

"Well, I guess I can't disappoint Evelyn. Not to mention her beef stew and pecan bread are absolutely superb."

"Yes, they are," Mona agreed. "So, we're on for tonight?"

"We're on for tonight."

Dillon couldn't contain the surge of excitement that erupted inside his chest. It was a sensation he hadn't felt in years.

Stop it, he told himself. *Mona is not into you like that.*

But when he noticed the slight smile on her face, his detective instincts told him otherwise.

Nevertheless, Dillon knew he needed to stay focused so not to compromise the investigation. Circumstances surrounding the case were growing more dangerous.

Despite his undeniable feelings, he was determined to remain diligent until an arrest was made.

Chapter Nine

Mona sat on a corner stool near the window of Silvia's Speakeasy. She stared out at the dark, desolate street that appeared more like an alleyway. There was no sign of Dillon or Oliver.

She took a sip of her cranberry old-fashioned, then grabbed her cell phone.

Hey, she texted to Dillon. I'm at Silvia's. Been here for almost an hour. Still no sign of Oliver yet. Are you on your way?

Mona sent the message, then swiveled around in her burgundy leather barstool. She glanced around the small, dimly lit jazz club, wondering whether she'd missed seeing Oliver.

None of the faces lining the distressed brick walls looked familiar. The crowd ranged in ages from early twenties to late sixties. Various nationalities and genders dressed in outfits spanning from sweat suits to cocktail dresses filled the room.

Mona was glad she'd chosen to wear her fitted wool magenta dress and nude patent pumps. The look fell somewhere in the middle of the diverse club goers.

A large group of patrons shuffled through the heavy vintage steel door. They stopped and stared at the black-and-white photos of famous jazz musicians hanging along the entryway.

Mona stared anxiously at the group, hoping to catch a glimpse of Oliver. But when they shuffled farther inside and stopped at the bar, she realized he wasn't among the crowd.

Please show up, she thought to herself while once again checking his Instagram page.

"I hope I'm at the right place," she muttered aloud.

Mona double-checked his latest post.

What's up, my peeps? Who's meeting me at Silvia's Speakeasy tonight? It's open mic night! So come through and check out some of the best musicians in all of Louisiana. Mico will be at the bar serving up his handcrafted holiday cocktails, too. So don't miss out. See you there!

"Okay, I am definitely where I'm supposed to be," Mona said to herself.

She was actually surprised that Oliver was attending yet another social event.

*If he shows up, that is...*she thought, taking another look around the bar. *Where are you?*

Neither Mona nor Dillon had heard from the Whitmans since visiting their home. She'd tried reaching out to them but got no response. So she had resorted to doing what she did best—stalking Oliver's social media to find out where he'd be.

Now all you need to do is make an appearance.

Mona's cell phone buzzed. A text message from Dillon popped up on the screen.

Hey, Chief Boyer and I had to make an unexpected run to the forensics lab. New DNA results came back on a cold case he'd worked on years ago. He was so pumped that we drove out to Vincent Parish to pick up the report.

Heading back that way now. I'll be there as soon as I can. Think you can hang tight until then?

I guess I'll have to, Mona replied. The band will be going on soon. I'll just sip my drink and enjoy the music until you two arrive.

Mona sent the message, then spun around in her stool when she saw a commotion in the back of the bar.

Hands were waving in the air. Shots were being passed around. Patrons were toasting and hugging one another.

Mona stood up to get a better look at the group. As they began to scatter about, Oliver appeared. He was standing off to the side of the crowd, sullenly staring down at the worn hardwood floor.

She quickly grabbed her drink.

Play it cool. Act casually.

Just as she stepped away from the bar, Mona heard a loud voice boom into a microphone.

"Hello everyone, and welcome to Silvia's open mic night!"

Mona turned toward the stage. A heavyset older man with a bald head and triple chin stood front and center. He appeared cool yet jolly in his white button-down shirt, red bow tie, red suspenders and black corduroy pants. He was holding a bottle of beer in one hand and swiping a checkered handkerchief across his forehead with the other.

"I'm your host, Sir LeBlanc. And I'll be keeping you entertained throughout the evening while introducing some of the best jazz bands in all of Louisiana. So sit back. Relax. Or get up on your feet. Whatever floats your boat. Just make sure you're having a good time and keeping the bartenders busy!"

As Sir LeBlanc announced the first act, Mona turned her attention to the back of the club. Oliver was still standing in the corner. But now, it appeared as though he was in the middle of a heated argument with a petite redhead.

Oh, maybe she's what brought him out tonight...

Mona watched as Oliver placed his hand on the woman's shoulder. She pushed him away, then pointed her finger in his face. After yelling something at him, she stormed into the ladies' room.

Another woman stepped in and grabbed Oliver when he tried to follow her. The two of them got into a shouting match.

"What in the hell is going on?" Mona muttered.

Several moments passed before the woman threw her arms in the air, then ran into the ladies' room.

Oliver spun around and exited the club through the back door.

No! Don't leave!

Mona practically threw her drink down onto the bar. She tucked her gold leather clutch underneath her arm and hurried after him.

"Excuse me!" she yelled at the tight crowd blocking her pathway.

She squeezed her way to the back. By the time she reached the exit, Oliver was long gone.

Mona burst through the door and almost fell down onto the dark alley's black asphalt.

She jumped at the sound of the door slamming behind her.

Calm down, she told herself. *Just find Oliver.*

Her cell phone buzzed. Mona ignored it and turned right, then left. The long alleyway revealed nothing but steamy darkness.

Oliver was nowhere in sight.

The sound of scurrying footsteps echoed off the brick walls lining the alleyway. Mona's ears perked up. It sounded as though the heavy clicking was fading away toward her right.

She set off in the direction of the footsteps echoing against the asphalt.

Mona almost lost her balance when her heels skidded along the damp ground. But she kept going, determined to find Oliver.

She wrinkled her nose after passing a foul-smelling dumpster that reeked of rotten food.

Maybe you should've just stayed inside the club...

A gust of hot steam rushed up from the ground. Mona hopped over a manhole cover, choking on the stifling vapor.

The air cleared. She'd reached the end of the alleyway.

Oliver was still nowhere to be found.

"Dammit," she whispered.

Mona peered down both ends of the unfamiliar street. Aside from a few run-down shacks and small, swampy marshes, the road was deserted.

She parted her lips to call out Oliver's name. But she was interrupted when her cell phone buzzed again.

Mona grabbed it from her clutch. Dillon's name flashed across the screen.

Finally, she thought. *You're here...*

Right before she accepted the call, Mona felt a presence looming over her.

She dropped the phone in her clutch and paused.

Someone was approaching from behind.

Mona spun around.

A masked man grabbed her arm and pulled her in close. He was dressed in all black, just like the shadowy figure out in Beechtree.

Mona screamed, struggling to free herself from his grip.

"What are you *doing*—?"

"Shut up!" the man growled.

Mona clamped her lips together, resisting the urge to scream once again.

Do not show any signs of fear. Do not show any signs of fear...

"What do you want?" she asked, her strong tone contradicting the terror running through her body.

"The better question is, what do *you* want? Why are you still here in Lake Landry, Mona Avery?"

She grimaced when he spoke her name. The thought of being stalked by a maniac chilled her to the bone.

Stand strong. Do not let this man know you're afraid.

"Who are you?" she boldly asked. "And why are you following me?"

"Following you?" he repeated. "Like I did that day you were roaming aimlessly around Beechtree?"

The man's grip on her arm tightened. He moved in closer. Mona cringed when his hot breath blew on her neck.

"To answer your question," he whispered, "I'm following you because I want you to get the *hell* out of Lake Landry!"

Mona winced as an intense pain ripped down her arm. She blinked rapidly, trying to find a familiarity in his voice. She didn't.

His hand slid from her arm down to her waist. Suddenly, Mona was overcome by the urge to fight.

She shoved him as hard as she could, then spun around to run back down the alley.

But before she could move, he threw his arm around her neck, forcing her into a tight choke hold.

"You *bitch*," he barked. "You think you can hurt me? I should kill you just for trying!"

Mona whimpered as the man dragged her toward a dark corner of the alley's entryway. She grabbed his forearm, struggling to loosen his grip. Her heels screeched along the pavement as she fought to stay on her feet.

"Listen to me," the man continued, "and listen to me good. I want you out of this town. *Immediately.* Now, you can do it the easy way and hop on the first flight back to LA. Or you can do it the hard way and simply disappear, just like your girl did…"

Mona gasped at his harsh words. She jerked her head away when his lips brushed against her ear.

"Please," she pleaded, "leave me alone. Let me go!"

"Don't worry, I'll leave you alone. Just as soon as you leave Olivia Whitman's case alone. You're in over your head, Mona Avery. Get out while you can. Consider this your final notice. Got it?"

She remained silent, too stunned to speak.

"No response, huh?" her attacker spewed before pulling a switchblade from his pocket. He waved it in front of her face, then grazed her cheek with the cold, sharp blade.

Stinging tears burned Mona's eyes. She stiffened up, numb with fright.

The man tightened his grip on her neck.

Get to your phone, she thought. *Try to call Dillon back.*

Mona gasped for breath while fumbling for her clutch. She shoved her hand inside and grabbed hold of her phone.

As her trembling fingers struggled to unlock the cell, Mona heard a door open. The sound of voices and footsteps filled the air.

She fought to turn her head and look down the alleyway. *Get noticed. Scream for help.*

Through the corner of her eye, she saw club goers exiting Silvia's and spilling out into the alley. They were laughing and lighting cigarettes.

The attacker loosened his grip on Mona's neck. She inhaled deeply, choking as the air rushed through her lungs.

She once again tore at his arm, struggling to free herself. But he refused to let her go.

"Do the right thing, Mona Avery," he growled. This time, his sinister tone had lowered several octaves. "Get the hell out of Lake Landry. Unless you want your fellow journalists reporting on *your* disappearance."

Just as she felt herself giving up on being freed, the man pushed Mona against a brick wall, then took off running.

She quickly swiped open the camera app on her phone. Mona tried to take a picture of the man. But he had already disappeared into the darkness.

She spun around and stumbled back down the alley. Her hand scaled the wall as she struggled to hold herself up.

"Excuse me, ma'am?" a woman who was standing near Silvia's back door asked her. "Are you all right?"

"I—I'm fine," Mona groaned.

The woman walked over and placed her hand on Mona's arm.

She grimaced, still sore from her attacker's vicious grasp.

"Are you sure you're okay?" the woman probed.

Mona stood straight up and cleared her throat. A small crowd began to gather around her.

Don't make a spectacle of yourself, she thought. *Just get back inside and call Dillon.*

"I'm positive," she managed. "Thank you for asking."

Despite her wobbly legs, Mona was able to make her way back inside of Silvia's. She dialed Dillon's number. The call went straight to voice mail.

"Nooo," she moaned.

At the sound of the beep, she began leaving a message.

"It's Mona," she yelled over the music. "I was—I was just attacked! I'd stepped outside to—"

She stopped abruptly at the sight of Dillon standing near the entrance.

"Dillon!" she screamed.

When he failed to look her way, Mona pushed through the crowd toward the front of the club.

"Hey!" Dillon boomed as she approached him. "Sorry I'm late. You know how long-winded Chief Boyer can be. Did Oliver ever show up?"

Mona just stood there, staring at him.

"Uh-oh," Dillon said. "He's not here, is he? Don't worry. Let's just find a table, have a drink and enjoy the music—"

Before he could finish, Mona collapsed in his arms.

"What—what's going on?" he asked, his heightened tone filled with confusion.

"I was attacked when I went out back to try to find Oliver!" Mona cried into Dillon's chest. "The same man who threatened me in Beechtree followed me here tonight. He pulled a knife on me in the alley behind the club."

"Hold on, hold on," Dillon said, wrapping his arms around her. "Slow down. I can't understand everything you're saying. You were *attacked*?"

Mona looked up at him. "Yes. Can we please get out of here?"

"Wait! Do you think he's still in the area? I can call backup and search the perimeter and—"

"Dillon, no. He's long gone. Trust me, you won't find him. Now, please, I have got to get out of here."

"Of course. Come on."

Dillon held her tightly while leading her out of the club. "Did you drive yourself here?" he asked.

"No. I took an Uber."

"Okay. Let's get you back to the inn."

They took the short walk down the block to his car in silence. Once they climbed inside and Dillon pulled off, Mona was overcome by a wave of emotion. She leaned her head against the back of the seat and closed her eyes, stunned that she'd been assaulted.

"I cannot believe this happened to me," she whispered.

"I can't either. And I'm so sorry. Can you tell me exactly what happened?"

Mona opened her eyes and took a deep breath. "I was sitting at the bar inside of Silvia's when I spotted Oliver. After getting into an altercation with a couple of women, he ran out of the club's back door. So I went after him."

She paused, her voice shaking with fear.

Dillon reached over and took her hand in his. Her fingers tightened around his palm. His reassuring touch gave her the strength to continue.

"When I ran out into the alleyway, Oliver was nowhere in sight. So I made a right turn and followed what I thought was the sound of his footsteps. And then, out of nowhere, I was attacked by the same man who followed me out to Beechtree."

"How do you know it was the same man? Did you get a good look at him?"

"No. He was wearing a ski mask. But I recognized the outfit and build. Not to mention he told me that it was him. Thank God I'm okay. He did, however, rough me up and pull a knife on me. And he said that if I don't stop investigating Olivia's disappearance and leave town, I'm going to go missing, too."

Mona felt Dillon's grasp on her hand tighten. She looked over at him.

His expression was tense.

He suddenly slammed on the brakes and turned the car around.

"What are you doing?" she asked.

"Going back to Silvia's. I've gotta track this maniac down."

"Dillon, I'm sure he's long gone by now."

His lips twisted in disappointment. "You're probably

right." He slowly turned the car back around and headed in the opposite direction.

"I'm so sorry this happened," Mona told him.

"No, *I'm* sorry this happened," he insisted, pressing down on the accelerator.

She turned and looked out the window, watching as they sped past The Bayou Inn and made a sharp left turn down Robinson Avenue.

"Where are you going?" she asked.

"To the police station. I know you may not feel up to it, but after tonight's assault, I want to file a report ASAP. Do you think you can do that?"

Mona's heart began to race at the thought of going to the station and repeating the details of the attack. But she knew it was necessary.

"Yes," she told Dillon. "I can do that. And afterward, I think we need to come up with a new game plan."

"Okay. Do you already have a strategy in mind?"

Mona looked down and pressed her shaky hands together. "I do. For starters, while I fully believe Blake is behind all this, I don't think he's the one who attacked me."

"You don't? Are you sure?"

"I'm positive. The assailant's voice and physical stature are the complete opposite of Blake's. But I wouldn't put it past him to send one of his guys after me. So, with that being said, I want to approach Blake again and request an on-air interview. This time, I'll present it as if I want to help him prove his innocence to the people of Lake Landry."

"*What?* But…*why*?"

"Because I really want to get him in front of the camera. And when I do, the entire country will witness me eat him alive. By the time I'm done, he will have admitted to the crimes he committed against Olivia *and* me without even knowing it."

"Whoa," Dillon said, cracking a smile as he pulled in front of the station. "Somebody got their chutzpah back."

"It never left. It was just buried underneath a layer of terror. And that's quickly fading, by the way. Now I'm bound and determined to prove Blake's guilt."

"Okay, well, if you can pull the confession out of him that law enforcement couldn't, which we all know Mona Avery is perfectly capable of doing, then I say go for it."

"Thank you. I will. Oh, and even though tonight was a total bust, I still haven't given up on scoring interviews with the Whitmans. Especially Oliver."

"Good. You shouldn't give up."

Dillon reached for his door handle, then paused.

"Listen," he continued. "Before we go inside, let me assure you I'm going to do all that I can to protect you from here on out. If that means escorting you everywhere you go, and having a patrol car keep watch over The Bayou Inn, then so be it. And if you land that interview with Blake, I will be tagging along. Also, no more roaming around in desolate areas or down dark alleyways."

"But this time, I was—"

"Hold on," he interrupted. "Let me finish. I'm not blaming you for what happened tonight. I'm just saying that we need to take extra precautions to help keep you safe now that we know you're being followed. My partner back in Baton Rouge had a habit of going out on his own to investigate cases. One night when he was by himself, he ended up getting severely injured. That was another reason why I left town. It got to be too much. I don't want to end up in a situation like that with you."

"Understood," Mona replied quietly. "And thank you."

"You're welcome. But I like where your head's at regarding Blake and the interview. I think it's a good idea. You've got my full support."

"Thanks, Dillon. That means a lot to me."

"Of course. Now, let's go inside and get this report filed. Then we'll go back to the inn, have a drink and decompress."

Mona took a deep breath and opened her car door.

"You good?" Dillon asked her. "Are you sure you're up for this, or would you rather wait until tomorrow?"

She could still feel her limbs trembling from the aftermath of the attack.

Pull it together, she told herself. *You can do this. Nobody said your job would be easy. You were built for this.*

"Yes," she said, holding her head high as if that would pump confidence into her veins. "I'm good. Let's do this."

Dillon gave her arm a reassuring squeeze. Together, they walked inside the police station.

Chapter Ten

Dillon sat in the corner of Blake's study, staring up at the elaborate dome-shaped ceiling. Soft yellow recessed lights shone down on rich, sandalwood walls. The curved shelves were packed with antique books, family photos and expensive heirlooms. Tufted cream leather furniture surrounded an intricately carved, custom-built desk.

He took a sip of ice water. He glanced over at Mona, whose makeup artist was busy dusting bronzer across her cheekbones. A cameraman adjusted the light hanging above her chair as she straightened the sleeves on her lavender cape-back dress.

Blake walked over and took a seat across from Mona. As soon as he settled in, a producer approached him and attached a lavalier microphone to his navy blue blazer's lapel. He appeared calm and collected while sipping coffee from a marble ceramic mug.

Dillon shifted in his chair. He adjusted his tan suede sports jacket, then smoothed his dark denim jeans.

Between Blake's designer suit and Mona's elaborate getup, he felt severely underdressed. But he quickly reminded himself that he wouldn't be the one in front of the camera. He'd simply tagged along to support Mona and make sure things went smoothly during the interview.

Just as she'd planned, Mona was able to convince Blake

that going live on air and openly discussing Olivia's disappearance would help salvage his reputation. His attorneys, who were sitting across the room quietly eyeing their cell phones, thought otherwise. But there was nothing they could say to convince the narcissistic Blake Carter that doing a live broadcast with Mona was a bad idea.

Dillon was still shocked that he'd agreed to it. But at the same time, he wasn't. Blake believed he could outsmart anyone. That included Mona, law enforcement, the community, and anyone else who dared to go up against him.

"But this is Mona Avery we're talking about," Dillon had overheard one of Blake's attorneys telling him when they first arrived at the house. "The woman is a pro. She can catch you up and have you twisting your words, then confessing to things you had nothing to do with."

"Not me," Blake replied before popping his crisp white collar. "Around here? *I'm* the pro. Now step aside and watch me work, gentlemen."

And that was it. Blake's attorneys backed off and took a seat in the corner. Considering how much they were probably getting paid, Dillon wasn't shocked that they'd given up so easily.

"How are we looking on time?" Mona asked her producer. "Are we just about ready to go live?"

"We are," she replied, stepping back while the makeup artist swooped in and brushed a curl away from Mona's face.

Dillon watched as Mona stared at Blake. He could see the glint in her shining eyes. He knew she was probably thinking of the attacks she'd endured.

May God have mercy on your soul, he thought, knowing that Mona would live up to her words and eat Blake alive.

"Okay, everyone," the producer said, "going live in five, four, three, two…"

She pointed at Mona, who turned and looked directly into the camera.

"Hello, everyone. Thank you for joining me during this special broadcast. Today I am here with Blake Carter, a well-known businessman who lives in Lake Landry, Louisiana. As many of you know, I've been in Lake Landry for the past few weeks investigating the disappearance of my good friend Olivia Whitman. Blake is the husband of Olivia, and many believe that he is involved in her disappearance."

Oh! Dillon thought. *So you're just gonna come out swinging. Okay...*

He turned to Blake, expecting to see some sort of reaction. But he just sat there, his expression appearing steadfast and unruffled.

"Blake has agreed to sit down with me to discuss Olivia's case," Mona continued, "in hopes of clearing his name and leading investigators to the real perpetrators. Blake, thank you for joining me."

"Thank you for having me," he replied coolly.

"So, I'm just going to go ahead and ask the question that everyone wants to know. Did you have anything to do with Olivia's disappearance?"

Blake's eyebrows shot up into his forehead.

"No, I did not," he responded, his quiet tone tinged with pain. "And I resent you even asking me that."

"Do you have any idea what may have happened to her?"

"No, I do not. But I hope that she will return home soon, safe and sound."

"*Humph*, do you now..." Mona replied, her wide eyes filled with skepticism. "Let's go back to the day that Olivia went missing. What was her mood? Did she seem worried? Or had she mentioned anything about feeling unsafe?"

Blake turned his head slightly, staring at Mona through

the corner of his eye. Dillon was baffled by his silence. But then he remembered Mona telling him that Blake hadn't seen Olivia the day she went missing because he'd spent the night at his mistress's house.

"Oh wait," Mona said. "That's right. You told me during an earlier conversation that you didn't see Olivia the day she went missing. You weren't home that morning."

"No. I wasn't. I was away on business."

Mona threw Blake a doubtful look before continuing. "All right, then. So anyway, how long was Olivia missing before her disappearance was reported to police?"

Blake paused. Dillon could see his jaws clenching from across the room. It was clear that Mona was getting under his skin.

You've been fooled, man, he thought to himself amusingly. *Mona came here to take you down, and she's doing just that...*

"About a week, I believe?" Blake said, crossing one leg over the other.

"A whole week? *Wow.* That's a pretty long time, isn't it? Why'd you wait so long?"

Mona glared at Blake so fiercely that Dillon felt an outbreak of sweat form along his own hairline.

"Oh wait," Mona continued without allowing him to respond. "You can't answer that, can you? Because you weren't the one who reported Olivia missing. Her mother was. Why is that, Blake? Why didn't *you* inform police that your wife was missing? If you had, maybe she would've been found by now. I'm sure you know that the first forty-eight hours into an investigation are the most important, don't you?"

"I'm sorry," one of Blake's attorneys interrupted as he stood up. "But we're going to have to stop this—"

"No, no," Blake said, holding his hand in the air without taking his eyes off Mona. "It's fine. We can continue."

The attorney shook his head from side to side before slowly sitting back down.

"As you know, Mona," Blake said, "my marriage to Olivia wasn't in the best place. We got together when we were fairly young. The stress of our jobs, the pressure of upholding our prestigious families' names, our desire to start a family—"

"*Your* desire to start a family," Mona interjected. "From what I understand, Olivia did not want to have children with you. As a matter of fact, she was preparing to file for divor—"

"I'm sorry," Blake smirked, interrupting Mona's scathing rant. "But were you a part of my marriage, Mona? How would you know the intimate details of our relationship? Idle gossip doesn't compare to conversations between a husband and wife. However, you probably wouldn't understand that. Because you don't have a husband, do you?"

Dillon felt his breath catch in his throat. He peered over at Mona.

"No. I don't," she replied, staring icily at him.

"Exactly," Blake continued condescendingly. "So see, if you're ever blessed enough to actually find a husband, you'll realize that things occur within a marriage that aren't shared with outsiders. My wife and I love one another, Mona. And while we may have been having a few issues, we were in fact discussing starting a family."

"So then why wouldn't you have immediately reported your beloved wife missing, Blake?"

"Because I just assumed she'd gone off to clear her head. You know, take some time to be alone. But here's my question to you, Mona. As her friend, how come *you* didn't realize Olivia was missing? Since you seem to know so much about my marriage and what she was going through, you should've known she'd disappeared. Then *you* could've been the one to contact the police."

"This isn't about me, Blake. And I am not a suspect."

"Last time I checked, neither am I. Am I right, Detective Reed?" he asked, pointing over at Dillon.

Dillon wished he could've fallen through the floor as the camera turned toward him.

"No," he replied quietly. "You're not."

"I didn't think so," Blake gloated before turning back to Mona. "Maybe you need to reevaluate your friendship with my wife. Sounds like you two aren't as close as you may have thought. Next question."

Dillon looked over at Mona. The anger underneath her steely glare was apparent. She sat up in her chair, her back rigid.

He wanted to go over and embrace her reassuringly. Let her know she was doing a good job. But he couldn't. So he remained seated, hoping she could feel his support from the sidelines.

"Blake, what have you done to help find your wife?" she asked.

Nice comeback, he thought. *Stay on track. Don't let this man rattle you...*

"I've actually done a lot," he boasted. "Leo Mendez, who is Transformation Cosmetics' director of operations, has done a tremendous job in helping to plan a couple of search party efforts. He even assisted Olivia's family in planning a vigil shortly after she went missing."

Mona cocked her head to the side. "Wait, this Leo Mendez, he did all of that work on your behalf?"

"Yes, he did. At my request, of course."

"Wasn't he also Oliver Whitman's boss when he worked at Transformation Cosmetics?"

"That is correct. And per usual, Leo stepped up to the plate and showed immense leadership when he terminated Oliver."

Dillon leaned forward, intrigued by Blake's version of his encounter with Oliver. He hoped Mona would allow him to delve a little further.

When Mona propped her hand underneath her chin and stared at Blake curiously, he knew she was just as intrigued as he was.

"I don't want to get too off track with this interview," she stated, "but do you think Oliver has a good relationship with his sister?"

Blake sat back in his chair and crossed his arms. "Not at all. His parents had threatened to cut him off financially. He still depends on Mommy and Daddy, and they're sick of it. So he was growing more and more resentful by the day. His jealousy toward Olivia's success was eating away at him, too. It's no secret she's the Whitmans' golden child and he's the black sheep. As a matter of fact, you probably need to be questioning *his* involvement in her disappearance—"

"Hold on," Mona interrupted. "Let's reel it in. I don't want to discuss Oliver's possible involvement. He's not here to defend himself. So why don't we get back to you and the missing person events Leo coordinated. Did you assist him in *any* of the planning?"

Blake shifted in his seat, glancing over at his attorneys. After several seconds of silence, he turned back to Mona.

"No. I didn't."

"Did you attend any of the events?"

"I, um…no. I had a couple of unexpected work emergencies pop up." Blake paused. He raised his head and stared down his nose at Mona. "But wait, did *you* attend any of the events?"

"I hadn't arrived in town yet," she quickly shot back.

"However, now that I'm here, I am doing all that I can to help find Olivia."

"Good. So am I."

"Really? How so?" Mona probed, tapping her alligator leather fountain pen against her cheek.

"For starters, I've cooperated with law enforcement one hundred percent throughout this entire investigation. When they asked to come and search our house, I let them. When they asked to search our vehicles, I let them. When they confiscated our computers, I let them. When I was asked to turn over my cell phone, I did. When they asked for a DNA sample, I gave it to them. There is nothing I haven't done to assist in the effort to find my wife."

Mona's eyes squinted. She stared daggers at Blake while pursing her lips.

Dillon watched her closely, rubbing his hands together while anxiously awaiting the next question.

"And that polygraph test you took," she continued.

"Yes, what about it?"

"You didn't pass it."

"The test came back *no opinion*."

"Meaning?"

Blake sighed heavily. His eyes diverted to the floor as they quickly filled with tears. "Mona, I got so emotional while trying to answer the questions that the examiner kept having to stop and restart the test. As a result of that, he couldn't get an exact reading."

"So again, you didn't pass the test," she said, appearing unmoved by his show of emotion.

"The point is, I didn't fail the test."

"Yet the entire town of Lake Landry believes you had something to do with Olivia's disappearance."

Blake ran his hand across his face and opened his

mouth to object. But Mona kept going before he could get a word out.

"What about Olivia's life insurance policy? Can we talk about that?"

"Sure," he sniffed. "What about it?"

"You increased the amount of your wife's payout. A *week* before she went missing."

"Yes. *We* did."

"But you didn't increase yours. Why is that?"

Blake emitted a condescending chuckle.

"Mona, here's something else you may not understand as a single woman with…no children, isn't that correct?" he asked, tilting his head while scratching his scalp.

"Oh boy," Dillon whispered, hoping Mona wouldn't implode live on air. He noticed Blake's attorneys over in the corner, smirking and nodding their heads at one another.

Idiots, he thought before turning his attention back to the interview.

"Once again, Blake, this isn't about me. This is about you and your missing wife. Now please. Answer the question."

"Well, as a husband who's planning a family with my wife, Olivia and I wanted to increase the amounts on our life insurance policies for the benefit of our future children."

"But that still doesn't explain why Olivia's policy was increased and yours wasn't."

"Olivia was able to contact our insurance agent and adjust her policy before I did." He shrugged nonchalantly. "It's as simple as that. You do know that I am the president of Transformation Cosmetics. So, I'm a pretty busy man. But trust me, I was planning on increasing my payout, as well."

The room fell silent. Mona shuffled the papers sitting in her lap. Dillon could see her hands trembled from where he was sitting.

Uh-oh, he thought. *Come on, Mona. Hang in there. Don't lose your cool.*

"You okay over there?" Blake asked her, the snark in his tone apparent.

"I'm fine," Mona said. "Just looking for my next question."

Blake leaned forward, sneering at her.

"Wow," he breathed. "Mona Avery, getting thrown off her game by little ole me. What is the world coming to?"

When Blake turned to the camera and smiled, Mona tossed her papers down onto the floor.

"What about Olivia's bloodstained necklace, Blake?" she spat. "Why don't you explain *that* to me and my viewers?"

"Excuse me?" Blake asked, gripping the arms of his chair. "What are you talking about? What bloodstained necklace?"

Dillon jumped up. The producer ran over and grabbed him before he could interrupt the interview.

"The necklace that I found in Beechtree near the water source where Olivia went missing," Mona continued. "Her blood and *your* DNA were found on it. Now, how can you explain that?"

"I have no idea what the hell you're talking about!" Blake yelled, standing up and ripping off his mic. "Frank," he said to his attorney, "what is going on here?"

"I don't have a clue," he replied, approaching the pair.

"Don't stop rolling tape," Dillon heard the producer say to the cameraman.

"That's enough," Dillon said, brushing past the producer and stepping in between Mona and Blake. "This interview is over. Steve, could you please cut the camera?"

"Detective Reed," Frank said, "I think you've got some explaining to do. Is there any truth to Ms. Avery's claim?"

"I'm sorry, but at this time, I am not at liberty to discuss the details surrounding the investigation. If I need to bring your client in again for questioning, I will do so."

Blake snickered sarcastically while buttoning his suit jacket. "So what you're saying is, after Mona's little outburst, you still don't have any viable evidence linking me to Olivia's disappearance. And while I have not formally been named a suspect, I'm not even a person of interest. Is that correct?"

Dillon turned to him, fighting the urge to knock the arrogant grin off his face. "Mr. Carter, if there is any information that needs to be shared with you, I'll do so. In the meantime, we're done here. Mona, let's go."

His chest heaved as he watched Mona pack up her things. He couldn't believe she'd lost her cool and revealed intricate details of their investigation, not only to Blake and his attorneys, but to all of her viewers.

When Blake's lawyers pulled him to the side, the cameraman turned to the producer. "Should I stop filming now?"

Dillon threw his arms out at his sides. "You're still taping all of this?"

"Yes," Steve replied sheepishly, his eyes darting back and forth between Dillon and the producer.

Dillon turned back to Mona. Every nerve in his body was burning with anger.

"Could you please hurry up? I need to get out of this house. *Now*."

"I'm coming," she snapped.

As Mona continued gathering her things, the producer approached her.

"I know this interview didn't go as you'd planned, but it is ratings *gold*. Viewers are flooding our social media sites with questions and comments about Olivia's disappearance."

"Yeah, well, hopefully in the midst of all the chatter, we'll get some solid tips that'll lead to Blake's arrest."

Dillon shook his head in disgust.

"What it'll likely lead to is the media circus and public frenzy that I've been wanting to avoid this entire time," he interjected. "Now can we please get the hell out of here?"

Mona ignored him and turned her attention to her producer. "Sarah, would you mind wrapping up this segment for me? Maybe cut back to the reporters who are on standby back at the studio in LA? They can announce that due to unforeseen circumstances, Blake's interview had to be cut short, then move on to another story that I had on the docket."

"Of course," Sarah replied without looking up at Mona. Her head was buried in her phone. "Wow, the social media team has already uploaded a clip of the interview to Instagram. The post has over two thousand comments! This is wild…"

Steve peered over Sarah's shoulder and stared at her phone.

"Ooh, that is so cool! Did they give me filming credit?"

Dillon balled his hands into tight fists and turned to Mona.

"Will you please—"

"I'm ready," she quickly told him. "Let's go."

He stormed through the study, turning toward Blake on the way out.

"I'll be in touch," he barked.

"Yeah, and so will my attorneys!" Blake shot back.

Dillon practically ran through the foyer. His vision was so blurred with rage that he almost crashed into the eight-foot-tall Christmas tree standing in front of a massive bay window.

Crystal bells hanging from its branches jingled when

his arm brushed up against them. But he wasn't concerned about damaging any ornaments. He was too focused on escaping the Carter residence.

Dillon swung open the wooden double front doors and hurried down the veranda's stairs two at a time.

"Dillon," Mona breathed as the pair walked along the winding driveway.

He ignored her, rushing toward the car and opening the passenger door without saying a word.

Mona paused before slipping inside. She stood in front of him, as if waiting to make eye contact. But he focused on the lush wooded area across from the house, unable to look her in the eyes.

"Look," she began. "I am really sorry about what happened in there. I don't know what came over me. You know I am a consummate professional. I *never* crack like that. Maybe I lost it because this case is so personal to me. Please know that I did not mean to bring up the necklace. But Blake just kept poking and poking and—"

"This isn't Blake's fault, Mona," Dillon interrupted. "So you can't blame him. And I *thought* you were a consummate professional, which is why I agreed to partner with you on this investigation. But once again, here I am. Having second thoughts."

"Dillon, please. Don't start second-guessing me. Today was a mistake. I'm human. I allowed my emotions to get the best of me. But trust me. It won't happen again."

"Oh, I know it won't. Because I'm going to talk to Chief Boyer about taking you off of this case. I think it's time for you to go home to Colorado and spend the holidays with your family. Let law enforcement take over from here. Not only have you become a loose cannon, but the investigation is getting too dangerous for you to remain on board anyway."

Mona stood there, her mouth falling open. But nothing came out. She just stared at him through squinting eyes.

Dillon felt bits of sympathy trying to seep through his wall of anger. But he was too upset to empathize with her.

"We should get going," he said, his cold, hardened demeanor reminding him of the days when he worked in Baton Rouge. "I need to get down to the station and do some damage control. Call a meeting with the officers to plan out a new strategy on how we're going to tackle Olivia's disappearance moving forward."

"Fine," Mona muttered. She climbed inside the car and slammed the door.

"I can't believe this…" Dillon said to himself as he walked around to the driver's side.

He hated the volatile way in which he and Mona's partnership had ended. But he could no longer afford to keep her on the biggest case of his career.

Chapter Eleven

Mona jumped at the sound of her pinging cell phone. She grabbed it, hoping Dillon's name would flash across the screen.

"Ugh," she sighed after seeing it was yet another text message from her boss.

She slid the phone across the black wrought iron table without opening the message.

She was sitting on the inn's quaint back patio, taking a much-needed break over a glass of spiced iced tea and a plate of charbroiled oysters.

It had been several days since she'd last spoken to Dillon. Mona had reached out to him numerous times, but he refused to return her calls and texts.

Mona's viewers, however, couldn't get enough of her. After the interview with Blake aired, her cell phone, email inbox and social media platforms had been blowing up.

But the increase in popularity had done nothing to assist authorities in Olivia's disappearance. It actually appeared to hinder it.

The public began treating the case as salacious tabloid fodder rather than a serious missing person investigation. Mona feared that potential witnesses were turned off by the spectacle that the case had become, and decided to keep pertinent information to themselves in order to avoid the circus.

Exactly what Dillon feared the most. All thanks to me...

Mona's cell phone rang. Her heart bounced into her throat at the thought of it being Dillon. She groaned loudly after seeing it was her boss, who'd resorted to calling instead of texting.

"Hey, Felix," she said after picking up the call. "What's going on?"

"You're what's going on, my dear," he boomed so loudly that she had to pull the phone away from her ear. "Who knew that my star investigative journalist could somehow manage to shine even brighter? You knocked it out of the park with that Blake Carter interview!"

"Yeah. So says the viewers, but... I'm kind of seeing things differently on my end."

"You are? How? Why?"

"I allowed Blake to break me, Felix. I lost my cool live on air. I am mortified by how I let that man get the best of me."

"Are you kidding? Mona, you broke exclusive news to our viewers that no one knew about. Not even Olivia's own family! Do you know how much credibility that has given CNB News?"

"Sure, but do you know how many times Olivia's parents have called me asking why news of the necklace wasn't shared with them first? And of course they're thinking that Olivia was murdered since I revealed that her blood was found on it. Mr. and Mrs. Whitman are absolutely hysterical, and it's all my fault."

"The truth hurts, Mona. I'm sorry Olivia's parents had to face that news, but you were just reporting the facts of the case. That's part of your job."

"Felix, you're missing the point. I have personal relationships with these people. And now, thanks to my on-air explosion, the Whitmans are demanding that authorities arrest Blake immediately. Of course they can't because there isn't enough evidence against him. So now they're getting their attorneys involved. I'm telling you, my interview has turned this case into an absolute mess."

"Sounds to me like you're worried about things that you shouldn't be concerned with. Come on, superstar. Your ratings are through the roof. Let's focus on that and let Lake Landry's police department handle the rest."

Mona threw her head back in exasperation. "You just don't get it," she muttered more to herself than her boss.

She stared up at the pale green petals hanging from the American fringe trees lining the patio's white wooden fence.

Where do I go from here? she asked herself.

"So, speaking of the Whitmans," Felix continued, "I've been reading the comments on CNB's website. Viewers really want to see you sit down with that brother of Olivia's. Do you think you can land an interview with him?"

"After what happened during Blake's interview? I highly doubt it. I was actually going to try to schedule an interview with Oliver the night that I was attacked."

"Yeah," Felix replied quietly. "I'm so sorry that happened to you. Have the authorities made any progress on an arrest? Or even identified a suspect?"

"Not yet, unfortunately. But I'm hoping that—"

Mona was interrupted when Evelyn walked out onto the patio.

"Hold on a sec, Felix."

"How's it going out here?" Evelyn asked her.

"Fine, thanks. Everything is delicious."

"Good, glad to hear it. Listen, there's a woman named Bonnie here asking for you. She said she's a friend of a friend. She was acting pretty peculiar, so I told her to wait in the lobby while I came back to ask if you know her."

Mona's eyes squinted as she stared at Evelyn blankly. "Bonnie, Bonnie... Oh! Yes, I know who she is. That's Olivia's coworker. She's here to see me?"

"Yes. Is it okay if I bring her back?"

"Please, thank you."

"No problem. Be right back."

After Evelyn walked off, Mona turned her attention back to her phone call.

"Felix, it looks like I may have a new lead. That coworker of Olivia's who I met with a couple of weeks ago is here to see me."

"Really? You think she's got more info to share?"

"I hope so. I highly doubt she would've just shown up at the inn unannounced unless she did. But we'll see."

Mona looked up and saw Bonnie following Evelyn out onto the patio. She was clutching her purse strap tightly. Her complexion appeared pale while her fallen expression was wrought with worry.

"Listen, Bonnie's on her way over. I'll call you back as soon as we're done."

"Please do. Talk soon."

Mona disconnected the call and stood up.

"Bonnie, hi. Nice to see you again."

"Yes, same here," she replied hesitantly before turning toward Evelyn. "Would you mind bringing me a glass of ice water?"

"Of course not. Would you like to see a lunch menu, as well?"

"Oh no. Food is the last thing on my mind. Just the water, please. Thank you."

"Coming right up."

As soon as Evelyn was out of earshot, Mona placed her hand gently on Bonnie's shoulder.

"Are you okay?" she asked.

"Yes. Not really. Actually…no. Mind if I sit?"

"Please do. What's going on?"

Bonnie practically crumpled into the chair across from Mona's.

"I've got some new information that may have something to do with Olivia's disappearance."

"Really?"

Mona's heart began to beat faster at the sound of those words. She slowly took a seat, her eyes glued to Bonnie. "What have you heard?"

"It's not what I've heard. It's what I read."

"What you *read*? What do you mean?"

Bonnie paused when Evelyn approached the table with her water.

"Thank you," she mumbled before grabbing the glass and taking several long sips.

"No problem. If you need anything else, just give me a holler."

"Will do."

Once Evelyn was gone, Bonnie continued.

"My supervisor handed over several of Olivia's files to me that she'd been working on before her disappearance. He asked if I'd review them to make sure the research had been completed."

Bonnie paused, reaching inside her purse and grabbing a tissue.

When she dabbed the corners of her damp eyes, Mona slid to the edge of her chair.

"So what happened?" Mona asked. "Did you see something in one of the files that upset you?"

"Yes," Bonnie sniffed. "One of the companies Olivia was investigating was Alnico Aluminum Corporation.

They're notorious for dumping harmful chemicals into residential water sources. I'm talking lead and chromium. Waste that could kill someone if it were to be consumed."

Mona slowly leaned back in her chair, her mind churning in several different directions. She watched as Bonnie reached in her purse again and pulled out a piece of paper.

"Olivia had recently received a third round of test results back from the lab," she continued. "Like the first two, there was proof that residential water sources located near Alnico Aluminum had been contaminated. They contained extraordinarily high levels of carcinogens. Coincidentally, Olivia was preparing to report her findings to the government right before she went missing."

"Oh wow," Mona breathed, her lungs feeling as though they were beginning to constrict. She crossed her arms in front of her and stared up at the sky. "Do you think someone at Alnico found out about Olivia's report and did something to silence her before it could be submitted?"

"Absolutely."

Bonnie unfolded the piece of paper she'd been clutching and slid it across the table.

"Olivia had printed out this email message and added it to the file. It was sent to her by an Alnico executive named George Williamson."

Mona leaned forward and quickly scanned the message.

"As you can see," Bonnie continued, "George told Olivia that he'd received disturbing news from an inside source at LLL Water Quality Laboratory. He doesn't say exactly what it was, but I'm assuming one of our coworkers leaked the information that was in Olivia's report to this George person."

"And I see here that he asked Olivia to meet with him so they could discuss Alnico's waste disposal process in person."

"Yes, which would be unethical according to LLL's company policy. You'd be surprised by the amount of bribery that goes on in this business. These corporations will do anything to avoid being reported to the government. But the act of illegally dumping waste is a common occurrence among these corporations. Doing it the right way, through a certified disposal service, can be costly."

"You'd think that wouldn't be a problem considering how much money these companies make."

"You would think," Bonnie agreed. "But some of them are greedy enough to cut costs by any means necessary. Even if it means poisoning residential water sources."

"That's a damn shame," Mona scoffed. "Not only is it corrupt, but it's just inhumane."

"Yes, it is. And Olivia wasn't having it. Flip the page over and you'll see her response to George's message. She politely turned down his request to meet."

Mona turned the page and skimmed the reply. "This is good. I'm glad Olivia thought enough to keep a paper trail of her interactions with the company, too."

"Oh, Olivia was the queen of maintaining paper trails. In this business, it's imperative that we keep track of all communication between the lab and our clients so as not to misconstrue our findings and their responses."

"Smart. Hey, is it okay if I keep this email?"

"Of course," Bonnie told her. "I made that copy for you. I kept the original in the file."

"Good thinking. Thanks."

Mona's first instinct was to call up her CNB producer and cameraman, rush into Alnico's offices and pay George a visit. Catching him off guard on camera would be priceless. That type of exclusive, investigative reporting is what viewers expected of her. More important, questioning him could lead to Olivia's whereabouts.

But then, Mona paused. She thought about Dillon. She'd

already messed up by revealing confidential details about the necklace live on air.

Despite being tempted to put her journalistic skills to work, Mona knew the right thing to do would be to take this information straight to law enforcement.

"So," Bonnie said, snapping Mona out of her thoughts, "has this new development changed your views on Blake's involvement in Olivia's disappearance?"

"Hmm…" Mona sighed, propping her elbows onto her chair's wrought iron arms. "Possibly. But I don't know if I'm ready to let Blake off the hook just yet. What about you? Knowing all that you do about their relationship, has it changed yours?"

Bonnie threw her head back and closed her eyes. "I'm torn, too," she moaned. "After seeing your interview with him, I still sensed a layer of guilt hidden underneath his smug demeanor. But I know more about his lifestyle than the average viewer, so I may be biased."

"Right. But what if the guilt you sensed was attributed to his infidelity? Just because the man is a philanderer doesn't necessarily mean he's a criminal, too."

"That's true. Overall, the interview was pretty explosive. I didn't know Olivia's necklace had been found near the water source she'd been researching. Did that provide law enforcement with any solid leads?"

"No," Mona replied quietly. "Not yet."

"So this necklace that was found. Did the DNA results—"

"I'm sorry, Bonnie. I'm not able to discuss the details of the investigation. I shouldn't have revealed what I did live on air like that. But that damn Blake had pissed me off so badly. I just… I lost control."

"Well, who could blame you! He's such a jerk. I have to admit, though, after hearing that Olivia's necklace was found in Beechtree, then seeing this email from Alnico, I am having second thoughts about Blake's involvement."

"Really? Why?" Mona asked before taking a sip of her tea.

Bonnie paused, staring across the table at Mona with her head tilted curiously.

"Because Alnico is located right outside of Beechtree."

"Wait, *what*?" Mona choked. "Alnico is located where?"

"Right outside of Beechtree. I'm sorry. I thought you knew that. The water source Olivia was researching is where Alnico had been dumping waste. That connection is why I copied this email and booked it straight over here to see you."

"And I'm so glad you did," Mona said before standing up and shoving the paper inside her tote bag. "Listen, I need to go. I've got to get down to the police station and share this information. It may very well take this investigation in a completely different direction. Bonnie, I can't thank you enough for sharing it with me."

"Of course," Bonnie replied, standing up and following Mona to the front of the inn. "I hope it helps. I just really wanna get to the bottom of all this. Olivia's disappearance has the entire town of Lake Landry shaken up. She was such a big part of this community. And she is sorely missed."

"I know she is. And I'm going to continue doing all that I can to help bring her back. Thank you again for this info."

"You're welcome. Just be careful with it."

"I will."

Mona waved at Bonnie and hopped inside her car, anxious to get to the station and share the new developments with Chief Boyer.

Maybe this'll get me back in Dillon's good graces, she couldn't help but think.

Chapter Twelve

"I know she messed up," Chief Boyer said to Dillon. "But I've known Mona for years. I can assure you that this was just a one-time slipup that'll never happen again."

"Chief, I hear you. But with all due respect, I just can't take that chance again. After she went out to Beechtree behind my back and could have gotten herself killed, she promised there would be no more mistakes. Then what does she do? Go live on air and reveal confidential details about the case that I did not want to get out. Now I've got the Whitmans calling me every single day, demanding answers and threatening to sue me. And have you looked outside?"

Chief Boyer leaned against Dillon's metal-framed doorway and crossed his arms over his protruding belly.

"Yes. I have. And a couple of officers are out there manning the parking lot, asking that the news media pack up and leave. But you know how those reporters are. They're like wild, rabid animals pursuing their prey. You do know they're waiting for you to come out and give a statement, don't you?"

"I do. I've had to utilize the good ole 'I have nothing to report at this time' several times today. And it's going to stay that way until I solve this case."

"Yeah, well, I still believe that Mona is one of your biggest allies. And let's be honest. She didn't do any real harm with that Blake Carter interview. Chalk it up to her being human. And upset that her friend is missing. And remember, you wouldn't have that necklace in evidence if it weren't for her. So don't count Mona out just yet."

"Yes," Dillon heard a woman's voice chirp. "Don't count me out just yet."

Chief Boyer stepped to the side, and Mona appeared in Dillon's doorway.

"I—um…*hey*," he stammered, caught completely off guard. "I wasn't expecting to see you here."

"I wasn't expecting to be here. Yet, here I am…"

"Well, Mona," Chief Boyer interjected after an awkward silence, "just know that you're always welcome. It's good to see you."

"Good to see you, too, Chief. I noticed there's a ton of news media swarming the station."

"Comes with the territory when you're investigating a high-profile case."

"That it does," Mona agreed.

Dillon watched from behind his desk as the pair bantered back and forth.

He couldn't seem to stop his eyes from penetrating Mona's sexy silhouette. Soft curls cascaded beautifully along the sides of her face. The gloss on her supple lips shimmered as she spoke to the chief. Her body swayed like a dancer when she shifted her weight from right to left, showcasing her curvy hips.

Mona's fitted peach turtleneck outlined her figure in a way that caused a rousing sensation to stir deep within Dillon. He shifted in his chair when she slid her perfectly manicured hands inside the pockets of her snug chocolate brown riding pants.

Get ahold of yourself…

Dillon loosened his gray wool houndstooth tie as waves of heat crept up his neck.

"Listen," Chief Boyer said to Mona, "I'm glad you stopped by. I'm sure you and Detective Reed have a lot to catch up on. So I'll leave you both to it."

He gradually stepped away from the door, glancing over at Dillon and nodding his head.

Dillon stood up and adjusted his pants.

"Thanks, Chief. I've got it from here."

After Chief Boyer closed the door behind him, Mona remained near the doorway, wringing her hands.

"Please," Dillon said, sensing her nervousness, "have a seat."

"Thanks."

Mona walked tentatively toward the desk and waited for him to sit down before following suit.

Dillon felt a pull of guilt in his chest. He wasn't used to seeing the normally confident woman so off-balance. But as a bout of nerves buzzed around inside his gut, he realized he was feeling just as uneasy in her presence.

"So," Mona began. "You're probably wondering why I'm here."

Dillon folded his hands on top of the desk.

Don't crack, he told himself. *Make her sweat. Ask her why she stopped by unannounced. And uninvited.*

But when he looked into her soft, seemingly remorseful gaze, he backed down.

"I am curious. My guess is that you're here to report some sort of breaking news?"

"Actually, I am."

"Really?" he asked, scratching his jaw. "I was only kidding."

"Well, I'm not."

Dillon scooted farther into his desk, watching as Mona

dug around inside her tote bag. She pulled out a piece of paper and slid it toward him.

"I just met with Olivia's coworker, Bonnie. She's been working to close out Olivia's files, and found some suspicious information on Alnico Aluminum Corporation."

Dillon skimmed the paper's contents. "And what is this?"

"An email from one of Alnico's executives. George Williamson. Apparently, he'd heard that Olivia was preparing to file a report with the government that contained damaging information against the company."

"I actually know George. He's a good guy. I met him through the community service initiatives he's sponsored in conjunction with the police department."

"Yeah, well, there may be two sides to Mr. Williamson. According to Olivia's file, Alnico had been illegally dumping hazardous waste into residential water sources. George tried to meet with her before she reported her findings. She refused, since that's against company policy. Then less than a week later, she goes missing."

"Hmm, interesting…"

Dillon ran his hand down his goatee as he read Olivia's response to George's meeting request. Then suddenly, he dropped the paper and looked up at Mona.

"Hold on. Alnico Aluminum Corporation is located right outside of Beechtree."

"I know. The very same area where Olivia went missing while she was collecting water samples. Coincidence? Maybe not."

Dillon jumped up from behind his desk, grabbing his keys and cell phone.

"Do you think you could get me a copy of that Alnico file?" he asked.

"I don't know. But I can ask Bonnie."

"Good. You do that. In the meantime, I need to get down

to Alnico and talk to George. Find out where he was the day Olivia went missing."

Mona hopped up from her chair and followed Dillon out of his office.

"Wait," she said. "Shouldn't I go with you?"

Dillon stopped abruptly, right outside of Chief Boyer's office.

"I, um—I think I'd better partner up with a fellow law enforcement officer on this one."

"But I'm the one who gave you the lead," Mona insisted, taking a step closer to him. "I didn't have to do that. I could've gone straight to Alnico with my camera crew and questioned George myself. But I didn't."

"And you shouldn't have. Now listen, I appreciate you doing the right thing by turning this information over to me. But…" Dillon paused, struggling to find the right words. "I just don't want things to go left again like they did during Blake's interview."

"So that's where we're at now? You're gonna keep hanging that over my head instead of forgiving me and moving forward?"

"Come on, Mona. It's not like that. My initial conversation with George should be official police business. I don't want him thinking I'm trying to ambush him with a bunch of media madness. This needs to be taken seriously."

As soon as the words were out of his mouth, Dillon regretted speaking them.

A veil of darkness clouded Mona's eyes. The pain in her steely expression was apparent.

"Wait," he said, "I didn't mean it like—"

"Oh, I know exactly how you meant it," she interrupted. "So now you don't take me seriously? I'll have you know that I—"

"Hey!" Chief Boyer barked from inside his office. "I'm

trying to watch a recording of the mayor's speech from last night. What's going on out there?"

Mona brushed past Dillon and stormed into his office.

"Chief," she huffed, "I just turned over a great piece of evidence to Dillon regarding Olivia's investigation."

"About?" Chief Boyer asked.

"It involves an executive at Alnico Aluminum who was illegally dumping waste into residential water sources. He requested a meeting with Olivia that she turned down, then shortly thereafter she went missing. I think I should accompany Detective Reed when he goes in to question him."

Chief Boyer sighed deeply, pausing the video he'd been watching. "Okay, so what's the problem, Detective?"

"Sir, while I am very appreciative of Mona's tip, I think it'd be best if I go down to Alnico and question George Williamson without her."

"Wait, George *Williamson*?" the chief asked, appearing perplexed as he rocked back in his chair. "Wow. I'm surprised to hear that. He's always come across as such a stand-up guy. So you two are thinking that he could be involved in Olivia's disappearance?"

"Yes," Mona replied. "He may have wanted to offer up some sort of bribe, or even threaten Olivia so she wouldn't report her findings to the government."

"Whatever the case may be," Dillon added, "I'd like to hear what he has to say for himself—"

"Yeah, so would I," Mona interjected.

Both she and Dillon stood rigidly in Chief Boyer's doorway, waiting to hear his verdict.

"I'd definitely like to hear what he has to say for himself." The chief glanced over at Dillon. "Are you sure you don't wanna bring him down to the station for questioning?"

"I'd rather not. I don't want him to think he's being detained. I'd like for him to feel comfortable. Or as comfortable as he can while being questioned by a detective about his involvement in a missing person case."

"Good idea," Chief Boyer replied. "You know what else I think would be a good idea?"

"What's that, sir?"

"For you to take Mona with you."

"Yes," Dillon heard her hiss underneath her breath. He ignored Mona and remained focused on his boss.

"But, Chief, hasn't there already been enough damage done to compromise this investigation? I'd like to maintain the last bits of its integrity."

"Hey, I take offense to that," Mona shot back.

"Look, I'm just speaking the truth, and—"

"Listen!" Chief Boyer interrupted, silencing them both. "You two need to pull it together. Now, Detective Reed, I've said it before and I'll say it again. Mona's reputation speaks for itself. Her involvement in any case is advantageous."

"Thank you," she slipped in.

"But," the chief continued, eyeing Mona directly, "while you have certainly been an asset to this investigation, you've also had a few…*mishaps*. I'm expecting that won't happen again."

Dillon glanced over at Mona, noticing that her satisfied smirk had transformed into a slight frown.

"No. It won't happen again, sir," she muttered.

"Good. Now, I recommended this partnership between you two for good reason. Reed, your detective skills are bar none. You don't miss. You're a patient, quiet storm who knows exactly when to move in on a suspect and make an arrest."

"Thanks, Chief."

"And, Mona, your people skills, instincts and attention to detail are invaluable. No other evidence was discov-

ered near the Beechtree water source where Olivia allegedly went missing, except for the necklace you found. Did
you know that?"

"Yes," she chirped. "I did."

Dillon could see her peering over at him through the
corner of his eye. He ignored her.

"Together," Chief Boyer continued, "I have no doubt that
you two will get this case solved. So get down to Alnico
and find out what George has to say for himself. And hey,
leave through the back door so that the reporters out front
won't try to stop you with a barrage of questions."

"Good idea," Dillon replied. "We'll report back to you
once we're done."

"Great. And I'm expecting you two will behave yourselves."

"Of course, Chief," Mona assured him.

Dillon stepped to the side and held out his arm.

"After you," he said to her.

She slinked past him, remaining silent while walking toward the back of the station. He followed closely behind her.

"You probably want to ride in separate cars," Mona said
when they exited the building. "So I'll just meet you in
front of Alnico."

"Don't be ridiculous. I can drive us both there."

"Really?" Mona asked, her staunch poker face softening.

"Yes. Really. Now come on. Let's go and speak with
George."

Chapter Thirteen

Mona could feel her blood pumping rapidly through her veins as she followed Dillon inside Alnico Aluminum Corporation.

The company's corporate offices were located across the street from the manufacturing plant. The vast lobby's floor-to-ceiling windows surrounded beautiful black-and-white marble floors. Sleek white leather furniture sat among modern steel-and-glass coffee tables. Pricey abstract artwork hung from the walls, and a massive, glossy white reception desk covered the back wall.

"Wow," Mona murmured. "Looks like a lot of Alnico's multibillion-dollar annual revenue went into decorating this lobby."

"It sure does," Dillon agreed.

Mona felt her tense muscles relax a bit after hearing his response. She was worried that he'd be annoyed after Chief Boyer forced him to bring her along to question George.

Just stay in your lane, she reminded herself. *Don't take over the conversation. Let Dillon take the lead...*

"May I help you?" she heard a woman ask haughtily from behind the reception desk.

Mona stayed back, allowing Dillon to approach her.

"Good afternoon. My name is Detective Reed. I'm here to see George Williamson. Is he available?"

"Is Mr. Williamson expecting you?"

Mona peered over Dillon's shoulder. The woman sitting behind the desk looked more like a model than a receptionist. Her long, bone-straight blond hair was slicked back into a severe ponytail. Beautiful translucent makeup covered her flawless porcelain skin. Her perfectly tailored jade green jumpsuit could've been taken straight off the runway, as could her snooty expression.

"No," Dillon replied, "he isn't expecting me. But I'm here on official police business and would like to ask him a few questions."

He eyed the receptionist as she remained silent, staring back at him.

Mona balled her hands into tight fists. Her palms burned with discomfort. She shifted her weight from right to left, wondering whether she should say something.

No! she told herself. *Do not overstep your bounds. Dillon can handle it.*

"I'm sorry," the receptionist finally said. "But Mr. Williamson isn't available right now."

"How do you know?" Dillon asked, his patient tone tinged with sprinkles of irritation. "You didn't even call him."

"I don't have to. I'm aware of his schedule and know that he is not able to speak with you at this time."

Mona cleared her throat, unable to hold back any longer. She stepped up from behind Dillon and approached the desk.

"Hello," she purred while smiling sweetly. "I'm Mona Avery. And you are?"

The receptionist gasped so loudly that the sound reverberated through the lobby. She hopped up from her chair and offered Mona her hand.

"I'm—I'm Em-Emily. Emily Bradford," the young

woman stammered. "And I am so sorry, Ms. Avery. I had no idea that you were here with this man."

"Detective Reed," he interjected.

"Yeah, okay," Emily said without taking her eyes off Mona. "Ms. Avery, I am your biggest fan. I'm in graduate school right now studying journalism in hopes that I could one day have a career half as successful as yours."

"Aw," Mona said while firmly shaking her hand. "That is so kind of you. Thank you. I have no doubt that you will one day have a career ten times more successful than mine."

"Ha!" Emily snorted. "I seriously doubt that. But thank you for the vote of confidence. I will carry those words with me always."

Take advantage of this moment, Mona thought to herself. *Go in for the kill...*

"So you said that Mr. Williamson isn't available, huh?" she asked. "Are you sure about that?"

Emily's eyes widened. She glanced around the lobby, holding her hand to her chest as she tiptoed around the desk.

Mona almost jumped back when the receptionist grabbed her arm and pulled her in close.

"Mr. Williamson isn't here," Emily whispered. "I don't know what's going on, but I've heard rumblings that after your *incredible* interview with Blake Carter, he skipped town."

"He *skipped town*?" Mona asked. "But...why? And where did he go?"

"After the way you interrogated Blake on national television, Mr. Williamson felt as though he might be next because of a report Olivia Whitman was getting ready to file against Alnico. So he fled to the Bahamas in hopes that everything would blow over soon."

"Do you have any idea when he's planning to return to Lake Landry?" Dillon asked.

Emily shot him a look of annoyance, as if he were intruding on a private conversation between her and Mona.

"No," she chirped, "I don't. But if Ms. Avery would like for me to find that information out for her, I'm sure I could."

"You could?" Mona asked, pressing her hands against her cheeks for added shock value. "For *me*?"

"Of course I could," Emily gushed. "Anything for you..."

"Oh boy," Mona heard Dillon sigh underneath his breath.

Don't be a hater, Mona wanted to tell him. But instead she pulled a business card from her bag and handed it to Emily.

"Here's my contact information," she told her. "Please feel free to reach out to me once you find out when Mr. Williamson will be back in town."

"Because I'm guessing he's completely off the grid and unreachable via phone or email," Dillon interjected.

"Of course he is," Emily shot back before turning her attention to Mona.

"Anyway, just between us, I may be able to get more information about Mr. Williamson. I'm really close with his executive assistant. So I'll see if I can dig around and find anything that might be pertinent to the investigation. If I do, I'll contact you."

"Emily," Mona sighed. "You are an absolute gem. Thank you. And, hey, why don't you send me your résumé. Maybe you can come out to LA and intern at CNB News next summer."

"What?" the receptionist squealed, jumping up and down while rapidly clapping her hands. "That would be so amazing! You'll have my résumé in your inbox later this afternoon."

"I look forward to reviewing it. Thanks for that exclusive scoop, Emily. Consider this moment your first experience in investigative journalism."

Mona gave her a wink and a wave, then spun around and headed toward the exit. She could hear Dillon shuffling behind her.

"Bye, Ms. Avery!" Emily called out. "So nice meeting you!"

"Same here!"

Mona stepped to the side as Dillon opened the door for her. The minute they reached the parking lot, she turned to him with a huge grin on her face.

"Don't even say it," he huffed. "I am not in the mood to hear any sort of gloating right now."

"Me? Gloat? Why I take great offense to that, Detective Reed."

"Get in the car," he said, opening the passenger door before chuckling softly.

"Not until you tell me how much of an asset I am to this investigation."

"Oh, now you're pushing it, Avery. Get me some solid evidence from your new best friend Emily, then maybe I'll consider it. But in the meantime, how about I treat you to lunch? I've had a taste for grilled bourbon chicken from the Cajun Cookout Café all week."

"Mmm, that sounds delicious," Mona replied. "I am a little full, though, after I devoured your pathetic little attempt to talk to George in there."

"Please get in the car, woman!" Dillon insisted before both he and Mona burst out laughing.

The twosome climbed inside and headed out of the parking lot toward the restaurant.

"Oh, before I forget," Mona began, "I did reach out to Bonnie and ask if she could send me the full file on Alnico."

"What'd she say?"

"I haven't heard back from her yet. Which is weird considering how eager she's been to help out with the investigation."

Dillon shrugged his shoulders. "Who knows. Maybe she's been busy after taking on Olivia's workload. Just keep trying."

"I will."

He glanced over at Mona. "Listen. You've definitely been an asset to this investigation. A huge one. And… I owe you an apology. I shouldn't have just cut you off like that after Blake's interview. He was completely out of line and acted like an arrogant ass. I could've been more understanding of your reaction."

"Thank you for that, Dillon. And again, I apologize, too. I shouldn't have let Blake get me to the point where I compromised the investigation. Now all this media is swarming around town, sensationalizing the case. It's exactly what you *didn't* want to happen."

"Yeah, well, we're moving on from it, right? We've got this new lead with George Williamson, and I've still got my eye on Blake. Things are definitely looking up with this case."

"Yes, they are."

Mona watched Dillon closely. He appeared so content, as if he were happy she was there. She resisted the urge to lean over and kiss his soft lips as they spread into a slight smile.

The moment was interrupted when Dillon's cell phone buzzed. He stopped at a red light and tapped the screen.

"Oh no," he moaned.

"What's wrong?"

He turned to Mona, the color slowly draining from his face.

"Bonnie is dead."

Chapter Fourteen

Mona sat straight up, raising her chin as the producer adjusted her mic.

She glanced around The Bayou Inn's modest conference room. It's where she'd decided to hold Oliver's interview, which they finally scheduled after he saw her sit down with Blake and insisted on clearing his name live on air.

The festive Christmas decorations that had been hung around the room were replaced by dark backdrops. Mona was seated in one of four black mesh ergonomic chairs surrounding a small round cherrywood table. Her production crew was busy setting up their equipment while Mona's stylist touched up her hair and makeup.

It had been a week since Bonnie's body was found floating in Rosehill Park's lily pond. She'd been shot in the back of the head. There was little evidence found at the crime scene, and no suspects were in custody.

The sinister turn in the investigation had shaken Mona to her core. But she was determined to press on until the case was solved.

Mona took a deep breath and straightened the hem on her navy blue silk wrap dress.

"Any word from Oliver?" her producer, Sarah, asked. "We're going live in fifteen minutes and I need to get him prepped and mic'd up."

"He texted me at three o'clock this morning confirming that he'd be here."

"And you haven't heard from him since?"

"No, I haven't. But I'll send him a message and find out what time he'll be—"

Before Mona could finish, Oliver came bursting inside the conference room.

"I made it!" he announced, holding his arms out at his sides as if he were waiting on a round of applause. He almost dropped the extra large coffee cup he was holding in his hand. "Let the phenomenon of my voice being heard all around the world begin."

Mona resisted the urge to roll her eyes.

"Good morning, Oliver," she said, struggling to sound pleasant as she motioned him over. "I'm glad you're here. This is Sarah, my show's producer. She'll be getting you mic'd up. My cameraman, Steve, is adjusting the lighting. Would you like for my makeup artist, Megan, to apply a little concealer under your eyes or dust a bit of powder across your T-zone?"

"What, and hide all this handsomeness?" he deadpanned. "No, thanks. I came here looking exactly how I want to appear on camera."

Mona stared at Oliver through the corner of her eye. He was dressed decently enough in a mustard yellow sweater and jeans that weren't ripped throughout.

But it appeared as though he'd made no attempt to tame his unkempt curly hair or trim his scruffy beard.

His eyes were bloodshot red, a clear indication that he'd been up all night. And he was jittery. Between the caffeine and his adrenaline, he could barely stand still.

"You're going to take a seat right here." Sarah pointed, directing Oliver to the chair across from Mona's.

"Got it," he said, plopping down so hard that the wheels gave way. It tilted dangerously onto its right-side legs.

He gripped the edge of the table for dear life, barely avoiding crashing to the floor.

Mona reached out and clutched his arm. "Are you okay?"

"Yep! I'm good. Just a little wired, I guess. I'll be all right once we get started."

Oliver bounced anxiously in his seat, tapping his fingernails against the table.

"So where's your boy, Detective Rivers?" he asked.

"*Reed.* He's on his way. Had a few things to take care of down at the police station."

"*Tuh!* You mean he had to shuffle a few papers around on his desk?"

Mona ignored the snide comment, refusing to let Oliver take her out of interview mode.

She took a deep breath and glanced down at her questions, then jumped at the sound of his booming voice.

"There's the man of the hour!" he roared.

Mona looked up at the doorway. Her chest pounded at the sight of Dillon swaggering into the room.

"Hello, everyone," he said.

His presence immediately put Mona at ease.

She was surprised to see him dressed in a slim-fitting charcoal gray suit, crisp white shirt and black cap-toe Oxford shoes. She'd never seen Dillon look so handsome.

"Hello, Detective Reed," she said, struggling to keep her voice steady. "You're right on time. We were just about to get started."

"Good. Glad I wasn't late. I'll just take a seat over here in the corner and let you and Oliver do your thing."

"Thanks, Detective Rivers," Oliver quipped.

"*Reed,*" Dillon shot back.

"Are we ready to get started?" Sarah asked.

"I'm ready," Mona responded. "How are you feeling now, Oliver? A little calmer?"

"Not really. But last night's tarot card reading confirmed that all would go well today. My seven chakras are perfectly aligned. And I'm depending on the universe to guide my words. So I'm good. Let's do this."

She stared across the table at Oliver as he took a huge gulp from his coffee cup. She had no idea what he was talking about and knew not to ask for clarification.

Lord, please don't let this interview go left...

"Okay, everyone, quiet please," Sarah said. "Going live in five, four, three, two..."

She pointed at Mona, who looked directly into the camera with a stoic expression on her face.

"Hello, everyone. Thank you for joining me during this special broadcast. In my continued effort to assist Lake Landry's law enforcement agency in finding Olivia Whitman, I have her twin brother, Oliver Whitman, here with me today. Oliver, thank you for agreeing to speak with me."

"Ah, it's cool. Thanks for having me. And for giving me a platform to speak my truth."

"Oliver, what do you think happened to your sister?"

"I don't know." He shrugged nonchalantly. "You're the expert, aren't you? What do *you* think happened to her?"

Mona froze. The response caught her by surprise. She clenched her jaws together tightly, searching her brain for a quick comeback.

"Well, I've got my theories," she replied. "But as someone so close to her, I brought you here today hoping you could share your thoughts with viewers. Maybe provide some insight into what was going on in Olivia's life shortly before she went missing."

"First of all, my sister and I aren't close. And you know that, because you've been in our lives since we were teenagers. Secondly, Olivia and I didn't talk on a regular basis. So I have no idea what was going on in her life before she went missing."

Mona just sat there, staring at Oliver in disbelief. She couldn't believe he'd come onto her show just to waste everyone's time with his short, vapid answers.

I should've listened to Dillon. I never should have gone live on air with this man.

"But I will say this," Oliver continued. "Things between Olivia and her husband, Blake Carter, were *not* good."

Mona perked up after hearing the comment.

Thank you for giving me something to work with! she almost yelled.

"What do you mean, things weren't good between them? Can you please elaborate on that?"

"Well, I worked at Transformation Cosmetics for a while before that *jerk* Leo Mendez fired me. While I was there, I'd see Blake fawning all over women around the office. I heard he was partaking in intimate lunches behind closed doors that didn't just entail eating food, if you know what I mean. Olivia heard about all that, too."

"Was she planning on leaving Blake?"

"That's what I heard. But before she could? *Boom!* She goes missing. Suspicious, wouldn't you say?"

"It's definitely an interesting coincidence," Mona responded, careful not to allow Oliver to bait her. "But while there's no denying that Blake is a philanderer, that doesn't make him a criminal."

"True. And Olivia isn't innocent in all this either. There are reasons why Blake couldn't stay faithful to a flawed woman like her."

Mona felt her stomach drop.

Do not let this interview go off the rails...

"But Olivia is our victim here. We need to be respectful of—"

"Respectful?" Oliver interrupted. "Please. I'd show some respect had Olivia not married Blake in the first place. She never really loved him, you know. How could she? He always treated her like crap! But Olivia is greedy. Money and power hungry. And—"

"Oliver," Mona interrupted, "we're getting off track here. This isn't about—"

"Excuse me, let me finish! You asked me to sit down with you so that I could share my take on Olivia's disappearance. Now please, allow me to do that."

"Can you do so without attacking her character?"

Oliver's lips twisted into a snarky smirk.

"I'll try. Anyway, my sister is more concerned about her image than love. Marrying into the Carter family was a good look for her. While we Whitmans can hold our own when it comes to big bank accounts, joining forces with the Carters took Olivia's status to a whole 'nother level. And being the superficial bi—*woman* that she is, my sister loved that prestige."

A wave of heat washed over Mona. Droplets of sweat covered her back. She was tempted to cut the interview short. But they were live. So she had to keep going.

"Oliver," Mona said calmly, "Olivia and I have been very good friends for years. The woman you're describing is far from the woman I know. Olivia is kind and loving. She cares a great deal for her husband. She wanted their marriage to work. It's never been about money for her, which is why she worked so hard to earn a master's degree in environmental science and land a job at LLL Water Quality Laboratory."

"Another power play, if you ask me," Oliver snorted.

"Olivia's position at LLL gives her the authority to shut companies down if she sees fit."

"Do you think that authority might have had something to do with her disappearance?"

"Who knows. It could. Or maybe it's Olivia's karma coming back to bite her in the ass."

Oh, please don't go there...

"As one of my fellow conspiracy theorists," Oliver continued, pointing across the table at Mona, "you believe in kismet, don't you? The idea that whatever is meant to be, will be?"

She nodded her head, remaining silent to discourage one of his rants.

"You can't be greedy," he rambled, "and marry a man for money rather than love, and think it's not gonna come back to haunt you. Oh! And let's not forget the fact that Olivia knew Blake wanted children. He'd been talking about starting a family ever since the day they met. But once he married her? *Bam!* She refused to give the man children!"

Mona glanced over at Dillon, who had a pained expression on his face. She could just feel the words *I told you so* coming off him.

"Let me ask you a question," she said to Oliver, desperate to take the interview in a different direction. "I recently conducted an interview with Olivia's husband, Blake. Did you happen to see it?"

"Yes, I did."

"In it, he admitted to his infidelity. He also alleged that you and Olivia have a complicated family history, and you may have had something to do with Olivia's disappearance. What do you have to say to that?"

Oliver ran his hands rigorously over his ratty beard. When he failed to answer the question, Mona kept going.

"Why would you sit here and defend a man who'd say

those things about you, all while slamming your own sister's character? You're in essence blaming her for her own disappearance."

"Look, don't get me wrong. I can't stand Blake Carter. But he and my sister were in a messed-up relationship. Because of that, I'm thinking maybe she pulled a *Gone Girl*–type of stunt on the world and disappeared on her own accord."

"Which is the conspiracy theorist in you."

"Possibly," Oliver said. "But it's plausible that Olivia faked her own kidnapping in hopes of getting some attention, which we all know she loves, and framing her husband out of spite. She could very well be exacting revenge on the man who broke his vows and publicly humiliated her."

"Let's switch gears for a minute here, Oliver. There's been a buzz around Lake Landry for years about your place in the Whitman family. It's been said that you're bitter toward Olivia and your parents. That you feel like a stepchild rather than a full-fledged member of the family. Is there any truth to that?"

Oliver's expression fell into a rumpled frown. He folded his arms in front of him, rocking back and forth in his chair.

"Hell yeah there's some truth to that," he spat. "Olivia gets treated like a princess. And me? Like a pauper. She has everything. The money, the big house, the big job, the prominent husband. What do I have? *Nothing.* I'm stuck getting mistreated by my parents, who don't even *try* to understand my elevated level of brilliance."

"Then why don't you move out of your parents' house and stand on your own two feet, Oliver? Get a job. Take care of yourself so you won't have to worry about being mistreated."

He slammed his hands down onto the table.

"Because it's not that easy for me, Mona! These people out here can't comprehend my celestial existence. I get ostracized for simply being supreme. But that's okay. Just know that once I collect my half of the Whitman family fortune, which I hope will be sooner rather than later, this world will see what Oliver Bernard Whitman is made of."

Mona's head swiveled at his callous statement.

"Wait, are you actually wishing your parents an early demise so that you can collect your inheritance?"

"I said what I said," Oliver replied defiantly. "Interpret it however you see fit."

"Wow," Mona murmured, pausing while glancing down at her notes. She needed a moment to regroup.

"Maybe if Olivia doesn't resurface," he continued, "I'll get her half of the inheritance, as well."

Mona fumbled her papers, almost dropping them to the floor.

"Oliver, please. I know you don't mean that."

"Oh, I totally mean it. And since I'm being honest here, I might as well admit that my life has been *so* peaceful since Olivia went missing. In fact, I'm actually glad she's gone. And I hope she never comes back."

Mona's mouth fell open. She stared across the table, trembling at the sight of Oliver's dark, lifeless eyes.

When she turned to Sarah to ask if they could cut to commercial, the Whitmans came bursting through the door.

"Oliver!" Mrs. Whitman yelled. "What in the hell do you think you're doing?"

"Airing out this family, *finally*," he defiantly replied. "I'm done living the Whitman lie. Acting like all is well when it's not. The world deserves to know that you two treat your only son like crap."

"You're a fool!" Mr. Whitman shouted before lunging at his son.

Dillon jumped up from his chair. He grabbed hold of

Oliver's father right before his fist connected with his son's jaw.

"Keep rolling!" Mona heard Sarah tell their cameraman.

"Steve, no!" Mona insisted. "Stop the camera. Now!"

"Yes, ma'am," he replied, immediately ending the recording.

Dillon continued to hold Mr. Whitman back as Oliver pulled out his cell phone and began recording the confrontation.

"This is gonna blow my social media *up*!" he exclaimed, laughing while Dillon struggled to detain his father.

"Oliver, I cannot believe you would betray your own family like this," Mrs. Whitman cried. "How could you say such horrible things about your sister?"

"Mom, let's face it. Olivia is a bitch. And I stated nothing but the facts about this family—"

"Oliver!" Dillon barked. "That's enough. Steve, can you please escort him out of here while I stay back with his parents?"

"I don't need nobody to escort me outta here," Oliver insisted, his wild eyes darting around the room. "I get it. I'm probably America's most wanted right now. But it's all good. At least I'm living in my truth. Unlike all you phonies. Peace out."

Oliver strutted toward the conference room door. Mona just stood there in a state of shock. She peered over at Dillon, who was busy consoling the Whitmans.

Her eyes filled with tears. She couldn't decide which interview had been worse, Oliver's or Blake's.

"What did you do to my daughter?" Mrs. Whitman whimpered at Oliver as he strolled out the door. "What did you do to my daughter?"

He turned around and aimed his camera at her.

"Aw, look at my mom," he said. "Hey, to all my followers out there, just know that this is the most attention my parents have given me in *years*. Years!"

"Cut that damn camera off and answer your mother's question!" Mr. Whitman yelled.

"Go to hell, Dad. See you all at home!"

Mr. Whitman balled his fists as he struggled to compose himself.

Mrs. Whitman turned to Mona and glared at her.

"How could you do this? Betray our family like this? You knew Oliver was in no condition to be interviewed live on television. Yet you did it anyway, exploiting the Whitman name for the sake of ratings. You should be ashamed of yourself."

"I—I, um…" she stammered. "But Oliver approached me asking if I'd provide him with a platform to speak after Blake's interview aired."

"I don't care!" Mrs. Whitman argued. "You and Detective Reed both witnessed how unstable Oliver is after I opened up my home to you."

"And what did you do with that information?" Mr. Whitman added. "The complete opposite of what you *should* have. See, this is exactly why we wanted to keep Olivia's disappearance out of the media and take care of matters privately."

Mona bit the inside of her jaw, struggling not to burst into tears.

"Mr. and Mrs. Whitman, please know that my only goal is to help find Olivia. That's all I want."

"No, you want ratings," Mr. Whitman told her. "And notoriety. Whatever positive traits you picked up during your time here in Lake Landry are long gone, young lady. You've obviously been corrupted by the underbelly of Hollywood."

"That is not true," Mona whispered, her raspy voice

trembling with pain. "Everything I do is done with integrity. And I agreed to conduct this interview with the best intentions."

Mrs. Whitman turned her nose up at her. "Well, as the saying goes, the road to hell is paved with good intentions. Detective Reed, could you please see to it that my husband and I get back to our home safely?"

"Of course."

Dillon followed the Whitmans toward the door. But his eyes were glued to Mona. When he mouthed the words *I'll call you*, she nodded her head and began gathering her things.

"I need to get out of here and get some air," Mona told her production crew. "Can you all wrap everything up and see yourselves out?"

"Of course," Sarah said without looking up from her phone. "We'll take it from here. And hey, I know you may not wanna hear this right now, but CNB News's social media platforms are on fire. According to the PR team, the website crashed after viewers hit the comment section."

"But it's up and running again," Steve, who was also scrolling through his phone, chimed in. "And boy oh boy, have the tables turned."

"What do you mean?" Mona asked.

Her makeup artist, Megan, who was peeking at Steve's phone over his shoulder, gasped loudly while jumping up and down.

"What is going on?" Mona asked, grabbing her own cell and pulling up CNB's website.

"Welp, according to this poll CNB took, everybody now thinks that Oliver is behind Olivia's disappearance. *Not* Blake."

"So Blake is no longer public enemy number one?" Sarah asked.

"Nope," Steve said. "Oliver Whitman is officially the nation's new suspect."

All eyes turned to Mona.

"Ugh," she moaned, tossing her phone inside her purse and grabbing her things. "This is insane. I cannot believe yet another one of my interviews turned into a complete disaster."

"But look at all the attention you're bringing to this case," Sarah told her. "And the viewership you're bringing to CNB News."

"I don't care about the viewership, Sarah! My reputation is on the line here, and more importantly, Olivia's safety. I'm trying to run a reputable news program, not some sensational trash show. Between Blake's interview and now Oliver's, that's exactly what my broadcast has become."

"Well, call it what you want," Sarah quipped. "Whatever you're doing is working, because according to your boss, your show just received the highest ratings in CNB's history."

Mona rolled her eyes and waved Sarah off.

"Under normal circumstances," she began, "hearing that would've been music to my ears. But after tonight? I couldn't care less. And with that being said, I have got to get out of here. I'll call you all tomorrow."

Mona hurried out of the conference room just as tears began to stream down her face.

MONA SAT ALONE on the inn's back deck, sipping a glass of much-needed red wine.

It had been a couple of hours since her interview with Oliver. Even though her phone had been buzzing nonstop, she refused to respond to most of the texts, emails and phone calls.

The one message she did check was Dillon's. He was still

with the Whitmans, trying to convince them that they'd get to the bottom of Olivia's disappearance after they threatened to contact the FBI and a private investigator.

Mona asked if he could come by once he was done. She wasn't in the mood to be alone. He said he'd be there as soon as he could.

She drained her glass and set it down on the table. She slipped off her shoes, then walked out onto the lawn.

The soft, cool grass felt good underneath her bare soles. She dragged her feet through the thick turf, walking farther into the darkness.

Mona was overcome by a sense of peace. The calm, wooded area hidden behind the inn helped soothe her rattled nerves. She sauntered farther toward the dense brush, inhaling the aromatic scent of pine needles.

Just when she thought she'd heard tree branches rustling in the distance, Mona's cell phone buzzed. She pulled it from her pocket. A text message notification from Dillon appeared on the screen.

Hey. Wrapping things up with the Whitmans now. Finally got them to calm down and convinced them to give us a little more time to solve this case. The fact that Oliver isn't here definitely made things easier. I'll be there as soon as I can.

"Thank goodness," Mona muttered to herself as she composed a response.

Good. Glad you were able to buy us more time. After Oliver's interview, I definitely think we need to take a closer look at him. I can't believe the things he said about his own sister. We have a lot to discuss. See you soon.

Right before Mona sent the message, she heard what sounded like someone rustling through the trees.

That's when she realized she was not alone.

Mona spun around and shot off toward the inn. Twigs that had fallen from the trees sliced at her feet. She ignored the pain, determined to get to safety.

When shallow puffs of air failed to fill her constricting lungs, she choked. The lack of oxygen slowed her down.

She could feel a dark presence looming behind her. The predator was getting closer.

She ran as fast as she could. A gust of humid wind propelled her forward. When the tips of her toes got caught underneath a jagged branch, Mona stumbled.

She fell forward, plunging to the damp ground.

Her attacker pounced.

She tried to scream out when his heavy body landed on top of hers. But she couldn't eke out more than a feeble wheeze.

Mona parted her lips, once again attempting to scream. But he quickly covered her mouth with his dry, salty hand.

She bit down on his fingers, jumping at the startling sound of his animalistic growl.

"You *bitch*!" he grunted, mushing her facedown into the mud.

Mona struggled to catch a pocket of breath. A clump of dirt slipped inside her mouth. She forced her head out of the mud and spit it out.

"Who are you?" she cried. "Why are you doing this to me?"

The prowler grabbed a handful of her hair, pulling her ear close to his lips.

"We've been over this before, Mona. I'm doing this to you because you *refuse* to back off of the Olivia Whitman investigation. How many times do I have to warn you before I have to kill you? Olivia is not your concern. Why would you want to die over something that has nothing to do with you?"

Olivia is my concern! Mona wanted to yell. But when she felt the cold, hard end of a gun dig into her temple, she remained silent.

"Now, you listen to me," the attacker hissed, "and listen to me good. Go back inside that inn, pack your bags and get the hell out of Lake Landry. *Immediately.* Do you understand me?"

Before Mona could respond, she heard the gun cock.

You cannot let this man take your life. Fight back!

"Do you *understand* me?" the attacker repeated, more forcefully this time.

Mona frantically ran her hand along the ground until it landed on a rock. She grabbed it, reached back and slammed her assailant against the side of his head.

"Aaah!" he yelled.

Her attacker rolled over, gripping his temple while moaning in pain.

Mona quickly pushed herself up onto her knees.

The gun. Get the gun!

She reached down and grabbed the firearm.

He tightened his grip, then swung his fist toward her eye.

Mona ducked, barely avoiding the blow. She dug her fingernails into his hand, hoping the pain would release his grasp on the gun.

It didn't.

"You think you can get the best of me?" he grunted. "It'll never happen. You're too weak!"

"*I'm* weak? Correction. *You're* weak! You've been trying to kill me since I got to Lake Landry. It hasn't happened yet, and it's not about to happen now!"

Mona bent down, preparing to sink her teeth into the assailant's hand. And then...

Boom!

The gun went off.

Mona screamed, falling backward as the sound of the bullet ricocheted through the air.

She stared over at her attacker. He wasn't moving. But he was still holding the gun.

She leaned forward, checking to see whether he'd been shot.

"Gotcha!" he yelled, lunging toward her.

Mona quickly rolled over to the side. He landed on the ground, missing her by inches.

Just as she scrambled to her feet, the sound of a car engine roared in the near distance.

Headlights flashed across the darkness. Tires screeched over rough gravel.

Dillon!

When the headlights went out and a car door slammed, Mona's attacker began to crawl away.

Go after him. Get a look at him. Bite him. Scratch him. Get his DNA. Call out to Dillon. Do something!

But she was too afraid. Her assailant still had the gun in his possession.

Just stay calm. Help is on the way.

"I think she's still out on the back deck," Mona heard Evelyn say.

"Okay, cool," Dillon replied. "I'll meet her out there."

The inn's back door opened. Mona's attacker jumped to his feet and ran off into the darkness.

"Dillon!" Mona screamed out from the lawn.

"Mona? Where are you?"

"Out here!"

She struggled to walk toward him. Her wobbly legs could barely hold her up.

"Mona!" Dillon once again called out. "I don't see you!"

She opened her mouth to speak, but only managed to muster up a lingering sob.

The thumping of Dillon's footsteps drew near. Mona looked up and saw him hurrying toward her. She was overcome by a wave of relief.

"What happened to you?" he asked.

Mona responded by falling into his arms.

"Hey, hey," he murmured, gently embracing her. "It's okay. I'm here now. Come on. Let's get you inside."

She didn't budge. She gripped Dillon's back while crying into his chest. "I was attacked again."

"You were *what*?"

"I was attacked again," Mona sobbed, her voice cracking.

"Oh no," he moaned, embracing her tighter. "How long ago did this happen?"

"Right before you got here. He fled after hearing you pull up."

Dillon reached down in his pocket and pulled out his cell phone, shining the flashlight around the vicinity.

"What are the chances he might still be in the area?"

"Not likely. He ran off into the woods several minutes ago. Plenty of time to get a good lead."

"My God," he muttered. "I bet you it was Oliver. He never showed up at his parents' house. I'm gonna call for backup. Have the area checked. You never know what we may find."

Mona sniffled loudly while pulling away from Dillon and wiping dirt from her face.

"Are you okay?" Dillon asked softly, placing his hands on Mona's arms. "Do you need to go to the hospital?"

"No. I'm fine. Even though the attack was pretty physical. He had me pinned to the ground with all of his body weight. But this time, he had a gun. Things are getting worse, Dillon. We have to solve this case. *Now*. Because if we don't, I might end up just like…"

Mona's voice trailed off. Angry tears streamed down her face. Her body shook at the thought of her assault. Visions of Olivia being attacked flashed through her mind.

"Listen," Dillon said, "I am so sorry this happened to you. Do you think it's time to consider going home and—"

"No! I've never been one to give up and I'm not about to start now. I am determined to stay in Lake Landry until I get justice for Olivia."

He sighed deeply, leading Mona back toward the inn. "I can understand that. I just can't help but feel responsible for this because once again, I wasn't here to protect you."

Mona slowly climbed up the deck's stairs and slipped on her sandals.

"This wasn't your fault, Dillon."

"Yeah, well, I feel otherwise. Now let's get you inside. You can give me the details of what happened tonight and I'll file a police report."

"And what about Oliver? What are you going to do about him?"

"I will definitely be bringing him down to the station for questioning."

"Good," Mona said, leaning into Dillon as they headed inside the inn.

Chapter Fifteen

Dillon glanced down at his watch. It was a quarter past five. Oliver was over an hour late.

He had arranged for Oliver to meet him down at the station the day after his disastrous interview for questioning. Considering he had yet to arrive, Dillon was ready to report him to Chief Boyer as a no-show.

Just as his cell phone buzzed, there was a knock at his office door.

"It's open!"

Chief Boyer cracked open the door and stuck his head inside.

"Hey, just checking in to see if you've heard from Oliver."

Dillon grabbed his cell and checked the home screen. The only new notification that appeared was a text message from Mona.

"Nope," he told the chief. "Not a peep."

"Have you tried his parents?"

"I have. Neither of them are answering their phones."

"Hmm…" Chief Boyer sighed. "Welp, I'll give it a shot and call the Whitmans. See if they know where he is. You may have to hit the streets and find him. If he refuses to come to you, then you may have to go to him."

"That's fine with me. And good luck trying to get ahold

of his parents. After that interview, they see the writing on the wall. They probably don't want to face the fact that their own son may have something to do with his sister's disappearance."

"Who could blame them? I'd be devastated if I were in their shoes. Nevertheless, I'll try to reach out to them now."

"Thanks," Dillon said. "Let me know how it goes."

"Will do."

After the chief left his office, Dillon opened Mona's text message.

FYI, I just heard back from Emily at Alnico Aluminum. She didn't find any incriminating info in George Williamson's email account. She said she'll continue to keep an eye out for us. But at this point, I think you and I both know who's behind all this. Speaking of which, has Oliver come in for questioning yet?

No, not yet, he replied. I reached out to his parents to find out if they knew of his whereabouts, but didn't get an answer. Chief Boyer is contacting them now. Hopefully he'll have better luck—

Dillon's cell phone rang, interrupting his reply. It was Mona calling. He tapped the accept button.

"Hey," he said, "I was just responding to your message. Oliver isn't here yet, so Chief Boyer just went to call his parents—"

"Dillon!" Mona interrupted, her voice filled with panic. "Oliver has been attacked!"

"Wait, *what*?"

"Oliver has been attacked!" she screamed.

"Where? When? We haven't gotten any calls here at the station about an assault."

"That's because Oliver didn't call it in. He was severely

beaten in his parents' driveway on the way to the station. The Whitmans heard all the commotion and ran outside to see what was going on. But by the time they'd gotten to him, the assailant had fled the scene."

"Similar to the way it happened to you," he noted.

"Exactly. But unlike my attacks, Oliver's injuries are pretty extensive."

"How do you know all this?" Dillon asked.

"Surprisingly, Mrs. Whitman called and told me. After she and Mr. Whitman got Oliver back inside the house, he insisted that they not call law enforcement and asked them to call me instead."

"Really? So they're not mad about the whole interview debacle anymore?"

"I guess not," Mona sighed. "I asked Mrs. Whitman if I could come by and talk to Oliver."

"What'd she say?"

"She said yes. And of course I asked if you could come with me."

Dillon felt a pounding inside his chest as he waited for Mona to continue. When she didn't, his jaws clenched in frustration.

"She said no, huh."

"Well…she didn't say no. But she didn't say yes either. I think she's worried that Oliver may get upset seeing you there. She mentioned him rambling something about the attack being set up by the police. And he thinks Blake is paying off law enforcement, too."

"Good grief," Dillon muttered, dropping his head in his hand. "Oliver and his conspiracy theories. This entire investigation is getting more and more twisted by the day."

"That it is. I think you should just take your chances and come to the house with me. At this point, we don't have anything to lose. Up until Oliver's interview, I'd had a feeling that he held the key in helping us solve this case. Now that he's been attacked, I'm almost certain of it."

Dillon stood up and grabbed his keys. "I have to agree with you there. Did Mrs. Whitman happen to mention whether Oliver needs medical attention?"

"She did. Despite Oliver's objections, the family doctor is there now tending to his injuries."

"Good. I'm on my way to the inn to pick you up, then we'll head over there."

"I'll be ready when you get here. Oh, and, Dillon?"

"Yes?"

"I'm sure this goes without saying, but aside from Chief Boyer, don't mention the attack to anyone around the station."

"Wait," he said. "Did I just hear you correctly? Did the queen of investigative journalism, who leaked top secret information regarding this case to the entire nation, just tell *me* to keep my mouth closed?"

"Don't start with me, Detective Reed!" Mona shot back. "Now hurry up and get here so we can go check on Oliver. We've got a case to solve."

"Yes, ma'am. I'll stop by Chief Boyer's office to give him a quick update, then I'll be on my way."

"Great. See you soon."

And with that, Dillon charged out the door.

DILLON AND MONA approached the Whitmans' front door and rang the bell.

As soon as it opened, he heard Oliver yell out in what sounded like excruciating pain.

"Mo-o-om!"

"I'll be there in a moment!" Mrs. Whitman called out over her shoulder before turning to Dillon and Mona. "Thank you so much for coming," she sniffled.

"Hello, Mrs. Whitman," he said quietly, relieved when she didn't react negatively to him being there.

Mrs. Whitman's watery eyes were a dark shade of pink. The tip of her runny nose was red. Her hands trembled as she wiped away the tears streaming down her cheeks.

"Please," she said, stepping to the side, "come in. Oliver is resting inside the study. Mr. Whitman is upstairs consulting with our attorney. But he should be down soon. Oh, and just to warn you, Oliver has converted the study into his own personal command center. So beware of all the clutter."

Dillon and Mona entered the house and followed Mrs. Whitman down a long hallway lined with dark, shiny hardwood floors and family portraits.

"Thank you for calling me," Mona told her. "I am so sorry that this happened to—"

"*Mo-o-om!*" Oliver called out once again.

Mrs. Whitman approached the study door.

"I appreciate that, Mona. We'd better go on in. I'll see what Oliver needs, and you two can talk to him about the assault." She paused, her voice quaking. "You have *got* to figure out who's behind these attacks on my family."

When she broke down in tears, Dillon gently placed his hand on her arm.

"We will," he told her. "We're getting closer and closer by the day."

He glanced over at Mona. Her eyes appeared glazed over, as if her mind were elsewhere. Dillon sensed she was thinking back on being attacked at the inn.

As Mrs. Whitman led them inside the study, he gave Mona's shoulder a reassuring squeeze.

"You okay?" he whispered.

She turned to him and nodded her head.

"Good."

He walked inside the dimly lit study. The oval-shaped

room was lined with shelves filled with leather-bound books. A wrought iron chandelier hung from the high beam ceiling.

Piles of newspapers, file folders and computer printouts were scattered everywhere. Three laptops had been set up on Victorian-style walnut end tables. Half-empty glasses and crumb-filled plates were strewn on the floor around a dark brown tufted leather couch.

And there, sprawled out across the sofa, was Oliver.

Dillon stopped dead in his tracks at the sight of him.

Both of Oliver's eyes were blackened and swollen. A stream of dried blood drained from his broken nose. His neck had been wrapped in a foam cervical collar. His right arm and left leg were heavily bandaged.

Dillon felt Mona grip his arm.

As shaken up as he was over Oliver's condition, he forced himself to remain calm and collected.

He cleared his throat, slowly approaching the couch.

"Hey, man," he said quietly. "How are you feeling?"

"Like crap," Oliver moaned. "Mom! Bring me a glass of orange juice. With *no pulp* in it this time. And one of those painkillers Dr. Moore brought me."

"Sure, son," Mrs. Whitman breathed.

She walked over to the couch and collected a few of the dishes.

"Can you please hurry up?" Oliver yelled before wincing in agony. "I feel like I'm about to die!"

Mrs. Whitman covered her mouth. Dillon could tell she was struggling to hold back a sob.

"I'll be right back," she choked before rushing out of the room.

Mona took a deep breath and stepped forward.

"I'm so glad you called me over, Oliver. Thank you again. Detective Reed and I are determined to find out who did this to you. We both think the answer is going to get you justice, and also lead us to Olivia."

"Detective Reed," Oliver snorted. "What the hell is he doing here? I didn't invite him over. Just you. You're defying the fellow conspiracy theorist code, Mona. We're a secret society. You can't break the unspoken bond we're supposed to share."

"I know," Mona sighed dramatically, staring down at the floor as if she were disappointed in herself. "But considering the extenuating circumstances we're under, I didn't think you'd mind me breaking the code just this once. Time is running out, Oliver, and things are escalating. The perpetrator is getting more dangerous. We have got to get him off the streets before someone loses their life."

"If I worked for Lake Landry PD," Oliver said, "I would've had this case solved *weeks* ago."

Dillon bit his tongue, refusing to take the bait.

"Is it okay if we sit?" he asked, pointing over at the love seat positioned next to the couch.

"Whatever…"

Just when the pair sat down, Mrs. Whitman came scurrying into the room carrying a tray filled with orange juice, coffee and ice water.

"Mona, Dillon, I am so sorry," she said. "I didn't ask if you two wanted anything. I hope coffee and distilled water are enough for now. I need to get upstairs and speak with my husband and our attorney. But if you'd like anything else, just let me know."

"This is more than enough," Mona told her. "Thank you."

"You're welcome."

She handed Oliver his glass of orange juice and pain medication, then hurried out of the room.

As she closed the door behind her, Dillon pulled out his notepad.

"So did you get a look at your attacker?" he asked Oliver.

"Yeah. He was short and fat and dressed in all black tactical gear. Ballistic helmet and all. I should've been able to take him down. But he caught me off guard."

"How so?" Mona questioned while typing notes in her cell phone app.

"When I was getting inside my car, he rushed me from behind. I tried to pull out some of my Krav Maga moves on him, but he tackled me to the ground so fast that I didn't even get a chance."

"What is 'Krav Maga'?" Mona asked.

Dillon waited for Oliver to respond. But when he was hit with a coughing fit, Dillon turned to Mona.

"Krav Maga is an Israeli hand-to-hand combat system that was founded in 1891," Dillon said. "It was developed for defense and security forces."

"How do you even know that?" she asked.

"I actually learned about it not too long ago while watching an old episode of *Jeopardy*—"

"Dude!" Oliver interrupted. "First of all, the lady was talking to me. Secondly, why are you here again?"

Mona quickly reached over and placed her hand on Dillon's thigh before he could respond.

"Did you recognize anything else about your assailant?" she asked. "Despite the tactical gear, did his physique appear familiar? Or what about his voice? Did it sound familiar?"

"Mona, I'm not gonna lie to you. I smoked some weed before leaving the house. I wanted to be nice and mellow when I went down to the station to be interrogated. So no. I didn't recognize a thing. Not to mention I was busy getting beaten in the back of the head with the butt of a gun."

"Wait, he pistol-whipped you?" Dillon asked.

"Yes. But thanks to the almighty universe, I'm so mentally enlightened that my cerebral strength parlayed into my physical endurance. I took that beatdown like a *champ*, bro."

Dillon watched Oliver closely as he spoke. Despite his tough exterior, his teary eyes and quivering hands told a different story. He saw right through him. Oliver was terrified.

"What exactly did the attacker say to you?" Mona asked.

"Ahh!" Oliver moaned, turning over onto his side and rubbing his lower back. "He said all types of crap."

"Such as?"

"Stuff like, you'd better back off of this investigation. Your sister hates you, so why would you risk dying over her? Keep your mouth shut unless you wanna be killed. Then before he slammed my head into the concrete, he said this was my first and final warning."

Dillon and Mona discreetly glanced at one another. When she gave him a knowing nod of the head, he knew they were both thinking the same thing.

Oliver's assailant was probably the same man who'd attacked her.

"So you didn't get a look at the attacker?" Dillon asked.

"No."

"If you had to guess, who do you think was behind this attack?"

Oliver took a deep, labored breath.

"Let's be honest," he began. "A man like me is gonna have enemies. I'm pretty outspoken when it comes to my otherworldly beliefs and conspiracy theories. Some nonbelievers could be behind this attack, and using Olivia's disappearance as a cover-up."

"Do you really think that's the case?" Mona probed skeptically.

"No…" Oliver muttered before tossing the pills inside

his mouth and taking a gulp of orange juice. "I don't. I just thought it was worth mentioning. I fully believe that Blake Carter sent one of his goons after me."

"And why do you think he'd do something like that?" Dillon asked while vigorously scribbling notes in his pad.

"Because he's still mad at me for going off on his boy."

"Leo Mendez?" Mona chimed in.

"Yeah. That clown. Also known as Blake's lap dog. But really, if I may just cut through the BS, Blake probably killed my sister because he wants to be free and single. Marrying her was a good look for them both. But then the whole *marriage* thing got real. He was expected to be committed and faithful, but obviously he couldn't. Yet he also wanted it both ways. Cheat, but start a family. Pressure my sister to have a baby while entertaining a harem of women. Doesn't make sense, does it?"

Dillon stopped writing midsentence. He was shocked to hear Oliver say something sensible for once.

"It definitely doesn't make sense," Mona agreed.

Oliver struggled to prop himself up on his elbows before crying out in pain.

Within seconds, Mrs. Whitman came charging into the room.

"Mona, Dillon," she said, "I think that's enough for today. Oliver needs to rest. Were you able to get what you needed?"

"Somewhat," Dillon replied. "I think we were just on the cusp of getting some good insight. But I understand. Oliver does need time to recover."

He pulled out his phone and checked his text messages.

"A couple of my colleagues are out front processing the crime scene now. Mona and I will go check in with them, then follow up with you later today. How does that sound?"

"That sounds good," Mrs. Whitman replied. "Thank

you very much, Detective Reed and Mona. We appreciate you both."

"You're so welcome, Mrs. Whitman," Mona said before
approaching the couch. She stepped gingerly in between
Oliver's piles of documents.

"Thank you again for calling us over," she told him.

"Thanks for coming to check on me," he croaked, closing his eyes tightly while grabbing the back of his head.

Dillon waited for Oliver to make a smart remark about
not inviting him. When he didn't, Dillon knew he must've
been in an immense amount of pain.

As Mrs. Whitman exited the study, Dillon noticed Mona
bend down and pick a file folder up off the floor.

"Hey, what is this?" she asked Oliver.

He squinted, struggling to see what was in her hand.

"Some file I swiped off an exec's desk on my last day
at Transformation Cosmetics. I never bothered to look
through it."

"Would you mind if I take it with me? You never know.
It may contain some pertinent information."

"Yeah, whatever," Oliver sighed before slumping down
against the back of the couch.

"Thanks. Detective Reed and I will be in touch." Mona
gave his shoulder a gentle pat, then walked toward the doorway.

"What was that all about?" Dillon asked her as they
headed down the hallway.

"I spotted this folder labeled Transformation Cosmetics: Confidential *lying on the floor*. I have no clue what's
in it, obviously. But I figured it was worth checking out."

"Good call. Once we get back to the inn, we'll do just that."

Chapter Sixteen

Mona sat next to Dillon on the teal blue silk love seat inside her room.

"There's nothing here," she mumbled, shuffling through the papers piled inside the Transformation Cosmetics file.

"Nothing?" Dillon asked. "Are you sure?"

"Well, nothing pertaining to Olivia's disappearance. All I see are promotional materials for community service events that the company hosted, a few inventory lists and a bunch of shipment receipts."

Dillon leaned over and scanned the papers.

"Interesting. Look at the bottom of each page. According to the URL, each of these documents is linked to Leo Mendez."

"Okay, but I don't see anything incriminating here."

Just as Mona continued paging through the documents, her cell phone rang. She reached down and grabbed it off the coffee table.

"Oh, this is Mrs. Whitman. I hope everything's okay with Oliver," she said before answering the call. "Hello?"

"Mona!" Mrs. Whitman screamed. "Is Detective Reed still with you?"

"Yes, he's right here. Why? What's going on?"

Mona quickly switched the call over to speakerphone so that Dillon could listen in.

"Mr. Whitman and I just received an anonymous phone call from a man claiming to have Olivia in his possession. He said that in order for our daughter to be returned to us safely, we must wire five million dollars into an offshore bank account by midnight tomorrow!"

Mona grabbed Dillon's arm. Tears of relief filled her eyes at the thought of Olivia still being alive.

But her heart pounded out of her chest as she wondered what her friend had been through since she'd gone missing.

"Mrs. Whitman," Dillon said, "did you make any sort of agreement with the kidnapper?"

"No. He didn't give us a chance to. He just passed along the banking information and said he'd call back in an hour with further instructions."

"Did he provide you with any proof that he really has Olivia in his possession?" he continued. "Did he let you speak to her?"

"No," Mrs. Whitman sobbed. "And I asked, but he wouldn't allow it. He said all I need to be concerned with is getting the money together. And if in an hour I have proof that I've begun the wire transfer process, he'll let me speak with Olivia."

"Well, by the time he calls back," Dillon told her as he began texting away on his cell, "I'll have a recorder set up on your phone. I'm sending Chief Boyer a message now letting him know what's going on. He'll obtain an emergency court order so we can put surveillance on the kidnapper's phone. We'll trace where the call is coming from, either through the VPN or cell phone towers. Mona and I will be there to help walk you through the conversation when he calls back."

"Thank you, Detective Reed. I'd definitely feel better having you two here with us. And I think you've got a good plan in place. Mr. Whitman, however, thinks otherwise. He'd like to speak with you."

Mona heard the phone rustling before Mr. Whitman got on the line.

"Detective Reed, I don't think it's a good idea to entertain this…this *criminal*. What if he's lying? What if this is all a scam, and the person doesn't really have our daughter? See, I knew the minute we went to the media with this case, fraudsters would come out of the woodwork, lying and demanding money."

"Mr. Whitman, that's a chance we're going to have to take," Dillon told him as Mona nodded her head in agreement. "This is the first lead we've gotten of this nature. And we need to act on it. Because what if it *is* legit, and this person does have your daughter? The only way we'll find out is by taking the necessary steps to try to get her back."

When Mr. Whitman responded with a disapproving grunt, Mona chimed in.

"Detective Reed is right, Mr. Whitman. I've worked on several missing person cases that involved ransom demands. You don't have to go through with the wire transfer. But you should at least begin the process to show that you're serious about sending him the money and bringing Olivia home."

"I don't know about all that," Mr. Whitman grumbled.

"Listen," Dillon said, standing up and grabbing his keys, "Mona and I are on our way there now. We'll have the house and your phone lines under surveillance. Trust me, we will get to the bottom of all this and, ultimately, get your daughter back."

"And what about the money wire transfer?" Mr. Whitman asked. "What should we do about that?"

"I'll have my digital forensic specialist pose as your banker and send you an email making it appear as though the transfer is in motion. That'll buy us some time while we work on locating the kidnapper."

"Fine," Mr. Whitman replied. "We'll see you when you get here."

Mona disconnected the call and grabbed her laptop.

"Hey," Dillon said. "Why don't you bring that Transformation Cosmetics folder you got from Oliver? We'll take a closer look at it and see what we can find."

"It's already in the bag."

"I should've known," he told her as they hurried out of the room and down to the lobby.

"I cannot believe this," Mona panted as the pair climbed inside the car. "We're finally going to solve this case, Dillon. I can feel it."

"I hope so…"

MONA SAT AT the Whitmans' dining room table. Every muscle in her body was wrought with tension.

She peered over at Mrs. Whitman, who was on the phone with the alleged kidnapper. Mr. Whitman sat next to her with his arm wrapped tightly around her shoulder.

"This email looks legit," the assailant said.

"Turn up the volume," Dillon whispered to Donovan, his digital forensic specialist.

Donovan nodded his head and increased the sound on the speakerphone.

"But I'm going to have to look into the transfer routing number," the assailant continued.

Mona shivered at the sound of his deep, distorted tone. It was obvious he was speaking through a voice enhancer. His garbled pitch was disturbing to say the least.

Mrs. Whitman crossed her arms in front of her tightly. She eyed Dillon wearily. He gave her a reassuring thumbs-up. She took a deep breath and leaned into the table.

"The email *is* legit," Mrs. Whitman said. "The routing number and all. Our banker is working to get the five million dollars wired to your account as we speak. Now, *please*. We're doing our part. You must do yours. Let us talk to our daughter!"

The kidnapper chuckled into the phone. "Tsk tsk, not so fast, Mrs. Whitman. According to this email, the transfer is still in the very early stages. You'll speak to your daughter once I see those funds moving."

"Just let me hear her voice," Mrs. Whitman sobbed. "*Please.* I'm begging you!"

Mona heard a click. The phone went dead.

"Let me speak to my daughter!" Mrs. Whitman screamed.

"He hung up," Dillon told her. "I'm so sorry."

Mrs. Whitman jumped up from the table.

"I can't do this," she wept. "I'm going to check on Oliver."

Mona's heart broke as she watched Mrs. Whitman rush out of the room. She turned to Donovan, who was busy typing away on his laptop.

"Were you able to pick up on a location?" she asked him.

"I'm communicating with the caller's cell phone service provider now. Her software application is tracking his phone's GPS positioning. She's keeping me updated as she goes. I'll let you know as soon as she gets a hit."

"Great. Thank you."

Mona wiped her damp forehead and turned to Dillon, whose head was buried in his cell phone.

"Just texting back and forth with Chief Boyer," he told her, as if sensing her anxiety. "He's down at the forensics lab waiting on the results of the DNA that was collected from the area where Oliver was attacked."

"Well, unlike the areas where I was attacked," Mona said, "I hope they're able to recover some sort of evidence."

"Let's hope so. In the meantime, why don't you take another look at the Transformation Cosmetics file? Between that and this trace we've put on the assailant, we're bound to get a hit."

"Good idea."

Mona pulled the file from her tote bag, glad for the distraction. Even though there didn't appear to be anything worthwhile in the folder, she hoped that paging through it would help ease her racing mind.

A loud clapping reverberated through the room. Mona jumped in her seat.

"We got a ping off a cell phone tower!" Donovan exclaimed.

Dillon pumped his fist in the air.

"Yes! What area are we looking at?"

"The phone is pinging about fifteen miles west of Lake Landry. Looks like it's moving toward the town rather than away from it. So our kidnapper is heading this way. The cell phone service provider is working to get an exact location."

"Excellent," Dillon told him. "As soon as she does, let me know."

"Will do."

Mona felt her heart thumping out of her chest. A rush of adrenaline flowed through her veins.

They were getting closer. Olivia would be home soon. She hoped...

Dillon reached over and gave her hand a squeeze, snapping Mona out of her thoughts.

"Hey," he whispered, "I'm gonna step outside for a second and call Chief Boyer. He wants to discuss the likelihood of us recovering Olivia alive. I don't want to have that conversation in front of her family."

"Okay. While you do that, I'll continue combing through this file."

"Sounds good. Be right back."

After Dillon left the room, Mr. Whitman stood up.

"I'm going to go check on my wife and son," he muttered. "Maybe get a drink. Something strong, to help ease my mind. Would either of you like anything?"

"No, thank you," both Mona and Donovan replied in unison.

Her stomach churned at the sight of Mr. Whitman slinking out of the room. She and Donovan exchanged sympathetic looks. He turned back to his laptop, and she turned back to the file.

Mona once again thumbed through the random documents. Inspection reports and distribution plans were sandwiched between dispatch authorizations and fumigation statements.

"There is nothing here," she mumbled to herself.

Right before Mona slammed the file shut, she noticed a crumpled piece of paper stuck to the back of the folder.

Another receipt, she thought.

Mona pulled the document from the file, expecting to see a shipment confirmation.

But when she unfolded it, she laid eyes on a chain of email messages.

"I'm back," Dillon said, rushing into the room. He sat down next to Mona and flipped through his notepad. "Did I miss anything?"

"Nope," Donovan told him. "Mr. Whitman went to check on his family. I'm still waiting to hear back from the cell phone provider. And the creepy kidnapper hasn't called back yet."

"I may have found something," Mona said, sliding the email printout toward Dillon. "Take a look at this."

He leaned over, and together they scanned the document.

"You found this in Oliver's file?"

"Yes. It looks like several email exchanges between one of Transformation Cosmetics' general mailboxes and some random person who goes by the name GDub. The messages are short and cryptic. Like this one." She pointed. "'Materials picked up and discarded. Monies received.' There are several more that are worded the exact same way. The only difference is the dates they were sent to Transformation."

"Hmm, interesting…"

"Sorry to interrupt, guys," Donovan said, "but we've got movement."

Dillon hopped up from his chair and peered over Donovan's shoulder at the laptop.

"Talk to me. What are we looking at?"

"The kidnapper's phone is pinging on the border of Lake Landry. He's moving into town via St. Francis Boulevard."

Dillon grabbed his keys and cell phone.

"Donovan, Mona and I are going to track him down. Can you provide me with real-time updates while we head his way?"

"Absolutely, sir."

Mona felt a rush of energy jolt through her body. She shoved the email inside her tote bag.

"You ready?" Dillon asked her.

"I'm ready. Let's go."

Chapter Seventeen

Dillon turned up the volume on his car's Bluetooth.

"Talk to me, Donovan. Which way are we going?"

"Make a right turn down Armitage Street. But keep your distance. The kidnapper is slowing down toward the end of the block."

"You got it," Dillon replied.

He turned the corner and let up on the accelerator.

Mona leaned forward, squinting as she struggled to see through the darkness.

Streetlights were sparse on the upscale residential street. Sprawling lawns surrounded grand plantation-style homes.

The dark sedan that the kidnapper was driving decelerated up ahead.

Mona gripped the door handle. She resisted the urge to jump out of the car and rush his vehicle.

"I want to run up there and see if Olivia's inside of that car so badly," she told Dillon.

"Same here. But we have to be careful. If Olivia is in there, we don't wanna make a wrong move and jeopardize her safety."

"I know," Mona huffed. "We're just so close. My anxiety is through the roof. I need to know that she's okay."

"Me, too. Hey, Donovan, has the kidnapper called the house again?"

"No, not yet."

"Okay. Looks like he's coming to a stop up ahead. Mona and I are sitting back toward the opposite end of the block with our headlights off."

"Good," Donovan replied. "Be sure to keep your distance."

"How are the Whitmans doing?" Mona asked.

"The best that they can. They're still in the study with Oliver. I told them to just stay in there and relax. I'll send for them if the kidnapper calls back."

"Good plan," Dillon told him. "Their stress levels appear to be at an all-time high, which is understandable. Just reassure them we're doing all that we can to bring Olivia home safely."

"I will."

Mona jumped when she felt her cell phone vibrate inside her pocket. She pulled it out and saw a text message notification appear on the screen from a number she didn't recognize.

"Who is this?" she muttered before opening and scanning it.

"Got some new intel?" Dillon asked.

"Wait. Let me read this message again."

Mona held her breath, rereading the message twice before almost dropping the phone.

"You are *not* gonna believe this," she said.

"Believe what?"

"I just got a text message from Emily at Alnico. Apparently, George Williamson has been conducting official Alnico business from his personal email address. And guess what name he goes by?"

"What name?" Dillon asked.

"GDub."

"GDub... Wait, isn't that the name of the person who was exchanging messages with someone from Transformation Cosmetics?"

"Yes, it is," Mona confirmed.

"That's strange. Why would an aluminum corporation be doing business with a cosmetics company?"

"Good question. I have no idea. But I definitely think it's something we should look—"

Mona was interrupted by the sound of screeching tires.

She looked up and saw the kidnapper's sedan peel away from the curb.

"Dillon!" she yelled. "He's on the move!"

"I'm on it," he said, hitting the accelerator and speeding after him.

"Do you have eyes on our suspect, Detective?" Donovan asked.

"I do. I'm following him now."

"Good. I'm tracking him on my end, as well. So just know that you've got backup in case you lose him."

"Thanks."

"Looks like he's getting on the expressway," Mona breathed, her voice filled with panic.

"Where the hell is he going now?" Dillon muttered.

"I don't know, but I'm dying to get a look at him and see if Olivia's in that car."

"We'll both get a look at him soon enough. He has to stop off somewhere eventually."

Dillon trailed the kidnapper onto the highway. He expertly maneuvered his car while their suspect weaved in and out of traffic.

Mona gripped the dashboard. She and Dillon rode in silence, the chase too intense for conversation.

The abductor eventually exited the expressway and drove toward a swampy rural area.

"What in the world...?" Mona uttered. "Where is he going?"

Her racing heartbeat thumped sporadically. She stared

out at the vast, desolate fields. Her eyes were met with an eerie darkness.

Mona did not have a good feeling.

"I have no idea where we are right now," Dillon said. "Didn't even know this area existed."

"Me either," Mona told him. "Be careful. You're getting kind of close to the suspect. There's hardly anyone else out here, so we could easily be noticed."

Dillon eased up on the accelerator and put some distance between his car and the kidnapper's.

"Are you still with him?" Donovan asked.

"I am. This guy just turned down some narrow, bumpy road. There are no streetlights or signs. And as difficult as it'll be to see, I'm gonna turn off my headlights and do my best to continue following the subject."

"Good idea," Donovan told him.

Dillon hit the brakes as the car's tires dipped down into huge holes in the road.

Mona braced herself, struggling to not bang her head against the window.

"Damn," she murmured. "Talk about a road less traveled. These bumps feel more like craters. It doesn't seem like anyone should be driving out here."

"I agree. And that's probably why our perp chose this destination. Whatever crimes he's committed would be well hidden."

Mona dropped her head in her hand.

"Lord, please don't let this man lead us to Olivia's body…"

"Come on, now," Dillon told her. "Don't think like that. Believe that we're going to recover Olivia safely."

Mona looked up ahead and noticed red brake lights flashing. She reached over and grabbed Dillon's arm.

"He's stopping," she screeched. "He's stopping!"

"I see him," he told her calmly as he pulled over to the side of the road and cut the engine.

Mona slid to the edge of her seat and peered through the windshield.

"This looks like an abandoned sugarcane field," she said, eyeing the tall stalks leaning against the side of the car.

"It does. And I think I see some sort of shack up ahead."

Mona wrung her hands, once again anxious to hop out of the car and see if Olivia was inside the vehicle.

"I wish this man would hurry up and get out of his car so we can move in on him," she said, now rocking back and forth in her seat.

"He will. Just stay calm."

As soon as the words were out of Dillon's mouth, the man opened his car door.

"Okay," Mona whispered as if the suspect could hear her. "He's moving!"

Dillon reached over and opened the glove compartment. He pulled out a Glock 22 and a pair of handcuffs.

Mona inhaled sharply.

Uh-oh, she thought. *This just got real...*

"Donovan," Dillon said, "you still there?"

"Yes, I'm here, Detective."

"Listen, our subject is on the move. Mona and I are going to go after him. I need for you to give Chief Boyer an update on what's happening. Tell him to be on alert, but don't send backup to the scene just yet. It's too desolate out here. I don't want our perp to know we're on to him. He may panic and do something stupid."

"Like hurt Olivia," Mona added. "If he hasn't already."

"I'll call him now, sir," Donovan said. "Be careful, and keep me posted."

"Will do."

Dillon disconnected the call. He and Mona stared

straight ahead, waiting to see what the assailant would do next.

Within seconds, he jumped out of the car and ran toward the shack.

Dillon turned to Mona.

"You ready?"

"I'm ready."

"Okay. Stay low, step quietly and follow my lead. Got it?"

"Got it," Mona responded, her voice filled with determination. "Now come on. Let's go get our girl."

"Let's do it."

The pair quickly opened their doors and slipped out. They ducked down, watching as the kidnapper tore up the shack's rickety wooden stairs.

Mona looked over at Dillon. He motioned for her to follow him.

They tiptoed along the edge of the sugarcane field. As they got closer to the run-down gray cabin, Dillon pulled Mona back into the stalks' long green leaves.

The pair watched as the shadowy figure pushed through the door.

They heard a loud scream come from inside the house.

Mona gasped, covering her mouth to stop her own scream.

Dillon grabbed her hand and pulled her out onto the gravelly road.

"We're going in!" he declared.

Mona stayed close while they ran toward the shack. Dillon drew his gun as they hovered near the doorway.

The suspect had left the door wide-open. Dillon peeked around the corner inside the house. Mona stood next to him, discreetly peering over his shoulder.

It took a few moments for her eyes to adjust. Odd pieces

of dilapidated furniture were scattered around a shabby, dimly lit living room.

Mona recoiled when the kidnapper appeared from behind a closed door. He was wearing a black ski mask and tactical gear. She immediately recognized his silhouette. It was her attacker.

Dillon motioned to Mona that they were going inside. She stood straight up and gripped his arm.

The perp walked farther into the living room. There, standing behind him, was Olivia.

Mona willed herself not to run in and rescue her.

The kidnapper grabbed Olivia by the throat, pulling her face inches away from his.

"Those wire transfer details your parents sent?" he yelled. "They're fraudulent! Do those idiots think I'm stupid enough to release you before I get my money? How does it feel to know your family doesn't care enough about you to pay a ransom that wouldn't put a *dent* in their fortune?"

Olivia whimpered as tears streamed down her face. She clutched his hands, struggling to pull them away from her neck.

"Just hang tight," Dillon whispered to Mona. "I'm waiting on the right time to go in."

Mona nodded her head, her eyes glued to Olivia.

"Don't your parents know that if they keep playing games with me, I will *kill* you?"

Olivia's face twisted with terror. She screamed out.

He jerked her to the side in an attempt to silence her. That's when she noticed Mona and Dillon hovering in the doorway.

"Mona!" she yelled.

Dillon quickly pushed Mona behind him, then pivoted, pointing his gun at the suspect.

"Police! Get your hands up!"

The abductor froze. Olivia dropped to the floor and crawled over to a dingy floral couch in the corner of the room.

"I said get your hands up!" Dillon repeated.

The kidnapper slowly began to raise his hands in the air.

"That's it," Dillon said, carefully stepping inside the shack. Mona followed closely behind him.

"Do you have any weapons on you?" Dillon asked.

The perp remained silent.

"I said, do you have any weapons on you?"

Just when Dillon took a step toward him, the perp swiftly reached back inside his waistband.

Dillon cocked his gun.

The assailant pulled out a silver Beretta 92FS.

Just as he aimed it at the detective, Dillon blasted a shot. The bullet hit the wall right behind the assailant's arm.

Mona screamed and dropped to the floor.

The assailant shot back. The bullet careened past Dillon's ear, barely grazing his lobe as it flew out the door.

"Drop your weapon!" Dillon demanded.

The kidnapper fired another shot. As Dillon fired back, the perp spun around and bolted out the back door.

"Stay here!" Dillon told Mona and Olivia before charging after him.

Mona stayed low, crawling over toward the couch.

Olivia's eyes were wide with shock. She remained crouched down, frozen in fear.

"Olivia," Mona whimpered, embracing her friend tightly. "You have no idea how happy I am to see that you're alive! Are you okay?"

"I—I don't know…"

She leaned into Mona, her frail body shaking as she sobbed uncontrollably.

Mona glanced down at her friend. Olivia had lost a considerable amount of weight. Her dingy white T-shirt and baggy gray leggings hung off of her feeble frame.

Olivia's long, wavy hair was pulled back into a tangled ponytail. Her face was red and puffy, and her tired eyes were swollen. It was clear that she'd been through hell.

"Is that Detective Reed with you?" Olivia sniffled.

"Yes, it is. We've been working together for weeks trying to find you. He's been amazing."

"Well, then, let's go make sure he's okay," Olivia insisted, scrambling to stand up.

Mona had been so focused on Olivia that she'd forgotten Dillon was outside trying to capture the kidnapper.

A lump of terror formed in her throat at the thought of losing him.

She and Olivia ran out onto the shack's ragged back porch.

In the distance, Mona saw Dillon splashing through the dark, murky swampland. The gunman was several feet ahead of him.

"Be careful, Dillon!" Mona screamed at the sight of the chaotic chase.

She watched as he propelled his body forward and pounced on the kidnapper.

An intense brawl ensued. The pair thrashed about the muddy water. Fists flew in the air and vicious kicks were thrown.

Mona and Olivia clung to one another, looking on in horror.

The brutal attack seemed to go on forever. Mona covered her eyes, terrified of what would come next.

And then, a gunshot rang out.

Mona's eyes flew open. Both men collapsed into the water.

She gasped. Then froze. Waited to see if Dillon would stand up. When he didn't, Mona tore down the stairs.

"No, come back!" Olivia yelled, grabbing her arm. "You can't go out there. It's too dangerous!"

"But I have to check on Dillon," Mona cried.

"You can't," Olivia insisted, wrapping her arm around her tightly. "Detective Reed is perfectly capable of taking care of himself. He'll be fine. Let's just wait here, where it's safe."

Mona stumbled back up the stairs. She willed herself not to unravel as she waited for Dillon to reemerge.

He's okay. Don't worry. He's okay...

She kept her eyes peeled to the marsh, holding her breath. Finally, the two men resurfaced.

"Oh thank God!" Mona cried out.

"He got him." Olivia wept as Dillon put the assailant in handcuffs and dragged him back through the thick wetland. "He got him..."

Mona broke down in tears and turned to Olivia. The two friends embraced one another once again.

"I cannot believe this is finally over," Mona sobbed. "And I can't wait to find out who this maniac is behind the mask."

Olivia's arms fell down by her sides. She pulled away from Mona, her expression perplexed.

"What do you mean, find out who he is?" she asked.

"What I mean is, we've been trying to catch that lunatic for weeks. He's attacked me on more than one occasion, and even tried to kill me after I refused to stop investigating your case. Then he beat your brother half to death. I want this coward's identity revealed so I can look him in the eye and show him that he didn't get the best of us."

"Mona," Olivia said quietly, "I thought you knew who'd captured me, and law enforcement was just trying to hunt him down."

"I have no idea who he is. He's been running around town hiding behind that creepy ski mask."

Mona watched as a veil of anger covered Olivia's eyes. Her chin began to quiver as her chest heaved uncontrollably. It was then that Mona realized she knew her captor.

"Olivia, who is he?" she whispered.

"Leo. Leo Mendez."

Chapter Eighteen

"Just so we're clear," Dillon said, watching as Mona poured the bottle of red wine into their glasses. "Leo Mendez of Transformation Cosmetics had established an underground agreement with George Williamson of Alnico Aluminum Corporation."

"That is correct," Mona replied, handing Dillon his glass.

"And we're *sure* that Blake Carter didn't know anything about this agreement."

She nodded her head.

"Right. He knew nothing about it. And that can be proven through email messages and records Blake kept."

Dillon took a long sip of wine, then sat down on the love seat inside of Mona's hotel room.

"You know, I was so busy interrogating Leo that I really didn't get a chance to speak with Olivia. But I'm glad you and Chief Boyer were there with her while she shared her story. So, tell me again. What was the purpose of this agreement?"

Mona sat down next to Dillon and leaned her head against his shoulder.

As he waited for her to answer the question, he subconsciously began stroking her hair.

Once he realized what he was doing, Dillon paused, waiting to see how she would react.

"Don't stop," Mona said softly. "That feels good."

"I won't," he replied as he continued running his fingers through her curls. "Now, what were you saying?"

"So, according to Olivia, Leo cut an under-the-table deal with Alnico to illegally dump Transformation Cosmetics' excess chemical waste. Blake had the paperwork to prove that he'd instructed Leo to hire a certified disposal service to safely discard the lead and chromium being produced during Transformation's manufacturing process. But Leo's secret agreement with Alnico was a much cheaper option that allowed him to drastically cut corporate costs. This enabled him to come in under budget, and the money he saved went directly toward his yearly bonus."

"Wow," Dillon breathed, staring up at the ceiling as he took it all in. "So Leo Mendez, Blake's right-hand man, the one he's always bragging about and propping up on a pedestal, sold him out and jeopardized the integrity of Transformation Cosmetics. All for a check."

"Exactly. But the arrangement between Leo and Alnico got out of hand when Leo instructed George to dump the chemicals into residential water sources. That's how Olivia discovered the acts of contamination. George wanted to meet with Olivia so he could blow the whistle on Leo. But Leo kidnapped her before she could find out the truth *or* report her findings to the government."

"And I'm guessing he planned to collect the ransom money and skip town before the truth came to light," Dillon added. "Luckily, we intercepted that plan before it came to fruition."

"Yes, we did, *partner*," Mona said, giving his thigh an affectionate squeeze.

Her touch caused him to shift in his seat. He took several sips of wine, then cleared his throat.

"I'm just glad we finally solved this case," he continued. "I got Leo to confess to Bonnie's murder, and Olivia has returned home safely. Oh, and judging by the way she and Blake were acting toward one another down at the station, they may even try to reconcile."

"Yeah, I noticed all that lovey-dovey action. I was shocked. But obviously they're both extremely traumatized by all of this. So if they can get past their issues and work things out, then good for them."

"I agree. And speaking of their trauma, I hope they'll be relieved knowing that Leo is in custody and George is being extradited back to the States from the Bahamas."

"I hope so, too," Mona said. "By the way, what are they being charged with?"

"They're both being charged with knowingly discharging hazardous substances into a water of the United States. In addition to that, Leo's been hit with kidnapping, attempted murder and extortion charges."

"Good."

Mona exhaled, then looked up at Dillon.

"You know I have to leave town soon."

"I do know that. And I'm trying not to think about it."

"Really? Why?"

"Because," Dillon said, gently brushing a strand of hair away from her eye, "it's gonna be tough not having you around. I've gotten used to you being here. And I really enjoy your company."

"That's nice to hear. I really enjoy your company, too."

The pair fell silent. After several moments, Mona sat up and turned to Dillon.

"Come home with me for Christmas."

"Wait, what?"

"You heard me. Come home with me for Christmas. Evergreen, Colorado, is amazing during the holidays. There's ice skating, caroling, holiday float parades, festivals…"

Dillon reached out and gently caressed her cheek.

"I would love to. But are you sure? Won't your entire family be there?"

"Yes, they will. And I'd love for you to meet them. You and I have been to hell and back together. We'll be the stars of Evergreen with all the stories we have to tell."

"I bet we would," he chuckled.

He and Mona gazed at one another.

"Thank you for the invitation," he said. "I'd be honored to spend Christmas with you and your family."

"The pleasure will be all mine," Mona murmured before they leaned into one another and shared a long, passionate kiss.

Epilogue

Three Months Later...

"A toast," Mona said, raising her glass of champagne in the air. "To Leo and George being convicted, this entire ordeal officially being over, and new beginnings."

"Salud."

Dillon clinked his glass against hers, then took a sip of champagne.

Mona sat back in her lounge chair and looked out at the setting sun.

She and Dillon were sitting out on her LA loft's rooftop deck, enjoying the scenic views of the vast, twinkling city.

He reached out and took her hand, interlocking his fingers with hers. She turned to him and smiled, still feeling as though it was all a dream.

"Can you believe that you're no longer a detective?" Mona asked him.

"You know, I can, actually. I don't think I realized how burned-out I was when I took the job with Lake Landry PD. By the time we'd solved Olivia's case, I was *done*. Working as a private investigator and setting my own schedule suits me much better."

"And so does LA living, doesn't it?"

"Yes, it does. But I have to admit, I would've gone anywhere in the world if it meant being with you."

"Aw, babe." Mona smiled, leaning over and planting a soft kiss on Dillon's lips. "I'm so glad you decided to move here. I never would've thought investigating my friend's disappearance would lead to me finding love, landing my own nightly news show—"

"And don't forget getting your man a job as a CNB News on-air contributor."

"That, too. Let's just say that I'm happy. And finally fulfilled."

Dillon wrapped his arm around Mona.

"I love hearing that," he said. "And I can say the same for myself. I never would've thought I'd leave Louisiana behind and find happiness elsewhere."

"But since you're consulting with police departments all over the state of Louisiana, you do still have roots there."

"I do. However, my heart is now deeply rooted here. With you."

Dillon leaned over and nuzzled her ear.

"I love you, Mona Avery."

She turned to him, blinking rapidly as tears of joy filled her eyes.

"I love you, too, Dillon Reed."

* * * * *

AGENT COLTON'S TAKEDOWN

BEVERLY LONG

For Alex. Welcome to the family!

Chapter One

"I can't believe my life has come to this," Olivia Margulies said. She sat with her feet tucked under her, in the corner of her couch, a light throw over her to ward off the chill. An empty cup of hot chocolate sat on the end table next to the new hardcover that she'd purchased just last week.

Before all this had started.

"Uh-huh," said FBI agent Bryce Colton, who'd appointed himself her brand-new bodyguard, not looking up from his computer. He sat on the opposite chair, laptop open, cell phone beside it on the table. It was either ringing or lighting up with incoming and outgoing text messages with some regularity. Enough regularity that she'd put her book down. The cup of coffee next to him was still full.

Too busy to drink.

Too busy thinking of ways to capture Len Davison. The man who, just days before, late on a Saturday night, had broken into her pride and joy, Bubbe's Deli. She'd been alone and terrified by the intruder. He'd bizarrely insisted she make him a sandwich. She'd done it, and it was nothing short of a miracle that she hadn't sliced a finger off in the process. Her hands had been shaking as she'd pressed the knife through the bread, the pile of meat and cheese. She'd been confident that, ultimately, he would kill her, even if she didn't fit his usual pattern. But he hadn't. He'd taken money, from the cash register, from her purse, and the knife that she'd used. But then he'd run away, escaping from the FBI, US marshals and local police.

She'd been lucky. She knew that. Davison was believed to have already killed at least four times that the police knew of. And, if he stayed true to his pattern, he'd kill again soon. Both her brother, Oren, a marshal, and Bryce, a federal agent and brother of Oren's love, Madison, had told her that. She, of course, believed her brother, and Bryce had reason to know. He had been chasing Davison for months, following up on leads as far away as New York City.

"Why me?" she asked. It was the question that had been nagging her. "There are other restaurants, other people who know how to make a sandwich."

He didn't look up immediately. But seconds later, after hitting a few keys, he lifted his head and leaned back against the couch. "And you're not an older male in your fifties and sixties walking alone in the park," he said.

"Exactly." All the things she'd been thinking.

"I don't know why," he admitted.

"That's not terribly comforting."

"I'm sorry about that. If it's any consolation, I've been asking myself the same questions pretty much nonstop since it happened."

"Small consolation." She deliberately rolled her eyes.

He smiled at her reluctant acquiescence.

She had to ask her other question, the one she'd truly been afraid to ask. "Do you think he planned to kill me, but for whatever reason, it didn't happen?"

"Again, I don't know. But what I do know is that Davison is a dangerous man who has killed before. And what I can promise you is that I'm going to figure this out and I'm going to find him."

She really couldn't think about this anymore. It made her stomach hurt. "Your job would drive me wild," she said. "Chasing data, being chained to your laptop."

He reached both arms overhead. "I'm not chained."

"Well, not literally," she said. "But the effect is the same. I couldn't do what you do. I need people. Interaction. Conversation."

She got all that and more running Bubbe's. As the only Jewish deli in the small city of Grave Gulch, Michigan, she had a natural niche. But it was the quality of the food, the product choices and the customer service that had made them a hot spot for people wanting to dine in or take food to go.

She'd been nervous going back to the deli after her encounter with Davison. With good reason—he'd said he would return. Because of that, Bryce had promised Oren that he'd watch out for her and was evidently taking the promise seriously.

If she was at home and awake, Bryce was watching her. When she went to bed, he left, but the officers outside her door remained. He was back early mornings to follow her to work. He left her there, along with a rotating set of Grave Gulch police officers charged with watching the front and back doors of the deli. When she closed up at night, Bryce was back, to ensure she got home safely.

All that, plus Bryce had tapped into Bubbe's security system, and he could check it in real time on his computer or phone. It was likely not state-of-the-art enough compared to what he'd seen, but it had been plenty sufficient for her. Of course, that had been pre–Len Davison. A camera provided a view of everyone who came in the front door, and a second one covered the cash register. She had no doubt that Bryce was checking both regularly during the business day.

All of that resulted in her having deeply conflicting feelings. Gratitude for the commitment to her safety. Annoyance with the invasion of her privacy. Although, in fairness to him, he was not intrusive. He even brought his own thermos of coffee to drink so that he didn't consume hers. He was polite, quiet and earnest about his work. A regular Boy Scout.

A very sexy Boy Scout, with his short dark hair, alluring eyes and slim but muscular physique.

"When do you sleep?" she asked, throwing off the blanket. She felt suddenly warm.

"At night," he said, checking his phone.

"I hear you on the phone. You're meeting people after you leave here. Following up with others about Davison."

"The man has to be stopped. And you work a lot, too. You go in early mornings and don't leave until the place closes up at nine."

"It's my business. That's what people who own businesses do." It had only been in the last six months that she had managed to create a schedule that included one day off each week. Fortunately, she had her office upstairs, so during the slow times of the day, like midafternoon, she was able to go there, put her head on her desk and take a little nap. And now, thanks to a delivery just this week, which had been tricky because of the stairs, she had a beautiful new couch. She'd actually be able to put her feet up. It made her small office an even tighter fit, but she was sure it was a good purchase. Bubbe's really was her second home.

"Well, being an FBI agent is a lot like running your own business. You get a caseload and you're expected to work it until it's resolved. I'm not paid by the hour."

"Nobody judging harshly when a criminal remains on the loose?" she asked. This man was driven. Perhaps it was his boss putting pressure on him.

"The only person that any of us are judging harshly is Len Davison. He's a bad guy."

Davison's behavior did seem to defy logic.

What kind of criminal ate a corned beef sandwich and then promised he'd be back for a pastrami? Especially when he had to know he was a hunted man.

She yawned. "I think I'll…" She stopped. Bryce had picked up his cell phone to look at a text message, and he'd lost all the color in his face. "What?" she asked.

He was moving fast. Shoving his laptop aside, standing, attaching his phone to his belt. She saw the quick reach, to check the gun in the pocket holster that he was never without. Most people never saw it because he wore a suit jacket or sports coat over it. She'd gotten used to it this last week.

He was going somewhere where he wanted to be armed.

And he didn't seem inclined to tell her where. Instead, he practically ran to the back door and had a few words with the officer there before heading to the front door to do the same. Finally, he turned to her. "I have to go. Len Davison has been seen in Grave Gulch Park."

"The same place where he's killed before?" she whispered.

"Yeah. He's either getting braver or stupider. I don't care which, as long as we get him. Both officers know that I'm leaving. You'll be fine."

Yes, but would *he* be? In a short time, she'd gotten very used to having him around. Bryce was too serious, too quiet. But also oddly funny sometimes, as if he was holding back a good sense of humor. Perhaps he thought it was undignified for an FBI agent. "Be careful," she said.

"I will be," he promised. "He's not getting away again."

BRYCE COULD ALMOST feel the heat of his blood running through his veins. They had expected Davison to strike again. He was due. The man had been killing every three months. Generally, the first hint of his horribleness was a dead body. But now, likely due to the dozens of watchful eyes around Grave Gulch, they had a chance to prevent a death and capture a madman.

Who for some strange reason had left Olivia unharmed, after demanding that she fix him a late-night snack. Olivia had sensed the man's depravity and had feared for her life. Her gut had been spot-on.

Bryce had jumped at the chance to watch over Olivia Margulies. She was a concrete link to Davison, inasmuch as the killer had promised to come back for another sandwich. Bryce had promised her brother that he'd keep her safe. Oren had taken him at his word, likely because the two men respected each other, and now they had a family connection, too. Oren was engaged to Bryce's older sister, Madison.

It wasn't a hardship assignment, by any means. Olivia Margulies was gorgeous, with her long dark hair and her blue eyes. And he had appreciated both the grit and determination she had demonstrated in the aftermath of Davison's visit as police had descended upon Bubbe's Deli. She'd told her story clearly, concisely, and by the end of the night, she had recouped enough of her confidence that she was offering coffee and honey cake to the police.

It was interesting how something that had started out as a task—watch out for Olivia—had become more. He found himself waking early, looking forward to seeing her first thing in the morning when he escorted her to work. Then throughout the day, when it seemed as if the monthslong search for Davison might finally pull him under, the thought of seeing her that night had been enough to keep him focused.

She talked a lot. He was getting used to that. And she was eternally optimistic about all things, a real glass-half-full kind of person. Yes, she was too trusting. He'd found her car unlocked outside Bubbe's, and she'd not been as concerned as he'd thought appropriate. But after working for years in law enforcement, with an intense focus on criminals, it was nice to spend time with somebody who saw the good in others.

She'd gotten lucky with Davison. And it bothered Bryce that he didn't understand why. He liked data. Liked that criminals were predictable when there was good data available. The capricious nature of the event at Olivia's deli grated on Bryce's nerves. Just when he thought he was close to knowing everything there was to know about Len Davison, he'd gone and done something so out of character. It was maddening.

Maybe he was going to have a chance to ask him about it tonight. When the man was in a jail cell. That thought had him racing his vehicle down the street.

He got to the park, parked and found two officers of the Grave Gulch Police Department. He flashed an ID. "Bryce Colton, FBI. What do we know?"

The older man spoke up. "I'm Officer Fuentes and this is Officer Howser. Tell him," Fuentes instructed the very young man standing next to him.

Howser wiped a hand down the leg of his trouser. He was nervous. "Davison was seen near the fairy statue. The woman who recognized him said that he looked right at her, smiled and said, in a singsong manner, 'They can't find me.'"

"A singsong manner?" Bryce repeated.

The young officer sang it back. "'They can't find me.'"

Bryce held up a hand. "I got it. Where is he?"

"We don't know," Fuentes said. "He took off. We're searching the entire park."

Damn. He'd been within their grasp, and he'd managed to slip away once again. He was going to kill again. But first he was going to play with them a little bit. Agitated by Davison's boldness, Bryce started pacing, at first staying on the paths and then straying off into the short grass. It was a cold night. He could see his breath.

But fire raged through him, keeping him warm.

There were too many things in his life that were out of his control. Just last month, his father, the man he'd thought dead for more than twenty-five years, had been discovered alive and well. That news had been startling and had left Bryce more shaken than he was likely to admit or show.

It wasn't as if the man hadn't offered up an explanation. He'd been in witness protection. He said he'd done it to save his family—Bryce and his two sisters, Madison and Jillian. And their mother, Verity Colton—the woman who was never legally his wife but had borne three of his children.

The authorities, including Oren Margulies, who had been his father's handler, had confirmed the story. All should be forgiven and forgotten, right?

It just didn't work that way. The threat had significantly diminished twenty years ago when the man who'd issued the threat, a notorious gunrunner, had died in prison. But Richard Foster hadn't come back. And likely would have stayed away if Bryce's sister Madison hadn't stumbled upon him. The result of said stumble had thrown Madison and Oren together, which was a good thing. His sister was happy, and Oren would make a fine brother-in-law when the two of them married.

But the jury, as far as Bryce was concerned, was still out on his father. Others in the family were welcoming him, if not with open arms, at least with an olive branch. Bryce couldn't do that. Maybe it was because he'd been the man of the house long before he was ready. Maybe it was because Richard Foster had already brought trouble back into their lives. His reappearance had led the gunrunner's son, looking for vengeance for his father, to Madison. If not for Oren's efforts, she might have been killed.

So, no olive branch. Maybe a rose thorn. Maybe a—

He heard footsteps. Turned. It was a man walking, listening to something on his phone. Bryce could see the white earbuds. He had a leash in one hand and a German shepherd at the end of it. He was midfifties.

The target age. Walking alone in a dark park. Not paying attention.

Bryce got close and ripped on the cord, dislodging the earbud. "Hey," the man said, putting up a hand to push him away.

Bryce flashed a badge. "FBI. What the hell are you doing, buddy? You don't watch the news? Men just like you have been killed in this park. If you think your dog is going to save you, you're wrong. Canines, even the kind you're walking, aren't any protection against a bullet."

He was being harsh, almost nasty. But the next time he saw this man, he didn't want it to be on a morgue slab. He should apologize. "Listen, I'm—"

Someone was running up to him. It was Howser. "We have picked up a scent," the officer said.

"Let's go," Bryce said. He gave the man with the earbuds one more quick look. "I'm sorry. Just go home. Please. Be safe."

Then he started running. A half mile later, they were off the trail, in an isolated area of the big park. Dread was almost choking Bryce. They were going to find another dead body. Len Davison had been here, he'd found his prey and he'd killed.

And now he was likely laughing at them.

They came over the small hill, and Bryce stopped short. The K-9 officer, who was less than thirty feet ahead of him, was on full alert. His tracker and Bryce trained their flashlights on the spot.

There was no body. No blood.

Just a knife. A large butcher knife. Its end stuck into the ground. He got closer. The blade was pinning a note to the ground.

And even before he read the note, he knew. Knew that the knife was the one that had been taken from Bubbe's Deli. Knew that the note was from Davison, about Olivia.

Knew that he'd fallen for Davison's trick. And that he'd left Olivia alone to face the murderous bastard.

The message was brief. *Thanks for the head start.* No signature. Just a crudely drawn smiley face.

"Olivia," he whispered, knowing it might already be too late.

Chapter Two

She was upstairs, in her bedroom, brushing her hair, when she heard a noise. Firecracker? Not this time of year. Car backfiring? Maybe. But did cars really do that anymore, or was that a fictional contrivance?

Gunshot? It took her just seconds to get to that option, even though in her quiet residential neighborhood, that would be practically unheard-of. Perhaps she made the leap because she'd been thinking about Len Davison too much lately, and a gun was his weapon of choice.

You're fine, she told herself as she carefully put down the brush. She had armed guards at both her front and back doors. Officers who were alert and anticipating danger. They wouldn't get caught unaware by Davison. They knew that Bryce was away. He'd checked with both of them prior to going.

Still. She reached for the light and shut it off. Then, in the dark bedroom that she knew like the back of her hand, she walked to the window and carefully turned the wand on the wooden blinds, just enough that she could see out.

Her street was quiet. Somewhere down the block, a dog barked. Farther away, ever so faintly, she could hear the sound of trucks on the highway, using the cover of night to go fast.

She was at the wrong angle to see the agent outside her front door, with no view whatsoever of the one at the back. She left the window, walked across the room and opened her bedroom door. Standing there, in the dark upstairs hallway, she listened. She heard nothing unusual.

She was being ridiculous. And weak. If it had been someone else, she'd have shaken them and said, "Stop letting Davison get in your head." The dog had stopped barking. See, there was nothing out there.

Her brother was a US marshal, for goodness' sake. A really brave guy. And they shared blood. A Margulies did not shrink in terror at a small noise. She walked downstairs, intent upon confronting her fears.

She turned the corner and walked into her pretty kitchen. And realized that sometimes the very worst fears could come true.

"Hello, Olivia. So nice to see you again."

She put her hand on the wall. She was not going to faint or swoon. She was going to fight with her hands, her feet, her teeth. "How did you get in here?"

Len Davison, who stood by the back door, waved a hand. "Child's play."

A wave of sadness passed through Olivia. The officers had to be dead. Brave men, like her brother, killed. Protecting her. Thank goodness Bryce was away. He, at least, would be safe. "What do you want?" she asked, hating that her voice quivered.

"I like you, Olivia. In truth, I've developed a little crush on you." He grinned, rather sheepishly, she thought. If not for the knowledge that he was a cold-blooded killer and the sight of the horrible-looking gun in his hands, she might have thought the older man with the white hair and the friendly brown eyes standing in her kitchen was sort of sweet.

A little crush. Just her luck. She thought about what Bryce had told her about Davison. Up until he'd started his killing spree, he'd been a mild-mannered accountant. Not a star employee but generally regarded as an average, solid guy. Those who knew him best felt some empathy toward him, because he'd lost his wife of some thirty years to cancer the previous year.

"You need to leave," she said, summoning up the voice she'd used with the few unruly customers at Bubbe's that she'd encountered over the years. Stern. Uncompromising. It had worked surprisingly well on most everyone.

But did not seem to impress Davison. "No, I don't," he said simply. "There's no one around to stop me. I've seen to that." He walked over to the kitchen window and pulled back a curtain. "See, nobody is coming to help you."

She couldn't see into the backyard, but she believed him. Fear skittered along her spine. She'd been lucky that first time at Bubbe's. He'd robbed her, but he'd left without harming her physically. She didn't think she'd be so lucky a second time.

"It's all going to be fine, Olivia. We are meant to be together. I have feelings for you. I want you with me, sharing my life. I have a bun—"

The dog that had quieted down the street started up in a frenzy. Davison's eyes changed, and fury crossed them.

"That's Bronco," she said. "He's just a puppy. A labradoodle. A real cutie," she added. "Can't get enough of squirrels." She was rambling. But she was scared. Scared that he'd get spooked and kill her. "I came downstairs to get a snack. I've got a pound of pastrami, some fresh-baked rye and excellent sour pickles, if you're interested in joining me."

He drew back. Perhaps he was remembering his first sandwich at Bubbe's. Or perhaps a wife of many years offering to make him a sandwich after a long day's work at the office.

She walked over to the refrigerator, turning her back on him. If he was going to shoot her, she'd rather not see it anyway, she thought to herself. She opened the door, pulled out the items she'd just listed and set them on the counter.

"You do make a lovely sandwich," he said.

She focused on breathing. Where the heck was Bryce? Had Davison simply lured him away, or had he done something more sinister? Had he killed Bryce?

The thought of that weighed heavy on her as she finished layering the meat and the pickles and smearing some whole-grain mustard on the bread. This time her hands were not shaking, but her heart was racing in her chest. Summoning up a smile, she turned and extended the sandwich to him.

He took it and carried it to the table. Pulled out a chair and sat. He put his gun down on the right side of his plate. Picked up his meal with his left hand. He took a bite. "As excellent as you promised," he said.

"Thank you." She'd bought herself some time. Now she just had to figure out a way to either get out of the house or get the gun away from him. She could—

The distant blare of police sirens had Davison's head

jerking up from his plate. The fury was back. "As good as this is," he said, pushing back his chair, "it's for another time. I promise you that, sweet Olivia." He picked up his gun and headed for the back door.

BRYCE HAD CALLED 911 from the park, and when he got to Olivia's house, he saw that they'd already arrived. A female GGPD officer assisted the man who'd been guarding Olivia's front door, who was lying on the ground. He had blood oozing from a head wound.

"Olivia?" Bryce asked.

The officer shook her head. "I haven't been inside."

Bryce bounded up the fronts steps and opened the door. The living room was dimly lit, light spilling in from the kitchen. He heard nothing. He entered quietly and quickly. Heard the scrape of a chair, raised his gun and checked himself when he rounded the corner and saw her sitting at the table. A second female officer stood at the stove, heating the teapot.

Olivia stood up. "Bryce," she said.

She looked healthy. Whole. He grabbed both her arms and held her steady. "You're not hurt? He didn't hurt you?"

"No. Get him," she said. "He went out the back door."

He saw the sandwich on the table, and it sickened him to think that Olivia had once again been made to wait on Davison, to serve him. The murderer was not getting away. What kind of brazenness had made him think that he could waltz in and terrorize Olivia in her own home? Likely the kind gained from successfully eluding law enforcement for months. The kind that came from being a step ahead all the time.

It needed to end. Tonight.

Outside the back door, he saw the officer who had been guarding that door. He was sitting up, being assisted by a paramedic. The cop raised a hand. "That way." He pointed.

Bryce ran through the backyard, got to the street and stopped short. He had no idea which direction Davison had gone. But then he heard gunshots. Two. Several blocks away, to the right. He started sprinting.

When he got there, he saw a man he didn't recognize on the ground, looking shaken. "What happened?" he yelled.

A police officer stepped forward. "We saw Davison and attempted to apprehend him. Mr. McKinley here, out for an evening walk, was in the wrong place at the wrong time. Davison grabbed him as a human shield while firing at us. We had to take cover. His vehicle must have been parked behind that garage," he said, pointing. "He pushed McKinley away and got in his vehicle before we could apprehend him. We got a partial plate and know it's a dark sedan. We've radioed it in. Everybody will be looking for him."

Bryce wanted to join the search. Wanted to be the one to stop Davison, the one to cuff him, read him his rights and then throw him in a cell. But the knowledge that Davison had so easily created a diversion earlier and then focused his attention on Olivia had him running back to her small house.

She was still in the kitchen. Still sitting at the table. The tea had been made, and a steaming cup sat in front of her. Her head jerked up, and her eyes met his. He understood the unasked question—had they gotten Davison?

He shook his head.

Olivia stared at her cup again, her shoulders slumped. It seemed as if the life had gone out of her. It bothered him. She was funny and vivacious and so full of natural joy that it shook him to see her this way.

The female officer who stood at the sink, looking out into the dark backyard, turned her head. "You got this?" she asked. "I'd like to check on the man who was guarding the back door. He used to be my partner."

"Go," Bryce said. He wanted a minute alone with Olivia before more from the Grave Gulch Police Department descended upon the house to process the scene.

"How are the officers?" Olivia asked.

He'd checked on his way in. "They're both going to be okay. The guy in the front got knocked in the head. He'd got a cut and will be monitored for signs of concussion, but it looks fine right now. The officer at your back door was shot in the leg. He lost blood pretty quickly and passed out. But he's conscious now and coherent. He was the one who pointed out to me where Davison had gone."

"I'm so grateful they're going to be okay. I'd have felt terrible if they'd have been…" She stopped. "*Killed* is the right word, isn't it?" she asked, sounding so distressed. "People, good people, could get killed because of me."

"No," he said sharply. "Because of Davison."

"Who got away."

"For now. But he's in a vehicle, and every law enforcement officer and agency will be looking for him even harder now."

He heard the front door open and quickly shut. Seconds later, Olivia's brother stepped into the kitchen.

Worry. Pain. Fear. It was all there on Oren Margulies's face. He let out a visible sigh when he saw Olivia.

He hugged her tightly. Looked over her shoulder and made eye contact with Bryce. A clear message was there. *This guy cannot keep doing this to my sister.*

"How did you know?" she asked.

"I know everything," he said, teasing her. Bryce suspected that Interim Chief Brett Shea had called him. "I got an update on the way over that told me you were okay, but I really needed to see it myself."

"I'm fine," she said. "I'll be even better once they've caught Davison."

Oren pulled back. "It's not looking good. They've lost him. He can't have just disappeared, so there's some hope yet."

Bryce knew that Davison was remarkably skillful at slipping out of sight.

"What happened?" Oren asked.

Bryce filled him in on the sighting in the park. The futile search. Finding the knife and the note. "Once I realized that we'd been had, I called 911 and came back as quickly as I could."

"I can probably fill in the rest," Olivia said. "I was upstairs and heard a noise. I came downstairs and found him in the kitchen, by the back door. He…" She stopped, looking embarrassed.

"Did he touch you?" Bryce asked, filled with a sudden and intense rage. She'd told him no earlier, but he had to ask again.

She shook her head. "He told me that he has a crush on me."

The words seemed to hang in the air. The two men

looked at one another, each clearly uncomfortable with Davison's admission.

"He said that he wanted me to go away with him. That he had a bun…" Her voice trailed off. "He stopped midsentence. Maybe midword, because there was a barking dog. I finished making him his sandwich, and he started to eat it. But when he heard the approaching sirens, he bolted. He said that he'd be back." She paused. "What do you think he meant by 'bun'?"

Bryce ran to get his computer in the living room. "I'm going to do a search for words that start with 'bun.'"

A list popped up, and Oren looked over his shoulder at the screen. "Bunker," Bryce exclaimed, pounding a fist on the table. "Could it have been 'bunker,' Olivia?"

"Yes. But I don't know for sure."

"It's something. More than we had before. Bunker. The bastard is hiding underground." Bryce leaned forward, reached for her hand. Her skin was warm. So alive. "We're going to get him, Olivia. We will."

Oren cleared his throat. He was staring at their linked hands. Bryce pulled back. He understood brothers. After all, he had two sisters. And he didn't want Oren or Olivia herself getting the wrong idea. He was just thankful that Olivia hadn't been hurt. The same way he'd be thankful that any person hadn't been hurt.

Liar.

He ignored the voice in his head. It was easy enough to do when he could hear conversation from outside wafting in. Officers were gathering.

Oren likely heard it, too. "I'm supposed to be delivering someone into witness protection tomorrow. But I can call my boss. Explain the situation. They can find someone else. I'm staying here with you."

"Absolutely not," she said.

"My choice."

"I get a vote, bro."

The two of them would be wrestling on the floor before long. "There's no need for you to change your plans, Oren," Bryce said. "By Davison's own admission, he's fixated on Olivia. As her brother, you're perhaps too close to her. You're an obvious obstacle. That makes you a target."

"I'm a marshal. I can take care of myself."

"I'm not questioning that, but still, it diverts resources that could be solely focused on protecting Olivia. To that end, I'm moving in. I'm going to be with your sister 24/7."

"What?" Brother and sister spoke at the same time.

"We have to take Davison at his word. He told Olivia once before that he'd be back, and sure enough, he showed up. He said it again tonight. So we wait. We watch. We stay ready."

"I don't know," Oren said.

"I think that's my decision," Olivia blurted.

Bryce understood. His sisters respected him and listened to him but were very capable of making their own decisions, thank you very much.

"Of course what you want matters," Oren said.

Again, a wrestling match was not out of the question. "There's a spare room here," Bryce said. "I'll take it." He wanted to make his intentions clear. "I will try my best not to get in the way."

"Olivia?" Oren asked, looking at his sister.

"I…uh… Are we sure that's necessary?"

He could make it happen one way or another, but it was always better when the solution wasn't shoved down someone's throat. "I'm sure. And, hey, we're practically family," he reminded them. He was still a bit shocked at how quickly Madison had fallen for Oren, but if he could use it to his advantage now, he wasn't above that. Catching Davison was the priority.

"You're going to be bored at Bubbe's all day," Olivia said.

"Are you bored?" he asked.

"Of course not. But I'm working."

"I'll be working, too. I'll have my computer, my phone. And… I can help you, too."

"Do you have any restaurant experience?" she asked.

"My uncle Geoff owns the Grave Gulch Grill," he said. Everybody in town knew the rather expensive but lovely restaurant.

"Do *you* have any restaurant experience?" she repeated.

"No," he admitted.

She looked at Oren with a raised eyebrow.

"He could babysit Mrs. Drindle," her brother suggested.

Babysit. Mrs. Drindle. None of that sounded good. "Tell me more," he said, not wanting to immediately shut any doors.

"Mrs. Drindle is the third customer of the day," she said.

"The third customer of *every* day?" he asked.

"Yes. Since we opened."

"That's pretty exact," he said. "How does she manage that?"

"She's inventive," Olivia acknowledged. "And bold. Sometimes, a group of four, dining together, might be waiting when we open our doors. Mrs. Drindle has no compunction about asking them to separate as they enter so that she can maintain her standing as the third customer of every day."

He started to laugh but realized that Olivia was dead serious.

"And when you give her her coffee," she said, "every server at Bubbe's knows to make sure there are exactly three individual creamers on her table, in a row. No more, no fewer. She wants her check immediately upon receiving her food so that she can pay right away. That ensures that she'll be ready and prepared to leave after exactly—"

"Wait. Don't tell me. Thirty-three minutes."

"Unfortunately, Mrs. Drindle likes to take her time with lunch. So it's sixty-six minutes."

"So she's a pain. The customer from hell."

"No, she's lovely. A truly beautiful seventy-four-year-old woman who wears exquisite cashmere suits, heels and beautiful gold jewelry, as if she was on her way to a board meeting in New York City."

"But she's not," he said.

"She's retired from working at the library and lives alone, less than three blocks from Bubbe's. She's so sweet but so odd at the same time that everyone sort of fawns over her, in an effort to figure her out and to make her happy." She studied him. "If you entertained her, it would free up my staff to do other things."

He'd had worse assignments, he was pretty sure.

But now Olivia was shaking her head. "If she caught a glimpse of your gun, it would probably upset her."

She paused. "So, no restaurant experience, but do you like to cook?"

Not particularly. "I manage to feed myself. And occasionally others. I guess you could say that I have a limited repertoire. I don't venture outside my comfort zone very often."

"What's in your comfort zone?"

"Steaks. Burgers. Baked potatoes. Frozen French fries." He could tell that she wasn't much impressed. "Eggs, turkey sandwiches, fruit." He paused. "Okay, I basically eat the same thing over and over. But I work a lot. I don't have much time to cook. But I'm willing to learn. Don't be afraid to put me to work."

PUT ME TO *work*. Olivia was still thinking about that when she woke up the next morning. She hadn't slept well since her first encounter with Davison, and last night was no different. It had taken forever to actually get to bed. First, evidence, like the remains of the sandwich Davison had been eating, had needed to be gathered. She'd had to provide a written statement. Her brother and Bryce had stuck by her side through all of it. But in the end, Oren had left and Bryce had stayed.

She'd been emotionally spent. Had mumbled goodnight and gone to bed, only to toss and turn. No wonder she felt almost physically ill upon waking. But the deli didn't open itself. There was soup to make, bread to bake and desserts to create. Amid all that, she had to be a positive role model for her employees and a warm, welcoming host to her customers.

How long could she stay in bed before someone missed her?

When they came knocking, she'd have a note posted on the front door. *Be back soon.*

Her friends might go away but would Len Davison? Or would he make it his mission to track her down?

Truth be told, it would never work. Oren would go along with the plan. But it was hopeless to think that he wouldn't tell Madison Colton the truth. He'd fallen fast and hard for the lovely woman. Who happened to be Bryce's sister.

It all came down to Bryce. Again.

With that somewhat irrational, she admitted, thought firmly lodged in her temple, she forced herself to get out of bed. She opened the door, put one weary foot in front of the other and promptly collided with a hairy chest.

One so hard and muscular she practically bounced off.

"What?" she sputtered.

"Hey," Bryce said. "Careful."

Careful. She shouldn't have to be careful—she was in her own damn house. She meant to tell him so, but words failed her when she realized that he was naked with the exception of some very nice black knit boxer shorts.

"I didn't realize you were awake," he said. He had the good grace to look a bit self-conscious at being less than half-dressed.

She managed to make some kind of noise in response. The problem with meeting a naked somebody in your hallway who was six-two in their stocking feet when you were only five-six on a good day was that it put you at a definite disadvantage. His broad chest was right…there. And he smelled really good.

"Better get a move on," he said.

"I know what time the deli opens," she said peevishly. She had no experience with handling what was going on right now. Her limited sexual experiences had been of a certain duration that did not include morning meetings in the upstairs hallway. Dinner, drinks, sex and good night. All within the bounds of a single evening.

Maybe it was odd, but she'd never had a guy spend the night, and she'd never spent the night with a man. Her relationships had been…tidier than that. This was messy.

"Perhaps a schedule for the bathroom," she suggested. "Or a robe."

"Your house, your rules," he said. He stepped as far to the side as he could, motioning for her to pass. She did but couldn't resist one more look over her shoulder. His backside was every bit as nice.

A robe would be a damn shame, she thought a minute later as she eyed her reflection in the still partially steamed-up mirror. Shaking her head, she got into the shower.

Ten minutes later, she was back in her room, getting dressed. She pulled on a denim skirt, a gray-and-purple-checked long-sleeved button-down and some purple flats. She didn't take time to dry her hair. Instead, she wound it up in a bun and pinned it to the top of her head.

Makeup was a swipe of mascara and some lip gloss. Anything else would be a waste after a few hours of standing over steaming pots and in front of hot ovens.

She walked downstairs to find Bryce waiting for her in the kitchen. Fully dressed. More than fully dressed—he already had his winter jacket on and his keys in one hand. "Even though we're both leaving and coming back to the same place, I think we should continue to drive separately. Just in case I need to leave during the day. I'll follow you."

"Fine," she said, picking up her own keys. It appeared neither one of them was going to mention that *moment* in the hallway.

"As always, wait in your vehicle until I've checked in with the officer who watched the deli overnight. I'll signal to you when it's safe."

I know the drill, she wanted to say. But given the events of the night before, she kept her mouth shut. It was hard to blame him for being extra careful.

He waited for her to slip on her coat and sling her purse over her shoulder. Then they walked out through the door that led to the garage. She opened the big overhead door, and he continued on to his SUV, which was parked in the driveway. Both backed out, with her taking the lead as they drove to the deli.

Their actions were precise. Efficient.

A finely choreographed ballet.

Only if the ballerina felt as if the next pirouette was going to end in an epic face-plant. Because that was a bit how she felt right now. She was teetering. Her old life, pre–Len Davison, pre-Bryce, had ended less than a week ago. She'd liked that world. Following her graduation six years earlier from culinary school on the East Coast, she had relocated to Grave Gulch, a place that she'd loved to visit because it was the home of her own bubbe. She'd found the perfect spot, opened the deli, named it for the Yiddish name she'd called her grandmother and willingly poured her heart and soul into running it.

It was hard work, but in comparison to her new life, with Len Davison fixated on her and Bryce fixated on catching him, it was a cakewalk.

She wasn't exactly sure how she was going to be able to cope. But, as her bubbe used to say, the only way to get to the end was to go through the middle. She'd just have to do this, one day at a time. And keep her focus where it needed to be—on creating beautiful and delicious food and serving it in a way that delighted her customers.

She pulled into her parking place at the rear of the deli and saw the GGPD car. Bryce parked next to her and, within thirty seconds, had opened his door and was motioning her out. She did so, then unlocked the back door of the deli and stepped inside. There was just one light on, over the big butcher-block table. It was quiet.

Hernando, the chef who'd worked at Bubbe's for several years, sometimes beat her to work. When he did, he had his own key. The rule was that whoever arrived first relocked the door. Hernando walked to work, so there was never any vehicle in the lot to clue her in, but she always knew right away if he'd arrived—all the lights and the music, an '80s rock-and-roll station that she'd come to tolerate, would be blaring. He'd turn it down at first sight of her, but he wouldn't turn it off. Fair was fair, and she thought he'd likely grudgingly accept the country station she favored, on the days she beat him to work, but she never tested the hypothesis. Hernando was simply too important.

How he would react to Bryce being around all day was too difficult to predict.

"What happens between now and eleven o'clock, when you open?" Bryce asked.

"We bake and prepare the day's soups and specials. You might already know that the deli isn't kosher."

"I did. What's on the menu today?" he asked.

"Two soups—matzo ball and cream of broccoli. The specials are stuffed cabbage rolls and a vegetable quiche. There's also challah and rugelach to bake."

"What's rugelach?" he asked.

"Cookies," she said, pulling a clean apron out of the drawer. "Folded and crescent-shaped with different fillings, like chocolate and hazelnuts. Delicious. We sell out almost every day."

"You have one of those for me?" he asked, pointing at the apron.

"You're serious? You're actually going to work?" When he'd said it the night before, she hadn't really thought it would happen. "What about your own work?" she asked, motioning to his backpack.

"I'll get to it. For now, I'm at your disposal." He looked around, his eyes settling on a wooden block filled with knives. "I'm pretty good with a knife. I can hit center mass at thirty yards."

"That's going to be incredibly helpful," she said dryly. "I suppose I'm not likely to get the one back that Davison stole from Bubbe's and then left in the park last night, am I?"

He shook his head. "It's evidence."

"Well, then, I guess I'm grateful that he didn't take my food processor." She pulled bags of carrots and celery out of a big stainless-steel refrigerator. "If you want to help, you can start by cleaning vegetables for the soup and then putting them in the food processor."

He eyed the produce. "How much soup are you making?"

"Chef Hernando and I make ten gallons of each kind."

He looked shocked. "That's twenty gallons of soup."

She nodded. People who had never worked in the restaurant business were always surprised by the quantity of food. "Do the math. There's 128 ounces in a gallon. Each of our soup bowls holds ten ounces. That means that we get roughly thirteen cups to a gallon. So twenty gallons gets us 260 cups of soup."

"You sell that much every day?"

"Most days. Especially now that it's getting cold outside. At least half of our sales come from takeout, and soup is a very popular item. And—" she paused and glanced around as if someone might hear her "—the protesters have actually been very good for business. All that yelling and screaming makes them really hungry, to say nothing of the marching."

"We certainly don't want any of them wasting away," he said sarcastically. "Interim Chief Brett Shea has his hands full. Just like my cousin did before him."

Melissa Colton, the former chief of police, had had a good reputation. But things had soured for her when people in the town no longer felt safe from Davison, who'd been allowed to remain free to continue killing after evidence tampering and other crimes in her own department. "She has been in Bubbe's several times. I always liked her," Olivia said. "Which is good, I guess, since she's going to be a shirttail relative, given that my brother is engaged to Madison."

"Melissa is easy to like. It was unfortunate that she took some negative hits to her reputation that weren't entirely deserved. But she's happier now than she's ever been, so things work out. And Brett Shea will do a good job as interim. He'll probably have his hands full with protesters after news breaks about the Davison sighting in the park last night. People want him caught. Who can blame them?"

"I'm dreading seeing today's newspaper," she said. "I know that you and others were answering reporter questions last night. I do appreciate you keeping them away from me."

"You shouldn't have to deal with that. We tried to downplay his visit to your house, but two police officers were injured. There's no way that's not getting some coverage. We did, however, emphasize the sighting in the park. Hopefully, that's how the story will play out. If a reporter comes into Bubbe's today, there is no need to give them any comments. In fact, we'd advise against it."

A noise at the back door had Bryce instantly on guard. But then Hernando came around the corner. The chef gave Bryce a look that said *who the hell are you and what are you doing in my kitchen?*

"Hernando, this is Bryce Colton. He's an FBI agent." Hernando was the only one of the employees who knew the full story of what had happened almost a week earlier. "I had another interaction with Davison at my house last night, and my brother and others, well, they think it might be helpful to have Bryce spend some time here."

"Why can't you catch this guy?" Hernando asked, looking at Bryce. Since day one, he'd been protective of Olivia, saying that she reminded him very much of his own daughter, who lived in New York City. But she knew it was also likely the worst question that he could have asked Bryce, who was already so frustrated that Davison kept getting away.

"We're doing our best," Bryce said, his jaw tight.

"I think you need to do better." Hernando turned his gaze on Olivia. "You weren't hurt?"

"No. And I'm confident that Bryce and the rest of law enforcement are doing everything they can."

Hernando made a noise that might have been agreement or disgust. It was never easy to tell. He could be gruff and opinionated, but he was also an excellent chef and could step in for Olivia when she wasn't there. "Do what you need to do to keep her safe," he said, as he walked past Bryce. He turned on the radio, and Blondie blasted forth before he turned it down.

"I intend to," he said. He looked around. "Is there coffee?" His tone was rather pleading.

Olivia bit back a smile. She appreciated his restraint and effort to be pleasant to Hernando. Perhaps it was a skill he'd acquired while working at the FBI. "Coffee might be a good idea. Making a pot is usually my first task. I'll get it."

He practically sighed in relief. Then, without complaint, he picked up the peeler that she'd placed next to the carrots and started cleaning them. Ten minutes later, when she brought him his first cup, he'd already made a dent in the task. He stopped to pull some cash from his pocket.

"Oh, no," she said. "None of my employees pay for food or drinks."

"I'm not an employee," he said.

"No. You're free labor. You definitely should not have to pay." It dawned on her that it was going to be nice to have an extra pair of hands in the kitchen. Even though they arrived three hours in advance of when they opened at eleven, it was all they could do to be ready.

While Bryce cleaned vegetables, she put a big pot of water on the stove and turned the heat on high. Five minutes later, chickens were cooking. It would take them an hour or so, and then they'd have to cool a bit so that the meat could be plucked from the bones.

While she was doing this, Hernando was mixing up the dough for the many loaves of challah. First, he mixed some honey into a bowl of warm water. Then he added yeast. He set that aside and moved on to making macaroons. Customers loved the cookies, and why not—they were a lovely combination of eggs, sugar and coconut, with a bit of orange peel added for extra flavor. At the end, they'd be drizzled in dark chocolate.

Once he got the first batch in the oven, it'd be time to return to bread making. He'd need to add olive oil and egg and then, very carefully, cups of flour, one at a time, making sure the dough was tacky but not wet.

Then a bit of kneading on a floured surface, and the dough would be set aside to rise for ninety minutes. Then punched down and cut into smaller pieces that would ultimately be rolled in the traditional under-two, over-one braid.

Bryce, who was watching the early stages of Hernando's work, looked across the butcher-block table at Olivia. "I love bread."

"What's not to love about it?" she asked. "What's very cool is that, this afternoon, Hernando will take his very basic bread recipe and add chocolate and some cranberries and turn out some challah rolls that he'll dust with citrus sugar, and customers will literally line up for the chance to take them home."

"So his job is to do the baking?"

"Yes. And to precut all the meats and cheeses that we'll need for sandwiches. Plus get things like tomatoes and lettuce and pickles ready for quick assembly. He'll fit that in during the middle of his baking." She was fond of telling people that the secret to their success at Bubbe's Deli was the ability to multitask. Literally, both she and Hernando would be working on multiple things every minute. "While he's doing that, I make the soups, the salads and the daily specials. Speaking of that, I better get started on those cabbage rolls."

"I've always heard that the restaurant business is hard work," Bryce said. "But getting to see it up close convinces me it is."

"Here's how someone who had been in the business for years described it. Hardest they'd ever worked. Least money they'd ever made. And most fun they'd ever had."

"Paints an interesting picture," Bryce said.

"Indeed. And trust me on this—I'm not running a nonprofit here. I make enough money to pay my bills, pay my employees fairly and still have a little left over at the end of the month. More important, I have a community of customers here that I quite frankly wouldn't want to live without. I wouldn't mind, however, the occasional vacation," she added lightheartedly.

All the while, she was sautéing ground beef in a pan with onions and spices. It would be the basis of the filling for the stuffed cabbage rolls. She put the lid on and walked over to the coffeepot and refilled both her and Bryce's cups. "I'm not a breakfast eater, but if you want to make yourself something, there's eggs and meat in the cooler."

"I'll get myself some eggs."

By the time he'd made and eaten his eggs and toast, she'd finished getting the cabbage rolls ready for the oven. A half hour later, her chicken was ready to pull from the bone. Once that was done, she'd finish making the matzo ball soup and start making the cream of broccoli, which was a customer favorite.

"I think I heard somewhere that you'd been to culinary school," he said casually.

She gave him a side look. "Did you hear it, or did you do a background check on me?"

"You're in protective custody, not suspected of a crime."

It did not escape her that he hadn't answered the question. "I did. Loved it. Mostly."

"And did you think it was going to lead you here, or were you expecting it to take you... I don't know... somewhere fancy? A Michelin-star restaurant?"

"You think Bubbe's isn't fancy?" she asked, acting so very shocked.

"I'm sorry," he said quickly. "Of course it's fancy. I mean, not fancy, but really, really nice."

She laughed until her side started to hurt. "Oh my God. Your face," she said. *"Of course it's fancy."*

"Hernando is giving us a look," he hissed.

He was, indeed. Didn't have a tremendous amount of patience for foolishness in the kitchen. "Perhaps he's hurt that you think so little of us."

"That's not what I said."

"I know," she said, letting him off the hook. "Listen, I love Grave Gulch. I have ever since I visited my grandparents when I was young. And when I looked at what type of restaurant might be successful here, I wasn't terribly confident that another high-end spot was what was needed. I'm comfortable with my choice. And every day I use my training. Perhaps it's the white wine that I add to a cream sauce. Or the extra butter to a marinade. Or the fresh herbs and the citrus that will go in tomorrow's meat loaf. I like to think that I take food from my heritage and make it special."

"That's pretty cool," he said. "Not fancy, mind you," he added, showing his sense of humor.

"Right."

"What's next for me?" Bryce asked.

She tossed him one of the heads of cabbage. "Chop this up in the food processor. I'll teach you how to make the best and fanciest coleslaw ever."

BRYCE SAT IN a booth, his laptop open, when the doors got unlocked at eleven. He'd been there in that spot for the better part of an hour, reviewing the online statements from officers who had responded to the sighting of Davison in the park. He was double-checking information that he'd already looked at late last night after Olivia had gone to bed. But he'd triple-check it if necessary. They were missing something. He could feel it.

Davison had offered them an important clue last night when he'd slipped up and said *bun*, which, in the context of the sentence, was likely *bunker*. It opened up all kinds of new possibilities.

A young couple walked in and sat in a booth. Then in came a woman, thin and tall and dressed better than most people at weddings or funerals. She was the third customer. And she had a pleasant look on her face until she saw him.

She looked rather alarmed.

He checked to make sure his gun was safely hidden by his sports coat. He'd removed it when working in the kitchen but had put the coat back on once more employees arrived at Bubbe's and he'd moved to start his own work.

He offered the woman a smile. She did not smile back.

Whatever. He focused on his computer but then got distracted because Olivia had come from the kitchen. He watched her walk through the dining area, a quick look here and there to make sure everything was just so. All the front-of-the-house staff had arrived within the last half hour and had been busy rolling silverware and setting place mats and condiments on tables. They'd ignored him, likely thinking that there was no way that Olivia didn't know that he was sitting in the booth, and if she was okay with it, they were okay with it.

Olivia walked past his booth. "So that's Mrs. Drindle," she said as she paused.

"Does she order the same thing every day?" he asked quietly.

"No. You would think she might, given her other odd behaviors. Always has a cup of soup but then adds a sandwich or a salad or even the daily special. She's got a good appetite, given how thin she is." She looked at his empty coffee cup. "Can I get you anything?"

"No. I'll move back to the kitchen now that you're

getting busy. I don't want to take up space needed for a paying guest."

"Just try to stay out of Hernando's way."

"I probably didn't need that warning. He's…not that friendly," Bryce said.

Olivia smiled. "You just need to get to know him. He's a sweetheart. He lost his wife to cancer about five years ago, and his daughter lives in New York. He's a talented chef. I think he appreciates the opportunity to work a lot, because it fills up time. I'd be lost without him."

He didn't think she'd be lost, but after watching Olivia and Hernando this morning, he understood their relationship a little better. They barely needed to communicate verbally, but still, things got done. There had been a lot of balls in the air at one time, and by some stroke of luck or kitchen genius, they'd managed to catch them all. Now the take-out and deli cases were piled high with sliced corned beef, roast beef, pastrami and other meats, as well as several types of cheeses. There were the salads he'd helped prepare and some gefilte fish that Olivia had said was popular. Both soups were hot, and the two daily specials, the cabbage rolls and the quiche, were sitting ready in the steam table. The pastry case was full of freshly baked items, including a delicious-looking rye bread.

He gathered up his computer and phone and went through the swinging door that separated the kitchen from the dining room. Earlier on a pass through the kitchen, he'd met the young Black man, Trace, who had arrived to help Hernando while Olivia was in the dining room. He was friendlier than Hernando, which wasn't saying much, and not overly interested in Hernando's quick explanation that Bryce was a friend of Olivia's. "Trace's mom, Sally, is a waitress here," Hernando had said.

"Good to meet you," Bryce had said.

Now he nodded to both Trace and Hernando and took a position against the far wall. He kept an eye on the back door and an ear open, listening carefully for any unusual sounds from the dining area. Plus, he had his computer open and at an angle where he could see the screen. The security cameras were picking up all the activity at the front door and the cash register.

Even so, every once in a while, he took a look through the small window in the swinging door that separated the dining area and kitchen. And his eyes always came back to Olivia. She was able to do it all. She greeted everyone who came in and thanked them as they left after paying. In between, she helped clear tables and answered the phone that seemed to ring non-stop with requests for to-go orders.

By the time the lunch rush was over, he was properly impressed. "Now what?" he asked when Olivia finally came back to the kitchen. The dining room had mostly emptied out and the phone had stopped ringing constantly.

"We have a couple hours of relative quiet from 2:00 to 5:00 p.m. Then it picks up again for dinner. Hernando will bake a few things to replenish the pastry case and make sure that the other cases are freshened up, as well. I just checked on the soups, and we're in good shape. This is the time when I usually make myself a cup of tea and some lunch and take it upstairs to eat. Then I tackle the never-ending paperwork. There

are invoices to pay, new orders for food and supplies
to place, and payroll checks to cut."

She was like the bunny that never quit on that television ad. "Lunch sounds good," he said. "What are
you having?"

"Maybe a turkey Reuben."

"I don't remember seeing that on the menu," he said.
He'd had time to study one while he was attempting
to keep out of everyone's way and watch for Davison.

She smiled. "On the menu are regular Reubens
with corned beef. Now, I love most everything about
a Reuben. Sauerkraut, yeah. Swiss cheese and Russian
dressing. Wonderful. A dab of whole-grain mustard.
Excellent touch. Grilled rye bread. Bring it on. Just
don't care for corned beef. Please don't tell anyone."

"You're leading a double life, secretly preferring
turkey?"

"Let's just say that there are some expectations for
a Jewish deli, and I try not to upset that very delicate
balance."

"I see. Well, I'd like to try your secret turkey Reuben, and I'm willing to sign a confidentiality statement."

She laughed. "I don't think that will be necessary."
She pulled the sandwich ingredients out of the refrigerator and heated a pan. Within five minutes, they both
had sandwiches and a side of fresh fruit. "Follow me,"
she said. "Just make sure that nobody sees your sandwich up close," she added in a whisper.

She was fun. He liked that. He followed as she led
him to the stairs behind the cash register. When they
got upstairs, she pointed to a chair. "You can have that
one. We'll use my desk as a table," she said, taking the

leather chair behind the desk. "I'm sorry it's kind of cramped. I literally just had that couch delivered earlier this week. It's been on back order for a month."

There really was barely enough room. But it was a pretty flowered couch, with light pink roses. Very feminine. "You don't plan on sleeping here," he said.

"Not at night. But sometimes," she said, sounding a bit embarrassed, "I get tired and really want a little nap. I've been using my yoga mat, but the floor is really hard."

He laughed. "It's a great idea. And I read something the other day that said we'd all be better off if we took an afternoon nap."

"Makes me feel like I'm eighty. But sometimes I don't sleep well. I'll spend several hours awake at night, and that catches up with me."

"Why don't you sleep soundly?"

"If my mind is trying to process something, I have a hard time shutting it down. So, if there's a problem at work or with my family, I lose sleep."

"I'd be up every night," he said. "You know, with my complicated family dynamics. Dead father back from the undead and all that."

"Your family will work it out," she said optimistically.

He was pretty sure she was wrong but didn't want to have the argument. "It's delicious," he said moments later. "But I'm not surprised. I was watching the reaction of your customers to the food. You could tell, people are happy with what you're serving."

"That's nice," she said.

"Yeah, I overheard—" He stopped and picked up

his cell phone, which was buzzing. He read the text. "I don't believe this," he said, pushing back his chair.

"What?"

"Len Davison was spotted at the protest downtown. He was standing in the crowd, posing as a protester. Carrying a sign that said Catch Davison Before He Kills Again."

"No," she said. "The nerve of this guy."

"Yeah. But a woman recognized him and started screaming. He took off, but not before giving her a big grin. That all got the crowd really worked up, and the police have their hands full right now keeping order."

"He's making less sense all the time," Olivia said.

"He is," Bryce agreed. "But the son of a bitch is getting cocky. He's going to make a mistake."

"You should go. Talk to people who saw him. Talk to the protester who interacted with him."

"No," he said. "Others can do that. We can't assume that all this isn't a ruse to somehow get you alone again."

She pushed her sandwich away. Yeah, the thought of that did sort of ruin one's appetite.

"I'm not leaving," he reassured her.

She sighed. "There are officers at the front and back doors of Bubbe's. At my home, too, when I'm there. You're with me 24/7. How long can this last? How long can this much manpower be devoted to me?" she asked.

"At this point, you're the key to us catching Len Davison. So I'd say quite a while."

"A means to an end," she said, sounding terribly unhappy.

"Listen," he said, feeling bad. The minute he'd said

the comment about resources, he knew it had come out wrong. "That's not—"

"What happens next?" she asked, sounding impatient.

"I want to talk to Davison's daughter, Tatiana. Davison slipped up last night when he told you that he had a bun. We believe he meant bunker. Maybe she knows something that can be helpful to us."

"Fine. If you're worried about leaving me alone, I'll go with you after we close tonight. I've met both her and Travis before. He's another one of your Colton cousins, right?"

"One of Uncle Frank's kids. Co-CEO of Colton Plastics."

"Well, I don't know either of them well but can't imagine that they both wouldn't be interested in ending this. The sooner this all gets resolved, the better for all of us, right? Normal life can be resumed."

That was what he wanted, right?

But, suddenly, normal seemed pretty…empty.

No more days at Bubbe's. No more nights at Olivia's. "Yeah, of course," he said.

Chapter Three

Tatiana Davison opened the door for Olivia and Bryce. Travis Colton stood behind her, holding their new baby girl, Hope, who'd been born about a month earlier.

"Congratulations on the baby," Olivia said after both had greeted her warmly. "I hope it's not too late to come."

"Thank you," Travis said. "And it's actually really good. This little one has her days and nights mixed up, and she's ready to party at this time. Other than that, she's perfect."

"Like her mother," Tatiana teased. "Come in, come in."

"Thank you for seeing us," Bryce said. "We promise not to take up too much time."

"I'm happy to do it," Tatiana said, leading them to the living room. She looked at Olivia. "Coffee? Tea?"

Both Olivia and Bryce shook their heads. Tatiana and Travis were sleep-deprived new parents. They did not need to be entertaining.

"At least have some chocolate," Tatiana said, picking up a huge box that was sitting on the end table.

Olivia smiled and took a piece. "I never turn down chocolate," she said.

Bryce also took a piece. "Thank you," he said.

Tatiana leaned forward in her chair and looked at Olivia. "When Bryce called to set up this meeting, he filled me in on the two encounters you've had with my father. I'm terribly sorry that he's terrorizing you. I don't know why he does what he does."

It dawned on Olivia that while it was difficult to be the object of affection for a serial killer, it must be truly horrible to be *related* to that person. "You're not responsible for what he does," she said.

Tatiana gave Travis a warm look. "Others tell me the same thing. But still. It's what drives me to do whatever I can to end this."

"In that vein, we want to revisit the issue of places where your father might hide," Bryce said. "On his most recent *visit* to Olivia's home, your father talked about wanting to go away with her. He said he has a crush on her."

"A crush," Tatiana repeated. "Oh, this is so embarrassing. My mother is probably flipping over in her grave. It's more bizarre all the time."

"I know," Bryce said. "Your dad also said that he was looking forward to taking her away to his bun."

"His bun?"

"Yes. He got interrupted and didn't finish. We believe the word might be *bunker*. A hole, if you will, underground, where he could safely be hidden."

"Well, that seems rather unbelievable," Tatiana said, "but no more unbelievable than anything else that I've heard or learned about my father in the last few months. As I mentioned months ago, my father's favorite part of the city park was where it meets the Grave Gulch Forest. He would often take me for walks there, usually with our dogs, sometimes to collect rocks. We'd go home with bags of these moss-covered stones so that I could show Mom what I'd collected." She paused, evidently thinking of happier times in her family, then gave them a sad smile. "But I believe the area has been searched extensively by the police already."

"It was," Bryce said.

"Knowing my father, if he had a bunker, it would be far off a trail. He was comfortable going off the beaten path—actually preferred it. Used to tell me that was where you found the most interesting things. He always carried a compass and used to like to make maps, rather roughly drawn, of course, of new areas that we'd explored."

"You wouldn't happen to have any of those old maps?" Olivia asked, thinking of some of the odd things her parents had saved from her childhood. Her second-grade report card. The program for her fourth-grade recital.

"Good question," Bryce said, giving her a quick look.

"Unfortunately, no," Tatiana said. "I wish I could tell you more."

"The forest is large and backs up against Lake Michigan eventually," Bryce mused, maybe thinking out loud. "A bitch to search. But with K-9 officers and a focus on looking for a bunker-type structure, we might get the break we need."

No one said anything. Olivia figured they were all afraid to burst Bryce's bubble. But she gave him credit. He'd been searching for Davison for months across the country. Somehow the cunning murderer had always slipped through. But Bryce hadn't given up. That was dedication to your work and something she could appreciate.

"Well, if you think of anything else," Bryce said, standing, "please call me."

Tatiana nodded. Travis walked ahead of them to get the door. "How's your mom doing, Bryce?" he asked. "With your dad's reappearance and all that."

"She's doing okay," Bryce said. "You know Verity. She can always see the good in a situation."

Travis looked at Olivia. "Have you met Verity Colton yet?"

"No. I mean, she's a customer of Bubbe's. I would recognize her, but we've not been formally introduced."

"You'll have to do that, Bryce," Travis said. "You'll like her," he added, turning back to Olivia. "She was always a favorite of all of her nieces and nephews. And I'll bet she's a great teacher. Those second graders don't know how lucky they are to have somebody like that."

From what Olivia recalled of Verity, Travis's comments made sense. She was always very polite and friendly when she was in the deli. She was also very attractive.

They said their goodbyes, and Olivia and Bryce got in his vehicle. They had driven together. Now he would take her by Bubbe's to pick up her car before they drove to her house. "That has to be nice, to hear such good things about your mom." She figured this was a safer topic than talking about Davison.

"Yeah, well, I would introduce you and all that, but my mom's kind of busy right now...dating my dad. Again."

His tone was bitingly sarcastic, something she'd not previously associated with him. Obviously, this was not a safer topic. But now that she'd opened the door, it only seemed to make sense to try to understand what was behind it.

"Words you never thought you were going to say?" she asked, keeping her tone light.

Bryce drove without looking at her. He didn't seem inclined to respond, so she also sat quietly and let the miles slide by.

"It's just too damn late," he finally said, some ten minutes later. "The time for dating has come and gone."

"Because?" she asked.

He took his eyes off the road just for a second. "Because he had a chance to come back. I have accepted that he initially had to go into witness protection twenty-five years ago. But when the man who was threatening him and our family died in prison, he chose to continue to stay away. He *chose*," he repeated.

"Has he admitted that was a mistake?" she asked. She thought that was true.

"What else can he say at this point? And then when he finally did come back into the picture, after my sister Madison accidentally encountered him while bridal shopping for the wedding that never happened, thank goodness, he brought terror back into our lives."

"Good news is that Madison didn't marry Alec. Otherwise, she and Oren would not have gotten together. Bad news is that there was a son who was determined to kill the man who'd put his dad in prison. What's the chances of that?"

"I don't know about probability. What I know is that my sister and your brother almost lost their lives due to the son's long-simmering rage."

That was true. But Oren had been Richard Foster's

handler. As such, when it became clear that Louis Amaltin's son, Darius, was hell-bent on avenging his father and that Madison was going to be collateral damage, Oren had protected her. And fallen in love with her. Proving that some good could come out of very bad things.

"If Richard Foster is not accountable for that," Bryce continued on, "he can certainly be held accountable for leaving my mother to deal with three kids on her own. What I don't understand is why my mother and my two sisters seem inclined to let it slide." His tone was hard, making it seem as if the accusation had been ripped from somewhere deep inside him.

She'd known that Bryce was the least receptive to his father's sudden reappearance but hadn't been prepared for this level of animosity. By now, they had reached the parking lot behind Bubbe's. She hated that he was so tortured by this new family dynamic. She stretched her arm out, putting her hand on his shoulder. "Bryce," she said softly.

He shuddered. Literally shook under her touch. The tough FBI agent was truly wrecked about the situation.

Her natural compassion for others had her unbuckling her seat belt and turning to him. She reached for him, to give him a hug.

His body was big and warm, and he smelled really good. This felt…right. And she held on, accepting that her impulsive nature might be working against her. Theirs was a relationship born of necessity. And now the only thing that seemed very necessary at all was never letting go.

Mistake. She was making a mistake, she knew. She dropped her arms and started to pull back. But he didn't let her go. Instead, with two fingers under her chin, he lifted her face. Then he slowly bent his head and kissed her.

And certainly she was no longer thinking about offering compassion.

He was a most excellent kisser. Intense. Sensual. Tasting faintly of the hazelnut chocolate that he'd had at Tatiana's. Offering promises of something more that would be...

Oh, so wrong.

This time when she pulled back, it was with so much force that she almost hit her head against the window in the process. She put a hand to her throat, feeling the intensity of her beating heart, the unsteadiness of her breath.

What the hell were they doing, making out like two teenagers in a dark vehicle?

"I'm sorry," he said immediately.

"Not your...fault," she stammered. No, indeed. She'd started it. And she did not shrink from accepting responsibility.

"I..." He stopped. "That won't happen again," he said instead.

He did not have to make it sound as if that would be easy. It needed to be hard. He was acting like it was equivalent to giving up cauliflower, when it should be like...giving up cupcakes. She felt wronged. Or robbed. Or some emotion that she couldn't quite pin down or name. She reached for the door handle.

"Wait," he said, kicking fully into FBI agent mode. "Let me check your vehicle first."

"I locked it," she said, knowing she sounded angry.

"Let me just check," he said, his voice calm.

That kind of control really got under her skin. But she managed a nod.

He got out and looked in and around her vehicle. Then gave the lot and the street a quick look. Only then did he motion for her to join him. She moved fast and was in her car in less than thirty seconds.

"I'll follow you and blink my lights once I've got confirmation from the officer at your house that it's safe," he said.

She didn't answer. Just shut her door. Then she started the vehicle and pulled out of the lot—too fast. She hit the ridge where the street and the lot didn't meet up exactly even and felt the bounce jar her back teeth.

She needed to get a grip. It wasn't his fault. She'd turned to him, touched him first, literally melted in his arms. And truth be told, she could have kissed him for a very long time. She looked down and realized that she was doing forty-three in a thirty-mile-an-hour zone.

She reduced the pressure on the gas pedal and forced herself to remember the steps involved in assembling cabbage rolls. Then she drove home at a sedate twenty-seven miles per hour. She slowed down as she neared her driveway. She could see a Grave Gulch police car parked on the street, knew that Bryce would be communicating with them. Once she saw Bryce's lights blink, she pushed the button for her garage door and pulled inside.

It was quiet and dark, and she was tempted to spend the night in her car. But knew Bryce would never allow that.

By the time she got inside, he was already there, having come through the front door. "Everything okay?" he asked.

"Great," she said. "I'm going to turn in right away. It was a long day."

"Olivia…" he said.

She held up a hand. Nope. Not right now. She was torn up inside. Something had fundamentally changed in their relationship, and picking at it, analyzing it, looking at the data components, was asking just too much of her. "Good night."

IT HAD BEEN a long day, Bryce thought fifteen minutes later, as he sat on Olivia's sofa in the dark. From reporting to work at Bubbe's, through a full day of operations, to the meeting with Tatiana and Travis.

He'd stepped over a line tonight. He was assigned to protect Olivia. It was his *job*. A job that he, quite frankly, normally excelled at. But there was nothing in the job description that covered what had happened in his SUV.

Perhaps he should reread the manual on the appropriate handling of explosives. Because that was how the situation had felt. It had been all fast heat and friction. She'd touched him, and boom, the fuse had been lit.

Burn, baby, burn.

She, fortunately, had had the common sense to pull away, to break contact. In retrospect, the immediate loss he'd felt had been almost comical—it had been all he could do to avoid begging. *Please, please, let me kiss you again.*

He didn't want to be one of *those agents*, the ones who got talked about in hushed tones over drinks in a dark bar. The ones without the discipline to keep their head on straight for the duration of an assignment and avoid getting sidetracked in some way.

It did not escape him that he could have been talking about Oren and Madison. But, fortunately, for a whole lot of reasons, the case hadn't been compromised and nobody's career had been trashed. That wasn't how it usually turned out in those kinds of situations.

He'd slipped tonight, and he could either dwell on the mistake or simply be determined to do better. And right now, doing better meant focusing on the case. Regardless of how much he'd enjoyed the feel of Olivia in his arms.

He reflected upon their conversation with Tatiana. He felt as if they'd gotten at least a little more information that might help them find Len Davison. He picked up his phone. Not knowing if Interim Chief Brett Shea would still be up, he texted the pertinent details about looking far off-trail, deep in the Grave Gulch Forest. His phone rang in response.

"It's something…" Brett started out.

"It could be something," Bryce agreed.

"I can take Ember to search, and we'll get another pair of K-9 officers, as well. The dogs can cover a lot of ground quickly."

Brett and his partner, Ember, a black Lab, had joined the Grave Gulch Police Department just months ago. He and Ember had been part of the Lansing Police Department, and the bigger-city experience had served him well. Bryce had heard that it had not taken long for him and Ember to build up a great reputation within the department. "That would be great," Bryce said.

"We'll start tomorrow," Brett promised. "How is Olivia handling all this?"

Like a champ. "Okay, I think," Bryce said. "Bubbe's

helps her stay focused. And it's not all bad for me. I learned how to make matzo ball soup today," he added.

Brett laughed. "Always good to have a fallback position if the FBI thing doesn't work out."

"Right." Guys like him and Brett were lifelong law enforcement types. "Thanks for your help."

"Don't thank us yet. We haven't found him."

"Even the effort is appreciated. Sometimes when somebody has successfully evaded capture for a while, it's easy for some to give up, to think it's never going to happen."

"The name Randall Bowe comes to mind," Brett said, his tone serious.

Forensic scientist Randall Bowe was in the wind after having deliberately mishandled evidence, allowing certain criminals to avoid prosecution. As bad as that was, he'd done something even worse, from Bryce's perspective. He'd attempted to pin it all on Jillian, Bryce's younger sister, whom he had supervised. "I'm confident that you haven't given up trying to find Bowe," Bryce said.

"And I've got a feeling that I'm safe in saying the same about you and Davison," Brett replied.

"I'm going to get Davison if it's the last thing I ever do."

Chapter Four

The next morning, neither one of them mentioned the kissing that had occurred the previous night. Bryce told himself that he was grateful that Olivia wasn't the type who needed to talk everything to death. There was no need for armchair quarterbacking. It had been a lapse in judgment.

But, in truth, he'd wanted to know if she'd lost more than a bit of sleep over it, too. He had to admit, he'd thought about her confession earlier that day that sometimes when she was stressed over something, it caused her to lose sleep. More than once, he'd shot up in bed, thinking he heard her bedroom door open or close, or a footstep in the hallway.

He'd told himself he was just being a careful agent. In truth, he was looking for confirmation that her boat had been rocked. Just a little.

He was evidently the only one who was seasick. Which was…unexpected. He'd kissed women before. Plenty of them. The numbers weren't important. He certainly didn't keep a scorecard. And sometimes, there'd been more with women he cared about. And when those relationships or flings had ended, usually because of his commitment to his job, there had been…

well, if not sadness, then at least moments of self-reflection where he'd acknowledged that this was the life he was choosing.

There had been no lost sleep. And no overwhelming desire for some shared soul baring. He'd simply moved on.

And that was what he needed to do now.

That was what he kept tellling himself as they got up, got dressed for work and drove to Bubbe's. Once there, he got busy. More vegetables needed to be sliced and diced, this time for a beef barley soup. Then he peeled twenty pounds of potatoes that would need to be boiled and mashed to go with what appeared to be a mountain of meat loaf that Olivia was mixing up. In between everything, a big delivery arrived midmorning, and he helped put the food away and break down the boxes afterward. After that, he retreated to the dining room with a cup of coffee and his computer, where he pored over maps of the Grave Gulch Forest.

When the door was unlocked at eleven, he watched, with some amusement, as Mrs. Drindle, the third customer, made her way through the door. She stared at him, and he offered up a little wave. She did not wave back.

She was wearing a suit and heels and pearls. Her dark hair had no gray, and he suspected that was due to a trip to the salon versus nature. It was difficult not to be very curious about her. But she didn't appear to be interested in striking up a conversation, so he returned his gaze to his computer.

Before he knew it, they were in the midst of lunch, and the phone was ringing off the hook. He gathered up his things and went to the kitchen, where Hernando and Trace were keeping up without even breaking a sweat.

Then it was time for him and Olivia to retreat to her office for lunch. He was grateful that there were a few servings of the meat loaf left. He had that, and she ate an egg salad sandwich with a cup of cream of asparagus soup. On a side plate, she had a macaroon for dessert.

"Busy day," he said.

"Yes. The daily specials are going so well in this colder weather. People really want something substantial to eat."

"It's really good," he said, pointing to his plate.

"It was really quite lovely to be able to mash up those potatoes without having to peel all of them. I'm going to be spoiled when this is all over," she said. "Which needs to be sooner than later."

"What?"

"I mean, Davison is due to kill again, right? Every three months is his deal. I just meant that he needs to be stopped soon."

"I talked to Brett Shea last night. He's going to take his dog, Ember, along with at least one other K-9 officer, and search the forest. Maybe they'll discover this wonderful bunker that Davison is hiding in."

"Can you imagine, hiding in a bunker? It sounds awful, the idea that he thought that I'd willingly go there with him!"

"Yet Tatiana is so solid, so good-hearted."

"Proof that nurture is greater than nature."

He put down his fork. "Lately I've been giving that a lot of thought. Really wondering, you know, how important it is." Oddly, he wanted to talk to her about some of the thoughts that had been running through his head since the return of his father. He hadn't wanted to talk with his sisters or his mother about it, but Olivia seemed…safe. And he was fast realizing that she was a good thinker. "I've always thought of myself as a pretty solid guy. The kind of guy that takes responsibility for himself and others. The kind of guy who can be trusted to do what's right even when it's not expedient or fun or satisfying. The kind of guy who could inspire others, could lead, even."

"I don't know you all that well," she said, "but you seem to be that kind of guy."

He shrugged. "You *don't* know me. And last night, I didn't demonstrate that I was that kind of guy."

"Because we kissed?" she asked.

He appreciated her bluntness. "I'm responsible for protecting you. I gave my word to your brother, too. It is my job." He paused. "And when it was convenient, I seemed to forget all that. And it dawned on me sometime during the night that maybe I'm not so different from my dad, who conveniently was able to forget that he left behind a family. The kind of guy who abandons responsibility."

"I think you're comparing apples and…liver pâté. Two very different things."

"Different, sure. But for years, I thought my dad had been killed in the war—a hero, if you will. Now I know differently. Just like all these years I've thought I was a stand-up kind of guy, but maybe I'm really not. His blood runs in my veins. I am his son."

"It's a very fresh situation. I mean, you've all had just weeks, really, to adjust to a new world. And while you're reeling from it, think about it from the perspectives of both your mother and father. They must feel as if the earth is no longer turning on its axis. Everything is different than it was before. A bit like Alice falling down the rabbit hole."

"I never read *Alice in Wonderland*," he said.

"But you know the general story."

"Enough to know that some bizarre stuff happens to Alice. Like maybe she ate some bad mushrooms," he added. He didn't want to talk about his dad. He really didn't. But...

"Everyone in your family will find a way to deal with their new world. And it will be different for each person. Some people accept change easier than others. Some people deal with ambivalence better than others. But your family will find a way out of this. You just have to have faith and cut each other a little slack."

Everything she said made sense. But he had to be honest. "I'm dreading, absolutely dreading, the holidays. I just don't know how I'm going to be able to *pretend* that it's all okay. That he missed twenty-five years of turkeys, but now that he's here for this one, all is forgiven." He stopped. Swallowed hard. "You know who carved all those turkeys? I did. I was just a kid and I took care of it. I took care of lots of things, for my sisters, for my mom. I had to because he wasn't there. So no, he doesn't get to waltz back into our lives like it was nothing."

"It's not hard to imagine that you were a good brother and a son that your mom could be proud of and rely upon. And that's all the more reason why you're going to have to find a way past this," she said. "If not for yourself, it's for Madison and for Jillian. For your mother. Because you are that kind of guy you described before. The kind who is going to put the needs of others first."

He wanted to be that guy. But he wasn't sure it was possible. None of that was Olivia's fault or worry, though. "Thank you," he said. "Your own life is in turmoil. You can't even live alone in your own house or go to work without an armed guard at your side, and yet here you are, setting that aside so that you can offer up what I'm sure is good advice."

She smiled, a bit sadly, likely because she realized that he hadn't said he was going to take the advice. "You know who the very best listeners are?"

He shook his head.

"Bartenders, probably. But waitresses are right up there. Especially waitresses in a place where you have regulars. Over the years, I've waited on enough customers that I've heard all kinds of stories, all kinds of heartache, all kinds of joy. You learn a lot by listening. And you hear a lot of mistakes. And almost always, those mistakes are made by people who are hanging on to their anger, hanging on to feelings that should be shaken out like a sandy beach towel, left to drift away in the wind." She reached across the desk and put her hand on top of his.

Kind. Comforting.

His rational mind saw it that way, but his body reacted as if his short-term memory was the supreme ruler. Hot sizzle and flaring heat. From a pat on the hand.

Pathetic. Maybe. But it didn't matter.

He stood up fast, sending his chair rolling back across the floor. It didn't have far to go before it bounced off the new couch. But nobody was paying attention to that.

Because he was already around the desk and pulling her into his arms.

She tasted of coconut. It was intoxicatingly sweet. And so at odds with the heat of her tongue, the wetness of her mouth, the feel of her breasts against his own chest as their bodies strained against one another.

It went from a low flame to a roaring fire in sixty seconds.

He put his hand under her shirt, felt the bare skin of her back, knew that this was what had really kept him up the night before. He wanted her. Badly.

"Olivia," he said, lifting his lips.

"Yes," she said. "Touch—"

Knock. Knock.

He froze. Someone was at her office door. He straightened up fast, vertebrae clicking into place. She was tugging her shirt down. Pulling at her ponytail, as if to assure herself that it was still intact.

"Yes," she said.

She sounded so normal. His lungs felt as if he'd run a ten K.

"There's a Brett Shea here to see Bryce," Hernando said. "Is he…available?"

The question had been asked as if the man had the ability to see through the closed door.

"Of course," Olivia said. "We'll be right down. Pour him a cup of coffee, please." She stopped. "Thank you, Hernando."

"No problem."

The steps on the stairs were audible. "He didn't have to sound so damn satisfied," Bryce said.

Olivia smiled. "He doesn't know what he interrupted."

"He's a man. He knows." Bryce picked up both of their dirty dishes. "I really don't know what to say. I go from apologizing for my lack of self-control to demonstrating that I really have none. It's like being on a roundabout with no exit ramp."

"I'm not sure I know exactly what you mean by that, but no apology needed. We kissed. A second time. People do things like that."

"Not agents and the person they're assigned to protect."

"Those are rules and protocols that I don't know about or, quite frankly, care about."

But he had to. "It's not that simple. It will not happen again. Will not. Cannot. Won't."

"Okay. I believe you," she said, opening the door. She walked down the steps ahead of him. They were three from the bottom when she turned and very quietly said, "But I don't think it's me that you're trying to convince."

He was saved from having to reply, because Brett was waiting. He'd brought a big topographical map of the city park and the forest with him. The deli was almost empty, and Bryce led him to the booth at the far back where they could spread the map across the table and talk privately.

The interim chief walked him through his thoughts on a search process. It was interesting but not enough of a distraction, however, to keep Bryce from revisiting the comment in his mind.

Whom was he trying to convince? Her? Himself?

What was he trying to prevent? A further lapse in

judgment? A more serious digression that could change the trajectory of his life?

Wow. That was a little dramatic.

"What?" Brett asked, looking up from the map. "Did you say something?"

Could have been *I'm an idiot.* "No. Go on," he said, pointing to the map.

When the discussion was finished, Brett looked around. "This was one of the first places I ate when I moved here. Somebody recommended it to me, and I quickly could see why. The food is always really good," he said.

"I'm gaining a real appreciation for the work involved in making that happen." He saw Olivia at the cash register, checking out a guest who'd picked up a to-go order. She was chatting and laughing, and when she pushed a lock of her silky hair behind her ear, his fingers literally itched to be touching her.

"And Olivia seems to have a real knack for connecting with her customers."

"She's pretty amazing," Bryce admitted. "It's the little things. She remembers whose mother was going in for surgery and whose daughter was making college visits, and she takes the time to ask about it. I think every one of her employees would defend her to their last breath."

"Yeah. I got that impression when I came in. You'd said to come in through the back, but when I did, I think I upset the chef."

"Hernando," Bryce said.

"Fortunately, he recognized me because of some of the recent press coverage. Otherwise, I might have needed to worry about the sharp knife in his hand."

"He's very protective of Olivia."

"It's tough to see people that we care for being under threat," Brett said. "When Annalise was…" He stopped, still evidently finding it difficult to talk about. "Let's just say that I quickly realized that there wasn't much that I wouldn't do to keep her safe. It got personal rather quickly."

Annalise Colton was Bryce's uncle Geoff's daughter, with his second wife, Aunt Leanne. She had almost been seriously harmed by some idiot who'd made a career out of catfishing women. Brett had saved her. And fallen in love with her. Was Brett trying to tell him something? The man's relationship with Annalise, as well as the numerous positive professional interactions the two of them had had, made Bryce confident that he could trust Brett. But he wasn't ready to confide in anyone. "I won't let my personal feelings interfere with me doing my job," Bryce said. That was all he was willing to offer at this point.

Brett nodded. "Yeah, that's what I told myself. But Annalise made that rather impossible."

"Yeah," Bryce said. "I get that."

The interim chief smiled and folded up his map. "I'll keep you up to date on the search. I'm feeling hopeful that we really are going to stop Davison before he kills again."

"Or before he gets to Olivia again," Bryce said.

"Something tells me you're not going to let that happen," Brett said. "I think she can sleep peacefully at night."

BRYCE THOUGHT OF that comment later that night. Brett had been right. Olivia had gone to bed shorty after nine, and given that he didn't hear any tossing and turning from the room next door, he assumed she was indeed sleeping peacefully.

He, on the other hand, was likely not to sleep at all. Len Davison weighed heavily on his mind, of course. His inability to appropriately channel his feelings for Olivia, not just once, but twice, was a thorn in his side. But what had him really agitated tonight was the call he'd gotten from his mother.

She wanted him to come to lunch on Sunday. That, in itself, wouldn't be unusual. Verity loved having people to her house, and she was always a congenial hostess. He liked going back home for family meals, especially liked the opportunity to catch up with his sisters, who both had busy lives.

But then his mother had dropped her bombshell. *Your dad will be here, too.*

A couple of responses had immediately come to mind. And given that he was too old for his mother to wash his mouth out with soap, he might have gotten away with it. But her feelings would have been hurt, and, in general, she'd have been disappointed in him that he couldn't find a better way to express himself than being vulgar.

He'd settled with *that's a bad idea.*

She hadn't argued or pleaded. She'd simply said that it was important to her that he come. It was a low blow, of course. She knew that he'd do just about anything for her and that he sure as hell wouldn't want to fail to do something that was *important* to her.

"I'm providing protection for someone," he'd said, calling upon the only excuse that might work.

"I know all about that," she had said. "I've talked to

Madison. Bring Olivia with you. I've seen her at Bubbe's Deli but have never been properly introduced. It's high time, given that Madison and Oren are together. Speaking of Oren, however, he won't be able to join us, unfortunately. He's still out of town."

It really wasn't fair that Oren had a good excuse. Bryce had ended the conversation without expressly promising that either he or Olivia would be in attendance at Sunday's lunch. He didn't want to go. Didn't want to sit across from Richard Foster and pretend that everything was okay. Pretend that he'd forgotten all about the fact that the man had stayed away for twenty-five years. Practically all of Bryce's life.

But if he didn't go, his mother would be upset, and his sisters would be all over him. All the women in his family would think he was…what? Selfish? Stubborn? Hateful? None of the descriptors were flattering. And he would be running a very real risk that they would be so hurt by his inability to accept Richard Foster back into their lives that their relationship would be forever changed. Damaged.

That he couldn't bear. He and Madison and Jillian had been each other's best friends growing up. Maybe it was because they didn't have the normal family structure, or maybe it was just that they really loved each other. He would not risk ruining that.

He could get through a meal. Part of his FBI training had involved the ability to withstand various forms of punishment, even torture. Sharing a pot roast could not be that bad.

Olivia would have to go. He couldn't leave her alone. And there would definitely be a benefit—he'd be less inclined to act like an idiot if she was there.

And she had such a charming demeanor that she'd no doubt add to the civility of the occasion. Yeah, she was going. He closed his eyes. Definitely going.

Chapter Five

"I don't think that's a good idea," Olivia said. They'd arrived at Bubbe's just fifteen minutes earlier. Hernando had not yet arrived, and the coffee was still brewing. She was barely awake, and without warning, Bryce had announced that they were going to his mother's house for lunch the next day.

"I have to go, and I can't leave you. I looked at the schedule you have posted on the wall, and you're off."

He was sneaky. "So I will be home. Can't an officer from the Grave Gulch PD be assigned, just for a few hours?" She was trying to be reasonable. Finally the coffee was done, and she poured cups for both of them.

"I promised your brother. He would want you to be with me. I'm just sorry that he can't join us. I imagine that would make the whole thing more comfortable for you."

"That part is fine. It's just—"

"My mother is a really nice person."

"I know she is. It's not that. It would just be…weird sharing a meal with your whole family."

"Not weird. They know that I'm providing protection for you. They're going to expect you to be with me."

"I suppose." She really didn't have a good argument. But she'd gone to bed last night thinking that Bryce was right, that the two of them needed to keep things on the straight and narrow. The focus had to be on catching Davison. Nothing could interfere with that.

She heard the back door open. "Just me," Hernando called out.

Still, Bryce checked immediately.

He really was being so diligent. And what he was asking wasn't an impossible task. Difficult, perhaps. But not impossible. "Fine," she said.

"Fine, you'll go?" he clarified.

"Yes. But I'm not going empty-handed, so please call your mother and ask her what I can bring."

"You don't have to take anything," he said.

She gave him a look that was meant to have him think twice about so cavalierly dismissing her request. He evidently understood, because he picked up his phone. "I'm calling her now," he said.

She did not listen to the conversation. Instead, she took her coffee and walked to the front of the deli. It should feel powerful—she had an FBI agent on the ropes. But, in truth, she felt a bit desperate. In the short time since Davison had first broken into Bubbe's Deli, her life had changed so much. She felt out of control.

"She's delighted we're coming," Bryce said, coming out to join her. He, too, carried his coffee. "And she says that she adores the chopped salad at Bubbe's, the one with the olives and cheese, so if you want to make that, it would be wonderful."

That, at least, did not add stress to her life. She could make that salad in her sleep. "I better get busy," she said. "The specials don't make themselves."

"What can I do?" Bryce asked.

"How do you feel about meat slicers?" she asked.

"Respectful," he said.

She smiled. The problem with Bryce was that he really was quite charming. "That's a good perspective." Yesterday, she'd liberally seasoned big chunks of roast beef and then baked them all afternoon. The meat had chilled in the refrigerator overnight. She could keep Bryce busy slicing it paper-thin for Italian beef sandwiches. Then he could cut up the onions and peppers that would go on top at the customer's request. "Follow me," she said.

And for the rest of the morning, she threw herself into the work, barely looking up from her tasks. In addition to the two soups—cream of mushroom and vegetable—she made chili for lunch. The temperature was dropping, and people were asking for it.

By the time customers started pouring in, she'd almost forgotten about lunch at Bryce's mother's house. Almost. And she was pretty confident that Bryce also didn't want to talk about it when they had lunch upstairs; he spent the entire time on his computer and his phone, following up with others who were literally on the ground in the park, searching for Davison.

"Are they having any luck?" she asked finally.

"There are hundreds of acres to search. They're focused on some of the more remote areas, which slows the process. But no one is giving up," he added, as if he thought she might be thinking of that.

Hardly. With Davison expected to kill again this month, they were doubling down. It was mind-boggling to understand how one man could have successfully avoided capture, and she couldn't imagine how worn down Bryce and others must feel after all these months. She was beat up about it after a much shorter time.

"Have you ever had a chocolate egg cream?" she asked. They desperately needed something fun to think about.

"I have no idea what that is, but I'm assuming it has chocolate, egg and cream in it."

"Wrong in so many ways," she said sweetly. "Chocolate syrup, but no eggs or cream. Just whole milk and seltzer. Come on. I'll show you."

They gathered up their lunch dishes, and she led him downstairs. Then, behind the counter, she pulled a soda glass off a shelf.

"Is the glass important?" he asked, eyeing the tall soda glass that was narrow at the bottom and wider at the top.

"I think so. You'll see why." Then she added just a bit of milk, a cup of seltzer and, finally, two big tablespoons of chocolate syrup. She waited for it to settle to the bottom. Then she stirred the glass with a long-handled spoon. The seltzer bubbled up to create a fizz on top. She handed it to him. "And that is a chocolate egg cream."

He took a sip. "Delicious," he said.

"No self-respecting deli should be without these."

"Do they sell well?"

"Oh my gosh, yes. Especially afternoons and then evenings, almost as an after-dinner treat."

"Sort of like a milkshake, but not."

"Exactly."

He saluted her with the glass. "I've really learned a great deal in just a few days. Stuff that is just interesting, like how to make a chocolate egg cream, and stuff that could be very helpful, like how to boil down a sauce to thicken it and intensify the flavors. I think the next time I invite someone over for dinner, I'll feel slightly more competent. Will perhaps venture out of my *comfort zone*."

"I'll wait with bated breath for my next engraved dinner invitation," she teased impulsively. But then it hit her how that sounded. She held up a hand. "I'm not suggesting that you owe me a dinner invitation after this is all over. You don't owe me anything. I'll owe you. And all the other police officers and federal agents who are doing everything you can to protect me and everybody else."

"I'm not looking for gratitude, Olivia," he said seriously.

"I know. It just came out badly. I wanted to clear the air."

"Consider it cleared." The door opened, and Bryce immediately turned. He did that every time. She knew he was looking for Davison. Neither of them probably thought that the man would be so bold as to come in during business hours, but then again, they hadn't thought he'd be so bold as to join the protesters and let himself be seen. It was as if he was baiting the police, taunting them.

It would be his downfall, of course. Nobody could do that forever.

But how many would he kill first?

And how close would he get to her again?

All valid questions. But nothing that she wanted to think about right now. The customer coming in the door wasn't Davison, just a regular picking up a pound of pastrami and an extra-large container of coleslaw. Once she took his money at the cash register, she walked back to the kitchen.

She had a salad to make. And once she got home, she had to find the right outfit. She had a rust-colored cashmere sweater and a brown-and-rust tweed skirt that might be perfect with a pair of brown boots.

She was having lunch at Verity Colton's house. Meeting Bryce's long-lost father, the man in the center of so much controversy.

She hadn't seen this coming. And she had the strangest feeling that she better be prepared for anything.

OLIVIA LOOKED EVEN more beautiful than usual. He was used to seeing her with her hair up in a ponytail and a baseball cap when she was working in the kitchen at the deli. When she went to the dining area, she removed the baseball cap, but lots of times, the ponytail remained. She also didn't wear much makeup, likely due to the heat in the kitchen.

It wasn't that she didn't look good then. But right now, with her long hair curling over her shoulders in soft waves and her makeup perfectly applied, she looked amazing in a skirt that was just short enough to be really interesting. "I like the boots," he said. Was there anything sexier than a woman with great legs in a pair of midcalf boots and a skirt?

"Thank you." She reached into the refrigerator and pulled out the bowl of chopped salad that she'd brought home the night before from the deli. She gave it a stir, tasted it and smiled. "It's always better the next day."

"My family will love it. Well, I don't know about my dad. I don't know much about what he likes and doesn't like."

She let the comment pass. Maybe she sensed that, with each passing hour, his agitation was growing.

They drove to his mom's house. When they arrived, he saw that Madison's car was already there. When they got inside, he was surprised to see that Jillian was also there. As was his father.

"I didn't see your cars," he said.

"Mine is in the shop," Jillian said. "Dad hired a car to bring him here, so he picked me up on the way."

Weren't they all just one big happy family. He remembered his manners and turned to introduce Olivia for the benefit of everyone besides Madison. "This is Olivia Margulies. She owns Bubbe's Deli and is, of course, Oren's sister."

"How are you, Olivia?" Madison asked, hugging her. "I've been thinking of you."

"It's good to meet you," Jillian said, also offering her a quick hug. "I'm terribly sorry to hear about the stuff you're enduring with Len Davison. He would be in jail if not for my old boss."

"Someday both of them will be in jail," Bryce said. Randall Bowe had allowed Len Davison to literally get away with murder by making evidence against Davison disappear.

"That's right," his father said, looking at Jillian with pride. "And everyone will know the truth, that it was him, not you."

Bryce turned to him. "And this is… Wes Windham." It was the name his father had gone by in witness protection and the name he was choosing to continue to use. "Previously known as Richard Foster." There was no reason to add the last part. Olivia knew the details.

Everybody in the room probably assumed Olivia knew the details, given that Oren was her brother.

It was a petty thing to do.

"Bryce," his mom said, warning or plea in her tone.

His father stepped forward. "It's a pleasure to meet you, Olivia. Glad you and Bryce could both come today," he added, like he really meant it.

Verity, evidently seeing that Wes was going to overlook Bryce's little dig, must have decided to do the same. She approached Olivia with her hand outstretched. "I'm Verity Colton, and I am delighted to meet you. A little nervous to have you dine with us. Everything at your deli is always so delicious. I hope we measure up."

"I'm not worried," Olivia said.

It seemed to be just the right thing to say, because everybody drifted from the front door into the family room. Glasses of wine were poured, and a cheese platter was passed. Bryce sat in a chair, and Olivia took a spot on the couch with Wes.

"So tell me about this deli that I've heard so much about," he said to her.

"It's called Bubbe's. *Bubbe* is Yiddish for *grandmother*. The basics of many of the recipes that we use came from her, with a bit of updating on my part. She was a really great cook and I have great memories of cooking with her. Sadly, my grandparents are no longer with us. But they loved living here in Grave Gulch, and my grandmother continued to live here long after my grandfather died. My family was in Grand Rapids. We would come to visit, and those visits were always filled with good food. After high school, I attended culinary school and knew that I'd open my own place just as soon as I could. Grave Gulch seemed to be the right place to do that."

"I've done a little restaurant work over the years," Wes said.

That was news to Bryce, but then, there was probably a whole lot he didn't know about his father, given that the man hadn't been around for twenty-five years.

"It's really hard work," Wes continued.

"It is. Usually no need to go to the gym. I get enough of a workout every day."

"How is it," Jillian asked, "that you make those macaroons? I swear, if somebody from the department doesn't pick them up at least once a week, I'm officially in withdrawal."

Olivia laughed. "I'll tell you what. I'll arrange a private session between you and Hernando. He can show you. I guess that may be bad for my business, but you sound a little desperate."

"Oh, I'm desperate, all right," Jillian said.

"You loved cookies when you were a baby," Wes said, fondness in his voice.

Jillian was twenty-seven, just one year younger than Bryce. That meant that she'd been just two when Richard Foster had disappeared. How many memories of her could the man legitimately have? Bryce was about to ask when he saw his mother's face. She was smiling at Wes.

Bryce kept his mouth shut. "Smells good, Mom," he said.

"Thank you," his mother said. "Lasagna."

"I guessed pot roast," he admitted.

"A safe guess," she said, looking at Olivia. "I don't have a terribly broad range of things that I make."

"I love lasagna," Olivia said.

Whether she did or did not wasn't important. Her comment had made his mom relax. Or maybe it was because he'd stopped picking at his dad.

"How's school going, Mom?"

"I've got a mostly excellent class this year," his mother said.

"Mostly excellent?" Bryce followed up.

His mother smiled and looked at Olivia. "I've got a couple students who are struggling. They don't have regular attendance, and most of the time, I think they're probably coming to school hungry."

"So you're taking breakfast in for them," Madison said knowingly.

Verity shrugged. "I might be," she said evasively. "And everybody gets lunch at the school, whether they can pay or not."

His mother taught in a school where many of the families were economically challenged. Some of the stories she'd told about her students and their families were really heartbreaking. She'd provided everything from food to clothing to shelter over the years. Maybe it was because she'd been a single parent, raising three kids, that she had such empathy.

"Is there anything that others could do to help?" Olivia asked.

His mother studied her. "You probably have a food service sanitation certificate?"

"Yes, of course."

"You know what, Olivia? There might be something. Let me think about it for a few days and then I'll get back to you."

"Perfect," Olivia said.

NO FORKS WERE THROWN, no dishes were tossed at the walls and no one choked. If you were keeping score, that could be counted as a win, Olivia thought as they drove home. The lasagna had been good, they'd all raved about her chopped salad and there had been brownies with ice cream for dessert. Couldn't go wrong there.

But still, the tension had made chewing an absolute must as a stress-relieving tactic. She'd kept waiting for a blowup between Bryce and his dad, but thankfully, after the first few rocky minutes had passed, both men, likely not wanting to upset Verity Colton, had behaved.

"I always thought your mom was very nice when she was in Bubbe's, but she's truly lovely. So classy and such a warm personality. And your dad is…still very handsome. You look a bit alike, you know," she said tentatively.

Bryce rolled his eyes.

Olivia imagined that Verity was a really wonderful teacher. And she'd certainly raised three very polite and accomplished children, who seemed to genuinely love her and each other. All of that was, quite frankly, very impressive, given that she'd done it on her own.

"Did your mother ever date?" Olivia asked.

"She did. She was very young when… Wes disappeared. Man, that's still hard for me to get my head around. Wes Windham. Like a new name is going to make a big difference."

Now that they were away from his mother's home, Bryce wasn't being so careful to hide his attitude. His contempt was palpable.

"As difficult as this is for you, it has to be even more difficult for your mom and dad."

"How is it difficult for him?" Bryce asked. "He gets to waltz back in and pretend that nothing was odd about the twenty-five years that he was living somewhere else, pretending to be someone else."

"I obviously don't know your mom well. But I get the feeling that Verity isn't a pushover. I suspect there's been some very awkward and difficult conversations between the two of them. I doubt that your mom was willing to simply accept any excuse. I imagine your dad had to step up and admit where he was wrong." She paused. "If she can accept everything, then I think you likely have it within you to do the same."

Bryce said nothing, and Olivia thought she'd pushed too far, too hard. She felt bad about that, but really, it needed to be said. The situation as it currently stood was potentially explosive, and Bryce was teetering on making mistakes that could forever damage his relationships with his sisters and his mother.

"I wonder if it would have been different," he said finally, as they turned onto Olivia's street, "if they had been married. Could he so easily have walked away?"

Olivia had no answers to that question.

"And you asked before if my mom had dated. She did. She didn't make too big a deal out of it. But there were men around. Some had lots of money. As a little kid, that means nothing to you, but as I got older, I remember thinking that a few of them could have been a 'nice catch.'" He put air quotes around the last two words. "And they were all nice to me and my sisters. She didn't date jerks."

"But she never got serious with any of them?"

"She never married any of them. That's all I can definitively say. Why, I don't know."

"Because she'd had a great love and nothing else was going to measure up?" Olivia asked.

Bryce gave her a sideways glance. "Please, I know that the holidays are traditionally the time when sappy love-story movies permeate the cable channels, but can we refrain from that in my car?"

She believed in love. Had seen it with her own parents, her grandparents. And maybe in the movies it got depicted poorly, but that didn't mean that love wasn't real, that it wasn't wonderful, that it wasn't something to want and hope for. But she wasn't going to have that conversation with Bryce. "Love-story movies," she repeated. "That makes you sound really, really old."

The sun was setting, and he was using what daylight remained to check out her property, to make sure it remained undisturbed. He texted someone. She assumed it was the cop watching the house. "Let's go in," he said after about a minute. "Stay behind me."

She wanted to make a joke about Davison being inside, making a sandwich, but realized that she couldn't. The killer had demonstrated such brazen behavior lately that it wasn't that difficult to imagine that he'd be bold enough to be sitting at her table, with meat and cheese spread around him.

But her house was empty. It looked exactly how they'd left it hours earlier.

"Are you hungry?" he asked.

"No. I'll probably still be full tomorrow. It might be a popcorn-for-dinner kind of night."

He pretended to be shocked. "What would your customers think?"

"That I was bright enough not to have two big

meals in one day. But help yourself to whatever is in the refrigerator."

"I just have some of this if I get hungry," he said, holding up the plastic container of leftover lasagna that Verity had pushed on them. "I really do appreciate you being a good sport about going, Olivia. I think my sisters and my mom really appreciated that."

"Well, as you said before, we all are sort of family."

"So that means you have more of these family things to look forward to. What fun for you," he added, his tone dark.

"It will get better," she said. "You and your dad will come to terms."

Bryce shook his head. "I really don't think so. I just can't be like the rest of my family. I don't forgive that easily. I certainly don't forget that easily. And Wes Windham doesn't know me if he thinks that I'm not going to be watching him. He takes one step out of line, and I'll make sure he understands that no amount of begging or pleading will ever get him close to my mom or my sisters again."

She put her hand on his arm. She suspected that some of Bryce's reaction was due to the fact that he'd been the man of the family way before he should have taken on that responsibility. As such, he was used to protecting his mother and sisters. He wasn't stopping now. "Everybody missteps once in a while," she said.

"He better be extra careful."

She sighed. "Don't let resentment over the lost years prevent you from enjoying all the remaining ones. Don't let it diminish you. Parents die. Oren and I are fortunate in that we've not yet lost a parent. But when my grandparents died, I saw my mother's grief. I understood it. You don't want to be sitting shiva and only have regrets."

"This is different," he said, clearly not buying into her reasoning.

"Don't be foolish, Bryce. That's all I'm saying." She picked up some magazines that had come in the mail that week. "I'm going to my room. I'll see you in the morning."

"It's only six o'clock. You're going to bed?" he asked.

"I'm going to read and relax," she said. "Maybe take a bath." All she knew for sure was that it was probably for the best for them to each have a little space tonight. They looked at Wes Windham's return very differently, and more discussion about it didn't seem as if it was going to change anything.

She knew it had been a tough day for Bryce, suspected that he was filled with conflicting emotions. But she also knew that she was right. He was making a mistake by holding a grudge against his father. A mistake that had the potential to destroy his family.

Chapter Six

He'd checked the doors and windows twice. Had prowled the kitchen, had two bowls of cereal because it was less work than heating up the lasagna and had flipped through all the television stations without landing on a single thing that made him happy. What the hell was wrong with him?

He'd lived alone since college. He didn't get lonely. Or bored. Or needy for someone else's company. But, suddenly, all he could think about was what Olivia was doing upstairs.

She'd had her bath. Water had been run. And then drained. Old houses were good for hearing that kind of thing. Then the bathroom door had opened, then her bedroom door had closed. She was tucked in.

Reading? On her phone or computer? Sleeping?

Stop thinking about her, he told himself, rather sternly. It was…pathetic.

It bothered him that he was pretty confident that she was disappointed in him. Disappointed that he couldn't get past his distrust of and general irritation with Richard Foster, aka Wes Windham. When they'd been discussing the situation, he could almost hear her thinking, *Why can't he just go with the flow?*

It was insane that he wanted to march upstairs and explain in detail all the many times he'd done exactly that. He had the ability to adapt to change and to be flexible with plans. He had demonstrated a willingness to think outside the box and come up with solutions to unforeseen problems.

He had…

He stopped. He wasn't conducting a performance appraisal on himself. There was no promotion on the line or a big salary increase. He had nothing to prove and no reason to lose sleep over it.

Except that it mattered to him what she thought.

The idea of being a disappointment to sweet Olivia, with her sunny disposition and her natural ability to put others at ease, was not exactly palatable. If he had to invoke a food analogy, he'd say it was more like eating oversalted brussels sprouts versus enjoying a finely baked macaroon with a cup of good coffee.

He started through the television channels a third time when he heard her cell phone ring. It startled him and made him realize that this was the first time he'd heard it. He'd seen her on the telephone a bunch, but that was always on the landline for Bubbe's when she was taking to-go orders.

He was eaten up with curiosity about who might be calling her. Her parents? Her brother, Oren?

He quietly walked up the stairs and stood outside her door. And, like an anxious parent of a preteen girl, he tried to hear her side of the conversation.

But while the plumbing of the old house offered clues, the solid wood offered few. All that he could catch were bits and pieces and an occasional laugh.

Someone had called her who could make her chuckle.

The conversation lasted twelve minutes.

And had he not been fast on his feet, she'd have caught him lurking outside her door when suddenly her bedroom door swung open and she walked down the hall to the bathroom. He waited until he saw the door handle turn and casually sauntered out of his room.

"Oh, hey," he said. "I thought you were asleep."

"I was. An old friend from culinary school called. He's passing through Grave Gulch on his way to northern Michigan tomorrow, and he's going to swing by the deli. He should be there by seven."

Her old friend was a man, and it had taken him twelve minutes to say *that*? Of course, one had to add time for all the laughter. "What's your old friend's name?"

"Thomas Michael. One of those unfortunate ones who has two first names. For the first two weeks of class, one of our instructors got his name mixed up and called him Michael. After class, we would laugh about it."

She sounded very amused still. He didn't think it sounded that funny. "Does he come through Grave Gulch often?"

"No. Hardly ever. That's why this is so great."

Wasn't it. "I'll look forward to meeting him."

She shook her head. "I didn't want to go into the whole thing with Davison. It's just too much. I'm not going to tell him that I'm being protected from a serial killer. Can you...just lie low while he's here?"

It wasn't a huge request. She hadn't asked for any of this. It had all been foisted upon her because of Davison's perverse interest in her. Still. "I can do that," he said. Unless, of course, Thomas Michael gave him any reason to be a bigger presence.

"Thank you," she said. "Good night."

"Good night," Bryce said. He went back into his bedroom and booted up his computer. He used his password to access the appropriate FBI database and settled back on his pillows, content that he'd know everything there was to know about Thomas Michael before the night was done.

THE NEXT DAY passed in a blur. They were busy, running out of both lunch specials before the rush was even over. If this kept up, she was going to have to add a third special or increase the quantities of the two.

As usual, Bryce had helped for a while in the kitchen and then retreated to the dining room to do his own work, his cell phone and computer within easy reach. In the afternoon, once they'd shared lunch, she'd stayed in her office, and he'd gone back downstairs. She knew that he was in contact several times a day with Brett Shea and others about the ongoing search for Davison.

She refused to think about that man right now, however. Her friend was coming. Thomas had been a lifeline when she'd first gotten to culinary school. He was talented, had a good sense of humor and, quite frankly, didn't take it all as seriously as she did. That had helped her have some much-needed perspective on the days when things hadn't gone well.

She'd expected a few questions from Bryce today about Thomas, but there hadn't been any. In fact, Bryce had been really quiet the whole day. Maybe the lunch with his father was still bothering him.

At ten minutes after seven, the door opened. She

came around the end of the counter quickly. "Oh my gosh, it's so great to see you," she said, giving Thomas a quick hug. He looked good, even if his blond hair was a little shaggy. He'd always worn it short and now it hung over his ears and coat collar. But his light blue eyes were so very familiar, as were the dark-framed glasses he'd started wearing near the end of culinary school.

"You look beautiful. As always," he said, stepping back. Then he looked around the deli and nodded approvingly. "It looks as good as I remember it," he said.

"Has it really been two years since you've been here?" she asked, leading him over to an empty booth. "Sit, please. Have you eaten?"

"Of course not. I wanted one of your special pastrami sandwiches. And coleslaw. And one of every dessert that you have left."

"Come back to the kitchen with me. You can talk to me while I make it," she said. She would never make this offer to most of her customers, but she and Thomas had been through culinary school wars together. And both had survived. "How was your drive?" she asked, looking over her shoulder as she walked.

Which was a mistake, she realized, when she bumped into something rather large and solid. Bryce. Who was standing by the kitchen door, giving Thomas a look that would scare most people.

"Oh, this is Bryce. He's an FBI agent. Working with my brother on a few things," she said. "Bryce, this is Thomas Michael, chef extraordinaire."

Thomas held out a hand. "Pleasure to meet you. I haven't seen Oren since we were in school and he used to come see Olivia. I think I still owe him twenty bucks."

"Why is that?" Bryce asked, returning the handshake.

"Whenever he visited, the three of us would play cards. For money. On more than one occasion, he had to stake me a few bucks. I was a poor student and not able to bluff nearly as well as either of them."

Bryce was staring at Olivia. "So the two of you spent a lot of time together in culinary school?"

"That's right. And now we are in pursuit of the perfect pastrami on rye." She walked past Bryce with Thomas following him. She was surprised when she saw that Bryce had also come back to the kitchen. "Do you...uh...want a sandwich, too?" she asked.

"I've eaten."

This was weird. But Bryce took his professional responsibilities seriously, and she didn't want to make a big deal out of his presence. That would simply raise questions in Thomas's mind about Bryce's real purpose for being at the deli. Bryce had agreed to say nothing about the reason, and she was thankful for that. She simply wanted to enjoy her friend's visit and, if possible, forget about Len Davison and the havoc he'd wreaked on her life.

"Hernando," she said, "you remember Thomas?"

Hernando, who was across the kitchen working on orders for the other customers, waved. Olivia turned her back on both men and pulled the necessary items out of the refrigerator. Meat, Swiss cheese, Russian dressing, marbled rye bread and, of course, coleslaw—a little for the sandwich and more as a side dish. She lined everything up. She would make two sandwiches and join Thomas while he ate.

It dawned on her that the last pastrami sandwich she'd made had been for Len Davison. She pushed that thought away and smiled brightly at Thomas. "So tell me again about this great opportunity that has you cruising to northern Michigan." Last night, when they'd talked about him passing through to interview for a new job, Thomas hadn't said much, brushing off her questions with a casual "It's complicated and I'll tell you everything when we meet."

"Pretty exciting, huh?" he said.

"Uh, duh?" she teased. "We'd be in the same state. That would be fabulous." She glanced at Bryce. "Thomas has been the executive chef at a very chic inn in Maine."

"At the Water's Edge," Bryce said, surprising her.

She didn't think she'd told him that the previous night. But maybe she had. Thomas's phone call had woken her up. "That's right. Such a lovely place. And the food. It makes all of this look very humble," she said with a sweep of her hand.

"You could cook circles around me," Thomas said. "Top student in our class. She could have had her pick of opportunities."

"I knew what I wanted," Olivia said. "And I thought you were superexcited about your work. This must be a really great opportunity."

"It is," Thomas said. "And it just seems like the right time to leave."

Bryce cleared his throat, like he intended to say something, but he stayed mute. Olivia decided to ignore him.

"And the new job, tell me about it," she said.

"I will. But first, I want to hear everything about you and this place."

"Business is good," she said. "I have the nicest customers. Oh my gosh, let me tell you about Mrs. Drindle." By the time she was finished, the sandwiches were assembled. "Let's go eat," she said. She led him to one of the smaller booths, meant for just one person on each side.

Bryce followed them from the kitchen, but instead of looming over them, he took a position near the cash register, leaning against the wall.

"This is glorious," Thomas said, taking his first bite. "I knew it would be."

"I'll get us something to drink," she said. "What would you like?"

"Just water is fine. I might have one of those egg creams later."

She slid out of the booth. When she walked behind the counter to get two glasses of water, Bryce came over. "I didn't realize the two of you were so chummy."

"I told you we went to culinary school together," she whispered. "That's an intense experience. It helps to bond with somebody."

"So the two of you bonded?"

It suddenly dawned on her that Bryce wasn't simply being his usual protective self. He was acting...jealous. What the heck? "This is weird, Bryce," she said, pouring water into the glasses.

He said nothing. She stared at him. Seconds ticked by.

"Don't let me keep you from your little reunion," he said.

She was this close to reminding him that he was the one who'd made the big deal about the fact that the two of them couldn't kiss again. But she pressed her lips together. "Oh, I intend to," she said. And then she walked away.

She returned to the booth and focused her attention on her friend. She was going to ignore Bryce Colton and his glares. They were halfway done with their sandwiches when Thomas shared some startling news.

"Gwyneth and I are separated," he said.

"What?" Just the previous night, she'd asked about his wife, and he'd said that she'd started a new job at a hospital in Portland. "But—"

"I didn't want to say anything on the phone. It happened months ago. The divorce will be final in just a few weeks."

"Oh, Thomas." She reached a hand across the table and held one of his. "I'm so sorry." She had been at their wedding four years ago. "What happened?"

He shrugged. "You know. We just started going our separate ways. It's hard when people have careers that are very different."

"I'm sorry," she repeated. What else was there to say?

"I appreciate that," he said. "But you know, it's got me to thinking about what I really want out of life. And now that I'm here, I look around and I envy what you've built here, Olivia. I envy the simplicity of it."

It wasn't that simple—she had lots of things going on every day. But now wasn't the time to debate that. Her friend was hurting.

"I could do this," he said. "I could be happy doing this. And very happy doing it with you."

She was confused. "I don't understand," she said.

"We were a good team, you and me. I think we could be that kind of team again."

"I... I don't have a need for someone with your abilities, Thomas. I could never afford you, quite frankly."

"We'd work something out," he said. "I could take Hernando's spot."

Olivia straightened up in the booth. She pushed her half-eaten sandwich away. "Hernando hasn't told me that he's going anywhere. And I hope he isn't. I need him."

"Together, the two of us could make this place even bigger and better than it already is. More high-end catering. A second location. The sky is the limit."

She liked Bubbe's just how it was. He was being a bit condescending. But she put her hurt feelings aside. Her gut was telling her that there was something very wrong. "Thomas, I—"

"I wonder, sometimes, if we couldn't be a great team in another way," Thomas interrupted. "I should never have married Gwyneth. You and I really clicked at one time, Olivia. You know we did."

Her gut had gone from doing somersaults to backflips. She and Thomas had been very good friends, and at one time, maybe she had hoped for something more. But he'd met Gwyneth, and she'd accepted it was not to be. "Are you really on your way to a job interview?" she asked.

He shook his head. "No. I came to see you. Listen, Olivia. I care about you. I've always cared about you. And I don't want to waste any more time." He looked around. "I need this."

He sounded a bit desperate. And that drew her attention. But then she really thought about what he'd said. *I need this*, not *I need you*. "Why did you lie?"

"That's not important. I think that—"

"It is important," she interrupted him. "It's really important to me why my friend would lie to me." She realized, too late, that her voice had risen. Bryce was headed in her direction, moving fast.

She held up a hand in his direction. He ignored it and got close to the table. "Everything okay, Olivia?" Bryce asked, looking first at her, then at Thomas.

"Yes. Of course it is. Everything is fine," she said.

"Listen, I've got to go," Thomas said, pushing his own plate away. "I'll stop in tomorrow."

"Not tomorrow," she said quickly. She needed more time. This was too important.

"Okay. I'll kill a couple days kicking around the area. But I'm coming back," he said, reaching for her hand.

That was probably good. They needed to settle this one way or another. She looked at their linked hands and was struck by the realization that she felt none of the thrill that she'd felt when Bryce had touched her.

That's because you and Thomas are old friends. You have history. Fireworks can't be expected to last. She made the mental arguments fast and furiously. "That's fine." She pulled her hand away.

Thomas took a few steps toward the door. Then turned to look over his shoulder. "Just think about what I said."

It would be hard to think of anything else. It was *that* bizarre. "I will," she promised.

Then he was out the door. She stood, as well. "I'm going upstairs. I have some...paperwork," she said.

Bryce gently grabbed her arm. "Are you okay? Did he say or do something to upset you?"

She needed to think over what had just happened before she offered any explanations. Her friend had shocked her. First with his admission that his marriage was over. Then that he had lied about having a job interview. And finally with his suggestion that there was a place for him at Bubbe's. A place for him in her life. "Really got to get at that paperwork." She pulled away from Bryce, and he let her go.

He didn't follow her up the stairs, and she was very grateful. She needed a minute. One thing was absolutely clear—Hernando had helped her build the business. She owed him a debt of gratitude. And every day he proved his worth. His job was secure.

What a mess.

A half hour later, there was a knock on her door. "Yes," she said.

"Can I come in?" Bryce asked.

"Yes."

He took the chair in front of her desk. "How's the paperwork?"

She shrugged. "Still there." She hadn't opened any of the files on her desk.

"Want to talk about it?"

"What?"

"Whatever it is that idiot said to you that upset you."

"He and his wife are separated. They're getting divorced," she added. "And he lied about passing through on his way to a job interview. There's no interview."

Bryce didn't look terribly surprised. "He wasn't truthful about his employment situation," he said. "He lost his job at the inn three months ago."

"How do you know that?" she asked.

"I'm with the FBI. It's not that hard for me to find things out."

"You checked him out?" she asked, astonished. "You punched his name into one of your little databases and your computer spit out all kinds of things about him."

"My computer doesn't spit. But, yeah, I did some research. When somebody out of the blue suddenly wants to meet with the person that you're assigned to protect, you don't simply let them show up."

"But—"

"I won't apologize for trying to keep you safe."

It was hard to argue against that. And, quite frankly, she was too tired to argue about anything. The conversation with Thomas had sapped her. She'd been so excited about seeing her good friend. And it had all gone so differently than she'd anticipated. "I want to go home," she said.

"That's what I came up to tell you. All the customers have left, the door is locked and Hernando has the kitchen tidied up."

"I need to count the cash drawer. Get the deposit ready."

"I'll help you," he said.

"I can do it." She knew she sounded petulant.

Bryce held up his hands in mock surrender. "It seems to me if seeing Thomas Michael upsets you this much, you ought to just make sure that it doesn't happen."

"I might be seeing him a whole lot more," she said impulsively. Bryce had said the one thing that she'd been unwilling to think too hard about. That this might be the end of a friendship that had been important to her.

"Why's that?" he asked, his tone challenging.

"He…he's interested in working here, with me. With helping me take the business bigger. With…him and me being more than…" She stopped. She'd been spouting off, but, in truth, she was definitely not interested in discussing what her friend had said.

"More than?" Bryce repeated, his tone holding a challenge.

"Never mind," she said. And she walked out of the room without another word.

THEY DID NOT speak again. She counted the cash drawer, and he stared out the deli window, into the dark. Then it was time to drive home in their separate vehicles. Once he'd checked the house, she'd come inside and gone straight to her room.

Leaving him alone with his thoughts.

Thomas Michael wanted to work with Olivia. That was certainly newsworthy, but her admission that the idiot wanted the two of them to be *more than* had him truly pissed off. He wasn't surprised. Of course that was what the man wanted. Olivia was beautiful and sexy and smart. Plus, she had a personality that couldn't be beaten. She was the whole package. Plus, she had proved herself quite capable of running a successful business.

She'd be like winning the trifecta for somebody like Thomas Michael. The guy had lost his employment abruptly after there was a series of thefts at the inn that were suspected to be an inside job. Bryce had talked to the owner of the inn earlier in the day, and the man had been careful not to accuse his former chef but had broadly hinted that there was enough evidence that he'd made a prudent decision to cut ties with the man.

And while Bryce didn't claim to be an expert on resort operations, he knew that having an excellent chef was necessary. He didn't think the decision to end Thomas Michael's employment had been frivolous.

When the man had said that he was interviewing for the new job because he was ready for a new opportunity, Bryce had almost lost it. But he'd managed to keep his mouth shut. That had paled in comparison to the self-control it had taken when the idiot had reached out and grabbed Olivia's hand.

When he'd heard Olivia's voice rise, in obvious concern, he'd abandoned any pretense of simply happening to be in the dining room and marched over. He'd intended to pitch Michael out on his ear or whatever part of his anatomy landed first on the sidewalk.

But the look in Olivia's eye had stopped him. She didn't want a scene. It was consistent with how she'd acted since the day he'd met her. She didn't want to use Davison's actions to scramble up publicity for herself or for Bubbe's Deli, like so many might have done. They'd have been all over social media, attempting to tell their story, to elicit interest, to draw in customers who wanted to meet the woman Davison was fixated upon.

Instead, she'd literally begged to stay under the radar.

And causing a commotion in her own business, with customers certainly within hearing distance of raised voices, would have been mortifying for her. So he'd held back.

That did not stop him, right now, from wanting to go pound on Thomas's head for a bit.

Or pound on her bedroom door, demanding an answer to whether or not she was interested, intrigued or had any other form of interest in Thomas Michael's proposal, professional or otherwise. He didn't think for one minute that she was going to push Hernando aside. That was preposterous. He'd witnessed the close relationship between Hernando and Olivia and believed it could withstand any weasel-like intrusion from the man from Maine.

But if she was interested in pursuing a personal relationship, there were other restaurants that the chef could work at in Grave Gulch. A call from Olivia, who was respected within the culinary community, would go a long way. It would likely mitigate any poor recommendation from the inn in Maine. And, likely, Thomas's ex-boss would be careful about being too disparaging. He'd likely been as forthcoming as he was because Bryce had identified himself as an FBI agent.

Over my dead body. That was the thought running through Bryce's head as he popped the cap off a bottle of beer. He took a couple of slugs of it, but by the time he was two-thirds done, he set the bottle aside. He needed to be sharp. Vigilant. Olivia's safety was at stake.

Safety came in all shapes and sizes—sometimes as elemental as physical safety, but more often less easily defined in the form of emotional or mental security. Risks, too, could be tricky bastards, sometimes coming at you like a freight train, and at other times advancing so slowly and steadily that it was impossible to remember why you should be scared.

Thomas Michael was a risk to Olivia.

Bryce knew it.

Convincing Olivia, though, might be a different story.

Chapter Seven

Olivia turned over when she heard her alarm and, for the second time in less than a week, contemplated what might happen if she simply decided that it was too much effort to get out of bed to open Bubbe's.

Hernando would call the police. Mrs. Drindle would come looking for her. Both of those options scared her enough that she tossed back the covers. She'd slept poorly, waking up several times to reach for the water she kept on her bedside table. The nights were chilly in Michigan this time of year, and she'd turned on the furnace weeks ago. But that made the air dry.

Now she reached for her cup of water and realized it was empty. She sat up and reached for the robe that she'd tossed at the end of her bed. Living alone, she rarely wore it, but since Bryce had moved in, she'd made sure it was handy. As she put it on, she thought it was a shame she didn't wear it more. It was silk, with lovely dark pink roses. Her mother had bought it for her for her birthday the previous year and said it reminded her of the flowers that Olivia grew by her front porch in the summer.

She was quiet as she walked downstairs, not wanting to disturb Bryce if he was still sleeping. She rounded the corner of the kitchen and stopped short when she saw that he was already awake, dressed and drinking a cup of coffee. He looked…great, as usual. And rested. That irritated the heck out of her.

"I don't usually make coffee here," she said.

"I know. But I was up early. Didn't think I could wait until I got to Bubbe's for the caffeine hit. I'll replace anything I use," he said.

"That's not the point," she said. Then was immediately ashamed because she sounded…well, rude. And that wasn't her.

Under normal circumstances, she thought. Nothing normal about her life right now. But that wasn't Bryce's fault. He was trying to help. "I'm sorry. You are welcome to anything in my cupboards or my refrigerator, and you do not need to replace items used. You've disrupted your life to babysit me. A few supplies are a small price to pay."

"Thank you. Can I pour you a cup?" he asked, motioning to the coffeepot.

She looked at the clock on the wall. They had time. "Sure."

They sat at the table, sipping in silence. "My brother is expected back today," she said finally. "I got a text from him late last night."

"That will make Madison happy," Bryce said.

"I'm the one who is happy," Olivia said. "Happy that Oren found a woman as lovely as your sister. I always wanted a sister."

"Yeah, well, I thought they were a pain, growing up," Bryce said, clearly not meaning it. "It was two against one, all the time."

"The middle child and the only boy. What a terribly difficult life you had," she teased.

"At least with you and Oren, it was one against one."

"He was always a good brother. He'll be a good husband, a good dad."

"Do you think they'll have children?"

She looked shocked. "I hope so. I need to be Aunt Olivia. The sooner the better."

"How about you? You plan on having kids?" he asked.

"I...uh... I want to."

"A houseful?" he asked.

"Less than a litter," she said. She'd always imagined that she'd have a family one day. Had not been terribly concerned about her biological clock but knew that, at twenty-eight, with no marriage prospects on the horizon, time could be a factor. Was that what was nagging her about Thomas's suggestion that there could be a personal future for them? Was he offering her a path to a life that she'd envisioned? "You?" she asked.

He shrugged. "Add to the already burgeoning Colton clan? Why not? Lots in my extended family seem to have fallen hard this year. I imagine there will be many new babies in the coming years."

"Fun holidays," she said. "You asked me why I settled in Grave Gulch and I told you that it was because of my grandmother, that she'd lived here. Some of my very best memories are coming to her house for all the major Jewish holidays. My aunts and uncles and cousins would all come, too. It was always a houseful. When my grandmother had died, some of that stopped, of course. There was no longer a natural meeting point."

"Traditions die," he said.

"Traditions evolve. Now my own parents host holiday events. Oren and I are there, and in the coming years, as we marry and have children, those family dinners will grow. We'll be building the memories for the next generation. And if you look way out, someday, my husband and I will do the same for our family. It's important to remember that life goes on, more or less in the same fashion, regardless of what craziness is going on in the world."

He stared at her. "You're an optimist, Olivia Margulies."

"I am," she said. "But I'm not a fool. I understand that there are things in this world that are not good. Like Davison. But I refuse, absolutely refuse, to let him have the power to change my perspective. As dear Bubbe used to say, this, too, shall pass." She pushed her chair back. It really was time for her to get dressed for work. But the conversation, the coffee or the very warm memories of Bubbe's home had pushed away the dark cloud that she'd awakened under.

She was an optimist. If it was a character fault, she accepted it without reservation. Because to go through life as a pessimist must be terribly draining.

She was at the hallway, about to leave the kitchen, when she turned. "I don't think I'm the only optimist in the room," she said.

He made a point of looking in the corners and under the table. "I don't understand," he said finally.

"You forget that I grew up with somebody who has a lot in common with you. As worldly and jaded as you and my brother might like to come off at times, I think you're both optimists. Just like many others in public service. Otherwise, you all would not be able to do the work that you're called upon to do. You would not have the core emotional strength to get you through the really tough days."

He opened his mouth, then shut it.

She smiled and left the room, feeling good that she'd left him speechless.

SHE'D GIVEN HIM a lot to think about. One, what the hell was under that robe? He'd never wanted to untie anything so badly in his entire life. He'd practically had to sit on his hands.

Two, was he really an optimist?

And three, what did he see in his future in terms of children? Men, he thought, rarely got credit for thinking about kids. About the having or not having. It seemed that everybody acted as if that was a space reserved only for women. That men simply stumbled into the decision, led there either by the physical need to mate or by happenstance.

But he'd been raised in a single-parent family. And he'd taken on the role of father far earlier than some. He could still remember answering the door when Jillian got asked to her first dance. She'd been fifteen, so that would have made him sixteen. Hardly an authority figure. And the kid who'd been standing on the other side of the threshold was in his chemistry class.

But he'd leaned forward and very quietly, in a manner that would have convinced the most doubting, said, "I'm going to be watching you. And if you hurt her, in any way, I'm coming for you."

Jillian had gotten home that night, totally irritated by the fact that the kid had barely danced with her, and when he'd brought her home, he'd left her at the door without even a good-night kiss. Bryce had gone to bed happy.

He wanted kids. There. He'd said it. Well, thought it. He wasn't going to start talking to himself. Everybody would assume the hunt for Davison had finally put him round the bend. But, yeah, he wanted to take them to his mother's house and watch her spoil them. He wanted his kids to grow up with Madison's and Jillian's children and his other Colton relatives'—a bunch of happy cousins.

He wanted to take them apple picking in the fall and sledding in the winter. To baseball games in the spring and to the beach in the summer.

Hell, he even wanted his kids to know Wes Windham. A kid should know their grandfather. He wasn't at all sure, yet, what he might tell his children about Wes, but he imagined that he'd come up with something when the time came.

He'd always seen *the time* as sometime in the future. Had never felt the need to define it more closely or, quite honestly, to chase it more forcefully. But, suddenly, he felt a shift. And the shift had something to do with Olivia.

Who was probably upstairs right now, taking off her robe.

He poured himself another cup of coffee and allowed himself to enjoy that thought for a minute longer. When she came down to the kitchen ten minutes later, fully dressed, she looked lovely, as usual. Although, honestly, she looked a bit tired.

"Are you feeling okay?" he asked as they put on coats. "Why?"

He had lived with two sisters. He knew better than to say that she looked tired. "You've been going full speed for days," he said instead.

"My throat is sore," she admitted. "I'm worried that I'm getting sick. I'll wear a mask and gloves in the kitchen, just in case, but I'm not going to want to handle food. I... I know you have your own work, but you did offer and...uh... I'm going to need you."

That seemed a difficult admission. And maybe again, because he had sisters so close to her age, he understood. They were independent and strong, and it was important that be recognized. She was likely the same. "I'd be happy to help," he said simply.

"You'll want to keep your distance."

He supposed there was no use reminding her that it had been just recently that he'd kissed her. But his immune system was strong. "Do you get sick a lot?"

"Hardly ever," she said glumly. "Maybe it's my turn."

"Drink some orange juice," he said. "Lots of water. Get some sunshine and up your vitamins C and D."

"Thank you, Dr. Colton," she said. "I assume you finished medical school before you began your career at the FBI."

"Just saying," he said, holding the door for her.

"I'll have matzo ball soup for lunch," she said. "Or maybe just stand over a steaming pot of it."

"Whatever works." He didn't want her to be sick. He needed her healthy, alert, focused on being prepared if Davison came after her again.

Once they got to the deli and Hernando arrived, she didn't offer any explanation of why she was instructing versus doing. Nor for the gloves and mask she'd

By lunchtime, he was convinced that she was going downhill fast. She was talking less and even walking a little slower.

"How are you?" he asked.

"Fine," she said. "Can you be in the dining room when they unlock the front doors? When Mrs. Drindle comes in, would you tell her that I said hello but that I'm busy in the kitchen?"

So he was finally going to get to talk to the famous Mrs. Drindle. He went back to the dining room and sat in a booth, the same one he always used. Mrs. Drindle was the third customer in the door. He let the woman get situated in her booth and order before he approached.

"Mrs. Drindle?" he asked.

"Yes."

"I…uh… I'm Bryce, and Olivia asked me to tell you that she's unable to come say hello because she's busy in the kitchen."

She frowned at him. "Do you work here?"

He was usually the one asking the questions and making suspects or witnesses feel uncomfortable. Never relished relinquishing the role. But she was a favorite customer, and he *was* sort of working here. "Yes," he said.

"I haven't seen you before. Well, that's not true. I've seen you, in that booth. You've been messing up my numbers."

"I'm sorry. How did I do that?"

"I am always the third person in the door. But then, when I get inside, the first two customers through the door are here, which I expect, but then you're also here. Which makes four of us. Not three."

It was an absolutely ridiculous conversation, but she was dead serious and he understood the math. "I'm not a customer. You are the third customer. Everything is fine," he said, reassuring her.

"Thank you for the explanation," she said. "I had planned to ask Olivia about it today, and now there's no need."

"Happy to help," he said. "Nice to have met you."

"You, too, Bryce. Stop by anytime."

He returned to his booth, gathered up his computer and went back to the kitchen. "I spoke to Mrs. Drindle," he told Olivia. When he recounted their brief but odd conversation, he couldn't tell if Olivia was smiling or not, because she was still wearing her mask.

"She's something," she said when he was done. "I would miss her if she decided to go be someone else's third customer."

"I don't think there's any danger of that. She seems pretty happy. How are you doing?"

"Great," she said.

"Uh-huh."

During the lunch hour, Olivia did not step into the dining room. Instead, she handled the incoming orders from the phone in the kitchen. She didn't go near the food prep area.

Once the lunch rush was over and they went upstairs for their own lunch, it was obvious. She wasn't eating.

"Your throat is worse," he said.

She nodded. "I'm just going to rest for a few minutes," she said, sitting on her new couch. About thirty seconds later, she was lying down. "I knew this would come in handy," she said, closing her eyes.

She was sick—no doubt about it. "I don't think a nap here is going to do it. You need to be home. In bed."

She lifted her head slightly. "I'll be fine." Her head went back down.

He placed his palm on her forehead. "You're running a temp."

She didn't answer.

Now he was getting irritated. And worried. "Go home. And I'll go with you."

Again, no response. She didn't even open her eyes.

That did it. "Let's go. And please understand this—I'll carry you out of here if I have to."

Chapter Eight

"Hernando will have something to say about that," Olivia said. She wanted to open her eyes to confirm that two-way communication had been achieved, but it was simply too much effort.

"Come on. Give in now, get some rest and recover fast. Otherwise, you could be sick for days. Miss lots of work. That would be tough on Hernando."

That got her head up. It was one thing to be hard-headed about something. It was another thing to be selfish. "Maybe I could see if Sally could come in to cover for me."

"Now you're thinking."

By the time they left the deli twenty minutes later, she thought her head might explode. A headache had settled right between her eyes, competing with the ache in her throat and the overall stiffness of her joints. She was basically miserable. "I'll be here tomorrow," she promised Hernando.

Her chef looked at Bryce. "I couldn't manage to convince her to go home. Thank you for being more persuasive."

Bryce nodded.

She sensed a new peace beginning between the two

men over managing her condition. Of all the nerve. She'd be incensed if she could just work up the energy. She reached for her keys.

"I'll drive you home in my vehicle," Bryce said. "We'll leave your car here. Maybe we'll get it later, or it can stay in the lot overnight."

"Fine," she said. She really didn't care about much besides getting horizontal.

She closed her eyes as Bryce drove to her house. Then she dumped her purse and coat in the kitchen, grabbed herself a huge glass of water and went upstairs. "I'll be in bed," she said. She didn't wait to hear Bryce's answer.

She woke up many hours later, because it was already dark outside. Her phone was ringing. She looked for the time. Just after seven. "Hi," she said to her brother.

"Hernando told me you're sick," he said, not bothering with small talk. "Are you okay?"

Her throat was still sore and most every bone in her body hurt, but her headache was better. "I'm fine. Just being cautious."

"Uh-huh," he said, clearly not believing her. "Have you ever left work sick before?"

No. "I don't remember," she said.

"That's right. You haven't. I'm coming over. I want to see for myself."

"No, you'll be exposing yourself to whatever crud it is that I have," she said.

"I'm a US marshal. Crud is a condiment on our sandwiches."

"Not at my deli," she said, laughing. "But fine, come over if you want. I'll let Bryce know not to shoot you."

"I'd appreciate that," he said, hanging up.

She ran her tongue over her teeth and decided to brush them before heading downstairs. She took a minute to run a comb through her hair. She'd had a roommate in culinary school who believed in the theory that if you didn't look really sick, nobody believed you. So, basic hygiene came to a screeching halt. Olivia had dreaded when that girl got sick more than she dreaded being tested on making the perfect meringue.

She, instead, took the approach that the better you looked, the better you felt.

She walked down the steps and found Bryce at the kitchen table, with his computer and his cell phone. "Playing with your friends, I see," she teased.

He looked at her. So closely she began to wonder if she'd missed rinsing off some toothpaste. "How are you?" he asked finally.

"I slept," she said.

"I know. I checked on you a couple times."

That made her warm. Heck, now she was probably going to spike a fever. The idea of him standing at her door, watching her sleep. "My brother called," she said, wanting to think of something much safer. "He's on his way over."

Bryce sighed. "He called me first. I told him not to bother you, that I'd get in touch with him if there was any need to be concerned. I think he has trust issues."

"He trusts you to find Len Davison because that's in your line of work. He probably doesn't realize that you also went to medical school. I mean, I just learned that this morning."

Bryce rolled his eyes. "I'll let the officers outside

know to expect him." He sent a quick text. "You must be feeling better," he said, putting his phone down.

"I am. But I'm going to get a cup of tea."

"I'll make it," he said, standing up immediately.

"That would be nice," she said, feeling a bit awkward. She was so not used to someone waiting on her.

"Want a piece of toast with it?" he asked.

Her mother used to make her tea and toast when she was sick. "Yes, please. With butter and honey."

He got busy, and she sat and watched. And appreciated the way he moved. He was a tall guy, over six feet, and trim but not skinny. And damn sexy. She liked that.

Later, minutes after she'd eaten her toast and drunk her tea, her doorbell rang. "I'll get it," Bryce said.

"Wonderful. I'll just move to the couch and do nothing," she said. She might pretend to be sick for weeks.

It was her brother. He came in, carrying a bag of oranges. He shook Bryce's hand and hugged her. "You're alive, I see," he said.

"Punching above my weight," she said.

"I don't think so," he said, looking at her closely. He turned to Bryce. "She giving you any trouble?"

"Nothing but," Bryce said.

"Enough," she said. "I'm in the room."

Bryce rolled his eyes and Oren shrugged, as if to say, *What's a guy to do?* She might just go back to bed after all and leave these two goons to entertain each other. But then Bryce's cell phone buzzed. When he checked it, he frowned.

"It's the officer outside. Are you expecting a delivery?"

She shook her head. She started to unfold herself from the couch.

"I'll get this," Bryce said, standing up. He gave Oren a look that was easy to interpret. *Be alert.*

The minute Bryce was out the door, Oren leaned toward her. "Is this going okay?"

She loved her brother, a whole lot, but he was a typical guy—a fixer. If she confessed any of her convoluted feelings about Bryce, he'd be perplexed on how to quickly remedy the situation. That would make him unhappy, it would spill over to Madison and so on. She needed to just keep quiet. "Good. He's learning how to cook."

"I heard that you went to Verity's house for lunch. That Wes Windham was there and...well, that there was some tension between Bryce and his dad."

It felt wrong to discuss it without Bryce here to defend himself. "Guess who came to see me last night? Thomas Michael. Do you remember him from my culinary school days?"

"Yeah. I didn't know the two of you were still in touch."

He made it sound as if that wasn't a good idea.

"We don't see each other that often. But he's...anticipating a move to this area," she said.

Oren shrugged. "He's an okay guy. But I never got the opinion that there was that much substance there."

"He was fun," she said.

"Fun only gets you so far," Oren said.

She heard the door open, so she was prevented from saying more. It was Bryce, carrying a large bouquet of fresh flowers. He didn't look happy. "There's a card," he said.

The flowers were lovely. Truly. A beautiful fall arrangement with lots of yellows and oranges and deep purples. Had Thomas sent them? Never had before, she thought. But then again, he'd been married to someone else. She reached for the card.

It was handwritten. She read the words silently to herself and felt a chill. Thomas had not sent these flowers. She looked up, first at her brother, then a longer glance at Bryce. Then she slowly read the card out loud. "'Lovely Olivia, so very sorry to hear that you're ill. Please get better. I have so many plans for us. Love, L.D.'"

"That son of a bitch," Bryce said.

Oren said nothing, but the look on his face was murderous.

She dropped the card, feeling sick. Saw Bryce go to her kitchen cabinet and get a plastic bag. Then he carefully dropped the card inside.

"I'll be right back," he said. He left fast, slamming the door behind him. She understood the frustration. She wanted to slam her whole body against something.

"This is bad," she said to Oren.

"It's not good. But Davison is getting sloppy. He was seen in the park the other night and then again at the protest," he said, proving that he was keeping up with the investigation. "Now this. Sloppy people get caught."

She really hoped so.

Bryce was back a few minutes later. "We got lucky. The delivery driver and the officer outside know each other and were still chatting. The delivery driver put me in contact with the flower shop owner. They are closed for the day, but she was working the counter earlier this afternoon when a man came in and ordered these flowers. He insisted on a rush after-hours delivery. Paid extra. I described Davison, but she said it didn't sound like the man she waited on. Fortunately, they've got video. She's going to meet police at her store to take a look."

"I'll go," Oren said.

"Thank you," Bryce said. "I think it's best I stay here."

She got up and gave her brother a hug. "Be careful."

"Right back at ya," he said. Then he walked out the door.

"Davison is watching me closely enough that he knows I left work early today. Somehow he found out that I'm ill," Olivia said.

"Yeah," said Bryce. "And not that many people knew. You stayed back in the kitchen answering the phone, but you didn't make a big deal of why. Hernando knew, but I'm not even sure Trace caught on."

"I think you're right. But I did tell Sally when I asked her to cover for me."

"Did you ask her not to say anything?"

"No. I never thought about it. But I suppose if somebody came in and asked about me, she might have mentioned that I was sick."

"Okay, that's good."

"Why is that good?"

"More leads to follow up on. We're going to find somebody that can lead us to Davison."

She sat, thinking. "So he somehow finds out that I'm ill, goes to the flower store and orders what appears to be an expensive bouquet, which is even more expensive because he has to pay for a rush delivery. Oh, yes, and somewhere in there, he takes the time to pen me a personal note. Wow."

"Gets a lot done when his mind is set to it," Bryce said, sarcasm dripping from every word.

"That's what I'm afraid of," she said. Both times that she'd encountered Davison, he'd seemed a little lost, like he was making it up as he went along. But this, somehow, seemed so much more calculated. It was chilling.

"Maybe it's because I'm not feeling one hundred percent, but it almost seems overwhelming."

"I know. Sally would still be at Bubbe's, right?"

"Yes. She's staying until we close at nine."

"Let's call her. Ask if she remembers talking to anybody about you being sick."

She dialed the landline number for the deli. "Bubbe's Deli," Sally answered.

"Sally, it's Olivia," she said. "Thank you again for covering for me."

"No worries. It's been steady, and I can use the extra money for gifts. Happy to have the hours. How are you feeling?"

"Better," she said. "I wanted to ask whether you've had a conversation with anybody about me being sick."

"I talked to Hernando," Sally said. "He seemed to already know."

"Yes, for sure. Anybody else?"

"Well, there was one customer who asked for you. I've seen him before. Not like he's a regular, but he's definitely been in once or twice in the last week or two. It was probably midafternoon when he came in. He asked about you, and at first I just told him that you weren't available. Then he got a little pushy and said that he knew you were there, that your car was in the parking lot. I didn't want him posting something on social media that the owner of Bubbe's refused to talk to customers. So I told him that you were sick, that you'd left work earlier, leaving your car behind." She paused. "I'm sorry, Olivia. I hope I didn't do anything wrong."

"Of course not." She looked at the note that Bryce had passed her. *Get a description.* "Would you happen to recall what this guy looked like?"

"Yeah, I guess. White. Young. Maybe thirty. Not a very big guy. Dark hair, cut short."

"That's very helpful," Olivia said. "Anything else?"

"Had a café au lait and a chocolate croissant."

"Okay, thank you. And thanks again for working tonight." Olivia hung up. "Does that description mean anything to you?"

"Nope." He was already tapping keys on his computer. "But it's enough, given that we've got an approximate time, that it will be easy for us to pick him out on the security tape."

It took him just minutes. "This has got to be him. Do you recognize him?"

She studied the screen. She wasn't great with ages, but she thought the man looked about her own age. He was wearing blue jeans, a red sweatshirt and a red baseball cap. She did not know him. "No."

"I'm going to send it to Oren. Have him show the owner of the flower shop."

"Now what?" she asked after he'd done that.

"We wait. It won't be long."

It wasn't. His phone rang about ten minutes later.

"Oren," he said, looking at it.

"Can you put it on speaker?"

He looked reluctant, but he did it. "Hi, Oren. I've got you on speaker, and Olivia is here."

"Fine. I've talked to the owner of Fergie's Flowers and looked at their video. The man that came in to order the flowers that were delivered to Olivia was definitely not Len Davison. Although, oddly enough, the owner was familiar with Len Davison. He used to get flowers there for his wife."

She and Bryce exchanged glances. His now-deceased wife, who'd succumbed to cancer.

"Anyway," Oren went on, "good news is that there's definitely a match between the photo you sent and the video from the flower store."

"How did the man pay at the flower store?" Bryce asked.

"With cash," Oren said.

Olivia leaned forward. "I suppose there's no chance that the owner recognized him? That he'd been a customer before?"

"I asked. And no. Requests are already being funneled to other local businesses to see if there's any other street video that will be helpful in determining where the guy went after leaving Fergie's Flowers."

"That's good," Bryce said. "An accomplice. This is something new for Davison."

"Maybe not an accomplice. Maybe just some guy looking to pick up a few bucks," Oren countered. "Davison has cash to work with now, given that he stole some from Bubbe's."

"You could be right. Either way, we find this younger guy, we're that much closer to finding Davison."

"Agree," said Oren. "Any lead is better than no lead."

Bryce and Oren were both attempting to stay positive. She could do the same. On a limited scale. "Davison is…" She yawned. It was maddening to be still tired after sleeping all afternoon. She hadn't been lying when she'd said she was feeling better, but now fatigue was setting in. "Davison is no match for us three superheroes."

"Olivia, do you want me to come back over?" Oren asked.

"Nope. I'm going back to bed." She got up. "I'll talk to you tomorrow. Love you."

"I love you, too. Get well." Oren hung up.

ONCE OLIVIA WAS safely upstairs and in her bedroom, Bryce called Oren back. He stabbed the keys of his cell phone. He was no superhero. But he felt angry enough that just maybe he could toss somebody through a wall. Or drop-kick them through a set of goalposts. Maybe just Davison's head.

When Oren answered, Bryce pushed forward. "He's taunting us."

"Yeah," Oren said, sounding tired.

"I'm going to see if Tatiana can be of some assistance. I'll have her take a look at a photo of the man and see if she recognizes him as somebody from her father's past," Bryce said.

"That's a good idea. I have to tell you that I really appreciate you being there with Olivia. She told me that Thomas Michael stopped at the deli last night."

"He mentioned that he probably still owed you money from when you staked him in a poker game."

"Yeah, but I bet he didn't offer it up."

Bryce was a trained agent, used to detecting the smallest nuances in someone's tone or words. He didn't need any of those skills to understand that Oren wasn't a fan of Thomas Michael. "I got the impression that you, Olivia and Thomas hung around together when you visited your sister."

"We did. Olivia liked him. I think they were good moral support for one another. Everyone thinks how wonderful it would be to go to culinary school, but it's really a rigorous curriculum with lots of inherent stress as students compete against one another to produce the perfect dish. If there's a really zealous instructor, it's like a reality show with no prizes and too much reality. I was glad she had somebody who could make her laugh, and as such, I didn't make a big deal out of him being around. Also, I was confident it was never going to amount to anything more."

"Why?"

"I know Olivia. Thomas wouldn't be complex enough to keep her interest very long."

"I wouldn't be so sure of that. He and his wife are getting divorced. He said something to Olivia. I'm not exactly sure what, but it was enough that she's confident that his interest in her doesn't just have to do with his desire to work at the deli."

"What?" Oren asked, his tone harsh. "She didn't tell me that."

"I got the impression that she's not...repulsed by the idea of getting closer to him," Bryce said.

"This will be okay. I know my sister. She won't get fooled by him. Not when the stakes are high."

"I hope you're right," Bryce said. He thought about telling Oren that he really liked Olivia. But now wasn't the right time. "I'll talk to you tomorrow. Tell Madison hello for me."

After ending the phone call, Bryce wandered the house, checking windows and doors. Then he went upstairs but didn't turn off the light. He pored over topographical maps of the Grave Gulch park and forest.

Davison was even more closely linked to the park than he'd known previously. He could feel it.

And now he was linked to this other person.

It made sleep almost impossible. The good news was that Olivia seemed to feel much better. He suspected she'd be back at work tomorrow. He would not have to make the daily specials.

Which had turned out pretty darn good. He could now add potato knish with onion and spinach to his repertoire. Although he likely would need Olivia by his side to walk him through it.

What would she think when this was all over if he called her up and asked for some just-in-time instruction? Because of Oren's relationship to his family, she'd probably feel obligated.

He'd be a pity cooking lesson.

That had zero appeal. He closed his eyes, determined to focus on what was important.

Tomorrow, he was going to find the man who'd been at Bubbe's and later ordered flowers and attached the note supposedly from L.D. And Bryce was going to make him talk. One way or another.

Chapter Nine

Olivia felt much better physically when she woke up the next morning. Her throat had improved, she no longer ached and her headache was a dim memory.

Emotionally, however, she was shot. The idea that Len Davison had arranged for flowers to be delivered to her and had had the audacity to have his initials added to the card was a blow. She'd somehow managed to block it out and get some much-needed rest, but now, in the light of day, she was going to have to face it.

And it wasn't the only thing to face. There was Bryce's presence in her home. Quiet. Intense. Data focused. A serious man.

Next to him, she was flighty, too chatty and ruled by a gut instinct that could be significantly swayed by a person's likability.

Opposites attract. That was the little voice in her head as she pushed herself out of her warm bed. Maybe she'd run into his naked chest again in the hallway. That gave her step a little bounce as she headed for the door.

But the hallway was empty. And she found him fully dressed twenty minutes later, sitting at the kitchen table with, shock of all shocks, his laptop in front of him. "Do you sleep with that?" she asked.

He nodded. "Next to my pillow. And good morning. Feeling better?"

"Yes," she mumbled. "Good morning."

"You have a new review online," he said, showing her his laptop. "They loved the spinach-onion knish," he added.

She leaned over his shoulder to read the content. *Always enjoy my lunch at Bubbe's Deli but the spinach and onion knish I had there today was really excellent. Good taste, good value, good place to spend a little time.* It was posted by Sandie B.

"You don't live a double life as Sandie B, do you?" she asked.

"No, I do not," he said.

She straightened up and patted his shoulder. "You're feeling so proud of yourself, aren't you?" she said.

He shrugged. "FBI agents don't get many favorable online reviews."

"I suppose not. That's too bad. I really do appreciate it when people take the time to leave a review."

"Even when they're bad?"

She shrugged. "Fortunately, those have been few and far between. And would I prefer that someone air a grievance privately with me prior to posting the review so that I have time to fix the problem or make amends in some other way? Yes, of course. But people aren't always comfortable doing that. It's part of being in business. The goal is to never perform at a level where anyone thinks a negative review is warranted."

"Biggest fail?" he asked.

She thought about it. "Sauerkraut."

"Interesting. Tell me more."

"I have a few trusted food vendors. I get my sauerkraut from one of them. Now, sauerkraut can come in one of two ways. Already cooked or raw. Both can be eaten and they don't look all that different. The taste, however, is definitely different. Sadly, one day, the two got mixed up, and we served several sandwiches with raw instead of cooked sauerkraut. Not to be too graphic, but the customers were literally spitting out their half-chewed food into their napkins."

"Ugh," he said.

"Yes. Fortunately, they were nice customers and very understanding. We remade the sandwiches, gave everyone free dessert and didn't charge them for the meal. Service recovery."

"So no nasty review?"

"Definitely not. The nastiest online review I ever got was a backhanded compliment. Something that I don't think anyone would have ever said to my face but they felt comfortable putting it in print."

"What was that?"

In her typically chatty fashion, she'd shared too much. "Never mind."

"Tell me."

She rolled her eyes. "It said, *The desserts must be delicious at Bubbe's. I was in the deli recently and I'm confident the owner has put on ten pounds since they opened.*"

He opened his mouth. Then closed it. "Bitch," he said.

"Or bastard. I didn't know if a woman or a man had written it. There were just initials. T.B."

"You have an amazing shape," he said.

She felt warm. "I wasn't fishing for compliments," she said.

"I know that. I just think that T.B. was probably a

jealous crone. And I'm fairly confident it was a woman. No guy is going to find fault anywhere."

Warm had turned into molten lava. "The story has a happy ending. I had put on a few pounds, which is easy to do when you're working with food all day long. I started running again, and the weight came off. My psyche was not permanently damaged. In fact, I can't wait for all this to be over. I want to run again."

"I run," he said.

"Are you offering to jog with me?" she asked, hoping that she'd interpreted his response correctly. "Would it be safe?"

"Yes, to question one. I think so, to question two. Davison doesn't want to shoot you. We don't have to worry about an attack from a distance. We'll drive somewhere and then start our run. I can make sure we're not followed on the drive."

"It's supposed to warm up, be close to fifty this afternoon. It would be heavenly to get a run in."

"Do you feel up to it?"

"I do."

"Then it's a plan," he said. "Are you ready to leave?"

"I was, but now I'm going to run upstairs, pun intended, and get my running clothes and shoes."

"Mine are in my vehicle," he said.

"Always prepared," she teased.

"In that vein, I've already sent a photo of Mystery Man to Tatiana."

"Mystery Man," she repeated. "I like it."

"Anyway, she should see it on her phone when she wakes up. It's a long shot, but I hope that she can be of some help."

"Good thinking."

Just then, his phone dinged with an incoming text message. "Tatiana," he said, picking up his phone to read the message.

"Is the room bugged?" Olivia asked, to no one in particular.

Bryce put his phone down. "No luck. She doesn't recognize him."

"What next?"

"We'll run his face through recognition programs. If he's got a record or has in some other way gotten the attention of law enforcement, we might get lucky."

Something dawned on her. Something that she hadn't thought about before. "I'm going to have an FBI file, aren't I? I'm going to be one of those people."

He shrugged. "All kinds of people have FBI files. In the age of computers, when storage space is really infinite, many records exist. It's why data mining is such a specialty. The key is being able to use the appropriate search techniques to pull the data from this immense records stash to find helpful information. Otherwise, this treasure trove is about as useful as a stuffed filing drawer that never gets opened."

She glanced at the clock on the wall. It was time to go to work. "I guess I won't be too concerned about my file unless my picture is on the wall at the post office under 'Most Wanted.' And if that happens, you have to promise me that you'll make sure it's a flattering one."

"Pinkie swear," he said.

She smiled. "Sometimes I can so tell that you had sisters."

HE'D ALWAYS THOUGHT being raised with sisters was a blessing. Even when they were a pain, which both

Madison and Jillian had been at times. They, of course, would likely say the same thing about him. But disagreements had been rare. The siblings had gotten along, and there was never any doubt that they had each other's backs.

He wondered what they would say if he called them and confessed that he was falling for Olivia. What advice would they give him? Bide his time? Be assertive, make a move? Just tell her? Get the case settled first, then think about what might come next?

The possibilities were endless. What he didn't think they would say was to give up. Certainly not Madison, who had so recently fallen for Oren. She was so happy, and her nature was to want everyone else to enjoy the same contentment. Jillian had not yet found that someone special. And because of the work she did as a crime scene investigator, she'd seen some ugly things. He felt confident that she'd tell him if he had found something good and solid, not to let it slip through his hands.

Now, as they drove to work, together since her car was still in Bubbe's lot, he allowed himself to think about what life might be like once Len Davison had been captured and sent to prison. After being in circumstances that were literally life and death, could he and Olivia do something as mundane as date? Go out to dinner? A movie?

Have sex?

He felt way too warm, and he reached for the heater, finding the wrong knob and turning off the radio in his haste. Olivia gave him a funny look.

Excellent thing that she couldn't read minds.

He parked next to her car. It appeared to be undisturbed. Still, as they got out, he looked inside it, just to make sure that it was okay. As they entered the deli, they saw that Hernando had beaten them there this morning. The man's eyes warmed when he saw Olivia. "You're feeling better," he announced.

"I must have really looked bad yesterday," she said, smiling. "And, yes, back to normal." She turned to him. "I've got this. You can feel free to take your trusty computer and phone to a booth out front and data mine away."

"I'm going to count how many times you use the words *data mine* or some version of them today," he said.

She laughed. "I'll think of you with a hard hat and gloves and a little pick and shovel, digging for bits and bytes."

"Wow. More computerese," he said.

"I'm just getting warmed up." She whirled around the kitchen. "No need to call for *backup*. My *mainframe* is just fine, thank you very much. And my *memory* is superior. Although I think I would enjoy a *cookie*."

That last one got a smile from Hernando. Bryce thought she was about the cutest thing he'd ever seen. "I'm going to make coffee. You might want to watch your caffeine intake," he added.

She gave him a little wave.

By the time Bryce delivered her a cup in the kitchen, she was already hard at work. He went back to the dining room and settled in a booth. He opened his computer, smiling as he did. She'd been hilarious. He wasn't ashamed of being a computer nerd; he had skills that the FBI found very useful. He could also hit center mass at a hundred yards with his Glock. That made him a threat on many levels. It was good to have a wide array of skills.

Now he had an idea. Tatiana had not been any help in identifying Mystery Man. But Bryce believed there was some connection between him and Davison. He was going to go back through all the contacts of Davison that they'd interviewed over the past months. Review the notes again. See if there was some thread that could be picked up on that might lead them to identifying the mystery man. Olivia could poke fun at data mining, but the value of data was real. The ability to sort through it, organize it and use it to help in an investigation could not be underestimated.

That did not mean that he left his common sense at the door. A good agent needed all the tools in his or her tool belt. Davison was set to kill again this month. Something was about to happen. They just needed to get a step ahead of him.

By late morning, after he'd downed too much coffee, his confidence that they could get in front of Davison got a boost when he got a call from Brett Shea.

"We've got a partial plate on the man who was in Bubbe's and later ordered the flowers that got delivered to Olivia," Brett said.

"What? How? Tell me everything."

"We canvassed surrounding businesses and asked to see their security tapes. We thought we'd lost him, but then a hair salon at the corner of Winder Avenue and Spruce Street had something."

Bryce was pulling up a map as the other man was talking. It was at the far edge of the business district, where there was a mix of commercial spaces and housing. "That's more than four blocks from the deli," he said.

"Yeah. The guy snaked through businesses and backyards. Not the behavior you'd associate with an upstanding citizen. But we have him getting into a red Ford Focus and the last two numbers on his Michigan plate—they're seven and five. We're running a list of possible matches at this very minute."

It was good police work. If they'd stopped asking about security cameras after a couple of blocks, they'd have missed this. "This is great," Bryce said. "It could be the break we needed."

"I think you're right. Initially I thought it might be just some guy that Davison paid fifty bucks in order to get a couple errands run. But given how the guy tried to circumvent anybody following him, it makes me think that he's aware that he's helping somebody that he shouldn't be helping."

"We just need to figure out why," Bryce said, following the line of thought. "A relative or close friend? Someone paying back a debt of gratitude for something Davison did for him in the past? A sick sense of hero worship—he knows that Davison is a serial killer and it's something he respects and admires?"

"Any of those could make him a dangerous person."

"Agree."

"Once we get the list of potential matches, I'll forward it to you. It could be hundreds of names. Maybe we can coordinate our efforts to work through the list as quickly as possible," Brett said.

Bryce understood. Nobody had to tell him that time was not on their side. "Absolutely. I'll watch for it and be in touch." He hung up and put his phone down. His conversation had ended just in time. The deli would open in less than a half hour, and staff was arriving to put the finishing touches on the dining room. He did not want them overhearing his conversation.

As each employee arrived, he greeted them and then showed them a picture of Mystery Man. One waitress recalled seeing him before, maybe a week or so earlier. But she thought that was the first time. She recalled that he was pleasant. Sort of quiet.

With everyone, he left brief instructions: "If you see him again, don't let on that there's any interest in him. But immediately contact me. If I don't answer for some reason, contact Brett Shea with the Grave Gulch Police Department."

They'd all nodded in agreement, and he'd made sure that they had his information in their cell phone contacts. He wasn't going to miss an opportunity to catch the guy just because somebody couldn't remember his number.

It was during the middle of the lunch rush that he got an email from Brett with a listing of potential matches to a red Ford Focus with seventy-five as the last two license plate numbers. There were 167. Of that, fifty-one had a home address within sixty miles of Grave Gulch. He noted that there were both male and female names, and he was happy to see that Brett had not narrowed the search to just men. Mystery Man could have borrowed his wife's car. It was important to keep the search as wide as possible now.

After a few back-and-forth emails, they had a plan. The Grave Gulch Police Department would take the top half of the fifty-one-person list, and Bryce and whatever resources he could get from the FBI would take the bottom half. If they encountered no success looking within the radius, they would broaden the search to include the whole state.

He contacted his boss and the man immediately assigned two more agents to assist Bryce. In order to have a productive conversation with them that nobody could overhear, he went upstairs to Olivia's office. He and the two female agents further separated their list of twenty-six names into two groups and set a deadline of forty-eight hours for each of the agents to personally visit everyone in their cluster.

He felt bad that he wasn't able to assist in the effort. But it would have meant that he needed to leave Olivia behind, which he wasn't doing, or take her with him, which had inherent risks. While most fieldwork involved the almost tedious task of tracking down leads that quickly turned into dead ends, there was always the possibility that any contact could be the one thread that would unravel a whole case.

If the two of them happened to stumble upon the man who'd ordered the flowers, and he was more than Davison's errand boy, it could be bad. If the man or Davison really wished Olivia harm, having her along for the ride might be the equivalent of delivering the rabbit to the tiger's food bowl. He wasn't going to take that chance.

By the time Bryce got back downstairs, Olivia was back in the kitchen. She was working on a special order that was being picked up later that afternoon. Right now, she was surrounded by lettuce and other salad fixings.

"How much salad did they order?" he asked. He'd heard her and Hernando talking about the food order earlier. It was for an office party at the bank that was down the street.

"Chopped salad for fifty. Plus four platters of assorted sandwiches—pastrami on rye, turkey on whole wheat and chicken salad on croissants. That's on my plate. Hernando is handling the dessert platters."

"Does this happen often?"

She looked up and gave him a dazzling smile. "Only on the really good days."

"Cha-ching," he said, making the universal sound of money rolling in.

"Let's just say that special orders help the bottom line. We did a lot of the prep this morning, but I need to finish the salad and assemble the sandwich platters. Then I was hoping we might go for our run."

"We can do that," he said. "Are you going to eat something?"

"I just had some soup. That's enough. Especially if I'm running. But help yourself to whatever. I think there are some beef tips left from the lunch special."

He'd seen some of that getting served up before he'd gone upstairs for his phone calls. It had looked really good—tender tips of sirloin and mushrooms in a rich gravy over noodles. Certain to be significantly better than any frozen dinner he might have cooked for himself. "Okay, I will," he said. "Then I'll help you with the sandwiches."

"WHERE ARE WE GOING?" Olivia asked. Bryce had wanted to drive, and she'd been happy to let him. She felt gloriously free—the deli was in good hands under Hernando's watch, she was in her favorite running pants, shirt and hoodie, and it was a beautiful sunny afternoon, with the temperature in the high fifties.

"It's a place I found a couple years ago," he said. "We're almost there."

They'd left the town of Grave Gulch behind them ten minutes ago. Now they were in the open country. She had a feeling that she knew where they were headed. She'd heard about the old train track bed that bikers and runners raved about but hadn't yet been there. She'd not wanted to venture there on her own.

Sure enough, after another five minutes, Bryce pulled off into a small parking area that could probably hold twenty cars. There were six in the lot.

"How far is the trail?" she asked.

"From this point, we can go twelve miles south and four miles north. Both ways are fully paved and offer good scenery. The trail crosses the river about three miles that direction," he said, pointing south.

"Sold. How about we run to the river and back?" Six miles would be a good workout.

"Grab your water," he said, shutting off the car. They got out, stretched for a minute and took off. The trail was plenty wide enough for them to run side by side, even if they met someone coming from the other direction. She generally did about a nine-minute mile. She suspected he might usually run faster or harder but was holding back, letting her set the pace.

They didn't talk as they exercised. She appreciated that. She liked to let her mind empty out, to let her cares drift away on the wind. There was open farmland on either side of them. Acres and acres of freshly picked cornfields. The straggly stalks, the remnants of what had likely been a robust crop, danced in the wind, looking a rich gold in the bright sunshine. Off in the distance was a stand of trees, likely pines or cedars, with a few now-leafless maples standing in sharp contrast.

She lifted her face to the warm sunlight. A nice fall day was a truly glorious time to be outside. They ran steadily until they got to the bridge that crossed the river. She stopped to admire the view below. The water, probably thirty feet wide at this point, was still and dark, but as she looked out, there were spots where the sun was hitting it, making it almost reflective. It was beautiful. After a minute, she turned to him. "This is the best," she said. "The very best thing I could have done today."

He laughed. "You're like a little kid who got locked in the candy aisle."

"I know. It's weird. Like I said, I didn't start running until recently, and now I wonder why, since I love it. It makes me think about all the other things I don't do that I might also love."

"Skydiving?" he teased.

"Maybe?"

"Scuba diving?"

"Not on the list," she said.

"Downhill skiing?"

"This is Michigan, dude. Of course I can downhill ski."

"Okay," he said. "I'm out of options."

"Let's get closer to the water," she said. The riverbank was steep, but she thought they could do it.

"Let me go first," he said.

"To prevent me from sliding into the river?" she said.

"Something like that."

They scrambled down the grassy hill. Once they were level with the water, she searched for and found a flat rock. Then she expertly skipped it across the water. Oren had taught her how to do it.

"Impressive," Bryce said. He handed her another stone. "Let's see if you can do it twice in a row."

After five throws, Bryce held up his hands. "You are the undefeated champion of rock skippers."

"You didn't even try."

"I don't want to be shown up by a girl."

With the palm of her hand, she shoved his shoulder. "Chicken," she teased. "Cluck, cluck." It was how she'd teased her brother.

But when Bryce grabbed her in response and pulled her close, his body pressing against hers, all thought of sibling rivalry fled her head. He kissed her again, his lips warm, his tongue insistent.

"Oh, God," she murmured. The need to be close to him, to touch him in every possible way, was pulsating through her. It was all-consuming, robbing her of coherent thought.

And he clearly understood. Her silent plea. Her unspoken yearning. And when his hands went to her bottom and he pressed her close, she felt the thickness and strength of his desire. Now. Right here. Before all that nature offered.

"Yes," she said, even though he had not asked. She would do anything—

"Hey, get a room."

They sprang apart, Bryce immediately stepping in front of her. Above them, on the bridge, were three teenage boys on bikes. They were laughing hysterically.

And perhaps they saw the look on Bryce's face, or

the set of his shoulders, because they stopped laughing quickly. "Let's go," one said. The other two didn't argue. They pedaled off.

Bryce turned to her. She was busy nervously yanking at the hem of her sweatshirt. She didn't want to look at him. It was embarrassing to think that she'd almost been begging.

He put two fingers under her chin, lifted her face so that their eyes met. "Are you okay?" he asked.

"Swell," she said. Then let out a sigh.

"Just give me a minute," he said, walking away from her. He stood, twenty yards away, with his back to her, for several minutes. When he came back, he gave no explanation.

She couldn't let it go. "What were you doing?"

"Reciting the state capitals," he said. "And then I did a quick review of the history of the automatic rifle."

"Did it help?" she asked, not sure if she could name all the capitals and confident she knew next to nothing about guns.

"I think I can run again," he said.

She appreciated his lack of pretense, his willingness to admit that their *encounter* had left him physically charged. He was probably more honest than she was. "We should get to it," she said.

"After you," he said and motioned toward the hill they were going to have to climb.

"I go first, in case I come sliding back down." The minute she said it, she regretted it. The vision of her sliding bottom-first into him was too fresh a reminder of where they'd been.

"That's right," he said, letting it go.

Yep, no doubt about it. She might be able to skip

a few rocks, but he was going to take home the prize for most maturity. She marched up the hill, careful to keep her footing.

Chapter Ten

He'd now kissed her three times. Wasn't that number
supposed to be a charm? Well, he had…risen to the occasion. Supposed he should be thanking his lucky stars
that he hadn't spontaneously combusted.

Lord, he wanted her. On the butcher-block kitchen
table, on the glass-front counter, her desk, the couch
in her office. Maybe after that, he might feel civilized
enough to do it in a bed. But *it* likely wasn't going to
happen in any of those places, or anywhere, because
she had apparently lost the ability to look at him.

They'd been back at the deli for more than five
hours, had gotten through the dinner rush and the
slower hours after that, the drawer had been counted
and the deposit calculated, and not once, not one single
time, had she made eye contact. He was getting damn
sick of it. "Ready to go?" he asked.

"Yeah. Let me get my coat."

He heard a phone ringing and realized it was coming from the outside side pocket of her purse that she'd
left on the counter. He reached for the cell, looked at
the display and almost dropped it. It was his mother's number.

Olivia was nowhere to be seen. He grabbed for the phone. "Why are you calling Olivia?" he asked.

"Well, hello, Bryce," she said, not sounding put off. "Is that any way to answer your mother?"

"When you call *me*, I'm very polite."

"Yes, you are. And I'm returning Olivia's call."

What the hell? Why had Olivia called his mother? "She's not available."

"That's fine, Bryce. Just let her know that I do want to follow up with her and that I'll stop by the deli tomorrow after school is out."

"Follow up on what?" he asked.

She laughed. "If Olivia wanted you to know, I suspect she'd have told you. Goodbye, Bryce. I love you."

His mother hung up on him. He stared at the phone. Debated stuffing it back in the pocket of her purse but left it on the counter. When she finally came back, several minutes later, Olivia looked at it and frowned.

"My mother called. I answered the phone."

"Oh." She paused. "That's probably good, since we've been playing telephone tag."

"Why are you calling my mother?" he asked.

She frowned at him. "Because I want to be involved in her effort to feed hungry kids and families at her school."

He felt like an ass. He'd assumed the worst, not immediately trusting Olivia or his mother. Which was pretty damn stupid, since neither one of them had done anything to prove that they weren't trustworthy. He'd have liked to have blamed this tendency on his work as an FBI agent. But, more likely, not believing that others could have good intent was simply a place where he fell short.

"Why did you think I called her?"

"I don't know. I… I think my brain short-circuited when I saw her number. I thought maybe you'd called her to complain about me."

She looked…well, perhaps the word was *flabbergasted*. "You thought I would tattle to your mother that you…what…ravished me in the wilderness? What is this, 1880?" She paused, looking around. "Where is my chaperone?"

He held up a hand. "Okay, I get it. I'm sorry. That was stupid."

"You think?"

He bit down on his lip. "You haven't looked at me since we got back here this afternoon. What the hell was I supposed to think?"

"That I was busy?"

"I've seen you busy. Plenty busy. This wasn't that." He stopped. Because now she was looking a little embarrassed. That wasn't his intent. "I just want to clear the damn air. We're attracted to one another. That much is obvious."

"Clear the air," she repeated. "That's the second time we've used that phrase. So, please, yes, keep going. Clear the damn air."

"Both of us need to do a better job of making sure that we don't…that we don't slip up and let the moment get to us. I have a responsibility to you. To keep my head on straight and protect you."

"Well, I certainly don't want to stop you from doing your job," she said, sounding a bit frosty.

"Your safety is important. Catching Len Davison is important. Those are the things that I need to keep focused on."

"Of course," she said. She picked up her purse. "Let's go."

"Are we okay?" he asked.

"Consider the air so cleared that you might even think it's been purified."

VERITY COLTON SWEPT into Bubbe's Deli at four o'clock the following afternoon in a rush of cold air. She wore a stylish black coat with knee-high black boots and had a big smile for Olivia, who was at the cash register. "I was so glad and so grateful to get your call."

"I really want to help," Olivia said. "It breaks my heart to think that your students are hungry. That their families do not have enough food."

"I know. It's one of the hardest parts of my job, knowing that a child could be doing better, if only their basic needs were being met."

Olivia heard footsteps on the stairs behind her. She didn't need to turn around—she knew it was Bryce. He'd been working upstairs since the lunch rush had ended. They had not eaten lunch together. She'd claimed to be too busy for lunch, citing the need to do a physical inventory of supplies. He'd looked irritated with her excuse, and she'd thought he might call her out on such a flimsy pretext for avoiding him, but instead he'd fixed his lunch, taken it upstairs and stayed there. She'd known that he was ever diligent, watching his beloved screens that were synced with her security cameras, looking for Len Davison, for Mystery Man, for anybody who might be a threat to her.

That was what had, no doubt, brought him down

the steps now. He'd seen his mother arrive. She was no threat, of course.

"Hello, Bryce," Verity said, smiling when she saw him.

He hugged his mother. "How was school?"

"Exhausting. Tedious at times. Exhilarating at other times. Generally hilarious because, you know, they're second graders. The usual." She did not sound upset, but rather pretty satisfied.

Olivia understood the odd explanation. Work was not play, but when you loved what you were doing, it could be a very good thing.

"How was your day?" Verity asked, looking at both of them.

"Fine," Bryce said.

"Yeah, fine," she echoed.

His mother was too nice and too lovely to comment on the awkwardness that those three words, shared between the two of them, had evoked. "Shall we begin?" Verity asked.

"We can use my office," Olivia said. "It's upstairs."

"I'll need to move my things," Bryce said.

"If that's too much trouble, we can—"

"It's your office." He cut her off.

The three of them walked upstairs, and Verity and Olivia stood to the side while Bryce gathered up his computer, cell phone and tablet. Finally, when he was gone, they both took chairs.

"I'm sorry," Verity said, looking uncomfortable. "My son is normally well-mannered. I suspect his unhappiness with me because of Wes is simply too much for him to get past."

Olivia shook her head. There was already so much

cluttering up the situation with Bryce and his family that she couldn't let another thing be unfairly added to the list. "It's not you or Wes. It's me. Bryce is upset with me." She paused. "Actually, that's not even technically true. I think he's upset with the…situation that we find ourselves in." There, that was all she was going to say. But it should be enough that his mother didn't walk away feeling as though she was the cause of her son's irritation.

Verity studied her. "Your *situation*?" she repeated. Then she smiled. "That's very interesting, Olivia," she said, sounding rather amused. "You know what they say—the bigger they are, the tougher they want to be, the harder they fall."

Was that what they said? "I guess."

"Bryce was fiercely protective of me and his sisters when he was growing up," Verity said.

Just as she'd suspected. He had taken his role as man of the house seriously.

"But also fiercely protective of his own emotions," Verity continued. "We thought Wes, or Richard Foster, as we knew him at the time, was dead. Now, Bryce was only three when Richard disappeared, but he felt the loss, and it only intensified over the years, with the many events that occur where having a parent or not having one is noticeable."

"Like at school?"

"Oh, yes. All those years of Doughnuts with Dad programs, the perennial favorite of every school administrator. Most enlightened leadership has gotten smart in the past ten years or so and broadened the criteria so it's more akin to Doughnuts and Whatever Person Is Important to You in Your Life. But twenty years ago, when he was in grade school, we lived in a school district where the vast percentage of boys had dads or, at the very least, a stepdad. He had neither. But he didn't take the easy road, didn't try to pretend that he was sick that morning. No, he went to school, attended the event, with me at his side, and pretended that everything was just fine. But it wasn't."

It broke her heart to think of Bryce as a kid, sitting with his mom while most of his classmates were with their dads. That had to have hurt.

"In the car, on the way to school, he'd recite statistics of how many kids didn't live in a traditional two-parent family."

"Already making use of data," she said with a smile.

"Normalizing his world. Protecting his heart. Unfortunately for Bryce, it wasn't just school where there were reminders. The Colton family is big, and my long status as a single parent did not go unnoticed among the relatives. Every family event was a reminder that we were different. I have to tell you that, at times, I considered marrying someone just so that my kids didn't have to feel that stigma."

"But you didn't."

Verity shook her head. "Ultimately, I knew that whatever short-term benefits I might amass from building a more traditional structure would not outweigh the damage I'd do by adding someone into the mix that I didn't...that I didn't think would fit."

Olivia was pretty confident that she'd been about to say *that I didn't love*. And she was not at all sure how to respond.

Verity opened the leather portfolio she was carrying. "Now let's get down to business," she said.

Verity wanted to move on. Olivia certainly wasn't going to push. She understood having a certain reticence about sharing something so personal. At twenty-eight, she'd already endured questions from friends and family about her lack of a significant other. And when absolutely necessary, she'd developed a repertoire of lighthearted responses that all had something to do with her Prince Charming being late to the ball. And almost always, it was enough for the conversation to move on to safer topics.

In truth, maybe she was waiting for a prince.

She wasn't ready to settle for anything else. "I'm ready," she said.

An hour later, they had a plan. It wasn't just kids in Verity's classroom who were hungry. There were many more, in all grades. As such, they'd agreed that Bubbe's Deli would prepare and deliver one hundred sack lunches to the school every weekday. The meals would consist of some kind of sandwich, a side of fruit, a side of vegetables and a dessert. Once at the school, other volunteers would allocate the sack lunches to the neediest children and their families and pack each child an insulated case to take home. The food could be dinner for the child or could be used as breakfast for the child the next day. On Friday, the sack lunches would be a bit larger to provide extra to help get through the weekend.

"This is so wonderful," Verity said, closing her notebook. "You are the perfect partner for this effort. Now, let's not forget to talk about the money. We do not expect you to pay for the food itself. We have other very generous contributors who can help. Your preparation of the food is more than enough of a contribution."

Olivia had thought this through, had already looked at her financials. "I'll fund fifty percent of it."

"That's too much."

"I want to do it. And in the summertime, when there is no school, we can talk about a way to continue the program in some form. Kids don't stop being hungry just because the academic year ends."

"You're so right. I really can't thank you enough. You will be making a difference in people's lives."

"That's enough thanks right there."

Verity stood up. "I'll be in touch."

"Great. We'll be ready to start the program by the beginning of next week." That would give her time to get her kitchen organized. It would require Trace to work an additional two hours every day, ninety minutes to prepare the lunches and the remaining thirty to drop them off at the school. But she'd already spoken to him earlier in the day about the possibility of this, and he'd been excited for the extra money. She'd also need to up her regular food orders with several vendors.

She felt supergood about her conversation with Verity Colton and her efforts to help the kids and their families. She felt equally bad, though, about the awkwardness between herself and Bryce that Verity had witnessed. By nature, Olivia was a private person, and this felt very much like she'd allowed somebody to see something intimate and also allowed them to form an opinion about her based on that information. Some good had come from it, though. She'd gotten a glimpse into Bryce's past, a look that told her a lot about the man.

She'd expected to see said man in his regular booth, his computer in front of him, when she and Verity reached the front of the deli. Instead, he was behind the cash register, checking customers out, looking very at home. While she and Verity had been talking, the dinner hour had picked up steam, and now Bubbe's was bursting with customers. Most every booth was full, and there were at least four people standing in front of the glass deli case, trying to decide what they were going to take to go.

"It's busy. I shouldn't have taken so much of your time," Verity apologized.

"We're good," Olivia assured her. And she thought it was probably true. Bryce had stepped in and done the job that she'd normally have had at this time of day, allowing the rest of the staff to take care of customers.

His mother gave him a quick wave, smiled at Olivia and left. Olivia walked behind the cash register and stood behind Bryce. She waited until there was a break between customers to say something.

"Thanks for stepping in," she said.

"Happy to. And I'm sorry if I was a jerk earlier. I'm sure I'll hear about it from my mother. I imagine the conversation will go something like, 'I've got second graders with better manners than you.'"

"Your mother thinks the sun rises and sets on your shoulders. She knows that this is a stressful time for you. You're chasing Len Davison, you've got responsibility for my safety and you're coming to terms with your father's return." She deliberately left off the fact that they'd shared a number of smoking-hot kisses that had muddled their brains, because she didn't feel as if she could speak for him.

He shrugged. "She'd be right. I have better manners, and I know how to use them." A customer was approaching with cash in hand. "I'm sorry," he added quickly before stepping away.

That wound up being the last she talked to him for three hours. Soon it was almost eight o'clock, the deli had just a few late-night customers, and she was wiping down tables when she heard a noise from his customary booth. It had sounded very much like *about damn time*.

"What?" she asked.

"We have a good lead on the red Ford Focus." He looked up at her. His eyes were bright. "The owner used to work with Len Davison."

Chapter Eleven

She dropped the wet rag that was in her hands. And she didn't seem to notice. "What now?" she asked.

"They're bringing him in right now for questioning. I'm going to meet Brett Shea, and we'll do it together at the GGPD."

"Go," she said. "Go, go."

"You're coming with me," he said. "It's the safest place you can be. I'll send him a text advising that we can be there after nine." It was killing him to wait.

"Let's go now. Hernando can lock up."

"Are you sure? What about counting the cash drawer?"

"Hernando will put the cash in the freezer and I'll reconcile the drawer in the morning before we open. This has happened before."

That was all he needed to hear. "Okay, let's go," he said, closing his laptop.

His mind was working fast as he drove the two of them to the police station. The man's name was Timothy Wool. He was divorced, a father of two small children and had lived in Grave Gulch until about a year ago. Now his home address was a suburb of Chicago. Fortunately, he had not yet applied for an Illinois driver's license, so his name had popped up on their list of red Ford Focus owners living within sixty miles of Grave Gulch. He was currently staying in a local hotel, allegedly visiting family still in the area. Bryce knew all this from the quick summary that had been texted to him. None of that explained why he was helping Davison.

Brett was waiting for him and Olivia near the entrance of the Grave Gulch Police Department. It was now almost nine o'clock on a weekday. The inside of the police department was quiet, most of the offices dark, as employees had gone home for the day.

"Good to see you again," Brett said to Olivia. "I've got a conference room that you can sit in to wait. There's a television in there. Can I get you something to drink?"

"No, thanks. I have water," she said. "Don't worry about me."

Easier said than done, Bryce thought. When this assignment had started, it had been all about ensuring her physical safety. And he'd been confident that he could protect her from Davison. But now, as their personal relationship had gotten more complex, he had a host of new worries. What was Olivia thinking? Was Olivia upset with him? Disappointed in him? On and on it went.

But now he needed to put all that aside. Compartmentalize. Focus. Make data-driven decisions. "Where will we be?" he asked Brett.

"Interrogation room at the end of the hallway," Brett said, pointing.

It would take him less than ten seconds to reach Olivia if she needed him. "Keep your cell phone on and next to you," he said to her, likely proving to himself, her and Brett that expecting him to stop worrying about Olivia was akin to expecting him to stop breathing.

"We're inside a police station," she reminded him. "What could happen?"

The argument was logical, one that he'd made himself. But he also had learned the hard way to expect the unexpected from Davison. "Just stay aware," he said.

"Yes, fine. Go. Find out what this man knows," she said.

They left her in the conference room. As they walked, Brett turned to him. "Olivia seems to be holding up well."

"She's been a rock," he said. It was true. She was somehow able to compartmentalize the threat against her and manage to move on with her life. She was running her business, volunteering for new ventures in the community. Thinking of others.

Was it any wonder that he...?

"Be careful," Brett said as Bryce stumbled over nothing on the tile floor.

"Right," Bryce said, embarrassed. Hell of a time to realize that he might just be falling in love with Olivia Margulies. In the middle of an investigation—hell, in the middle of an interrogation. He needed to get his head back in the game. He needed his heart to *chill out*.

"It's good that one of us is," Brett said.

It took Bryce a minute to realize that the man was responding to his comment that Olivia was a rock. Now that he looked at Brett closer, the man seemed a little off. He was normally really solid. But maybe the stress had finally caught up with him. Bryce understood. They were all on edge, all fearfully waiting to discover Davison's next victim. All waiting to learn that once again they were too late. Was there something that Brett wasn't telling him? "Has something else happened?"

"Not related to this," Brett said. "I had just gotten off the phone with you earlier when I got a call from your sister Jillian."

Jillian was a crime scene investigator. She likely had reasons to have conversations with the interim chief. But he could tell from Brett that this hadn't been a routine work conversation. "About?"

"She got a text from Randall Bowe."

That couldn't be good. His sister had taken the man's abuse for months while he was her supervisor and then had been harassed and ridiculed by the public for the errors because Bowe had spread the word that she was incompetent. Everybody, including Bryce, who knew her work knew that wasn't the case. "What did he want?"

"To taunt her. Said that he messed with even more cases than has been discovered. Also spewed the usual garbage about the fact that she's incompetent. Said she should just quit."

"That's bull," Bryce said. "Bowe probably can't stand the fact that she's still got a job with the police department and he's never going to work as a forensic scientist again."

"I know it. I've already told her that her job is not in jeopardy. But I'm sure she'll appreciate her brother coming to her defense."

"Can the text be traced?"

"Not according to Ellie Bloomberg."

Ellie was the highly respected tech expert at the

Grave Gulch Police Department. If she couldn't trace it, nobody could. "Maybe this is a good thing. Maybe it means that he's going to surface again."

"Well, that would really be a great Christmas— locking Len Davison up before he kills again and flushing Randall Bowe out of hiding and holding him accountable for his misdeeds."

"We're a step closer to finding Len Davison," Bryce said. He hated that his sister was being trolled by Bowe, but right now, he needed to focus on the matter at hand. Before someone else died.

Brett opened a door and motioned Bryce in. Timothy Wool sat on one side of a plain wood table. They took chairs on the other.

"Mr. Wool, this is Special Agent Bryce Colton, FBI."

Wool nodded in his direction. He looked uneasy. That made Bryce uneasy.

"As I briefly explained, Mr. Wool," Brett said, "we're interested in talking to you about a flower delivery for Olivia Margulies that you arranged for."

"Last I checked, it wasn't against the law to send flowers to a woman," Wool said.

She's not your woman. Somehow Bryce managed to keep that thought to himself. He leaned forward. "Most times it's just fine. In fact, it can be a real good idea at times. But you ordered flowers, wrote a card and signed it 'L.D.' Those aren't your initials. I'm wondering what 'L.D.' stands for."

Wool said nothing.

They waited him out.

Finally, Wool tapped his index finger nervously on the table. For about fifteen seconds. Then stopped, evidently having made up his mind. "I ordered the flowers. I paid for them. But I didn't write any card. When the clerk asked me if I wanted to write a message, I told her yes. I pretended to do so, but what I really did was hand one to the clerk that was already written and ask her to include it with the flowers. I have no idea what the card said. If it was something bad, I'm not responsible. Not in any way."

"Who gave you the card that you passed on to the flower store?" Bryce asked.

"Len Davison."

Now they were getting somewhere. "How is it that you know Mr. Davison?" Bryce asked.

"I used to work with him. About ten years ago, I joined the same accounting firm that employed him. I was a lowly staff accountant intern. He was good to me, taught me a lot."

"And you and Mr. Davison have stayed friends since then?" Bryce asked.

"I guess. But we lost contact after neither of us was working at the accounting firm. I'd moved to Chicago. But he recently called me and asked me if I wanted to pick up some extra work, for cash. I could use it, with Christmas and everything coming up. I teach accounting classes at a local junior college, but the salary is ridiculously low. My classes are online, so I can basically teach from anywhere. So I told him that I could help him out for a few weeks. He's paying for me to stay at a hotel. I'm happy to be back in Grave Gulch, catching up with some family before the holidays."

"Are you aware that Mr. Davison is wanted by the law? That he has been officially named as a suspect in the serial killings that have occurred in Grave Gulch?"

"I wasn't when he contacted me. I don't follow the news here. But he told me about it."

"*He* told you?"

"Yeah. Said he was working to clear his name."

"And you believed him?"

"I don't see him as a killer. The poor man lost his wife. He's just…struggling with finding his way."

Bryce exchanged a glance with Brett. It was clear that Timothy Wool had literally had the wool pulled over his eyes by Davison. But he wasn't all that surprised. By most everyone's account, Len Davison didn't appear scary. That was probably what made him particularly dangerous.

"So once he told you what was going on and you were still willing to help him, what is it exactly that he asked you to do?" Bryce asked.

"To keep tabs on Olivia Margulies."

Bryce felt a chill go down his spine. And he resisted the urge to run down the hallway to check on Olivia. "How did you do that?"

"I started going to the deli, for coffee, sometimes for a meal. If I saw Olivia in the dining room, that was good enough. I never talked to her. Didn't want to draw any attention to myself. However, if she wasn't in the dining room, then I would ask a server about her. I did that the other day, learned she was home ill and reported that to Len. That's when he decided to send flowers to her."

"You didn't think that was odd?" Bryce asked.

Wool shrugged. "Len is a nice guy, but he was always a little strange. He was willing to pay me extra for ordering the flowers."

Len had regularly purchased flowers for his wife.

He'd told Olivia that he had a crush on her. It was sickening, but Davison might be somehow trying to replace his wife with Olivia. "You said that he wrote the card," Bryce said, working to stay focused. "You must have met with him before you ordered the flowers?"

"Yeah."

"Where?"

"In front of the south entrance to Grave Gulch Park."

"Have you met with him anywhere else?" Bryce asked.

Timothy Wool shook his head. "We talk on the phone. I wait until he calls me, and then I give him my report."

"How does he pay you?"

"Cash gets dropped off at my hotel room."

Hotels tended to have video of entrances, lobbies, hallways. Bryce saw Brett making a note and knew he was thinking along the same lines. "How does he communicate with you?"

"Cell phone. He always calls me."

"On that cell?" Bryce asked, pointing to the phone on the man's belt.

"Yeah."

"May I see it?" If the guy gave permission, there would be no need for a warrant.

"Sure. It's always from a different number. I don't like that. Makes it necessary for me to answer every call, and a whole lot of them are telemarketing idiots." He scrolled through his list of calls. Then very slowly identified the four that he recalled being from Davison based on the day and time of the calls. He handed the phone to Brett, who dutifully copied down the numbers. Bryce knew the FBI would review all of Wool's phone records, but he and Brett both wanted to make it appear that Wool was being very helpful and that they were appreciative. Those conditions encouraged a witness to be more forthcoming with information.

"He mentioned that he recently started biking," Wool said.

"Biking?" Bryce repeated casually. "As in bicycle riding or motorcycle?"

"I'm pretty sure bicycle. I asked him about his car. He used to have an old Corvette, from the early 1970s. It was in really good shape. I always wanted to drive it. He said that he didn't have it any longer, that he was doing more biking."

Bryce knew about the Corvette. There wasn't anything in Davison's past that he didn't know about. The car had been sold two years ago. But there hadn't been any history of Davison being a bike enthusiast. Perhaps a new passion. Perhaps a new necessity that allowed him to quickly get to places that might be difficult to get to in a vehicle and maybe explained Bryce's failure to find him in the many hours of street traffic video that he'd watched.

It also fit with Tatiana's thoughts that her dad preferred to be off the beaten path. Now they could include looking for bike tracks as they searched.

"When are you next expecting to hear from Davison?" Bryce asked.

"I have no idea. My room at the hotel is paid up until this weekend. I was anticipating going home after that, anyway." He paused. "Am I under arrest?"

"Let us confer for a minute," Bryce said. He stood up, as did Brett. The two of them walked out of the room.

"What do you think?" the interim chief asked.

"I think Len Davison was a trusted mentor to this guy at one point in his career, and when he denied being involved in the serial killings, Wool believed him."

"Yeah, I agree," Brett said. "I'll cut him loose."

"We need him to let us know if Davison contacts him again," Bryce said.

"Yeah. I'm concerned that Davison only paid his rent through this weekend. It almost makes it seem as if he intends to…end it before then."

Bryce said nothing. He understood the hesitation. It didn't feel good thinking that *ending it*, in Len Davison's world, might likely mean that he'd have killed his next victim—and he'd have successfully taken Olivia to his bunker.

"We know now to be looking for a bike or bike tracks," Brett added, probably wanting to put a more positive spin on things.

"Yeah, it's something," Bryce said. He wanted to take Olivia home and make sure she was safely tucked in for the night. "Let's finish this."

The two of them went back inside and sat down. "You are not under arrest," Brett said.

"So, I'm free to go?" Timothy Wool asked.

Bryce leaned forward. "Yeah. But we want to know if Davison contacts you again."

"Okay," Wool said.

"Don't tell him that you've been talking to the police," Bryce said. "See what he wants you to do and then call me. If you can't reach me, call Interim Chief Shea." Bryce added Brett's name and telephone number to his business card and passed it over to Timothy Wool.

The man stood up, shifted nervously from foot to foot. "You all think he really did this? Killed those men?"

Both men nodded.

"And I helped him," Wool said, not as a question but more as a statement of fact. The realization that he'd been used by his former mentor had hit hard.

"Now help us get him," Bryce said.

"I will if I can," Wool said. He took four steps toward the door. "This isn't going to be on the news, is it? That I was questioned, that I helped Davison. I... I've got two kids. One's a nine-year-old boy. Lives with his mother. He's bright for his age and reads the news online. I wouldn't want him to read that his dad... well, you know."

"Not on the news," Bryce promised. He and Brett pushed back their chairs and walked Wool to the front door of the police station.

After he left, Brett turned to Bryce. "That was worth a late-night conversation."

"Definitely. But I should probably get Olivia home." She was no doubt tired. It had been just a few days since she'd recovered from being ill, and she'd been on her feet for more than twelve hours today.

"Good enough. We'll talk later," the interim chief said, walking away.

Bryce had his hand on the doorknob of the conference room but hesitated, thinking of Timothy Wool's final plea to keep his visit out of the news. To protect his son. First of all, keeping their conversation with Wool quiet would hopefully benefit them. And Wool's kid shouldn't have to pay the price. Shouldn't have it shoved in his face that his dad was nobody's hero.

Nobody ever thought about the kids.

And in that second, he had a moment of clarity. One of the many things that galled him about his father's return was that his dad had yet to really sufficiently apologize for not coming home to the woman he supposedly cared about enough to father three children with. For not caring *enough* about his family.

Him. Madison. Jillian. Three little kids who needed a dad.

A dad to respect. Somebody to toss him a football. Somebody to show up at school or to cheer him on from the bleachers. Somebody who was willing to proclaim to the world that this child was important.

His sisters were all concerned about their mom. What was she feeling, thinking, hoping for? He understood. He had the same thoughts. *But what about us?* he wanted to scream at them. *What about the three of us? Does anybody care how* we *feel?*

He opened the door. Saw Olivia at the table, her head resting on her folded arms. She jerked up at the noise. "Oh, hi," she said. "How did it go?"

"Good. We're confident that Timothy Wool is no threat to you."

"That's good. But can he help you find Davison?" she asked.

"Not as confident about that, but he says he's willing to give it a try. Davison evidently initiates all the communication, so we'll need to wait for that."

She put her coat on and looped her purse over her shoulder. "The waiting is the hardest, isn't it?"

He wondered for a minute if she'd somehow been tracking with his own thoughts. Not about Davison but about his father and how Bryce had been waiting…just waiting…for so many years for his dad to come back somehow, even though the man had been presumed dead. Yeah, waiting was hard. And it took a toll on a person. "We're going to get him," he said, coming back to Davison. That was where his head needed to be right now. Until this was over. "Let's get you home. You've got to be tired."

"I am," she admitted. "Maybe it was all that fresh air yesterday."

Yeah, maybe. Maybe it was the tension that simmered between the two of them like a full pot of water on the stove. Increase the heat just a little and the water was going to boil over. Create a mess. Maybe even burn somebody badly.

It was his job to keep the burner on low.

"I heard from Thomas Michael," she said, stepping into the quiet hallway of the police department.

"Oh, yeah," Bryce said, visualizing the pot of simmering water, the heat carefully controlled.

"He said he'll be stopping back in tomorrow."

"And what are you going to tell him?" he asked, proud that he was able to sound detached, almost disinterested.

"I don't know," she said.

He could almost hear the clicks on the stove as the burner heat was increased. Low to medium to as high as it would go. The water was bubbling, about to turn into a foaming mass of heat.

And he was pretty sure he was just about to be scorched.

Chapter Twelve

The alarm rang at six the next morning, and Olivia still felt bleary-eyed and tired. But she got up, went directly to the shower and, ten minutes later, felt human. She was actually dressed and downstairs before Bryce. It gave her a minute to think.

She'd told Bryce about the text from Thomas because she didn't want any scenes at Bubbe's, and she was confident that giving Bryce a heads-up would support that goal. And just maybe she'd been a bit slimy, hoping that the announcement might prompt him to open up about his own feelings toward her.

But he'd seemed to shut down. They'd barely exchanged a word leaving the police station and once they were home.

She knew he was attracted to her. Physically. That had been obvious when they'd been at the river and interrupted by the laughing boys. And she wouldn't be honest with herself if she didn't admit that made her feel good. She turned him on.

Right back at ya, she could say. While it wasn't as painfully obvious, she'd been plenty needy and really angry at those kids. Had the trio not inconveniently interrupted them, would she have regained her senses at some point and decided that it wasn't a good idea to have sex on a riverbank? She thought maybe but wouldn't swear by it. Kissing Bryce Colton was a heady experience, and she might easily have chosen to simply forget the risks and grab for the pleasure.

When Brett Shea had parked her in the conference room last night, he'd encouraged her to watch television. She'd kept the set off. Hadn't picked up her phone to play any games. Instead, she'd taken the quiet moments to reflect on the last couple of days.

When they'd been running, it had been an absolute joy to be outside, with the warm afternoon sun on her face. She'd felt free and safe and whole. And it had been exhilarating when he'd taken her into his arms and kissed her. A superhigh on top of a high. Which had probably made the absolute despair when they'd been interrupted all that more jarring, harsher. Left her emptier than ever before.

In the quiet conference room, she'd grasped for perspective. Her glass-half-full self said thank goodness to the laughing teens—grateful that they'd come along when they had and not ten minutes later. They no doubt had cell phones on them and a fluency with social media. She and Bryce could have had way more *exposure* than either of them wanted.

Her glass-half-empty self said that, once more, she and Bryce had left things half-done, with absolutely no indication on his part that he was interested in talking about it. And he'd actually thought she'd called his mother to complain. It was ridiculous but spoke to the level of guilt that he was carrying on his very broad and sexy shoulders.

She didn't want Bryce to feel guilty. And she didn't want any more awkward moments between them.

The two of them were in a weird situation, to say the least. And there was really no one to talk to about it. She didn't want to confess her feelings to her parents, a friend or, even worse, to Bryce and have them dismissed because of the circumstances. Their concern would be cloaked in condescending statements that they likely wouldn't realize were condescending. *Of course you're grateful to him. He stood between you and death. But that's not love.*

Oren might be the one person who wouldn't automatically invalidate her feelings. After all, he'd fallen for Madison in similar circumstances. And he'd always been somebody that she could talk to. But having that conversation right now felt…premature.

Every day was filled with uncertainty about what Davison would do next. And uncertainty was an interesting condition. It prompted more glass-half-empty thoughts than she was comfortable with. But it also prompted thoughts of action. As in *take action now, because tomorrow is not guaranteed.* As such, she'd made a decision.

Enough of this advance-and-retreat foolishness.

The next time she and Bryce teetered on the edge, she was pushing them over.

The fat lady was going to sing. Or, in this case, they were going to have sex, and based on how she'd responded to his kisses, she'd likely experience two or three delightful orgasms.

And then maybe there'd be something to talk about.

"Good morning."

Olivia literally jumped. She had not heard Bryce

come down the stairs. "You should make more noise," she said, cross that she'd been caught unaware, with thoughts of mind-blowing orgasms on the brain.

He frowned at her. "I'll try," he said. He paused. "Is everything okay?"

"Just great." She put on her coat. "Ready when you are."

He looked at his watch. "It's still a little early."

She shook her head. "It's going to be a busy day. Good to get a head start on it."

He didn't argue. He put on his winter jacket, and they headed to their respective vehicles. When they arrived at the deli, he led the way inside. Hernando had not arrived.

"What can I do to help?" he asked.

Now that she'd made her decision, it felt too close to have him working side by side. "You know, I think I've got this. I'm sure you have FBI business that needs your attention."

"But you..." His voice trailed off.

She understood his confusion. At her house, she'd talked about a busy day. Now she was refusing help. As her mother used to say, she was talking out of both sides of her mouth.

Well, it couldn't be helped. "Don't you worry about me," she added breezily.

Something, maybe anger, flashed in his eyes. But when he spoke, his voice was level, calm. "I'll hang out until Hernando gets here," he said.

And then he would make sure the back door was locked. He took his job, his responsibility, very seriously. Hard to be mad about that. "Whatever," she said. "Maybe you could start the coffee."

"I'll do that."

They did not exchange another word until he brought her a cup. "Thank you," she mumbled.

"My pleasure," he said. He leaned against the three-compartment sink and sipped his own coffee.

She kept her eyes down, focused on the sharp knife in her hand. She had thirty pounds of potatoes to peel.

"So what time should we expect Thomas Michael?" he asked.

There was no *we*. She was expecting Thomas. But she could hardly anticipate that Bryce wasn't going to have questions.

She'd dangled the Thomas information to give Bryce a chance to prepare mentally, to avoid a scene, but also to distract him. Bryce was keenly observant, and she had a lousy poker face. He might sense that she was wound up tight about something. Better to let him think that it was about Thomas than to know the truth—that she was a woman with a plan.

"Late afternoon."

She expected some smart remark, but his attention was on the back door. There was the unmistakable sound of a key in the lock, and then Hernando came in. He glanced at Bryce standing by the sink, then at her peeling potatoes. Perhaps the tension in the air had a certain color, because he immediately asked, "Is everything okay?"

"Just fine," she said. "Expecting a busy day."

She thought Hernando might have rolled his eyes, but he said nothing. Simply grabbed a white apron off the shelf of clean linens, tied it around his waist and started pulling out his baking supplies.

Bryce went to the back door, likely to verify that

Hernando had indeed relocked it, then walked out of the kitchen without another word.

"In my mother's house," Hernando said, "the two of you would be required to sit next to one another and say two nice things."

"What?"

"That's how she solved petty bickering in our family."

"We're not four," she said.

"Perhaps not, but I'm not wrong, am I? You're upset with him."

"I'm upset with the situation. The Len Davison thing."

Hernando shook his head. "That's been going on for many days now. But this, this tension, is new."

"It finally got to me," she said. It was, in fact, a true statement. By omission, she would let Hernando think that *it* was the situation with Davison. Only she would know that *it* was an intense physical desire to have sex with Bryce Colton.

"I suppose that could be true." Hernando paused. "I think you could do much worse."

"What?"

"You could do much worse than Bryce."

It wasn't a ringing endorsement, but coming from Hernando, it was the equivalent of a five-star review. "I'm an 'assignment,'" she said, putting air quotes around the last word.

Hernando smiled. "Is that what you're telling yourself?"

"It's how *he* described it." God, she sounded like a petulant teenager.

"He's a man of honor. As I said, much worse."

"It's complicated," she said. "Maybe even risky." Her heart could be broken.

He smiled. "I am reminded of something my father used to say. A man who managed a grueling trip to get himself and my six-months-pregnant mother across the border between Mexico and America some sixty years ago."

"What was that?" she asked.

"That there are moments in our lives when we can no longer play it safe. The stakes are simply too high."

BRYCE WAS UPSTAIRS in Olivia's office, working at her desk, when he saw Thomas Michael come in the front door. Olivia was behind the cash register, and she smiled at her former classmate.

Bryce quickly shut down the file he was working on, closed his computer and walked out the office door. He sauntered down the stairs like a man without a mission. In truth, he was feeling agitated and thought one wrong look from Thomas in anybody's direction might be like a match to dry kindling.

Olivia and Thomas were already in a booth, chatting it up. Olivia had her back to him. He could see Thomas's face. The man was intently focused on Olivia.

He considered taking a position behind the cash register but knew that Olivia might not appreciate being hovered over. He would remain close, however. He walked back to the kitchen. Trace had left for the day already, so it was just Hernando.

Bryce opened one of the stainless-steel refrigerators, stared inside and shut it without removing anything. He wasn't hungry. He simply needed something to do, something to occupy his mind, which went in a bad direction whenever Thomas was nearby.

"Do you need something?" Hernando asked.

Bryce shook his head.

"Is there bad news?" Hernando asked. "About Davison?"

"No. It's... Thomas Michael is in the dining room, with Olivia."

"The *great* Thomas Michael."

Bryce thought he heard sarcasm. Hernando would definitely not think the man was great if he knew that he was lobbying for Hernando's job. And Olivia was being cagey about what she was going to tell Thomas. "He's a poseur," Bryce said, deciding to be honest. "Lots of expensive wrapping paper. Cheap gift inside."

"Fancy word, but I think you're right," Hernando said.

"I can't see what Olivia sees in him," Bryce said.

"But you quite clearly see what he sees in Olivia," Hernando said, leaning back against the counter.

Bryce thought about denying it. But Hernando had a look on his face that clearly said he wasn't wasting time with idle conversation. He had a point to make. Best to let him make it.

"Olivia is...an amazing person," Bryce said. "But she trusts too easily. I don't want her to get hurt."

"I guess we'll know if you're right soon. About the trusting too easily. If she agrees with what Thomas Michael is trying to sell her. Although that will mean that I won't be around to see you gloat."

The meaning of Hernando's words sank in. "You know?"

Hernando shrugged in an unconcerned manner.

"He's got a big mouth. In the last two days, he's hit three places that have all called to warn me that he's telling people that he's taking my place. That, in fact, he's taking *your* place."

"He's going to miraculously become an FBI agent?"

Hernando smiled. "Not that spot. He's hinting that he and Olivia have a thing."

"On his part, for sure. Olivia admitted as much to me. But she…she's not expressed that she's interested in him. Not outright."

"Has she dismissed it outright?"

"No," he said, miserably. "And anyway, that's not my place."

"So you say."

Neither man said anything for a minute. Finally, Hernando spoke. "So now the two of us wait. To learn our fate."

"Are you worried?" Bryce asked.

"No."

Bryce generally had an affection for concise answers, but some elaboration on Hernando's part would be helpful. When it didn't appear to be coming, he added his own. "He'd ruin Bubbe's. Could never do what you do."

"Why, that sounds like a compliment." Hernando studied Bryce. "Are *you* worried?"

"About your job?" Bryce asked.

"Don't be obtuse. It doesn't suit you. Are you worried that there could be a romance between Olivia and Thomas?"

Worried sick. "I think that would be a mistake."

"Why? Why do you think it would be a mistake?"

Because I'm the right guy. The words were right

there. But he found it difficult to voice something out loud that he'd not yet fully admitted to himself. "I just know."

"You know, there are all kinds of ways to get hurt," Hernando said, tapping his foot, as if that helped to make his point. "I worry that you'll hurt her."

"I would never hurt her. No way. Never," Bryce denied. Why would Hernando think that? "I would give my life to protect her."

"I don't doubt that last part. But that doesn't mean that you can't or won't hurt her. She cares for you."

"She said that?"

"I have eyes."

"I have a professional responsibility for Olivia."

"And it is interfering with...what? Your short-term wants?"

Bryce considered his words. "I'm not really a short-term-want kind of guy."

Hernando smiled. "I think not. Which is why I've not made a fuss about you being in my kitchen."

"It's a complicated situation."

"Odd—I've been hearing that word a lot lately. Affairs of the heart generally are. But you're good with information. Processing. Sorting. Deducting. Figure it out. But don't wait too long. Because beneath Olivia's sunny, welcoming exterior is a woman who has carefully protected her own heart for quite some time. If she invites you in, you'll not have too many chances to make the right decision."

What the hell did he mean by that? Bryce was prevented from answering, because the live feed playing on his phone captured the image of Thomas Michael leaving. It had been a very short visit. It was impossible to know what that meant.

Olivia had some explaining to do.

OLIVIA CONTINUED TO sit in the booth, nursing her coffee, long after Thomas had left. She felt sad and almost physically ill. She'd not been looking forward to the conversation. Had known from the beginning that she was destined to give him some disappointing news. One, Hernando wasn't going anywhere. The man had helped her build her business, and he had his job as long as he wanted it. And two, she wasn't interested in a personal relationship with Thomas.

He had been a good friend when she'd needed one. They'd had a common interest, and at times, when an especially difficult instructor would do everything in their power to intimidate, a common enemy. And that had made for some good times and lots of laughs. But there was a reason a romance had never blossomed, even though she'd thought, at the time, that she was open to the possibilities.

She'd known that he wasn't the right one. She was even more sure of that now.

She'd told him most of all this, using the kindest words that she could. But still, he'd gotten angry. And said some things that had hurt her.

She would not cry. That was what she told herself. She would sit here, drink her coffee and, in a few minutes, get up and go about the rest of the day. The deli wasn't busy. No one would bother her.

No one except Bryce, she realized just seconds later as he slid into the booth, taking up the spot Thomas had vacated. "Short visit," he said.

"Yeah."

He was looking at her closely. "You're upset."

"Yeah. He…uh…said some things." And damn her, the tears that she'd denied came anyway.

Bryce looked fairly alarmed. "I will find the son of a bitch and he will regret the day—"

"No," she interrupted, reaching for his hand. "No. It's done."

"The bastard made you cry. That is never going to be done." He paused. "Is he coming back?"

She shook her head. "And even though he hurt my feelings, I'm sorry about that. He was my friend. And it's hard to lose a friend." She tried to pull her hand back, but Bryce gripped it.

"You're better than he deserved," he said.

"I'd like to think so," she said, trying for a blasé tone that she wasn't really feeling. "But I couldn't give him the answers he was looking for."

The door opened, and Bryce quickly looked to see who was entering. He need not have worried. It was a couple of young women, each pushing a baby stroller. They made their way to the glass display case. No need for concern there. Just nice customers.

That was what she needed to focus on. She'd built a good business that financially sustained her and along the way provided steady employment for several others and was contributing to the overall viability of her community. She had purpose. And purpose gave direction. "I've got work to do," she said. "Tomorrow's special has to cook overnight."

"We're not spending the night in the kitchen?" he said.

"No. Cholent cooks on very low heat for a minimum of ten hours. Preferably more. Some do it in a Crock-Pot. We do it in an oven, at a low temperature."

"What is cholent?"

"Stew," she said. "You know, beef, beans, barley, potatoes. That kind of thing."

"Sounds delicious."

"It's good. And sells well, especially to those who value eating a traditional Shabbat lunch. And because all the prep is done in advance, I don't have to worry about someone else having to make the daily special when I have the day off."

"What are your plans for tomorrow?" he asked.

"Sleep in," she joked. "No setting of alarm clocks allowed. If you're up working on your computers and such, please be quiet."

"As a mouse," he said. He let go of her hand. "You're sure I don't need to go beat up Thomas Michael?"

He was joking. Or maybe not. "Nope. But thanks for being willing. That means a lot."

Chapter Thirteen

He really wanted to know what Thomas had said to Olivia that had caused tears. He also wanted to know exactly what she'd told Thomas, not the neat little summary she'd provided. *I couldn't give him the answers he was looking for.*

Answers, as in plural. He was left to read into that that she'd turned down his request to take Hernando's place and to have a personal relationship with him.

And because he was a jerk, he'd said things that had hurt her feelings. Instead of manning up and accepting that she had a right to make her own decisions. If Thomas did make the mistake of showing his face again, Bryce was going to make sure it connected with his fist.

Olivia had worked in the kitchen after Thomas's visit. The dinner hour had been really busy, and the flow of customers had stayed steady until just before they were ready to close.

Now Olivia was counting the cash drawer. Her phone rang, and she glanced at it. "Hi, bro," she answered.

He could only hear her side of the conversation, but

it sounded as if she was talking him through a recipe. When she got off the phone, she was smiling.

It was the first big and genuine smile he'd seen since Thomas had swept through. And he thought about all the things that he'd be willing to do to keep that same joy on her face forever.

"I swear," she said, "he could look up the same information online, but he prefers to call me before he makes a new recipe. He says I give him confidence."

"What's he making?"

"Baked macaroni and cheese with lobster."

"That sounds delicious."

"It's pretty good," she said. "I made it for him about six months ago, and he wants to surprise Madison with dinner. I could have made some money off the deal."

"I don't understand."

"When I told him I had tomorrow off, he said he'd pay me to make the meal. I told him no way. One, it wouldn't be as special if I did it. And two, I don't intend to cook anything tomorrow."

"I'll do it," he said quickly. "Anything that you want made tomorrow will be my responsibility. Breakfast, lunch and dinner. As long as you're okay with a limited repertoire."

"If I don't have to make it, I'll eat the same thing for all three meals."

She was still smiling. And Bryce felt good. "I said limited, not nonexistent," he defended himself.

"I was happy with tea and toast," she said, evidently remembering what he'd brought to her when she was sick.

"It'll be a step up from that."

She patted her chest. "My heart beats in anticipation."

Hernando came out of the kitchen. "I'm done," he said.

"Two minutes," Olivia said, "and I'll give you a lift home. It's too cold to walk tonight."

Hernando shrugged. "If you insist."

"I do." Olivia resumed her counting of twenty-dollar bills. It was five minutes later when the three of them left by the back door. Bryce got in his vehicle and Olivia and Hernando in hers. As they turned out of the lot, Bryce waved to the officer who was watching the back door. Then fell into line behind Olivia.

Hernando lived less than six blocks away. It wouldn't be far out of their way. But he wasn't letting her out of his sight.

He couldn't help but wonder what it was that Olivia and Hernando were talking about. Hernando did not need to ask her about Thomas Michael's visit. He knew the score, because after Bryce's chat with Olivia, he'd gone back to the kitchen ahead of her.

"So he's gone," Hernando had said, without referring to Thomas by name.

"Yeah. Olivia said that she gave him answers he didn't want to hear."

Hernando had nodded. "We live to fight another day."

"That's one way to look at it," he'd said. "You were never worried, were you?"

"I worry about the things I can control. And I cannot control Olivia. But I know her. Know her heart. I've been sleeping soundly. And I do not want her to know that I know. I want you to promise me that you won't tell her. It would bother her, and, quite frankly, she's got enough on her plate right now."

Bryce had nodded.

"Say it," Hernando had requested.

"I promise. Are we done here?" Bryce had asked, suddenly irritated.

"Almost. I want you to know that I understand that the stakes for me were not as high as for you. So, I do not fault you for the angst you must be feeling."

"Angst?"

"Yes. I'm nearing the end of my career. Will likely work another five years, ten at the most. I could do that somewhere else. It wouldn't be a job that I enjoy as much as this one, but I could do it. You are in a different circumstance. You have a life ahead of you. A life that literally depended on Olivia's decision." The man had crossed his arms and looked satisfied, as if he'd said his piece.

"That's a bit melodramatic," Bryce had argued.

"Is it?" Hernando had asked, smirking.

Bryce had retreated upstairs, to his friendly computer that didn't ask uncomfortable questions. He hadn't come back downstairs until all the customers had left for the evening and the front door was locked.

If Olivia had thought he was acting oddly, she'd said nothing.

And he'd offered no explanations. And he told himself that he hadn't spent the hours upstairs doing nothing. He'd been going back through the data they had on Davison from his working years, looking at names, cross-referencing them through available databases. He was working off the assumption that if Davison had reached out to Timothy Wool, then perhaps he'd done the same with another former coworker.

He'd thought he had a live fish on the line when he'd come across Davison's former secretary and looked at her banking records. She and her husband both had their payroll checks directly deposited to their accounts. That was an easy trail to follow. Similar amounts, every two weeks, like clockwork. But then there'd been an extra deposit, about two weeks ago, in the amount of $3,000. He'd thought it worth a follow-up. Not wanting to leave Olivia, he'd contacted Brett.

The interim chief had paid the woman a visit within the hour. Turned out, she and her husband were buying a house, and he'd sold some old and valuable baseball cards in order to increase their down payment. Brett was able to trace the buyer, who confirmed the story.

Another dead end. Brett had taken the list of former employees that Bryce was working through and said they'd finish it. Bryce had gracefully accepted the help.

He was tired. Was looking forward to some sleep. Olivia could not get Hernando dropped off fast enough, as far as he was concerned. He watched as she pulled into Hernando's short driveway. The man lived in a small brick bungalow with an unattached garage in the backyard. Bryce guessed the house had probably been built in the 1950s or 1960s and was maybe a two-bedroom, one-bath home. Plenty big enough for Hernando.

He waited for the man to get out of Olivia's vehicle.

But then suddenly Olivia was backing out, fast, Hernando still in her car. And Bryce's phone was ringing.

He grabbed it. "What?" he asked.

"Hernando thinks somebody either was or is in his house," she said, so fast that her words were almost running together.

"Why?"

"The blinds have been turned down."

If it had been anyone other than Hernando, he might

have questioned whether there could be some mistake. But he figured Hernando kept them just so, and he was the only one in his house who would change them.

"Keep driving," he said. "Go back to the deli parking lot. Stay in your vehicle. Both of you. I'll be right behind you." He was not taking a chance that this was another ploy to separate him from Olivia.

"What are you going to do?"

"Call Brett Shea. Don't worry. We'll figure this out."

"THERE'S NOBODY INSIDE right now," Bryce told her on the phone, thirty minutes later. She and Hernando were still in her car; Bryce was behind them. She'd put the phone on speaker so that Hernando could hear. "But there's some damage."

Her heart hurt for her friend. He'd been mostly silent in the passenger seat, saying almost nothing. She suspected he was angry that they'd had to drive away from his home, that he'd not been allowed to go inside, to immediately assess and, if necessary, defend his property. Even now, hearing this, he was quiet. But she could feel the tension radiating off him.

She had pulled into his driveway, and he'd already said good-night. His hand was on the door handle when he'd hesitated.

"Did you forget something at Bubbe's?" she'd asked. And then he'd told her his suspicions. Knowing that Bryce was behind her, she'd immediately backed out of the driveway and dialed his number. Bryce would know what to do.

"How bad?" she asked now.

"He's going to be busy cleaning up for a while." Bryce paused. "There was…"

"What?" Hernando demanded. His voice sounded loud and harsh in the vehicle.

"There was a warning on the wall. Red spray paint. *Stay away from Olivia. Quit.*"

She thought she might vomit. Hernando had been targeted because of her. "Who would do this?" she whispered. And then she had an awful thought. A truly horrible one. "Thomas Michael," she said. Had he seen Hernando as such a rival that he'd resorted to violence?

"I already thought of that," Bryce said. "Brett has people looking for him right now."

"When can I get into my house?" Hernando asked.

"Not yet. The police have not yet released the scene. I think you and Olivia should drive to her house. You can have my bed for the night. I'll take the couch."

Hernando barely hesitated. "No. Can I get my vehicle out of the garage?" he asked. "I have my keys."

"I don't know," Bryce said. "I'll check and call you back."

The line disconnected. "I will go to a hotel for the night," Hernando said.

"Bryce's suggestion was a good one."

"It's a hotel or the couch in your office," Hernando said. "Those are the only two options I'm considering."

Olivia knew it would be senseless to argue. Once Hernando made up his mind about something, there was almost no way to budge him. And she didn't have the heart to spar with him. She felt awful. Hernando didn't appear to question that Thomas Michael might want him to step aside. He had to know about Thomas's idea.

She immediately discounted the thought that Bryce

had told him. He wouldn't do that. But someone had. And they needed to talk about it. Now.

"See if there is a room somewhere," she said.

In minutes, Hernando had a reservation for a room at a nice, small hotel on the west side of Grave Gulch. Now there was nothing to do but wait to see if his vehicle could be retrieved.

"Hernando, I'm sorry," Olivia said. "I really can't believe that Thomas would do this, but if he did, it rests on my shoulders. He did it because he's upset with me."

"That you wouldn't turn me out to pasture and hire him in my place," Hernando said.

"How did you know?" she whispered.

"He's been talking to people in our industry all around Grave Gulch. Maybe he wanted it to get back to me. Maybe he thought I'd be upset enough to quit."

"I told him no. It was a silly idea. Born of desperation, because he'd lost his previous job." She paused. "I'd be lost without you, Hernando. I was just a kid who could make a smooth white sauce and a decent chicken stock when I met you, fresh from culinary school. You're the one who taught me the restaurant business. You're the one who really made Bubbe's a possibility."

Hernando shook his head. "You're giving me too much credit. And you're still a kid," he added, smiling.

"I am," she admitted. "And I don't know how you can be so good-natured when your property has been attacked like this."

Hernando shrugged. "Taking lessons from a kid. You. You've been under attack from Davison, both at your business and your home, and you're still in the ring, swinging."

"A bit dazed from a few punches," she said, quickly following along.

"That's living," he said simply.

Her cell rang. It was Bryce. "He can have his vehicle. Drive back to his house and park on the street. An officer will come get the keys and back the car out of the garage."

That was good news. But there was something in Bryce's tone that was different. In just the few minutes since they'd talked last, something had changed. "What's going on?" she asked.

Bryce sighed. "I just talked to Brett Shea. They've already located Thomas Michael. It wasn't hard. He'd used his credit card at a restaurant about two hundred miles away from Grave Gulch just fifteen minutes earlier, and he was still sitting at the bar when the Michigan State Police officer approached. He denies even knowing where Hernando's house is. Said he left Grave Gulch immediately after leaving Bubbe's. Gas and other charges on his credit card record support that." Bryce stopped. "Brett doesn't think it was Thomas."

"But then, who?" Olivia asked, both relieved that her former friend hadn't done it and worried that Hernando had an unknown enemy.

"A can of red spray paint was found in a dumpster about three blocks away. They checked at local stores that sell that red paint. Earlier today, a man who matches the description of Len Davison bought a can."

Len Davison. That news was even worse than if Thomas had done the damage. Len Davison was a killer.

"He evidently sees Hernando as a potential obstacle in getting to you," Bryce said.

"He's right about that," Hernando said. "For what it's worth, I'm glad it wasn't Thomas. And Davison better understand that I'm not going anywhere. Now, let's get this show on the road. All of us need to be in our beds."

"I'll take your shift tomorrow," Olivia said. "You're going to have your house to put back in order."

"Maybe," Bryce said, not yet having disconnected. "Now that it appears to be Davison, the Grave Gulch police are going to want to make sure they haven't missed a clue. They may or may not release the scene by tomorrow."

"Doesn't matter," Hernando said. "I'm working. I'm already scheduled to be off on Sunday, and I'll deal with my house then. You take your day off. Davison doesn't get his way. He doesn't get to upset everybody's plans, everybody's lives. He doesn't get to win. We do."

He doesn't get to win. We do. Bryce repeated the words in his head as he followed Olivia and Hernando back to the small house. Then Hernando, with Olivia following and Bryce behind both of them, drove to the hotel. He and Olivia did not leave until Hernando was safely in his room. Finally, they had driven home and walked inside Olivia's sweet house.

"I'm exhausted," she said. She sat on the couch and let her neck fall back until it rested at an odd angle.

"Yeah. Maybe it's a good thing that you've got the day off tomorrow."

"Davison is deadly," she said, still looking up at the ceiling. Maybe she was trying to see if the answers were written there. But there were no answers to explain why somebody who had lived a relatively normal, drama-free life suddenly became a serial killer, murdering people who, quite frankly, resembled himself in many ways.

"Understatement of the year," Bryce said. He also felt drained.

"Hernando knew about Thomas's plan to take his place," she said, surprising him.

"I know. Hernando and I talked about it."

Her head whipped down, and she stared at him. "You never said anything."

"He asked me not to. Made me promise. He didn't want you to feel bad."

"Too late." She sighed. "My life is a disaster, you know that? A real disaster. A category-five hurricane. Nine point three on the Richter scale. A tsunami. A..." She reached for a descriptor.

"An avalanche," he supplied.

"Yes. A freakin' avalanche."

Now she was smiling. "Want to know something?"

"Sure."

"I've made a decision."

"A decision," he repeated.

"Yes. I want to have sex with you."

If he had not been sitting down, he'd likely have fallen down.

She stood up, held out her hand.

There were a thousand reasons why it was a bad idea. Davison was still a threat. It was his responsibility to protect Olivia. "Listen," he said, holding up his hands.

"He doesn't get to win. We do," Olivia said, proving that she really could read his mind and that Hernando's words had also resonated with her. "Don't make me beg," she said, looking at her outstretched hand.

Never.

"There's no going back," he said. He needed to know that she understood. That this was not blowing off some steam—this was not casual.

"I'm only moving forward," she whispered.

He stood, reached for her hand and pulled her in close. "I thought you were tired," he murmured, his mouth close to her ear.

"Not *too* tired," she said before she raised her face and kissed him.

Hot, blazing need raced through him. *Slow down, slow down.* He would not rush this, would not...

She put her hands under his shirt, ran her fingers up his spine. Pressed her hips forward, connecting with him. He heard her low, throaty growl when she realized that he'd gone from zero to sixty in about ten seconds.

He lifted his mouth, took a breath. "Too important," he said before he crushed her lips again. He wanted to devour her.

"Bed," she said when that kiss ended. "Now," she added, reaching for his belt buckle.

She was not going to let him slow them down.

Happily defeated, he pulled her toward the stairs.

SOMEHOW, THEY MANAGED to make it upstairs, to her bedroom. He undressed her along the way, fumbling with the buttons on her shirt and swearing, something he rarely did, and that made her giggle. And then all laughing ceased when she stood on the hallway landing in panties and a matching lacy bra.

Time slowed. Touches become lighter, more reverent. Kisses lingered and traveled, and heat built. Finally they were both naked, in her bed, touching everywhere.

"You're so beautiful," he said.

"Take me," she begged. She felt as if she might truly die if that didn't happen in the next minute. She reached and opened the drawer of the bedside table. "I have condoms."

"More than one," he said, looking at the box. "Thank you, God."

And then he used his knee to gently spread her legs. And when he entered her, he held her face between his hands. "So damn beautiful," he repeated.

And then no one talked for a very long time.

She came apart in his arms not just once but twice, and only then did he take his own pleasure. Now she lay exhausted, spooned next to his still naked body, him curling protectively around her.

"I'm a changed man," he said, his mouth close to her ear.

"How can you tell?" she asked.

"How can I not be?" he responded. "After that."

It was the perfect thing to say. "Not upset that I wouldn't take no for an answer?" she asked, suddenly feeling unsure. She'd made her decision that they were going to have sex well before this. She'd had time to mentally prepare.

He'd had it sprung on him.

Had risen to the occasion, rather spectacularly, she thought. But still. She didn't want there to be regrets.

"I don't think I'll be including it in any of the status reports I hand off to my boss," he said, sounding amused. "And from an outsider's perspective looking in, I understand how they would condemn the action," he added, in a more serious tone. "But regrets? None. You?"

She rolled in his arms, turning to face him. "None. And do you know the very best thing?"

"That there weren't three of us in the bed—you, me and my computer?"

"Well, yes, that. And the fact that I have tomorrow off. Well, today, actually," she said, looking at the bedside clock. It was just after two in the morning. "And I'm not at all sure that I intend to leave this bed the entire day. We can do it over and over again."

He smiled. "Until we run out of condoms."

"How many do we have left?"

He thumbed through the box. "Six," he said.

She smiled. "That might be just enough."

"Food?" he asked.

That was perhaps more problematic. In truth, she didn't stock her home cupboards very well, because she ate almost all her meals at Bubbe's. "Delivery," she said.

"Chinese?"

"Sure." She was in an agreeable mood. Good sex had that effect.

"Pizza, too?" he asked.

"I only have today off," she reminded him.

"I plan on working up an appetite."

Indeed. "Pizza. Subs. Thai. I want you to keep up your strength."

Chapter Fourteen

Some eighteen hours later, Bryce was dressed and sitting in the living room, waiting for a pizza delivery. They'd spent most of the day in bed. Sleeping, making love, talking, laughing.

The real world had intruded a few times. Texts from Brett, the latest of which had come an hour ago saying that Hernando could return to his home, that the scene had been released. No new additional evidence had been collected that gave any indication of Davison's hiding spot.

Bryce had immediately sent a text to Hernando. The man's response had been brief. Thank you. Let Olivia know that we had a good day today. The cholent sold out. I'll see her on Monday.

He'd relayed the message to Olivia, who'd just emerged from the shower. She'd stood in front of him, naked, with her dark, wet hair hanging down her back. His body had responded in a most predictable way, and they'd made love once again. After that, he'd had his own shower, called the pizza order in and gotten dressed. He'd wake Olivia once the food arrived.

It had been an amazing day. For the most part, they'd managed to shut out Davison. The killer had had no place. It was a temporary reprieve, though. Days were ticking away, and with each turn of the calendar, the likelihood that Davison would strike again increased. How his plans for Olivia played into that was the unknown.

Not on my watch. And now, after what the two of them had shared, Bryce wanted every day, for the rest of his life, to be his watch. This morning, when they'd been nestled in bed together, he'd almost voiced those thoughts. But had managed to stifle them. They needed to concentrate on one thing at a time. First, get Davison. Then any plans for the future could be put in play.

He got a text from the cop watching the house that a car had pulled up outside. Minutes later, the doorbell rang. He verified it was the pizza delivery and then opened the door.

"Food is here," he yelled minutes later, after pulling out plates and napkins.

"Oh, thank God. I'm famished."

A few minutes later, as they sat in the living room, chowing down on the extra-large half cheese and sausage, half vegetarian, she reached for a second slice. "Everything is so much better when you don't have to make it yourself."

"You love to cook," he said.

"I do. But that does not mean that I don't appreciate an opportunity not to."

"You're back at it tomorrow. And I looked at the schedule. You don't have another day off until the holidays."

"I know. And it will be busy. Lots of catering orders, plus the new food program at your mom's school kicks off on Monday. Whew. And I can't even say I got a lot of rest on my day off," she added, with a teasing look in his direction.

There'd been periods of sleep. And with her in his arms, it had never been more restful. "Maybe I should sleep in the spare room tonight," he said.

"Don't you dare."

"Threatening a federal officer. You do have a wild streak."

"I'll show you wild."

He really could not wait. She'd been loving and giving and so responsive that it had made his own head feel as if it was going to explode at times, to say nothing for the effect on his heart.

Her phone buzzed. She picked it up. "My brother wants to stop over for a few minutes," she said.

Bryce felt his confidence drain away. The real world was intruding. More than an occasional text message. Oren was a good officer and a perceptive brother who loved his sister very much. He would not be easy to fool. "This should be interesting," he said, somewhat evasively.

"I imagine so," she said.

That was not helpful. "Are you…going to tell him?" Bryce asked. His need to have all available data pushed him to push her for an answer.

"I don't know," she admitted. "It's none of his business. But I also rarely hide things from my brother. Not important things."

He was important? The sex had been important? So many questions.

"I think I'll start by putting some different clothes on," she said, getting up. She wasn't naked. She'd put on cute little pink-and-white pajama shorts and a bright pink shirt with skinny straps before coming down to eat. But she was right. Oren would notice the casualness of her attire, the amount of bare skin, and immediately sense that things had changed.

"Good idea," he said.

"I really don't know why you're concerned about my brother," she said, frowning at him. "It's not as if Oren can claim the moral high ground. He did fall for your very lovely sister rather quickly."

"You don't understand brothers," Bryce said.

"Maybe not. But I get sisters. And I imagine that Madison would have told you to kiss off if you'd butted into what was going on between her and Oren. Why should I be any different? If our conversation goes in that direction and he's anything other than supportive, be prepared."

"Prepared for what?" he asked.

She smiled sweetly. "Just be prepared."

"Don't fight with your brother over me," he said. He would not be the reason the siblings squabbled. "I don't need you to stand up for me."

She walked to the stairs. "I'll make my decision," she said. "And when I do, I'll be standing up for myself," she added. Then she left him alone with his thoughts.

Ten minutes later, he got a text from the cop watching the door that Oren had arrived. The doorbell rang, and he answered.

"Hey, Oren," he said, opening the door. "Come in."

"Thanks. I can't stay long but just wanted to check in with Olivia. I heard about Hernando's house and that it's likely the work of Davison."

"Your sister is upstairs." *Getting dressed in a room*

where we had sex multiple times. "Should be down any minute," he said, grateful that mind reading was still not possible. "Pizza?" he asked, gesturing to the table.

"No, thanks." Oren sat.

In the past, Bryce would have made easy conversation with him. But now everything seemed high-risk. Thankfully, he heard Olivia's feet on the stairs.

"Hey, bro," she said, coming into the room. She was wearing jeans and a sweatshirt. "Want some pizza?" she asked.

"Bryce already offered," he said, smiling at her. "How was the day off?"

"Lovely," she said.

"What did you guys do?"

It was a reasonable question, Bryce thought. But it made his heart rate speed up. And maybe Olivia felt the same way, because she turned to him.

"Bryce, would you mind making me a cup of tea? The chamomile would be great. It takes a bit to steep and I like the water very hot."

In other words, *give me a few minutes.* It appeared that Olivia had decided.

IN THE END, Olivia had decided that it really wasn't much of a decision. She could trust her brother. He'd always supported her, even when they were both teenagers. "So, there's been a…development."

"With Davison?" Oren asked, likely thinking that he probably knew everything she did.

"With Bryce. We're…uh…you know."

Her brother said nothing. For at least a minute. And a minute of silence was a very long time, Olivia decided. But she physically pressed her lips together. She was not going to overexplain this.

"Are you happy?" Oren asked finally. He seemed very serious.

"Very."

"Is Bryce happy?"

"I think so. I mean, if he can't have sex with his computer, I'm probably a solid runner-up."

The comment did exactly what she'd intended. It made Oren laugh. And relax. "Madison is going to be surprised," he said. Then he looked worried. "Please don't ask me not to tell her."

"She can know. I trust her. She will understand the need for discretion outside the family."

Oren nodded. "I think he's a good guy."

"He's a very good guy."

"But you realize that you're in a really weird situation right now. And that when this all ends, things might change," he said.

It was sweet of him to want to protect her. "I'm a big girl. Much tougher than I look."

"You look like a cream puff, so that's not a high bar," he teased her.

She heard the slam of a cupboard door from the kitchen. "I think that's Bryce giving me the ten-second warning."

"Want me to play Dad and inquire about his intentions?" Oren asked.

"Only if you never want another free sandwich at Bubbe's," she said. She'd never been much of a live-in-the-moment kind of girl. Believed in the saying that luck occurred when preparation and opportunity collided. She almost always had a plan.

But not now. It seemed beyond her. And she was okay with that.

Bryce came around the corner, carrying three cups. "I made tea for everybody," he said unnecessarily, proving that he was likely more nervous about her conversation with her brother than she had been.

Oren held up a hand. "None for me. I've got to get going," he said, looking at Bryce.

Bryce did not look away. And Olivia was struck by the similarities between these two men who were both so important to her. What was it that Hernando had said about Bryce? *He's a man of honor.* Yes. He was honorable. It was an old-fashioned term, but it fit both of them.

"Are we good here?" Bryce asked. It was a loaded question. But the look on his face was easy to read. He clearly hoped that Oren was okay with what Olivia had told him, but if he wasn't, Bryce did not intend to duck and run.

Oren stood up. Extended his hand. "We're good," he said. "Best of luck," he added, with a wink in his sister's direction.

Bryce smiled and shook her brother's hand.

Oren left, and Bryce sank down onto a chair. "I didn't think it would matter to me," he admitted.

"I'm disappointed," she lied. "I was hoping for a duel in my honor."

"Now who is living in the past?" he asked, clearly remembering her earlier reference to a chaperone.

She shrugged. "With Davison, somehow the future seems tenuous."

He pulled her into his arms. "We're going to get Davison. I promise you."

She waited. Were there any other promises coming her way? But when he said nothing, she pushed aside her disappointment. If she didn't have a plan, how could she expect Bryce to have one? Simply existing, enjoying—that needed to be enough.

"I asked him not to say anything to anyone, that we're going to be keeping this to ourselves."

"Embarrassed by me?" he asked, with obviously forced playfulness.

"I don't want you to get into trouble at work."

"Is that the only reason?"

She stared at him. "I would tell everyone. Shout it from the rooftops. But the stakes are too high for you. I won't risk it."

"Thank you," he said simply. "Just until this is over."

"I understand." There was an awkward lull to the conversation. She understood. She really did. But there was something quite difficult about having to hide something so important.

"Let's go upstairs," she said, reaching for his hand. She could wallow in pity or she could *live*.

"Are you going to put on those little shorts and that pink top again?"

"Just so that you can take them off me?"

"Yes," he said, kissing her.

"I imagine I can be convinced."

HE'D SPENT THE next two hours convincing her in multiple ways. Finally, the two of them had slept. Now the alarm on his phone was ringing.

"Good morning," he said as she stretched in his arms. She was naked and warm, and he wondered if there was any way he could convince her to stay in bed.

She kissed the tip of his nose. "I get the bathroom first," she said, scrambling out of bed.

So much for that, he thought. The real world beckoned.

Once they were at the deli, there was little time for chitchat. On days that Hernando had off, Trace came in early. They'd taught him how to slice meat and cheese and prepare the deli salads. He was not a baker. So Olivia took over those responsibilities.

"You have flour on your nose," he said. Her cheeks were pink from the warm ovens, and a few strands of her long hair had escaped from her ponytail. She looked a bit like she did after she'd come in his arms. "How's the baking going?" he asked. Perhaps there was time to sneak upstairs and put that flowered couch in her office to good use.

"Good. Although I'm not happy with the rugelach dough. Too sticky. I might have overworked it."

They were definitely not on the same wavelength. He was focused on sex and having more of it.

But that wasn't all, he thought. More sex would be wonderful, but just spending time with Olivia was pretty damn nice. "I'm sure they'll be delicious. Can I do anything?"

She looked around. "I think we're in good shape. Go do your thing. I'm sure your computer misses you."

When she'd been sleeping, he'd checked his phone and email. Almost all of Davison's former coworkers going back at least ten years had been reviewed, and some who'd had especially close professional relationships with him had been interviewed. There was nothing to suggest that Davison had contacted any of them recently except Wool. There had been some risk to having those conversations. It might get back to Davison, and he might put two and two together and realize that law enforcement had discovered his connection to Timothy Wool. But given that Wool was reporting that there had been no additional contact from Davison, that connection might be blown anyway.

"My computer understands that there are sometimes competing priorities," he whispered. They'd agreed to keep the…relationship, or whatever it was they had, on the Q.T., and Trace was working less than ten feet away. He'd tell his mom, who'd tell the rest of the dining room staff, and within days, most of Grave Gulch would know.

"How lovely," she said, also whispering. "No one has ever told me that I'm a competing priority before."

"I've got the moves," he said.

"Yeah. Take your moves and get out of my kitchen."

BRYCE WAS IN the dining room, sitting in his favorite booth, when the doors were unlocked. A family of four came in. The kids were small enough to need booster seats, and it took them a minute to get settled. Bryce watched covertly. And thought about having a little girl with dark hair and blue eyes. A mini Olivia. He'd have to beat the boys off with sticks. It did not escape his attention that this was the very first time he'd ever had a similar thought. But now, picturing a family with Olivia didn't seem like that big of a stretch.

Still, no doubt he was getting ahead of himself. He forced himself to look away. Two men had come in and taken a booth across from him. They paid no attention to him.

It was at that moment that he realized what was

wrong. Mrs. Drindle was a no-show. Maybe she was out of town, on vacation. He closed his computer, not wanting to take up space in the event that the deli got busy. Olivia would stay back in the kitchen today since Hernando wasn't there. He'd go see if he could help. Maybe he could take the phone orders.

By the time he got back there, tickets were hanging for the family of four and the two gentlemen. Olivia looked at them and frowned. "Is Mrs. Drindle eating with someone?" she asked, sounding shocked.

"No Mrs. Drindle," he said. He looked at the tickets. The little kids were having grilled cheese sandwiches.

"What?" Olivia put down the spatula that she was holding. "No Mrs. Drindle! Did she call?"

"Not that I know of. She's probably on vacation. Or maybe sick."

"No. She goes to see her son in Portland every year. She makes sure we have it on the schedule. She's never been sick."

The phone rang. Likely a to-go order. "Want me to get that?" he asked. "So you can...make that food," he said. She appeared to be frozen.

"Yeah, sure," she said.

The pace picked up, and servers hung more tickets. And every time it was a single order, Olivia would ask if it was Mrs. Drindle. Every single time it was a shake of the head.

By one thirty, the lunch rush was over, and Olivia was obviously agitated. "We need to check on her," she said, taking off her apron. She motioned for him to follow her to the far side of the kitchen, away from Trace. "I know the building that she lives in. Not the condo number, but there's only a few units. Maybe she fell. Or…"

The possibilities were really endless. But it seemed as if she had one in mind. "Or what?"

"Davison."

"What? Why?"

"He got to Hernando. If he's been watching the deli, then he knows Mrs. Drindle is a regular. Might guess that she's important to me. I have to go check."

His mind clicked through the options. "No. Because if you're right, and I hope to hell that you're not, it could be a ploy to draw you out, to get you into an environment where you'll be less protected than what you are here. We can't take that chance. *I* won't take that chance with your safety."

"She could be in danger. Because of me."

"I'll call Brett. He can have an officer do a wellness check."

"Right away," she demanded. "Tell him that it needs to be now. It's the Ford Center Condos on Park Street. It's one of the second-floor units. She told me once that she does the stairs several times a day."

And Olivia would have listened and remembered. "I'll let him know our suspicions. I don't think that I'll need to convince him to do it quickly." Everyone was acutely aware that time was not their friend. Davison needed to be stopped before he could kill again.

Chapter Fifteen

Olivia almost leaped across the desk when she saw the text from Brett Shea light up Bryce's phone. But he was equally quick. He read the message. "No one at her apartment. No signs of struggle, either," he added, likely thinking that would make her feel better. It did not.

"Can they check street cameras, other cameras? Something?" she implored. Her gut was telling her that something was very wrong.

"They are. Also, do you know her son's name?" Bryce asked.

"Yes. Paul Drindle. Portland. I don't have his address."

He texted that information to Brett. "We'll be able to find him. I know it's hard, but I think you just need to relax until we've verified that she's not there or that he doesn't have some other knowledge of her whereabouts. Maybe she suddenly decided to take a cruise?"

"I will never forgive myself if something has happened to her because of me."

"Not because of you."

"I should have figured out a way to stop him that night he came to my house."

"He had a gun. You stayed alive. That was your only job," he said.

"He's not getting away the next time," Olivia promised. "I'm going to end this."

"There's not going to be a next time. He'll never get that close to you again."

"Maybe that's the problem," she said. "I'm too well protected. Police watching the front and back door of Bubbe's. The same at my house. You with me 24/7. So he's attacking others because he can't get to me."

"If you think the solution is for us to let up on our protection of you, you're wrong."

She'd made him angry—could tell by the tone of his voice. Thank goodness they were upstairs in her office and no one else could hear. "I know, I know. I'm just frustrated. The man is running our lives. He's in control. We're not."

"He's not in control of everything," Bryce said. "Not in control of…what happened between the two of us."

Bryce was right. And she needed to hang on to the positives. There was no bad news about Mrs. Drindle. Maybe she was just visiting her son and had forgotten to tell anybody. There could be all kinds of reasonable explanations.

Perspective. She needed to keep everything in perspective.

And right now, she had a few treasured moments alone with the very sexy Bryce Colton.

She pushed her chair back, walked around the desk and boldly raised her skirt so that she could straddle Bryce.

He smiled big.

"Yesterday was a good day," she said. "Can we just go back to my house and stay in bed?"

He kissed her. "That's a hard request to say no to. But I'm not sure it's a great long-term solution."

"Killjoy."

He kissed her again, and his hand reached all the places that it could reach with her skirt up around her hips. And she pressed against his palm. "We have time," she whispered.

"I daydreamed of doing it on your couch," he whispered in her ear.

"You daydream about us having sex?" she asked, pretending to be shocked. "Again, where is my chaperone?"

"In the parlor, having sex with the butler."

"Excellent. Have your way with me."

THE SEX WAS pretty damn wonderful. After it was over, Olivia righted her ponytail, double-checked to make sure everything was tucked in and zipped, and walked downstairs, her skirt a discreet two inches above her knees. But it was going to take Bryce a good long while to forget the sight of her hiking up said skirt.

Now he had to wait an appropriate interval before following her down the stairs. It was actually a bit humorous, given her joking about the chaperone. They were acting a little Victorian, hiding their illicit little affair. He suspected that in the old days it had been more to protect the woman's reputation. She wasn't concerned about that, but she was afraid that his bosses might react poorly to the news that he'd crossed a professional line.

He was just about to start downstairs when he got

another text from Brett. Reached Paul Drindle. Mom is not there. Paul not aware of any travel plans. Will canvass neighborhood.

It was not good news, and he sure as hell didn't want to tell Olivia. But keeping it from her wasn't a good option, either.

He found her in the kitchen, alone, because Trace was eating his lunch in the dining area. "I heard from Brett again," he said. And then because he figured she'd appreciate firsthand information, he showed her the text.

"This is bad," she said, her tone dull.

"Maybe," he said. He needed to be truthful. "Not necessarily." There was no harm in having some optimism.

"Is there anything that we can do to help?" she asked.

"I don't think so. Of course, if you think of any other place she might be, let me know. But beyond that, we let the local police do their thing. Brett will keep his eye on it."

She nodded, almost absently. Her mind was elsewhere.

"I'm going to call my brother," she said suddenly. "Tell him to be extra careful. Madison, too." She started pacing around the kitchen. "I need to say something to my employees. Put them on notice that they should be extra watchful."

"Don't you think that might be a little premature? You might be getting people upset for no reason."

"I've thought of that. And that's a real risk. But you know what is a bigger risk and one that I'm not willing to live with? The risk that Davison is targeting people that are important to me and someone else might be harmed because I didn't say anything."

"How do you plan to go about it?" he asked.

"I'm going to ask everyone working tonight to stay after for a few minutes and will send quick emails to all the other staff inviting them to attend."

"So, now I'll reverse the question you just asked me. Is there anything that I can do to help?"

She winked at him and leaned close. "Thanks to you, I'm feeling very relaxed, very capable of taking on the world. You're an excellent stress reliever."

"And I thought I was the only one with a poetic soul," he said.

She laughed. "I've got to get busy. There's a lot to do."

Hours later, the staff started arriving after eight. They immediately pitched in to help with closing duties, and thus, at the strike of nine, when they locked the doors, everything was done. Even the cash drawer had been counted after the last customer had left at fifteen minutes till the hour.

Every single staff member came, including Hernando, who said he'd made good progress on getting his house back in order that day. He had some insight into the meeting because Olivia had not just invited him via email but had taken the time to call him, too, to make sure he was aware of her plans. It was just one more way she demonstrated his importance to the overall operation of Bubbe's.

"Thank you all for being here," she said. She'd gathered the group in the kitchen, away from the windows of the dining room, where passersby might see them. "I'm sorry about the last-minuteness of this, but I thought it was really important." She licked her lips.

He wanted to jump in, take over, save her from having to do something that she should never have been called upon to do. She was an innocent pawn in Len Davison's murderous crusade, and it truly wasn't fair.

"I know that you are all aware that Len Davison, a serial killer, broke into Bubbe's Deli approximately two weeks ago. Subsequent to that, he came to my home. I was not hurt, and I had hoped that maybe that was the end of it." She took a breath. "But on Friday, Hernando's home was vandalized. The police have reason to believe that it was Davison. I am left to believe that it is because of his association with Bubbe's. With me."

Bryce glanced at Hernando. His face showed no emotion, but the man's eyes were chock-full of anger. Not at Olivia. At Davison. Bryce thought if the man walked in there right now, Hernando would likely kill him with his bare hands.

"And today, as some of you are aware, Mrs. Drindle unexpectedly did not show up."

That sent a murmur through the people who had not heard the news.

"The police have visited her home, and she's not there. There are also no signs…that anything bad happened there. That's good news, of course. The police have also been in contact with her son, who lives in Portland, and verified that she is not visiting. Nor was he aware of any travel plans."

The staff was looking at one another. One of the servers raised her hand. "Did the police talk to anyone at the Delightful Cup?"

"Why?" Bryce asked, already making a note of the place.

"Remember last year, when it got so cold, and we were having trouble with the heat? We were offering customers coffee on the house."

"That's two days I'd like to forget," Olivia said. "But, yes, I remember. Free coffee and pastry, as I recall."

"So I offered Mrs. Drindle a cup. I mean, we all know she never drinks it at lunch, but since we were supposed to offer it to everybody, I included her. She told me that she drinks exactly twelve ounces of coffee a day and not one drop more. She knows it's twelve ounces because she gets a large coffee from the Delightful Cup every morning."

"That's excellent information," Bryce said. "I'll share that information with the police."

"If anybody thinks of anything else that might be helpful, please let me or Bryce know," Olivia said. "Now, we have no idea whether Mrs. Drindle's disappearance is related to Len Davison, to Bubbe's or to me. But given that you are all members of the Bubbe's family, I thought it only fair to tell you everything that we know up to this point. I want you to be watchful, to be careful."

The meeting broke up shortly after that. He thought that Olivia had done a good job. Factual. Caring. Had achieved a fine balance. And he told her so when they were finally all alone in the dark kitchen.

"You've got a good group," he said. "They listened well, didn't get too excited. I think a lot of that goes to the fact that they trust you, that they know you care about them."

"They have really become my family over the years," she said simply. She yawned.

"Let's go home. I mean, let's get you home," he corrected himself.

She smiled, letting his gaffe go by unchallenged. It was his home. Temporarily. But what would happen once this was all over, once Davison was captured? She would no longer need his protection, need him.

That ugly thought nagged him as they got into their respective vehicles and headed to her house. He liked being with her. For the first time in his life, could easily imagine coming home to someone. Not just to someone, to her.

When they arrived, he checked the house. Once inside, Olivia dumped her purse and coat on the kitchen table and walked directly upstairs. "I'm going to take a shower," she said, looking over her shoulder. "I'll leave the door unlocked."

A fist pump would definitely be inappropriate. "Are you sure?" he asked. It had been a tough day. Maybe she just needed a minute.

"I'm sure."

"I'm going to check in with the officers outside, and then I'll be up."

"Don't blame me if I use all the hot water."

He was plenty warm at the prospect of what would happen tonight and definitely ready to shed the dark thoughts he'd had on the drive. First things first. Catch and stop Davison. Then worry about the rest. He sent his text and waited for a response. Once he got verification, he double-checked that the door was locked and then shut off the lights and followed her upstairs.

The bathroom door was closed, and he could hear the shower running.

He stripped his clothes off and walked into the bathroom. The shower had a frosted glass door, and he could see she had her head tilted back, likely rinsing shampoo from her long hair. Her back was slightly arched, her breasts high.

And his body responded.

She smiled when he joined her, and with her wet hand, she reached down and caressed him. "No warm-up needed," she said. "Impressive."

He returned the favor and slipped two fingers inside her.

She gasped. "Oh, God. Yes."

And there were no more words.

And the hot water did indeed run out.

Chapter Sixteen

On Monday, everything seemed almost normal. Hernando was back at work, and Olivia was making last-minute preparations to ensure that the first delivery of meals to the grade school went off without a hitch. However, there was an underlying tension in the air. Everyone was waiting to hear from Brett Shea. He'd promised that the police would follow up with the coffee shop once it opened this morning.

It was just after nine when Bryce got the call. He was in the dining room, sitting in a booth. There was no one around to hear the conversation. "Hey, Brett," he said.

"Your lead was a solid one," the interim chief said. "Mrs. Drindle is indeed a daily customer of the Delightful Cup. Arrives at seven forty-five every morning, gets a coffee to go. She was there yesterday as usual."

"And she appeared okay? Nothing suspicious was noted?"

"No. But I've got some bad news. We were able to get some street video from the gas station on the corner. A man in a hooded sweatshirt approached Mrs. Drindle and grabbed her. There was a limited struggle, but it appeared as if she suddenly stopped fighting. She was tossed into the back of a four-door sedan. The man got into the driver's seat and took off."

This was going to kill Olivia. "Davison?"

"We never got a good look at his face. We did see his hands and know that he's white. Based on the guy's height and weight, I think there's a very high likelihood that it was Davison."

"Did you get a license plate on the vehicle?"

"Yeah. It was stolen last night. The owner had left an extra fob in the glove compartment. A fourth grader could have figured it out. We've already located the vehicle. It was found in a parking lot, almost a mile from where Mrs. Drindle was taken. No signs of Davison or his captive."

"He's never killed a woman," Bryce said, thinking out loud.

"Yeah, I know. I guess that's good."

There was nothing good about any of it. "Can I tell Olivia?"

"Yeah, but ask her not to say anything to anybody else. The press isn't aware of this yet, and I'd like to keep it that way. We don't need more panic on the streets."

"Keep me in the loop," Bryce said.

"Will do." Brett hung up, and Bryce went to find Olivia. He got her attention and motioned for her to come to the dining area.

"What?" she asked, the look on her face telling him that she was expecting bad news.

He told her everything. When he finished, she was quiet. "This is not your fault," he said.

"I know that. It's Davison's fault. But poor Mrs. Drindle. She has to be so frightened."

"Probably just pissed that her schedule has been disrupted," he said, trying to lighten the moment. "Maybe we should feel sorry for Davison."

"Do you think he'll hurt her?"

"She doesn't fit the profile of his victims. And I think if he wanted to kill her, he'd have done it."

"I'm going to hang on to that."

"Remember, you can't say anything to anybody."

"I hate that."

"I know," he said. "How about if anyone asks, you just say that the police are actively investigating? That's not the whole truth, but it's not a lie, either."

She nodded. She didn't like it, but he knew she wouldn't hinder the police's progress in any way. "What time do we leave for my mom's school?" he asked.

"By one thirty. That will give us plenty of time to get to the school, check in with your mom, unpack our food and help load up the backpacks that I've been assured will be waiting for us. All before 3:00 p.m., when the bell rings."

"This is a really great thing you're doing," he said. It was no small effort. She, Hernando and Trace had all picked up additional responsibilities, to say nothing of the expense.

"I feel good about it," she said. "Of course, I'll feel better once we're a couple weeks into it and everything is running smoothly. There will be some bumps at first. We have to expect that and be ready to correct and keep going. Your mom asked if we wanted anybody from the *Grave Gulch Gazette* there today, and I told her no, that it's too early. We'll publicize the program later, with the goal of giving other businesses an incentive to help out in their own ways and to encourage more families to raise their hands if they are in need."

"Maybe Dominique de la Vega can help," he said, mentioning the well-known reporter. "I think my mom would have an inside track with her."

"Likely. She's with your cousin Stanton Colton now, right?"

"Yeah. I think she'd like what you're doing here. I know *I* like what you're doing here." He looked around, making sure that they were still alone in the dining room. Then he leaned in and kissed her. "You're pretty damn special, Olivia Margulies."

A flush of pink swept over her face. "Just a small-town girl," she said.

"Never *just* anything," he said.

Just a bit in love, thought Olivia, as she scooped fruit salad into plastic serving cups. How could she not be? He was…perfect.

She knew that wasn't fair. Because nobody was perfect, and if she put him on a pedestal, he was bound to fall off. And then she'd be disappointed and have only herself to blame.

Intellectually, there was no argument. But in her heart, right now, he felt pretty darn perfect. And in an hour, she was going to have to face his mother and try to hide it.

Yikes.

She filled the last fruit cup and put the tray into the cooler so that it could chill. "I'm going out to the dining room," she said, whipping off her apron and her baseball hat. It was time to open the doors for lunch. And while it was illogical to expect Mrs. Drindle after what Bryce had told her, she still had a bit of hope. Maybe they were wrong. Maybe she'd be the third customer in the door and the world would continue spinning on its axis.

But she wasn't. The third customer was a small, gray-haired man who ordered six soups and six croissants to go. "We're protesting the police failure to capture Len Davison," he told her as he paid his check.

For a quick second, she wondered if he'd deliberately said something because he knew of her role in the ongoing saga. But he didn't seem to be watching for a reaction.

"Lots of folks down there?" she asked.

"There's probably about a hundred of us. Good for a Monday. It's cold. This will help warm us up."

"Good luck," she said.

"They've got to get this guy," he said. "Nobody feels safe."

If you only knew. Olivia forced a smile in his direction before turning her attention to the next customer. It was almost two hours later before the rush let up. They were out of matzo ball soup and the lunch special of beef and noodles. The bakery case was looking sadly depleted, and Hernando would be busy replenishing for the evening.

"We should probably get going," she said to Trace.

Bryce, who was standing off to the side of the kitchen, finishing a tuna salad sandwich, stepped forward. "Eat something first. You have time. I already ate so that Trace and I could load the van while you do that."

He was probably right. It was going to be stressful enough making sure she got this new program off the ground and interacting with Verity Colton. Risking getting light-headed with hunger was something she didn't need. "I'll make myself a turkey sandwich and eat it on the way," she said, compromising. Bryce rolled his eyes but didn't say anything.

Trace would drive the company van, and she and Bryce would follow in Bryce's vehicle. She knew this because they'd gone over the plan this morning. Bryce, worried that Davison might attempt to strike while she was outside her two normal environments, Bubbe's and her home, had arranged for police to be in the parking lot of his mom's school in advance of their arrival. Doors would be watched the entire time Olivia was in the building.

Ten minutes later, they were on their way. She ate while he drove. She'd grabbed a bottle of iced tea, and she washed the sandwich down with that.

"I imagine you've been to your mom's school before," she said.

"Sure. And to Madison's classroom. I did origami for the kids the last time."

"I'll bet they loved that. Another hidden skill of yours?"

"Just something I mess around with. I'll make you a dinosaur later."

"I'll bet that works on all the girls," she teased. "It's kind of cool that Madison took after your mom and became a teacher, too."

"I think they're both natural educators. They love helping kids learn."

"It's a noble profession," she said.

"It is. They end up being teacher, family counselor, referee, nurse, custodian. Whatever it takes to keep their little classroom chugging along."

"And now your mom is taking on feeding hungry kids and their families."

"With your help," he said, taking a visitor spot near the door. "There's a doorbell and a camera. The office will buzz us in. We have to stop there first to get a pass and a name badge, and then we can go down to her classroom."

"Wow. Good to come with somebody who has the inside track."

"Stick with me, kid," he said.

If I can. She kept that thought to herself. He'd been teasing; she didn't need to be serious. Instead, she gave him a thumbs-up. "Can I get out?" she asked. She could see the Grave Gulch police officer's vehicle.

"Hold on," Bryce said. He sent a couple of texts and waited for replies. "Okay, we're good," he said a few minutes later.

They walked up to the building, rang the bell and told the woman who answered their names and that they were here to see Verity Colton. The buzzer rang, Bryce grabbed the door and they were inside.

It had been a very long time since Olivia had been in a grade school. But it looked much how she remembered. Artwork on the walls and the windows of the offices. They walked past classrooms, where the doors were open, and they could see students inside. Some at desks. Some at tables holding four or five kids. She could smell chalk. "I'm nine again," she said.

"I'll bet you were a cute kid," he said.

"I was a tomboy. You know, I had an older brother and I thought I could do everything he did, only better."

"For sure," he said. "And Oren treated you like you were a pain, but then when his friends were mean to you, he kicked their asses."

"Pretty much."

He motioned toward a set of stairs. Once they got to the second floor, Verity's classroom was right around the corner. Bryce stood at the door and waved to her. Verity finished her instructions and then joined them in the hallway.

She hugged both of them. "I am so excited about today," she said. "This has been a dream of mine for some time. The principal is going to take over my classroom for the rest of the day."

"Trace is here with our van and the food, so we're ready to go. He's waiting in the parking lot right now," Olivia said.

"There's a garage door on the rear side of the building where we get our deliveries. Let him know to drive there. We'll meet him there."

And five minutes later, they did just that. Then Trace, Olivia and Bryce carried the food in and handed it off to at least ten volunteers in the gymnasium, who were ready to distribute the food into the newly purchased insulated backpacks. Verity had done her part.

It was well organized, and Olivia watched, feeling satisfied that everything on the school's end was going to go well. It was the thing that she didn't have within her control, and it was a great relief. "I'm so happy," she said to Bryce.

He wrapped an arm around her shoulder and squeezed. "And I love seeing you happy."

He dropped his arm quickly, likely regretting that he'd gotten caught up in the moment and forgotten their need to keep things private. But, too late, Olivia realized that Verity was looking in their direction.

"Your mom saw that," she said, almost under her breath.

"I should have high-fived you. Maybe she won't think too much about it. I think she's got plenty on her mind right now."

Olivia certainly didn't have time to think much about it, because the backpacks were packed and several of the volunteers wanted to thank her. "The serving sizes are so generous," one woman said.

Olivia had done that on purpose. She doubted the child was the only person in the family who might be hungry. If it fed another child or a parent who was making do with less so that their child could have what food there was, then she was all the happier.

When the doors were opened and the kids came in, it was a blur of noise and confusion. But Verity was clearly in charge, and she quickly sorted things out. There were a few kids who accepted the backpacks like it was no big deal, sauntering out with them slung over a shoulder. But there were many others who were so excited that they opened the backpacks right there and started taking items out, examining everything.

The joy was palpable. About food. Something that a kid should simply have. A given. But for these students, and their families, that wasn't the situation. And now these pupils were literally screaming in joy.

She overheard one little girl, maybe eight or so, ask one of the volunteers who had done all this. When the volunteer pointed at Olivia, the little girl ran up and threw her arms around Olivia's waist.

"Thank you so much," she said. "I love you."

She hugged her back, not saying anything. It was hard to talk when your heart was bursting.

"BRYCE, DO YOU have a minute?"

His mother had asked politely, and someone overhearing might believe that he had a choice. But he knew better. He checked to make sure that Olivia was busy. She was talking to Macy, the school's internal coordinator for the program.

"What's up?" he asked as his mother led him to the far side of the gym.

"I couldn't help but notice that you and Olivia seem...closer than what I previously observed."

"You previously observed me being an idiot," he said.

She smiled. "And now?"

"And now I've smartened up."

"Is that it?" Verity asked.

"Did you talk to Madison?" he accused.

She shook her head. "No. What does Madison know?"

Bryce ran his hand through his short hair. "Listen, Mom. You're right. Things have changed between Olivia and me. In a big way. I really like her. A whole lot."

"And she feels the same way?" Verity asked.

"Pretty sure she does," he said. "She wanted to tell her brother, and, well, we couldn't expect him not to say anything to Madison. That's why I thought my big sister might have had loose lips."

Verity smiled. "She did not. And, trust me, no need

for details. I am your mother, after all. But it seems as if you're happy. I like seeing that."

"I… I haven't been as gracious to you," he said, his throat feeling tight. "In fact, I've been just the opposite. Making sure you and everybody else knew that I wasn't happy about Dad coming back, about you welcoming him."

She put her palm on his cheek. "I believe that everything you've said or done has to do with the fact that you love me. You protected me and your sisters when you were far too young to have that responsibility. But you never wavered in your commitment to us. You do not ever have to apologize to me for caring that much."

"I can be less of a jerk," he said.

"Always a worthy goal," she responded, giving his cheek a pat. "Can I give you a little motherly advice?"

"Of course."

"I know you like your data. You want information, then confirmation that the information is correct and an opportunity to test those assumptions again later. Only then are you satisfied. But love doesn't always work that way. It can happen fast and it can stand alone, without any other supporting facts. Because it's that strong. That can be scary to some people. And they decide to wait, to let the love be tested, to have it demonstrate its strength over and over."

He waited. His mother was beautiful and gregarious, and that caused some people to underestimate her. That was always a mistake. She had a point to make.

"But sometimes life throws you a curve that knocks the pins out from beneath you. You get no warning. You wake up and think that it's going to be an ordinary day. But then something or someone threatens the love that you've been…counting on. Believing it would be there forever. And that is a loss that you may never recover from."

Something like his father witnessing a murder and having to go into witness protection to shield himself and his family. "Mom," he said, wishing he could give her back all the years she'd believed Richard Foster was dead.

She shook her head, giving him a smile. "The moral of my story is not to feel sorry for me. It's to know that love is a great blessing. Don't take it for granted."

ON THE WAY back to Bubbe's, Olivia thought Bryce looked a little preoccupied. "Did something happen?" she asked, priming herself to hear more bad news. It would be hard, coming off the wonderful experience of the meal program at the school. Too many highs and lows really did make a person feel sick to their stomach.

"No," he said.

Was he lying to her? That wasn't his style. "You seem very deep in thought."

"I guess I am. I had an opportunity to talk to my mother. She saw me hug you, and she accurately guessed that our relationship has shifted."

"Shifted," she repeated.

"Changed. Grown."

"Blown up," she added with a smile.

"Yeah, that, too," he said, sounding satisfied.

That made her happy. "Did she say anything that I'd be interested in hearing?" It was a lame question. She wanted to hear everything his mother had said, but she didn't want to seem too needy, as if it was all-important to her what other people thought of their situation. It wasn't, truly. But his mom…well, that was different.

"She's happy for us. She likes you."

"That's it?"

"Yeah."

She doubted that was all that Verity had said, but it was probably enough. Approval. "Our bubble is growing. One more person knows. Will she tell Jillian or your dad?"

"I don't know. I didn't think to ask her. I suspect not. She is aware that Madison knew and didn't tell her. She wasn't mad about that. She understands that sometimes secrets really are important."

She was glad that Bryce had told her the truth. While she didn't intend to return to the school anytime soon, since that would be Trace's responsibility, she knew there was always the possibility that she'd be called upon to fill in. Now, if that happened, she wouldn't be surprised if Verity looked at her a bit differently. And, of course, Verity could be a customer at any point in the future. Forewarned was forearmed.

They parked in the lot behind Bubbe's and went inside. She briefed Hernando on how the trip had gone and visited with staff in the dining area to make sure the day was continuing to go well. Bryce had retreated upstairs to her office. She noticed that the coffeepot was low and started another brewing. Her back was turned to the door when she heard the light tinkle of a bell, signaling that someone was coming in.

She turned. And gasped.

Chapter Seventeen

Bryce saw the flicker of movement on his computer screen and turned his head to better see who was coming in Bubbe's. He did this a hundred times a day when he was working upstairs. And normally he saw nothing that concerned him. But now the image on the screen irritated the hell out of him.

Thomas Michael. What the hell was he doing here again?

He watched Olivia's reaction. Total surprise. She had not known he was coming. And there was no spontaneous hug or other warm greeting. She stayed behind the counter, near the coffee station. Thomas gave her an awkward wave.

And then they were talking, their bodies turned in such a way that he wasn't able to make out the words. But he could assume what was said when Olivia nodded and came out from behind the counter. The two of them headed to the rear of the restaurant.

The second he lost the camera view, he shoved his chair back. It would be nice to be able to toss the man out on his ear.

He ran down the stairs, stepped into the dining room and saw the two of them sitting across from one another in a rear booth. Olivia didn't look upset. She was listening to something that Thomas was saying.

Hernando, who had come from the kitchen to refill the soup canisters at the far end of the counter, finished what he was doing and then came to stand next to Bryce. "So he returns."

"Yeah," Bryce said. He did not take his eyes off the booth.

"Olivia would be unhappy with a scene," Hernando said, as if sensing Bryce's mood.

"I wouldn't make a scene," he said. He'd kick the man's ass out the door quite quietly.

"I don't think you're going to have to," Hernando said. "It appears that he's already leaving."

Hernando was right. Thomas was sliding out of the booth. Olivia did the same. And then she leaned in and gave the man a quick hug.

Rage swooped through Bryce, a hot, living flame. But he tamped it down. She could hug whomever she wanted.

And then Thomas walked past Bryce and Hernando, gave a nod in their direction. The two of them did not respond. He went out the door and disappeared into the cold, dark night.

Olivia walked behind the counter and stood next to Bryce and Hernando. "Well, that was a surprise," she said.

"What did he want?" Bryce asked. *And why did you touch him?* He managed to stop himself from asking the second question.

"To apologize. He felt bad about how we'd ended our conversation the other day. And to tell me that he's taken a position at a resort in Wisconsin. He starts next week."

It wasn't as good as him being on the East Coast, but at least he hadn't decided to stay in Grave Gulch. "So that's the last we'll see of him?" Bryce asked.

"For a good long time, I suspect. He'll be busy getting acclimated to his new job, and then it will be spring and summer and he'll be too busy to take time off." She paused. "I'm glad he came by. I hated that we'd parted on bad terms."

He'd known that was tough for her. "I'm glad he'll be busy," he said grudgingly.

Hernando rolled his eyes, letting him know that he was definitely sounding lame. "I've got work to do," the man said, leaving him and Olivia standing in the dining room.

"Okay, I wasn't happy with him being here," Bryce said. He needed to get it off his chest.

"I thought I was clear, on several occasions," she added suggestively, "that I'm not interested in Thomas. Someone else has my full-time attention."

"The *several occasions* were the only thing that kept me from shooting him."

She smiled. "I appreciate that. Not interested in more great publicity for Bubbe's."

"I'd probably have had to clean up the mess." Now it was his turn to roll his eyes.

"Undoubtedly. I'd suddenly have lots of paperwork to do. No time for wiping up blood and body parts."

"You think I'm ridiculous, don't you?" he asked.

"It's a bit sweet."

"I've never thought of myself as the jealous type before," he admitted. "But this...what we have... I don't want some other guy stepping in and messing it up. I'm not going to sit back and let that happen."

"He's on his way to Wisconsin. And I wasn't interested. I will admit that I was grateful that he didn't return for another confrontation. On top of the news about Mrs. Drindle, I think it would have been more than I could bear. I'm assuming there's no new news about her."

"No. That doesn't mean things are worse."

"I know, I know. I'm trying to stay positive. If it's a ploy to get my attention, he's not likely to hurt her. But I don't want her to be frightened. All this time, I've been anxious to prevent any contact between the two of us, but now I say bring it on. Let's get this over with."

He felt a frisson of fear run down his spine. "We're going to end this without him getting close to you."

She shrugged, as if she'd accepted the inevitability of her fate. "My brother said I look like a cream puff. I need a tougher image. I'm going to invest in some leather. Pants, jacket. Something that says 'don't mess with me.' And boots. That I can use to kick the living hell out of anybody who tries."

"I happen to like cream puffs," he said, his mouth near her ear. "Although you've painted a very fine picture in my brain of you wearing a pair of thigh-high leather boots and nothing else."

"Men," she muttered.

"You started it. Come on. You've earned a chocolate egg cream," he said, reaching for the sundae glasses.

"You're making it?" she asked.

"You bet. I learned from the best."

Hours later, when they'd finally locked up for the

night, Bryce had almost forgotten about Thomas's visit. Almost.

Because now, with the prospect of hours in Olivia's bed, he had much better things to think about. As he drove home, staying close behind Olivia's vehicle, he thought about his conversation with his mother and his subsequent talk with Olivia. He'd not been all that forthcoming with Olivia, certainly hadn't told her everything that his mother had said.

Was his mom right? Did he look for too much confirmation? Require too much logic before he'd simply accept feelings? Need too much proof?

Since college, he'd told people, *I'm a data guy.* It was a badge of honor, of sorts. Other people might be swayed by emotion, but he was driven by facts, numbers, proven science.

It was a lot to unbundle, he thought, as Olivia pulled into her driveway. Too much for right now, when they were in the middle of the Davison investigation, with each and every day potentially bringing them closer to another victim.

OLIVIA WOKE UP, her heart racing. Bryce was next to her, breathing deep, still asleep. She knew she couldn't close her eyes again. She'd been dreaming about Mrs. Drindle. The poor woman had been locked inside a giant watch, and every time the second hand turned and struck the three, Mrs. Drindle shed a tear the color of blood.

Very carefully, Olivia slipped out of bed. She was naked. She grabbed her robe that was on the end of the bed and slipped it on. Then she quietly padded downstairs.

And made herself a cup of decaf tea.

She sat in her dark living room, legs tucked under her, and sipped. She picked up her phone and scrolled through her email. There was one from her mom, asking what they could bring when they came to Grave Gulch for the holidays. All of the initial planning had happened before Len Davison had become fixated on her, before Bryce had moved in. Before she and Bryce had become lovers.

She needed to talk to Bryce about it. If this thing with Davison wasn't over by then, she needed to make sure that it would be okay for more people to be in the house. She wanted him there, of course. Not as an FBI agent, responsible for her safety. But as her...what? They'd not discussed labels. Her friend? Her special friend? Her boyfriend?

Ugh. This was where relationships got complicated. When it was just the two people, it was simple. No need for explanations or labels. But when others got into the mix, it got complicated fast.

"Olivia?" Bryce was standing at the bottom of the stairs. He'd pulled on his jeans. They were zipped but not buttoned, as if he'd dressed in a hurry. He wasn't wearing a shirt.

"You're very quiet," she said. "I didn't hear you on the stairs."

"What's going on?" he asked, walking into the room. "Are you okay?"

"I am," she said, patting the cushion on the couch next to her. "Want some tea?"

"No, thanks. I don't like waking up and not finding you there."

"I dreamed about Mrs. Drindle," she said.

"Want to talk about it?"

"No. But I knew I wasn't going to be able to sleep. I was checking my email and was reminded that my parents are intending to come to Grave Gulch for the holidays. I'm hosting. Or at least that was the plan before all this."

"And that's keeping you awake now?"

"No. Yes. I don't know. It dawned on me that if they come and you're here, it means there will need to be more explanations."

"We'll figure it out," he said.

Would they? "Maybe if you've caught Davison by then, you'll want to spend time with your family. I get that."

He reached an arm around her shoulders and pulled her close. "We can do both. Lunch here, dinner there. You can't have too much turkey."

"I think you can."

"Well, you definitely can't have too much pumpkin pie. Listen, it's three in the morning. Can we solve this once the sun is up?"

"I can't sleep," she said.

"Who said anything about sleeping?" And then he kissed her. Leisurely.

"I've dreamed of untying this robe," he said. And with a quick tug, he did just that.

"Just as I thought," he said, bending his head to take a nipple in his mouth. "Perfection."

WHEN HER ALARM woke her up, Olivia was cradled in Bryce's embrace. They had managed to make it back to her bed, and then the lovemaking had been slow and tender, and when it was over, she had slept and not dreamed.

"Good morning," she said, turning to face him.

"Good morning. Any more bad dreams?"

"Definitely not. Too bad you can't bottle what we did last night into a sleeping pill. It would fly off the shelves."

"Happy to oblige. Race you to the shower."

He won but shared the space, which resulted in them almost being late for work. Hernando was already there when they arrived. The minute Olivia saw him, she knew something was terribly wrong. The man's face looked swollen, and his eyes were shadowed with pain. And her first thought was that he'd been attacked. "Davison?" she asked.

He shook his head. "I have a bad tooth."

"Bad as in infected?"

"I imagine it is," he said.

"You think a dentist might be able to tell for sure?" she asked dryly, feeling bad for him, yet terribly relieved that it wasn't Davison.

"I'm trying to get an appointment," he said. It was at that moment that his phone rang. He looked at the number. "My dentist."

"Answer it. And take whatever they have available. We'll be fine here."

Three minutes later, Hernando had an appointment to see his dentist in an hour. It would take him fifteen minutes to get there. "I'll do what I can in forty-five minutes," he promised, already moving fast to pull out baking supplies. "I'll be back before we open for lunch."

Bryce looked up from the carrots he was peeling. "That should be fun," he said. "I'm going to make sure I have my cell phone. A video of you, loopy from painkillers, should entertain me for some time." He looked at Olivia. "Check with your workers' compensation carrier and see if there's coverage if he cuts his fingers off with a knife when he's high."

Hernando held up a big stainless-steel knife. "Even without all my fingers, I suspect my aim is still true," he replied, no malice in his tone.

"I suspect I can still run faster," Bryce said, smiling.

Olivia stared at the two men. Something was different between them. Something had changed. She'd first sensed it last night when she'd walked up to both of them after Thomas's quick departure. And now here it was again. She suspected, however, if she asked either one of them, they would deny it.

Forty-two minutes later, she walked up to Hernando and pointed to her watch. "Ticktock."

He punched his dough one last time. "Let this rise for an hour. Then—"

"I've made challah," she said gently, pulling him away from the table.

"I know you have," he grumbled. "You're a good baker."

"Yeah, yeah," she said. "Have a lovely dentist appointment. Do not hurry back. Take your time."

He didn't bother to answer her. But he glanced at Bryce, who was across the kitchen, stirring his coleslaw mix. The communication was brief but instantly recognizable. *You've got this, right?*

Bryce simply nodded and kept stirring. Again, though, it was telling. Just days ago, he might have bristled at the implication that there was a question whether he was able to keep Olivia safe. Now he seemed to accept that Hernando's worry was, if not justified, certainly understandable.

"I'll get the door behind you," she said. They had always kept it locked, but now everyone was being superdiligent to make sure that nobody could unexpectedly waltz through the back entrance.

As she was doing that, she saw that the produce delivery truck was at the end of the street, turning in their direction. "Delivery," she called over her shoulder.

Bryce immediately dropped what he was doing to come check. The semi took a bit to get in place, its back end facing the door. They waited as the driver got out. It was Pete, their regular delivery person. He waved at them and then walked to the back of his truck and opened the big door.

"He's early," Olivia said. "I better make some room in the cooler."

"I'll do it," Bryce said. He knew some of the things were heavy. Normally Hernando would have handled it for her.

"Thank you." She watched as Pete pushed a dolly loaded high with produce boxes down the ramp that led from the truck to the ground. Once he was there, she unlocked the door. "Good morning," she said, holding the door for him.

"Good morning, Olivia," he said. "Smells good in here."

He'd been her delivery person for years. He was one of the reasons she loved doing business with his company.

"Thank you. Can I get you something? The cranberry-orange rolls are already out of the oven."

"Sold," he said, moving toward the cooler. "I've got one more load after this."

"Want a coffee to go, too?"

"Absolutely. With cream."

She busied herself getting his order ready. Heard him exit and knew he would be bringing in the second load. As a surprise, she added a few cookies to the bag. They could be his afternoon snack.

She heard the door open and turned.

And the coffee cup she was holding slipped through her fingers. Hot liquid splashed onto her legs, but she barely registered it. Hard to think of something so mundane when her worst nightmare was standing in her kitchen, gun pointed at her head.

"Olivia," Len Davison said, his voice soft. "So nice to see you again."

Chapter Eighteen

Bryce had just moved the last box in the cooler when he heard a noise he couldn't pin down. He stuck his head around the corner.

Davison. Gun pointed at Olivia.

How the hell had this happened? It didn't matter, he realized. What mattered now was getting Olivia away from the man. He pulled his phone off his belt. Sent a quick text message that would reach several people. Somebody would see it and help would come.

There was no way to get the drop on Davison. He was going to have to confront the man directly. He pulled his gun and swung around the corner. "Let her go," he ordered, aiming his weapon at Davison.

"I wondered where you were," Davison said, not taking his own gun off Olivia. "I couldn't believe my luck when I saw the cook leaving. I thought I'd probably just have to shoot him. This is so much…cleaner. And that's important in a restaurant, isn't it, Olivia? Sanitation rules and such."

Olivia didn't answer. Pale-faced and rigid, she looked frightened, as to be expected, but she also looked angry. He wanted to reassure her that help was probably already on its way, but there was no way to do that without spooking Davison. *Stay calm*, he willed.

"As lovely as Bubbe's is, I don't have time to dawdle today," Davison said. "Put your gun away, Agent Colton. Or I shoot her."

He wouldn't. Would he? No, he was obsessed with Olivia. Kept coming back. Had sent others in his stead to track her movements.

But Len Davison was a wild card.

"There's no need for this to end badly," Bryce said. He just needed to buy some time.

"I really don't want it to end badly for Olivia," Davison said. "But it will. And it will end badly for the old woman."

"Mrs. Drindle?" Olivia asked.

"Yes. She's a pain in the ass. She was a backup plan if I couldn't get into the delivery truck. I'd heard she was important to you. Why, I don't understand. She's fussy and has an opinion about everything. But she's living on borrowed time. If I don't return home within the hour, the bomb she's attached to will explode and all you'll find is little pieces of her."

He was lying, Bryce thought. Not about having Mrs. Drindle. They suspected that. But he'd never used a bomb before. Guns were his weapon of choice. Still, with Davison, he couldn't be sure. "We can talk about this," Bryce said. "Figure something out."

"No. And if you don't put your gun down, right now, I'm going to shoot Olivia." Davison's voice had risen at the end. He was getting agitated. A gun going off by accident could be just as deadly as one shot with purpose.

"Okay, okay. I'm putting my gun down." He lowered his weapon, put it on the metal shelf where the flour and sugar were stored, and walked a few steps forward, attempting to close the gap between himself and Olivia. He just needed to get her safely out of the way. "We can talk now." He was still too far away to grab for Olivia.

"Stop," Davison yelled. "Not one more step."

Bryce kept his hands in the air and tried to look harmless. "So you were hiding in the back of the truck," he guessed. Pete had not returned, which likely meant that Davison had harmed him in some way as he'd exited from the back.

"All night," Davison said. "It was very cold and very dark. But the smell of fruit and vegetables, like the smell of rocks and moss, is a comforting thing, almost seductive."

Yeah, he didn't think so. But he was reminded of what Tatiana had said about her father, that he'd loved to show her moss-covered rocks.

"Come here, Olivia," Davison instructed, his gun pointed at her heart.

"Stay where you are," Bryce said. Help had to be nearby. They would come without lights or a siren, he thought. "You're on foot," he said, looking at Davison. "You won't get away."

"I'm not that stupid," Davison said. "I have a car." Then the man moved faster than Bryce had anticipated, grabbing for Olivia and swinging her toward him. Bryce lunged forward. No way in hell was he letting this killer take her.

The bullet hit Bryce, knocking him back. He staggered into a shelf of pots and pans, and they went tumbling, hitting the floor at about the same time he did.

The pain was intense.

He heard Olivia's scream, and he fought to stay conscious.

"No," he cried. "No."

Far away, it seemed, he heard a door close. Was that help? No, it had been Davison and Olivia leaving. He dragged himself up to a sitting position, leaning heavily against the wall. Blood was spreading from the wound in his left shoulder.

Feeling uncoordinated and light-headed, he managed to untie the strings of the white apron from around his waist. He roughly folded the cotton so that it resembled a long scarf, then wrapped it very tight around his shoulder and under his arm, using the strings once again to secure it in place. Pressure would reduce the blood loss. Earlier he'd willed Olivia to stay calm, and now he summoned up the same thoughts for himself.

Help was imminent. Davison could not get far. Olivia was smart. She'd stay alive, knowing that he'd do everything in his power to find her.

Reason after reason flitted through his head.

He focused on that rather than the thought-swamping guilt of knowing that once again he'd underestimated Davison. Hiding in the back of a delivery truck. *But the smell of fruit and vegetables, like the smell of rocks and moss, is a comforting thing, almost seductive.* That was what Davison had said.

Smell. The word evoked a sudden memory, one that he hadn't thought about in decades. But it came back to him now. He and his father had gone for a walk deep in Grave Gulch Park, well into the forest, in the late fall. He could not have been more than three. And while he had almost no other memories of that age, he suspected the traumatic nature of what had happened had cemented the memory in the core of his brain.

They'd been out for hours. But yet he hadn't wanted to go home. He was with his dad. They'd crossed several small streams, and his shoes were wet and his feet cold. Like it had happened yesterday, he could see the slick, moss-covered rocks that he'd picked his way across. Could feel the security of his hand safe within the hollow of his dad's big paw.

When they'd come to a wider stream, too deep and fast-moving for his small legs to make it on his own, his dad had picked him up to carry him across. But then he'd slipped. Bryce had fallen from his arms and gone under.

The water had been shockingly cold and dark, and it was perhaps the first time that he'd ever known fear. And the stream had turned around him, and he'd felt it pushing his body.

As he thought about it now, he had no idea how long he was under or how far the current had carried him. What he did have a clear remembrance of was the raw fear in his father's eyes after he was scooped up.

He'd hugged him, so tight that Bryce had been barely able to breathe. Then his dad had taken off his big coat and bundled Bryce in it before burying his cold face into Bryce's neck and saying *You're okay* over and over. In retrospect, Bryce thought that his dad was perhaps reassuring himself, not Bryce. But it was what he said next that was now making Bryce's head whirl. *You smell like rocks and moss and that damn river.*

He'd known that *damn* wasn't a word he was supposed to say. Which was probably why, when they'd gotten home and his mother had insisted upon hearing the whole story, he'd repeated what his father had said. *I smell like rocks and moss and that damn river.*

He'd said it repeatedly for days. But then had never said it again once his father had left, never to come home again. He'd been about thirteen, with his mom and sisters in the park, when his mom had reminded him of the incident. *This is where you fell into that damn river,* she'd said. *And came out smelling of moss and rocks.*

Then she'd told him that that day was the only time she'd ever seen his father scared about anything. He had blamed himself for the accident, saying that he'd known it was the part of the forest where the moss grew heaviest, and that he should have anticipated how slick the rocks in the river might be. She'd said that he'd still been shaking when they'd gotten home and continued to as he'd recounted the story for her.

Maybe the fear he felt now, with the very real prospect of losing Olivia, was akin to what his father had faced that day. Maybe that was why the memory had suddenly sprung from the recesses of his mind.

He heard the back door open, and the first face he saw was Brett Shea. The man's eyes were moving fast, taking in the scene.

"Olivia?" Brett asked.

"Davison has her," Bryce said. "And he has Mrs. Drindle. The way he talked, she's still alive."

"Any other casualties here?" Brett said, already kneeling to look at Bryce's shoulder.

Bryce heard one of the officers clearing the way for paramedics to enter. "I suspect the driver of the semi-truck is injured or dead," Bryce said.

"Not dead. Unconscious. Appears that he might have been drugged. Paramedics are already helping him."

That was good to hear. Hopefully Pete would be okay. "Help me up," Bryce said. He needed to go after Olivia.

Two paramedics came in. "No, no, no," the one in the front said in response to Bryce's plea to Brett. "Nobody's getting up."

"How's the driver?" Bryce asked, ignoring his direction.

"Better than you, I'd hazard a guess," the older paramedic said, sounding distracted. He was busy looking at Bryce's shoulder. "Today appears to be your lucky day. Entry and exit wounds. Looks as if the bullet passed through, obviously missing the subclavian or the brachial arteries or you'd have bled out by now."

The man's bedside manner needed work.

"Patch me up," Bryce said.

"At the very least, it needs to be disinfected and stitched. I wouldn't rule out surgery to repair torn ligaments."

"Not happening," Bryce said. "Not right now." He had to get Olivia back. "I think I know where he might be hiding," he said, looking at Brett. "He said something that triggered a memory of something that happened to me in the park. I can take you there."

He could tell Brett was undecided. The man wanted Davison every bit as much as Bryce did. He wanted to save Olivia and Mrs. Drindle. "You do that and then you're going to the hospital."

"Fine," Bryce agreed. He'd say most anything to follow Davison. "Work fast," he said to the paramedics.

Five minutes later, he was on his feet, his left arm

in a sling, a thick bandage on the wound. It hurt like hell, but he wasn't telling anybody that. "You're driving," he said to Brett.

The interim chief was giving instructions to the other officers. There would be plenty of police searching the park.

He thought about calling Olivia's brother. Somebody in the family should know. But he knew Oren was out of town and couldn't do anything to immediately help. No, he'd wait until there was definitive news to report about Olivia.

"I really didn't expect him to come in the daytime," Bryce admitted when they were speeding toward the park. "When he first came to the deli and then to her house, it was always at night, under the cover of darkness."

"Either he's getting more careless or more desperate," Brett said.

Neither was an appealing thought. But Bryce pushed those thoughts away. They would find her in time. They simply had to.

Chapter Nineteen

Olivia could feel warm sun on her face. And there was a dog barking. Close by. Like right in her ear. It was the equivalent of nails on a chalkboard. She struggled to open her eyes, to wake up, to get away from the noise.

When she finally surfaced, she was surprised to see that she was in a vehicle. She remembered seeing the car but had no recollection of getting inside it. The barking dog that had been in her ear was real, running back and forth on the back seat. Davison was driving. And the memory of what had happened hit her hard, making her chest feel tight.

Bryce, she thought. And she said a quick prayer that he had not been seriously injured, that he'd been able to call for help. It was too horrible to contemplate another alternative.

She was half sitting, half lying in the front passenger seat. She summoned her strength to sit up straight. She felt sluggish and sick to her stomach. She stared at her captor, who was busy parking the car. She looked around and thought that they were on the far eastern side of Grave Gulch Park.

She needed to get out of the car, get away. She

reached for the door handle, but her movements were uncoordinated and her hand had no strength.

Davison turned to her. "You wouldn't get five feet on your own. But never fear—it'll wear off eventually."

Eventually seemed way too far away. But with every second, her mind felt as if it was clearing. She remembered what had happened. After shooting Bryce, Davison had put one hand over her mouth and literally dragged her from the back door of Bubbe's and around the corner. She'd prayed that somebody would see them, would call the police. But the street had been empty.

She'd initially struggled until he'd reminded her that he had Mrs. Drindle. If she didn't cooperate, the older woman would pay the price. Less than a block away from Bubbe's, he'd stopped beside a vehicle, and she'd felt the sharp poke of a needle in her arm. It had been lights out. She remembered none of the drive from the deli to the park.

"You have a dog," she said. It was an insignificant detail, certainly didn't matter. But it was the first thing that she thought of to say. It just didn't match what she knew about Len Davison.

"Not mine," Davison said. "Belongs to an old lady. She leaves him outside all the time. Never even realizes when I borrow him. Nobody gives me a second look when I have a dog." He reached into the back seat and pulled some things off the floor. The first one was a red sweatshirt. He pulled it over his head. And then added a black stocking cap. Then he handed the remaining item to her. "Put this on. Put the hood up."

It was a navy blue sweatshirt with a big yellow *M*

and the words *University of Michigan*. It would hang on her, at least two sizes too big.

"We walk from here," Davison said.

She wasn't feeling overly optimistic that her legs would cooperate. "Someone will see us. They'll see that I'm not willingly going with you."

"If you make a scene and someone attempts to intervene, I will shoot them. You know I've killed before. And I'd decided that I was done with all that. But if you don't behave, I will do it. And that will be on your conscience, Olivia. You will have to live with it."

Oh, God. She definitely could not live with that. But perhaps she could signal to them in some way so that they would know something was wrong but would call the police rather than attempt to stop Davison. She had to try that. It might be the only way to keep herself and Mrs. Drindle alive.

"What's the plan?" she asked as she zipped up the sweatshirt and pulled up the hood. He got out his side, walked around the car and opened the back door first. That was when she noticed that he had a leash in his hand. He hooked it to the dog's collar and then opened her car door.

"The same one it's been since the first moment I saw you. I felt it, and I know you did, too. We belong together. One with nature. One in our togetherness." He sighed. "It's going to be so wonderful not to be alone anymore."

She could summon up no sympathy for him. He'd killed, many times over. Who knew what had happened to Pete, and the vision of Bryce, brave man, stumbling backward after being shot would never leave her. This man was a monster.

And maybe she was the only thing standing between him and the rest of the world.

So for now, she would walk quietly next to him. Let him think she'd given up. Let him think that she would go along with his ideas. Let him think she was weak.

But when she got her moment, she was going to strike. And strike hard.

For now, she tried to keep track of their path. When she got away, she wanted to be able to lead the police back. Fortunately, her mind seemed sharper than her body, which seemed to be struggling to catch up.

"I'm curious," she said. "Why is it that you kill certain people?" When she got away, she wanted to be able to give Bryce something of significance in his search to understand Davison.

Davison took his time answering. When he finally did, his admission was stunning. Even though it was exactly what the police had speculated.

"Because they remind me of myself," he said. "I am nothing. Not now. And when I see them, I *know* they are nothing."

His emphasis on the word *know* was chilling. He hadn't known his victims at all. It had been their dumb luck to be in his path and to have been near his same age and gender. It was just so terribly sad. Senseless losses.

"I'm sorry that your wife died," she said. Perhaps the woman had been his moral compass and talking about her would remind him that this wasn't what she would have wanted. "What was her name?"

"I don't want to talk about my wife," he snapped. "She left me."

In a manner of speaking. But she didn't press. She'd find the right button to push.

Davison had the dog's leash in one hand and the other arm around her, gripping her tight, holding her up, propelling her along. The good part of him being that close was it actually helped steady her, and if she focused very intensely, she could manage to put one foot in front of the other. Her hopes of attracting someone's attention were dashed, however. There was absolutely no one in this remote part of the park. After about ten minutes, the trail ended and the patchy grass was brittle, the result of several frosts. They were well past the manicured acres of grass and into the heavily treed forest. No raking of leaves occurred in this area, and there were piles and piles all around. The temperature was in the low forties, and while she hated being grateful for anything that came from Len Davison, the sweatshirt was a godsend.

Almost as if he could read her mind, he turned to her. "I've got coffee," he said. "I fill a thermos every morning at the gas station on Handel Street."

Two thoughts hit her simultaneously. One, that he was so bold to think that he could move freely around after having terrorized the community. And two, if he was buying coffee, that likely meant that wherever they were headed either had no electricity, no running water or neither. It was not a pleasant thought. But it did mean that there would be times during the day that either she'd be dragged along or she'd be left on her own. She was determined to look at every piece of information she could glean as an opportunity.

Data. That was what Bryce would have said. *Everything is data.*

"I bought you a dress," he said.

She stumbled, and he tensed. "For what?" she asked.

He looked vaguely surprised. "You can't wear what you have on to be married."

"A wedding dress," she said, willing her brain not to shut down.

"You'll be my wife," he said. "I was happy when I had a wife. And you're young. We'll have children. It will be a fresh start. That's what I want. That's what we'll have."

It was so absurd that she was tempted to laugh. But knew that would be a mistake. He was well past the point of seeing his own ridiculousness. "I... I'd want my parents, my brother, at my wedding," she said.

"From now on, Olivia, it's just the two of us. We matter. No one else." He'd stopped walking.

There was nothing around them, save trees and leaves and piles of brush.

"We're here," he said, sounding happy. He dropped the leash onto the ground, but the dog did not run.

Too late, she saw the syringe in his hand. Had no time to react before she felt another needle in her arm.

BRYCE HAD HIS seat belt undone and his car door open before the vehicle was fully stopped. He'd directed Brett to the far eastern side of Grave Gulch Park.

"If I'm right, it's about a mile in, well off the trails," he said.

Brett looked at a text on his phone. "K-9 officers are right behind us."

Bryce wasn't waiting. His shoulder wasn't bleeding through the bandage, and that was good enough for him. He'd stay upright and save Olivia if it was the last thing he ever did.

All the way from Bubbe's Deli, he'd been attempting to recall that day in the park when his mother had pointed out the rocks. He remembered seeing the sharp bend in the stream and the stand of cedar trees in the distance on a small rise. He remembered the woodsy smells—of moss and decaying leaves and damp earth—so strong that the scents seemed to settle in his throat.

He was moving fast, and his head was spinning. Likely from the blood loss and the shock of being shot.

"You okay?" Brett asked.

"Yeah." No need to elaborate. They were ten steps from the top of a small hill that might offer a better view. He needed to save his breath, his strength.

He took the steps and then stopped so quickly that Brett, who was behind him, almost plowed into him. He reached back with his good arm, put a hand on the man's shoulder and pushed him to the ground. Then knelt beside him.

"Look at that," he said.

Three hundred yards ahead of them, they could see the back of somebody wearing a red sweatshirt and jeans and a black stocking cap. He was bent over, clearing brush. Near him, on the ground, was something blue. Dark blue on the top, lighter on the bottom. It was really hard to tell what it was from this distance. "That's a dog," he said, pointing at the movement nearby the blue thing on the ground.

"Yeah. Davison doesn't have a dog," Brett said.

He'd killed men before who were walking with their dogs and always left the pets alone. Maybe he liked the animals. And it would be a great disguise. All Bryce knew for sure was that he was never going to underestimate the man again. Moving forward would put them in plain view of whoever it was clearing the brush should they decide to turn around.

Could it be Davison? Olivia? Oh, God, if it was, did that mean she was already dead?

No, Bryce reasoned. Davison had threatened to kill her but in the end had shot him rather than her. Davison didn't want her dead.

"Let's get closer," he said.

They moved fast, both with weapons drawn. As they got closer, Bryce knew he was right. The blue shapeless thing on the ground had arms and legs, and he was confident that it was Olivia.

The person clearing the debris from the ground chose that moment to reach for Olivia, likely to drag her into the opening he'd created in the earth.

"No," Bryce yelled. He wasn't going to let that happen. There was no telling what booby traps Davison might have set underground, what peril awaited anyone who ventured into his bunker. He wasn't letting Olivia out of his sight again.

Davison dropped Olivia back to the earth and whirled around. He had a gun.

By this time, Bryce and Brett were charging down the hill at full speed. "FBI," Bryce yelled. "Put down your weapon."

Davison raised his gun. Bryce dived for the ground and rolled. From the corner of his eye, he saw the interim chief do the same.

Davison fired two shots. There was no doubt which path the man had chosen.

Bryce raised his own weapon, steadied himself and fired.

Davison went down.

"Are you okay?" Bryce asked Brett.

"Yeah. Be careful as we approach," Brett replied.

But when they got to the man, Bryce realized that any danger Davison might have posed was over. His aim had been true. Davison was dead. He spared the man no more than a quick assessment before rushing to Olivia's side. She was facedown in the dirt. He carefully lifted her.

"She's breathing," he yelled. "Get me a medic."

He looked for injuries but saw nothing. He pulled back the blue hood, and sitting on the ground, with Olivia in his lap, he cradled the woman he loved.

"Olivia, Olivia," he said. "Sweetheart. Wake up. I love you. I need you. Come back to me."

Chapter Twenty

Maybe it was his voice. Maybe it was the cold. Maybe it was simply the drug wearing off, but Olivia's eyelashes fluttered. Her eyes opened. "Bryce," she said before closing them again.

"No, no. Come back," he said. "You're okay. We've got you."

She opened her eyes again and stared at him. This time she seemed to understand. "Mrs. Drindle," she said.

He gently turned her head so that she could see the woman, whom Brett had successfully retrieved from Davison's underground bunker. She'd been tied up, but there had been no bomb. She'd been complaining about the rude interruption to her schedule when she and Brett had emerged from the hole in the ground. Seeing an unconscious Olivia in Bryce's arms had shut her up. Now she was twenty feet away, wrapped in a blanket, talking to an officer. When she saw motion from Olivia, a smile broke across her face. "Welcome back, dear," she said.

"I'm so sorry," Olivia said.

Mrs. Drindle waved a hand. "Not your fault. Insufferable man. No respect for other people's time."

To say nothing of being a serial killer, thought Bryce.

Olivia turned to him, offered up a half smile. "On behalf of Mrs. Drindle and myself, let me just say that you have remarkable timing."

His heart sang. She was okay.

"Oh, no. You're hurt," she said, looking at the bandage on his shoulder. She struggled to sit up, but her efforts were clumsy.

"Calm down. It'll be fine," he said. "I'm worried about you. Medics are thirty seconds out."

"Davison?" she asked.

He had turned her so that the first thing she saw when she awakened was not Davison. She'd had enough trauma. But she needed to know that he was no longer a threat. "Dead. I shot him. He's never going to harm you or anyone else ever again."

A shiver rippled through her entire body. "Oh, Bryce. Someone needs to tell Tatiana. He was a horrible man, but he was still her father."

"I'll talk to her," he promised. A whole army of people were running toward them. The first officers on the scene had already strung up police tape that would keep most everybody back. But the paramedics were waved through.

"You're going to need to step back, sir," the first paramedic to reach them said.

He was happy to do that. He wanted her fully checked out. "She was most likely drugged," he said, carefully releasing her. He leaned down and kissed her gently, not caring if anyone saw. "Let them check you out. Please."

She reached up and stroked his cheek with her cold hand. "Thank you," she said. "For everything."

"My duty," he said. "And my distinct pleasure."

OLIVIA'S BLOOD PRESSURE was dangerously low, and after a quick exam on the cold ground, she was lifted onto a stretcher, carried to a waiting ambulance and unceremoniously loaded. Mrs. Drindle was going into another ambulance. In the distance, she saw a paramedic giving Bryce and Brett Shea an update. Right before they closed the back door, Bryce was there.

"You're going to be fine," he assured her. "Just do what they say."

"Did you do that? After you got shot?"

He smiled. "No, but I'm an FBI agent. You're a cream puff." He squeezed her hand. "The toughest, bravest cream puff I've ever met."

"And you're a prince," she said.

He looked alarmed, as if maybe he thought she was hallucinating from the drug Len Davison had given her.

"My prince," she clarified. "As in Prince Charming. I've been waiting for you."

"I'm hitting the pause button on the fairy tale," the paramedic said.

Bryce gave her hand one more squeeze. "I'll let Hernando know what's going on," he said. "And Oren and Madison, too."

She wanted to ask if he'd come to the hospital, if he'd be with her. But like he said, he was an agent who'd just shot and killed a known and dangerous criminal. There had to be some loose ends to tie up. He was being brave. She'd seen his poor body slammed up against that metal shelf, had seen him hit the ground. He had to be in pain. But he was focused on what needed to be done.

Nobody was going to accuse her of being a clingy vine.

"'Bye," she said, making sure her voice didn't quiver.

"Yeah, 'bye," he said, his voice husky.

The doors closed. "It's Bryce who should be in an ambulance," she said, unhappy with her lack of control over the situation.

"Uh-huh," the female paramedic said. "Right now, I'm not responsible for Prince Charming. I'm responsible for you."

"I have a restaurant to run," she said as the ambulance took off, siren wailing. She had no idea if Hernando was back from the dentist. Right now, it could be just Trace in the kitchen. While he was bright and hardworking, he wasn't ready to handle a busy lunch.

"Bubbe's Deli is one of our favorites," the young woman said, not seeming at all concerned about Olivia's protest. She was busy checking her blood pressure once again.

She'd thought she recognized her. "Thank you," she mumbled. She needed to stop acting like a baby. Didn't want it to get around Grave Gulch that she'd been an ungrateful patient.

She wished she'd had the good sense to get taken with her phone in her pocket. Then she could at least make some calls. She thought about asking the paramedic to use her phone but decided to wait until she got to the hospital.

But once she arrived there, she had no time. She was whisked away for blood work and an exam. Bryce had said he'd call Hernando and her brother. She just needed to have a little faith.

"I HAVE FAITH and confidence," Tatiana said, standing in the doorway of her house, "that my father wasn't always a bad person. Something inside him snapped."

She glanced over her shoulder to the corner of the room where her baby played on a blanket. "You know why we named her Hope?"

"No."

"Two reasons. One, we thought it was a beautiful name. And two, because I never gave up hope that this whole nightmare with my father would come to an end. This isn't the end that I wanted, but maybe it's the only ending that means it's truly over. He might have died today, but I truly lost my father many months ago when this all started. He wasn't ever coming back to me."

She was dry-eyed and rational, as if she'd contemplated this day more than once. He'd known there was a possibility that she'd have heard before he got there, because it had taken longer at the scene than he'd wanted. But it had also been important that he give a statement immediately, given that he'd discharged his weapon.

There had been news media at the scene, and while they'd been kept back, he understood their frenzy to tell the story that they'd been chasing for the better part of a year. Fortunately, Tatiana hadn't heard anything. He'd told her the straight-up truth—that he'd been the one to shoot him.

"Now you need to get to the hospital," she said. When he'd first arrived, she'd invited him in, but he'd declined, telling her that it was a quick stop, that Brett Shea was waiting in the car, adamant that if he didn't report to the hospital within five minutes, he was calling in reinforcements to make it happen.

Bryce hadn't bothered to tell him that reinforcements wouldn't be needed. Brett would be hard to handle if Bryce were 100 percent. Right now, Bryce felt he was barely clinging to 60, maybe 65 percent. A good strong wind might blow him over. But he'd needed to do this.

"I'll make sure someone lets you know when the body can be claimed," he said. "Goodbye, Tatiana."

"Goodbye, Bryce. I hope Olivia is okay."

He'd given her a brief rundown of the morning's events. She'd expressed gratitude that Olivia hadn't been hurt worse.

He walked down the sidewalk and got into Brett's vehicle. "Did you hear anything?" he asked immediately.

"No. And you can ask for yourself, because the Grave Gulch hospital is your next stop."

"You're touchy," he said, settling into his seat. God, he was so tired. And his shoulder was burning.

"You better not die," Brett said. "That's all I can say. Be more red tape than one man should have to deal with in his career."

"I'm going to call the hospital," Bryce announced, knowing that Brett was kidding. He desperately wanted to talk to Olivia. Knew that it would do no good to call her phone. He'd seen it on the table when he and Brett had run from the deli. But he needed information. He was at his best when he had data.

He dialed the hospital, identified himself and asked to talk to the administrator in charge. When the person came on the line, he explained why he was calling. He was asked to hold and given some really irritating music to listen to while he did.

When someone finally came back on the line, it wasn't the administrator in charge. It was a person who identified himself as Dr. Finley. "I examined Ms. Margulies," he said. "Lab tests and CT scan were normal.

She has been released. As was Mrs. Drindle, the other patient brought in at the same time."

Bryce almost tossed the phone in his excitement. "Thank you. Thank you very much, Dr. Finley. I really needed to hear that."

He hung up and realized that Brett was staring at him. "You've got it bad, don't you?" the cop said.

Bryce was done denying it. "I love her."

"I thought so." He drove for a minute. "I'll let her brother know what's happened here."

"Thank you," Bryce said.

"By the way, Dominique de la Vega broke the story online in the *Grave Gulch Gazette*. Now it's popping up everywhere—Grave Gulch Serial Killer Dead."

"People will be happy."

"You would think. But there's already a protest getting planned to draw attention to our failure to capture Randall Bowe. In the amount of time you were at Tatiana's, I heard from the mayor, the police commissioner and the district attorney, who said almost the same thing—that we need to catch Bowe now in order to save the city and the police force and to recapture trust with the public."

"No pressure," Bryce teased. This all would cause his sister Jillian stress, because all eyes would be on the crime investigation unit. That made him realize that he was going to need to loop his sisters and his mom into what had happened this morning. They'd be frantic with worry and would likely demand to see him so they could verify with their own eyes that he was fine. And he'd need to tell his dad. That was an unfamiliar feeling—the need to go to two parents.

It was the memory of his father and him in the Grave

Gulch Forest and when he'd fallen into that stream that had spiked his memory of one of the most remote areas of the forest. If not for that, well, Olivia might have been dragged into that hole in the ground and disappeared forever. That thought had him pressing his good arm against his stomach. Brett would likely be angry if he vomited in his car.

Fathers. Fathers and daughters, like Len Davison and Tatiana. He'd been a good dad who had gone bad. But she could forgive him, at least enough that she wasn't going to let it erode the warm memories that she had.

Fathers and sons. Like Wes Windham and him. He'd been an absent dad, only to resurface with a strange story and what appeared to be a sincere desire to reconnect with his children and with Verity. Could Bryce be as brave as Tatiana and forgive past hurts and actions? Could he focus on the good?

Olivia wanted him to. Told him that it was a mistake to hang on to his anger and his feelings of betrayal. Told him that, in the end, it only would diminish him.

He didn't want anything to diminish him in Olivia's eyes.

He wanted to marry her. Have a family with her. Love her forever.

But first, he needed to get his shoulder stitched up and talk to his father.

IT WASN'T LIKE the Old West, where they poured some whiskey on the wound and used some thread and maybe a clean needle, thought Bryce. The event became much more complicated. Blood was drawn. Both an ultrasound and a CT were done. He was put in a blue gown, on a gurney, and wheeled into a room with bright lights.

Then it was lights out for him, and he didn't wake up until sometime later, when he was in the recovery room. His shoulder didn't hurt. Probably because he couldn't feel anything in that arm.

"Welcome back," a male nurse said.

"Nice to be back," Bryce said. "What time is it?"

"You just missed lunch," the nurse said by way of reply. "If you do well over the next forty-five minutes or so, we'll kick you loose and you can track down your favorite fast food."

He wanted a turkey Reuben, and he wanted to share it with the woman he loved. "Surgery went well?" He needed to have full use of his arm in order to stay in his job.

"The doctor will be in. I'll let her know that you're awake."

When the doctor came in, she was reassuringly calm. "We were able to successfully repair the damage the bullet caused on its path through," she said. "You've got at least six weeks of physical therapy ahead of you, but I'm confident that you'll have a full recovery."

"Thank you," he said.

"You're welcome. And thank you. I understand you're the agent who fired the shot that killed Len Davison. The whole community of Grave Gulch owes you a debt of gratitude. My dad walks in that park. Well, he did. Months ago, I told him never again until that killer was stopped."

It felt good to think that people could now go back to their lives.

"Your sisters and your parents are outside. Can I let them in?"

"I told them not to come," he said, shaking his head. He'd called them between the blood work and the CT scan. "Yes, let them in." He might as well get this over with.

Madison and Jillian came in first, followed by his mother and father. Verity looked worried, and Bryce noticed that his dad was holding her hand. Strangely, it didn't bother him like it might have before.

"You'll do anything for attention," Madison said, patting the side of his bed.

Jillian said nothing. She immediately examined the readings on the monitors at the side of the bed. They must have reassured her, because her eyes cleared and she smiled at him. "This is my lunch break."

His mother leaned down and carefully hugged him. "My poor boy," she said. "A mother should never have to hear on the news that an FBI agent has been shot and wounded."

"I'm sorry. I meant to get to you quickly. But I had to see Tatiana first. I had to tell her."

"Of course you did," Verity said. "Poor girl. We'll be there for her."

"Glad to see you're okay," Wes said.

"Can the three of you go get me a sandwich from the cafeteria?" he asked, looking at his mother and sisters. Verity's head snapped up. Her eyes were full of questions. Jillian and Madison were looking at each other. But none of them were dummies, and they immediately got the hint that he wanted a minute alone with Wes.

After the women left, Bryce motioned for his father to take the lone chair in the small room. His dad sat.

"Maybe we should wait to have any conversation until you're feeling stronger," Wes said.

Bryce shook his head. "I… I know that I haven't been the most welcoming to you since you came back into our lives."

"I make no judgments about that," Wes said.

"Perhaps not. But I've had the opportunity to assess my behavior, and, quite frankly, I'm not sure it's flattering. I did it with the best of intentions, to protect Madison and Jillian and Mom."

Wes said nothing.

"And I was angry. So very angry with you when I realized that there had been years and years that our family had been without a father because you hadn't seen fit to return. And then when you did, you brought danger to our door. It was just too much."

"I will always be sorry for any danger that I put Madison or the rest of the family in."

Bryce was silent for a minute. "I thought of something this morning. It was the day that we were in the Grave Gulch Forest and we were crossing the river. You slipped on the rocks, and I went under. Do you remember that?"

His father's eyes grew serious. "Do I remember it? I had flashbacks to that day for years. Not being able to grab you. Not being able to get you in time. I almost lost you. It would have killed your mother."

"And you?" Bryce pushed.

"It…it would have broken my heart. I don't think I could have lived with it."

He wasn't lying.

"You loved me," Bryce said.

"I loved all of you," Wes said, his eyes wet with unshed tears. "That doesn't excuse—"

"It's enough," Bryce said, interrupting. "You loved us and we loved you. And so we all lost something in the years when we were separated. Now that you're back, I'm not going to spend another minute being angry about it. Life is too short. I just wanted you to know my feelings and that I won't be in opposition to any relationship that you and Mom choose to have."

The tears that had been pooling in Wes Windham's eyes spilled down his face. He made no effort to wipe them away. "I love your mother. I always have."

"I think I have a better understanding of what it means to love that way," Bryce said.

"Olivia?" Wes asked.

Bryce nodded.

"Good luck, son."

"Thank you, Dad."

OLIVIA REALLY SHOULDN'T have worried about getting back to Bubbe's for the lunch rush. There was no rush. No lunch. Only locked doors and police tape. Even the parking lot was off-limits.

The taxi let her off on the street. She paid with the voucher that the hospital had given to her for just that purpose. As she walked toward her back door, she saw Hernando standing outside, hands in his pockets. He turned when she approached.

"It's too cold to be out here without a coat," he said.

The University of Michigan sweatshirt had been taken from her at the hospital. She suspected it was part of a growing body of evidence. "So, how was the dentist appointment?" she asked.

"I leave for five damn minutes," he said, not bothering to answer her sad attempt to lighten the mood. "And this happens." His harsh words belied the concern in his dark eyes. He was busy unzipping his own jacket.

"I'm okay," she said.

"I got that much from Bryce," Hernando said. "Put this on," he added, handing her the jacket.

She did as instructed. "You talked to him?" she asked, feeling hesitant.

"I did. He's out of surgery, and the prognosis is good."

She'd asked at the hospital. No one had been either willing or able to tell her anything. She'd clung to the belief that he'd seemed invincible when she'd awakened in his arms at the park. Surely he would recover. "He shot Davison," she said. It was the first time she'd said the words out loud. But they'd been running through her head, almost nonstop. He'd killed a man to save her.

"Hard to be sorry about that," Hernando said.

"Yeah." Maybe someday she'd work up some sympathy for the man, but right now, the memories of being led sluggishly across the forest, knowing that with each step she was closer to horribleness, but being too drugged up to fight, were too fresh. "Now what?" she asked, looking at the parking lot full of police cars.

"I start thinking about tomorrow's specials, because I think we're going to be busy. Everyone is going to want to hear the story. And there's rumors of another protest about the police's inability to bring Randall Bowe to justice. That will up the to-go orders, for sure. But let me worry about that. You go home and sleep."

Her brother had managed to track her down in the hospital, right after she'd finished giving her statement to the police, and he'd given her the same advice about getting some rest. He'd be back in town tomorrow, and she was confident that his first stop would be at Bubbe's to see for himself that she was okay.

"We'll be able to open tomorrow?" she asked.

"He seems to think so," Hernando said, motioning to Brett Shea, who stood in the back doorway, talking to another police officer. "He also told me that Mrs. Drindle was treated and released at the hospital. She was already talking about coming back to Bubbe's for lunch tomorrow."

Tomorrow would be the first time she'd unlocked the doors of Bubbe's without Bryce at her side in what seemed like a very long time, although it had really just been weeks. So while she was elated to hear the news about Mrs. Drindle, it was hard not to focus on the loss.

Bryce had so easily managed to become a part of everything she did. But who knew what would happen now? Circumstances had forced them together, but now the circumstances had changed.

For the better, she reminded herself. A deadly menace had been stopped. He'd said he was going to stop killing, but who knew if that was true? He'd had no compunction about shooting Bryce, and it could have been deadly.

If her relationship with Bryce was meant to be, it would...what? Survive? Develop? Burn hot for fifty years?

I'll take the last option, she told herself. She wasn't going to be satisfied with anything else. She'd admitted as much to him at the park when she'd told him that he was her Prince Charming.

In other words, if he came back and gave her some

version of the *I really want to be friends and continue
to explore our relationship while I gather some more
data* speech, she was going to hit him with a cast-iron
pan. She would allow that there was a time for data collecting. But then there was a time for action. And once
that line had been crossed, there was no going back.

She was surprised when Hernando leaned in and
hugged her. "I'm grateful that you're okay," he said, his
voice gruff. "What does this mean for you and Bryce?"

"I don't know," she said. She did not try to explain
the relationship. She knew that Hernando had figured
it out.

"He and I came to an agreement," Hernando said.

That surprised her. "What kind of agreement?"

"That I wouldn't come after him unless he hurt you."

"Hernando, he's an FBI agent. You can't threaten
him."

"And I'm a protective SOB. We understand each
other."

"You're a step ahead of me," she said. "I'm not so
sure I understand…everything. I love him," she added.

Hernando did not look surprised. "I am not likely to
think that anyone would be worthy, but, on the whole,
he is definitely at the head of the line."

Olivia smiled.

"Now, go home. I suspect Bryce will be there as
soon as he's able to."

"I'm scared," she admitted.

Hernando shook his head. "You're the bravest person I know. Go get him."

OLIVIA STOOD IN the very hot shower and enjoyed the
feeling of being warm. Before she'd left the parking

lot of Bubbe's, she'd given Hernando back his coat and retrieved her purse and cell phone from Brett Shea. She'd looked immediately at the missed calls. None had been from Bryce.

She must have been fairly transparent, because the interim chief had immediately informed her that Bryce had known she didn't have her cell phone. "I imagine he'll be in touch," he had promised. "He'll have some things he needs to tie up."

Loose ends. She hoped she didn't fall into that category.

"How did the two of you find me?" she'd asked.

Brett had simply shaken his head and said, "Ask Bryce about that. It was all him."

Suddenly so weary, she'd thanked Brett for everything he'd done that morning and all the other days to bring the search for Len Davison to a close. Then she'd gotten into her car and driven home, like a normal person, on a normal day. Feeling decidedly not normal, or at least not the same as before.

Her car had been quiet, her house even more so.

She needed to hear from Bryce soon.

She turned off the water, dried off and put on her flannel bunny pajamas and slippers. Then she made herself a cup of hot tea and sat on her couch. Waiting was not her strong suit.

Finally, an hour later, her doorbell rang. She used the peephole and saw that it was Bryce. His arm was in a sling. But otherwise he looked healthy and whole and absolutely wonderful.

She opened the door. "Hi," she said.

"Hi, yourself."

"You have a key," she reminded him. She stepped back to let him in.

"Cute jammies," he said.

That was what he'd said the first time he'd taken them off her. "Can I get you coffee or tea?"

"Whatever you're having," he said, looking at her cup.

They were being so polite to one another. Almost as if they were strangers. "So your shoulder is okay?"

"It'll be good as new after some physical therapy. How are you feeling?"

"Fine." She got his tea from the kitchen and delivered it to him. She sat on the couch; he took the chair. This was feeling so odd. She picked up her own drink and realized that her hand was shaking. Of course, he noticed.

"Are you sure you're okay?" he asked.

"Yeah. This—" she motioned between the two of them "—just feels weird."

"Yeah," he agreed, running his hand through his short hair. "I'm sorry that I let Davison take you."

"Don't lose one minute of sleep thinking about that," she immediately protested. "He shot you." She paused. "I still don't know how you managed to find me. I asked Brett, and he said it was all you."

Bryce shrugged. "Davison gave me the clue. Remember what he said about being in the back of Pete's truck? He said the smell of fruit and vegetables, like the smell of rocks and moss, is a comforting thing, almost seductive. Long story, but suffice it to say, the word *smell* triggered a memory of me and my dad being in the forest. And I had a good feeling that was exactly where Davison had his bunker."

"And with a hole in your shoulder, you ventured forth," she said. "Amazing."

"I would never have given up. Whether it took me an hour, a day, a week, a year to find you. I would never have given up."

She knew that to be true.

"I would have been here earlier, but in addition to getting my arm stitched up, I went to see Tatiana."

"How did she take the news?"

"She's sorry to hear of her father's death but also relieved that he cannot harm anyone else."

"She's had a heavy burden these last few months."

"Yeah. And speaking of burdens, I also talked to my father."

"You did?" The words came out rather breathlessly.

"I told him that I wouldn't be an obstacle to him pursuing a relationship with Verity. I also told him that I was sorry for the years that had been lost and that I accepted that he was, as well. I pledged to move on from it."

"Oh, Bryce." That had to have been a tough conversation. Bryce had been struggling with the issue for so long.

"I did it because of you," he said. "Because you were right. It was what needed to be said. What needed to be done."

That humbled her.

"I made one other stop," he said. Then he moved from his chair and knelt in front of her. He pulled a small jewelry box from his pocket. Opened it. Inside was the most beautiful diamond ring.

"I love you and can't imagine my life without you in it. Marry me, Olivia Margulies."

Chapter Twenty-One

"It is not going to be a long engagement," Olivia said, sipping her coffee.

Hernando mixed his dough and glanced at Bryce. "I imagine you can check your computer and concoct some program that will spit out the optimal day and time."

"Any day, any time," Bryce said, sipping his own coffee. All he knew was that yesterday she'd said yes without any hesitation. His heart had soared then. He was ready now. But he also understood that she probably had an idea of the perfect wedding, and he wanted her to have it. As long as it didn't take too long to orchestrate.

"Valentine's Day?" Olivia asked. "Is that corny?"

"Who cares?" Bryce said. It was a few months away.

"June weddings are always beautiful," she mused.

He raised his hands, palms a foot apart. Then deliberately brought them closer.

"Too far out?" she asked.

He nodded.

"Well, this is fascinating," Hernando said. "Can't wait to hear this same discussion every morning for the foreseeable future."

Olivia put her coffee down, walked over to the chef and kissed his cheek. "You're happy for us. Admit it?"

"Pleased as can be," he said. His voice was gruff, but his eyes were warm. "But last I checked, we still have a restaurant to run. I suppose you'll be shoving off," he said, looking at Bryce.

"Yes." He had already wrapped up much of the investigation. Very late the previous night, after getting a yes to his question, he'd gone back to the Grave Gulch police station to review and put the finishing touches on witness statements. He'd been almost done when the door to the conference room he was working in had opened.

Much to his surprise, he'd met Baldwin Bowe, a man he'd heard of, of course. He was Randall Bowe's estranged brother. Bryce had introduced himself and asked him what had brought him there.

Professional courtesy, Baldwin Bowe had claimed. Then he had gone on to explain that he'd been hired by an unnamed client to find his brother, Randall. This person was someone who had been harmed by Randall Bowe when the man had fabricated evidence against him. The man had lost two years of his life fighting the charges, and while now exonerated, he was frustrated that the Grave Gulch police had yet to apprehend Randall. He wanted him brought in alive to face charges.

Baldwin had been unemotional as he'd discussed his brother, as if the family connection had absolutely no relevance for him. It made Bryce's own family situation, with a father returning from the grave after twenty-five years, seem almost normal.

Bryce had attempted to ascertain Baldwin's credentials, but the man's explanation had been wholly unsatisfactory. *Consider me a ghost bounty hunter* was all he'd said. Then added that he worked without the limitations that constrained the police. He and his client had determined that it was now time for a more mercenary approach.

Bryce had warned the man to leave it to the Grave Gulch police, had tried to assure him that Interim Chief Shea was as committed as could be to apprehending Randall. Bowe had simply shaken his head, said he'd do the job he was hired for and walked out.

Bryce had been left with a feeling that Baldwin Bowe was going to shake things up. Not necessarily for the better.

"You do get a lunch once in a while, don't you?" Olivia asked, bringing him back to the present. "We could eat upstairs and…" Her voice trailed off.

Bryce clearly remembered what else they'd done on her new couch. And he had a feeling that Hernando had a pretty good idea, by the look on the man's face.

"I'll do my best to work in an occasional…lunch," he said.

She slapped her hand onto the counter. "I'm going to love being married to you."

He leaned in and kissed her. "Valentine's Day, cream puff. No later."

"Deal," she said.

* * * * *

COMING SOON!

We really hope you enjoyed reading this book.
If you're looking for more romance, be sure to
head to the shops when new books are
available on

Thursday 1st
December

To see which titles are coming soon, please visit
millsandboon.co.uk/nextmonth

MILLS & BOON

THE HEART OF ROMANCE

A ROMANCE FOR EVERY READER

MODERN
Prepare to be swept off your feet by sophisticated, sexy and seductive heroes, in some of the world's most glamourous and roma[n...] locations, where power and passion collide.

HISTORICAL
Escape with historical heroes from time gone by. Whether your passio[n...] for wicked Regency Rakes, muscled Vikings or rugged Highlanders, a[...] the romance of the past.

MEDICAL
Set your pulse racing with dedicated, delectable doctors in the high-p[...] sure world of medicine, where emotions run high and passion, comf[...] love are the best medicine.

True Love
Celebrate true love with tender stories of heartfelt romance, from th[...] rush of falling in love to the joy a new baby can bring, and a focus o[...] emotional heart of a relationship.

Desire
Indulge in secrets and scandal, intense drama and plenty of sizzling [...] action with powerful and passionate heroes who have it all: wealth, s[...] good looks…everything but the right woman.

HEROES
Experience all the excitement of a gripping thriller, with an intense r[o...]mance at its heart. Resourceful, true-to-life women and strong, fearle[ss...] face danger and desire - a killer combination!

To see which titles are coming soon, please visit

millsandboon.co.uk/nextmonth

MILLS & BOON
Desire

Indulge in secrets and scandal, intense drama and plenty of sizzling hot action with powerful and passionate heroes who have it all: wealth, status, good looks…everything but the right woman.

Four Desire stories published every month, find them all at:

millsandboon.co.uk